THE MAGNIFICENT
LIES OF
MADELEINE BÉJART

THE MAGNIFICENT LIES OF MADELEINE BÉJART

RICHARD GOODKIN

Boston
2025

Library of Congress Cataloging-in-Publication Data

Names: Goodkin, Richard E. author

Title: The magnificent lies of Madeleine Béjart / Richard Goodkin.

Description: Boston : Cherry Orchard Books, an imprint of
Academic Studies Press, 2025.

Identifiers: LCCN 2025025518 (print) | LCCN 2025025519
(ebook) | ISBN 9798887198446 (paperback) | ISBN
9798887198453 (adobe pdf) | ISBN 9798887198460 (epub)

Subjects: LCSH: Béjart, Madeleine, 1618-1672--Fiction | Molière,
1622-1673--Fiction | Actors--France--History--17th century--
Fiction | Theater--France--History--17th century--
Fiction | Théâtre illustre--Fiction | LCGFT: Historical
fiction | Novels

Classification: LCC PS3607.O56375 M34 2025 (print) |
LCC PS3607.O56375 (ebook) | DDC 813/.6--dc23/eng/20250718

LC record available at https://lccn.loc.gov/2025025518
LC ebook record available at https://lccn.loc.gov/2025025519

ISBN 9798887198446 (Paperback)
ISBN 9798887198453 (Adobe PDF)
ISBN 9798887198460 (ePub)

Cover design by Andree Valley
Book design by Kryon Publishing Services

Published by Cherry Orchard Books, an imprint of
Academic Studies Press
1007 Chestnut St.
Newton, MA 02464, USA
press@academicstudiespress.com
https://www.academicstudiespress.com/cherryorchardbooks/

This book is dedicated to my dear, dear friend Sharon Cohen. She shares many of the traits of Madeleine Béjart: extraordinary intelligence, dignity, integrity, perfectionism, humor, compassion, and a truly loving heart. Since kindergarten she has been an unsurpassed source of wisdom, support, comfort, and loyalty; in short, a perfect friend.

Contents

Author's Preface

The Magnificent Lies of Madeleine Béjart is a work of historical fiction set in France in the seventeenth century, the Golden Age of French theater. All of the main characters in the novel existed; indeed, the four playwrights, Molière, Pierre and Thomas Corneille, and Tristan L'Hermite, were among the most prominent cultural figures of their day. I carried out considerable research into their lives—and, above all, into those of Madeleine and Armande Béjart—during a Guggenheim Fellowship I held in 2005–2006. There are gaps in our knowledge of the life of Madeleine Béjart, a lesser celebrity at the time and the least well known of the main characters today; I have endeavored to fill those gaps with plausible and moving fictional events that develop Madeleine's story of a magnificent love carefully curated with magnificent lies.

As is true of all historical fiction, this work does at times diverge from the historical record—for example, the character of Madeleine's grandfather, Pierre Béjart, is actually based on an uncle—but I have generally tried to fill in unknowns rather than modifying what historians have clearly established. I have been especially attentive to the timeline of the story, a crucial issue in this tale of, among other things, Madeleine's pregnancies, which to this day remain veiled in mystery. I have also done my best to respect the major landmark events of Madeleine's and all of the playwrights' lives, especially Molière's.

I originally wrote the book in French—it appeared in France in 2013 with the publishing house Feuille de thé under the title *Les Magnifiques Mensonges de Madeleine Béjart*—and translated it into English myself. Translations of passages from the plays of Molière, the Corneille brothers, and Tristan L'Hermite are my own. I am extremely grateful for the support of Ghislaine Brault-Molas, the managing editor of the Feuille de thé Press, and of Daniel Frese at Academic Studies Press, whose support of the English translation has been invaluable.

Richard Goodkin
Madison, WI
February, 2025

PART ONE

WHEN FIRST WE PRACTICE TO DECEIVE

CHAPTER 1

In Which We Learn of the Salvation or Perdition of Madeleine Béjart, a Poor Misguided Soul

---

No sooner had Father Anselme left Madeleine Béjart's sickbed and clattered down the stairs than she gave herself over to laughter. Wiping away tears of mirth, she mused that it was one of the few remaining pleasures accorded the very ill. Her merriment subsided into a smile of satisfaction. She had concealed her indignation at what the priest had made her say for as long as was necessary, and it was a relief to have expedited the first item on her list of things to be attended to before her death. Act One of the drama of her demise had been more entertaining than she would have imagined.

Appearances notwithstanding, Madeleine Béjart was not an impious soul, but neither was she a conventional Catholic. As a renowned stage actress who, until her illness, had exercised her profession in spite of the Church's condemnation of all individuals connected to the theater, she had long flirted with excommunication and the refusal of last rites. But shortly before dawn on January 8, 1672, her fifty-fourth birthday, she had been roused by a sharp pain in her upper torso each time she drew a breath. She had pulled herself into a sitting position, which usually improved her respiration, but the discomfort had worsened. Many around her had been ravaged by consumption and she knew its rhythms more intimately than she cared to: the first droplets of blood; the slow early progression; the false reprieves; and the final decline. It now appeared that the end would come sooner rather than later. She wouldn't live to see fifty-five.

Madeleine Béjart had fallen back onto the satin sheets and shut her eyes to sort out the implications of this unwelcome turn of events. She had no fear of death, no bitterness in her heart. But she had unfinished business. Just as the dénouement of a play could make or break its entire success, the story of her life needed a proper conclusion.

The bells of Saint Germain l'Auxerrois announcing lauds seemed to be warning her to delay her reconciliation with the Church no longer. The idea that an actress would eventually run out of breath had a certain poetic justice; before hers was depleted, she must do what was required. While she considered her existence no more sinful than most, the matter was viewed quite differently by the priests. And it was they who would decide what would become of her earthly remains, they who might, although there was no knowing for sure, have an influence on the fate of her immortal soul. Why should she too not enjoy the few niceties offered to the dying?

So it was that when Madeleine's daughter, Armande, also an actress, called on her to wish her a happy birthday, the ailing *comédienne* asked her to walk to Saint Paul's and invite Father Anselme to the house. There was no hurry, she added to avoid causing alarm. In response to Armande's inquisitive look she stated with dignity that she had a *theological* question to discuss. Accustomed to the whims of this woman she and all of Paris had been led to believe was her older sister, Armande kept her thoughts to herself. The chambermaid having gone to the market, Armande lifted a cast-iron pot from the hearth, poured steaming wine into a cup, and set it down on a stand next to the bed. She then stoked the fire and departed.

Father Anselme had been pressing Madeleine for so long to repudiate her profession that she was not surprised to see Armande return an hour later with the ancient curate in tow. She shooed her daughter off to her rehearsal of Molière's new comedy, *The Learned Ladies*, which was to open on Mardi Gras at the Palais Royal, and turned her attention to the waiting cleric.

He surveyed the luxurious trappings of this famous actress's residence and then, having taken a seat next to Madeleine's bed, directed his gaze toward her. An unpleasant gleam in his eye made her wonder whether he was pondering the indecent activities that lay behind such conspicuous wealth. To collect herself before proceeding, she let her eyes sweep over the room.

There was no disputing its opulence. Carved furniture upholstered in burgundy velvet was set off by embroidered Rouen tapestries covering the walls. The January gloom was illuminated by the tapers of two bronze chandeliers suspended from the panelled ceiling and a fire dancing beneath a mantelpiece of Siena marble. She turned back to face Father Anselme. His forehead glistening and his eyes lit with anticipation, he resembled a long-suffering suitor waiting to see if his fair lady was about to grant him his heart's desires. Madeleine relaxed at the thought. An impatient lover was a type of individual with whom she had a certain experience.

Projecting her voice to the back of the room to compensate for Father Anselme's poor hearing, she declared that soon she expected to come face to face with her Maker and that she was ready to do whatever she was told to regain her good standing in the eyes of the Church. The priest's heavenward glance combined gratitude for the return of a lost sheep with irony at this pragmatic approach to atoning for a lifetime of sin; Madeleine was clearly not the first actress over whose last-minute change of heart he had presided. She kept her face from betraying the unorthodox notion that his doubts about her good faith were not her concern.

He sighed, reached into a pocket, and handed her a single sheet of paper covered with words printed in a tremulous hand evocative of a timid lover or an old, old man.

> *I, Madeleine Béjart, an avowed actress by profession, now realizing that my foremost consideration in this life must be my judgment before God in the next one, do hereby formally condemn and renounce the lie-mongering métier of the stage . . .*

If anything she'd underestimated to what extent Father Anselme had foreseen this moment. The document went on and on but the gist of it was that she, Madeleine Béjart, one of the most acclaimed actresses of her century as well as the former mistress of the great playwright Molière, must now turn her back on everything that made her what she was.

Illness having drained her complexion, Madeleine didn't give a thought to how Father Anselme might interpret the pallor caused by the offensive declaration. A deep breath proved of little use in calming her anger, the fresh pain that cut across her chest enhancing her rage. She fought for control but was about to show him the door when she found herself wondering what Molière would do in such circumstances. Not that he would consider renouncing his profession; her intention to do so for the sake of the Church had fueled many an argument between them. But were he to find himself in her shoes at this moment, how would he react?

As had often happened in a life filled equally with tragedy and comedy, her indignation dissipated in the emerging awareness of absurdity. What the priest asked her to do was revile the playing of roles. And to accomplish this, she would have to recite one last role!

Madeleine adjusted her smile of amusement into one of Christian humility. Reciting the insulting words in a convincing manner would be a final test of her acting prowess. Staring at the ceiling for divine inspiration, she declaimed the text with a fervor that left the cleric speechless. That boded well, for in her experience priests loved nothing better than to hear themselves talk. The performance fatigued her and she was overcome by a fit of coughing. Assuring him she simply needed to rest, she instructed him to slip the key under the door after locking it. She maintained a semblance of sobriety until he was out of sight, then granted herself the pleasure of that good long laugh.

She closed her eyes, delighted in the plush damask beneath her head. It was a pity to have been less than forthcoming, but what other choice had been left her? However Father Anselme might view her life's path, she had always tried to do the right thing—well, almost always. By becoming an actress, had she not only saved her family from destitution but also given a great many perfect strangers precious diversion from their human suffering?

"I wasn't lying, I was merely quoting," she said aloud. No, she couldn't fool herself into believing that what she had recited had not been a falsehood. She shrugged with the resignation born of a lifetime of compromises. In spite of the numerous lies she had told, Madeleine Béjart continued to believe that she was, at heart, a woman of integrity. She now reminded herself that nearly all of her lies, including the most recent, had been spoken with the best of intentions.

The theme of lying conjured up in Madeleine's mind the impish features of her mother, Marie Hervé, a veteran prevaricator who had died two years earlier at an age known only to herself. Unlike Marie Hervé, Madeleine was not a born liar but rather had learned in her years that life was less a dream, as the Spaniard Calderón had put it, than an extended series of unavoidable lies. Some fell flat; others were merely competent; only a few were magnificent. Some lies she was not proud of. Others were among her greatest achievements.

She shook with coughing once again and this time her handkerchief had more red in it than she had ever seen. It wouldn't be long before Father Anselme returned to the house for a more solemn ceremony than the one he had just carried out.

For a moment the pain eased and Madeleine allowed herself to draw in a lungful of air that brought clarity to her weary mind. The only remaining question of substance was how much she should tell Armande and Molière. It was in fact Molière, not Marie Hervé, who had first taught Madeleine that one could lie not to save one's own skin but to assist in the salvation of others. Yet again it struck her as implausible that this genius of a playwright and actor was her former lover. But even he, supreme sovereign of the *lie-mongering métier of the stage*—the words echoing in her mind were mercifully starting to lose their bite—hadn't the faintest notion of how skillfully she had combined lies and truths to create not so much her own life story, which would not matter to anyone once she was gone, as his, to be revered by the ages.

She reached for a second pillow to place under her aching neck. Would she ever find the courage to fling into Molière's face the magnificent lies upon which his good fortune, such as it was, had been constructed? Would he survive the revelation? Intrepid where her own safety was concerned, Madeleine was quick to harbor fears for those she loved. It had taken her years to know her own strength. To see her life's work destroyed would be too much, even for her.

A deep sigh brought on a fresh spasm. The pleasant lull was over.

Suddenly, as had occurred countless times in a relationship defined by mysterious comings and goings, there he stood, a vision from a dream: Molière. Dressed as the henpecked husband in *The Learned Ladies* for the rehearsal taking place at the Palais Royal Theater across the street, he panted from sprinting up the steps with a speed his legs could still manage but his lungs could no longer support. One ability he had not lost over the years was that of making an entrance with a horse's great clatter or, as today, because of her illness, the stealth of a cat.

At his advanced age he was not a man who drew the eye by comeliness, his attractiveness now residing in his voice and movements. Of average height, he was nonetheless shorter than Madeleine, a fact for which he'd long compensated by stuffing rags into his shoes. The bewigged head sat on a frame grown frail, the face dominated by a nose well proportioned in youth but now large and somehow plaintive. The eyes, Prussian blue or hazel depending on the light, remained arresting, the sensuous mouth, sulking lips jauntily set off by a chin dimple, utterly enticing.

She compared what she saw to her memory of the young man who'd come to her rescue not once but twice in the early days of their acquaintance. How could that valiant youth have metamorphosed into the poignant, irresistible shell of a man that stood before her, his bravado poorly concealing the tender lost boy who she alone knew lived on inside of him? She couldn't help but wonder what would have become of him without her, how he'd fare after she was gone.

"Armande tells me you sent for a priest," he tossed off in a mocking tone. "She said he dashed here so quickly she could hardly keep up. *Is Mado breathing her last?* asked I. *Not that I am aware*, said she. I expected to find you departed for the great beyond."

The final euphemism was pronounced with peerless understatement and not a soupçon of anxiety. When Molière was playing a role, sentiment crept into his voice only when he felt none.

He hadn't the faintest notion Madeleine knew this. She reached out a hand and he knelt by her bedside clutching it to his lips, shoulders heaving, the mask dropped. She could barely make out his words.

"Is it the end?" he croaked between sobs.

"Not quite," she replied.

"Then why frighten us with priests?" he managed to get out.

"If you must know," she said airily, "Father Anselme kindly oversaw my conversion. It was a touching scene. Had I known you planned to attend I'd have held the curtain."

She expected a sharp reaction: although Molière's belief in God was not feigned, it couldn't compare with his loathing of hypocrisy. But he wiped his tears on a white lace sleeve and, stepping back into a role, said, "You've been putting off spilling your heart to that priest for months to avoid displeasing me." He patted her hand, then dropped it abruptly. "It was foolish of you, my dear," he went on as if addressing a misguided adolescent. "You're free to do as you please. If only you'd believe that all I wish for is what's best for you."

She assumed her gravest expression. This tyke playing a great man knew her not at all! A priest was the last person on earth in whom she would confide.

She gestured majestically, her arms being the only parts of her body that retained their former strength, and said with a voice half-serious, half-comical, "I'm saved—yet again!"

"Yet again?" he echoed, his eyebrows knitting.

"Already you've forgotten?" she demanded with a pout.

Molière's eyes became veiled, whether in an attempt to grasp this allusion to their youth or in reminiscence of it she couldn't tell. Suddenly he eyed the clock, a gift from the Corneille brothers, Pierre and Thomas, before his falling out with them a decade earlier.

"I must return," he said. "The rehearsal is not all it should be. But how could I refrain from coming when Armande told me of your *visitor*?" To cover his concern he began to chant:

> *I hope you don't mind, Armande's lent me the key,*
> *So you'd not have to rise and be bothered by me.*
> *In case you were wondering, and why should you not,*
> *As I let myself in I shall let myself out.*

He kissed her hand again and dashed away. Soon she heard the return of the frenetic step that remained his trademark but was now accompanied by wheezing. Once again he stood at the foot of her bed, and though his cheeks still glistened he teased, "You may think you're about to die, *Marie-Madeleine, Sinner and Savior*. But you may not do so without my consent."

She smiled at this fresh evocation of an episode from over thirty years ago. He crouched next to her ear and intoned his final couplet in a stage whisper.

> *You may ask my permission but I never shall give it.*
> *And as for your life, you have only to live it!*

The door slammed for a second time but there was no sound of a key. As usual, Molière had forgotten to lock the door behind him.

Madeleine groaned, pushed the covers aside, and hoisted herself up. Like her late father, Joseph Béjart, Molière always seemed too preoccupied with more important matters to bother about security. She'd have no choice but to collect the key Father Anselme had pushed under the door that morning and lock it herself.

* * *

She dragged herself across the room, leaning heavily on her cane. Molière's reaction to Father Anselme's visit, alarm yielding to condescension and then a teasing dismissiveness, was evidence that it would be no mean task raising serious concerns with this master of the sleight-of-hand for whom locks were redundant. Molière had long been convinced he could gain access to her innermost thoughts, indeed open any door by playing the proper role. The one place of concealment in which he believed was his own inviolable heart. Madeleine was not all that different, but while he was a conspicuous mystery begging to be plumbed, not the least of her accomplishments was that the world assumed she felt only the sentiments she allowed to appear.

Yes, her revelations would come as a shock to Molière, and she shrank from disabusing this magnanimous soul of what he so touchingly thought was the truth about her. But time was growing short. Wouldn't it be simpler, while she had the strength, to write her secrets down, leave them for him to read once she was gone? And if at the very end she decided against it, she could stage a final *coup de théâtre* for her own amusement, cast the document into the fire and die laughing.

So, rather than going back to bed after locking the door, she hobbled over to the ebony writing table on which the chambermaid had laid out sheets of gilt-edged paper, a quill pen, and a bottle of ink. Supporting her arms on the table, she let her weight fall onto an armchair.

"Mado! How many times have I told you not to lean on the table? It's on its last legs and the Seine will turn to wine before your father gets around to repairing it!"

Her mother's voice came from an obscure recess of her memory and she felt a pang of nostalgia as she recalled the wobbly table upon which her family had eaten their meager fare when she was a girl growing up in the Marais district of Paris. And it was with a mixture of satisfaction and wistfulness that she ruminated on what a long way she had come.

She took up the quill in one hand and ran the other through her hair, no longer so red as it had been but still thick for a woman her age. Dipping the pen into the inkpot she wrote:

> *Paris, January 8, 1672*
> *Before I die there are things I wish to reveal.*
> *I don't know how to express them but I must find a way before I die.*

She frowned. She had not dabbled in poetry since she was a young woman, but it was clearly a bad sign to have started and ended with the same phrase. It appeared she wasn't quite ready to tell her tale.

Madeleine sat back, her thoughts adrift. So many secrets, her own and others'! What man had access to the information women possessed? Only women knew if men's reputations in love, whether laudatory or scornful, were deserved. Only they understood how to tend to others in the way of a mother, a sister, a daughter or a wife. Only they knew who was the father of their children.

And decided whom to tell about it.

From a nearby house, the noise of a child crying transported her back to the evening of Armande's birth, and her meditation turned to the events surrounding the conception of this young woman who'd been passed off as her sister. Armande's shrieks as the midwife pulled her from Madeleine's womb had sounded to her exhausted ears like iterations of the very question that had been running through her mind ever since she'd discovered she was expecting: who? who? who will be the father? Madeleine recalled the words she'd whispered into her daughter's ear. "I promise you a father, my darling," she'd said. "All in due time, my sweet. Not now."

Back in the present Madeleine stared at her quill poised above the paper and said aloud, "Not now," borrowing her earlier phrase, this time to give herself a reprieve in writing down what she could only think of as her final confession. To her mind, more important than whatever she might say to Father Anselme on her deathbed were the words she would either speak to Armande and Molière or leave in their hands to be read after she was gone. The priests never tired of intoning that one's final confession was part of what determined the fate of one's immortal soul. But having spent five decades assuaging those around her, Madeleine couldn't help but believe that she would muddle through with God as she had with her fellowmen. Armande and Molière, on the other hand, were another matter altogether. They'd never known how to placate anyone, not even each other. Soon Madeleine would no longer be there to watch over them, to assure that their lives, too, have proper endings. What she told them before she died was their last, best hope for salvation.

She limped across the room and settled down for a nap. A woman of faith in her own way, she fervently believed that however short her days were growing, a solution to her problem would come. The message of postponement she'd delivered to Armande so many years earlier assumed special poignancy on the lips of an actress. For if there was one lesson life had taught her, it was that in the theater, as in motherhood and love, timing was everything.

CHAPTER 2

In Which the Bad Old Days Are Remembered and Paris Is Swept by an Implausible Sea Breeze

---

In later life Madeleine Béjart often thought that if she hadn't had the reddest hair in all of Paris when she attended her Aunt Marion's wedding at the age of eighteen, none of it would have happened. Not her long and illustrious career in the theater. Not her relationship with Molière, almost as long but much more difficult to characterize. And certainly not the tragicomedy of errors that the question of who would be selected to play the role of Armande's father would turn out to be.

At the time of Marion's wedding in March of 1636, Madeleine's family was renting a ramshackle dwelling on the Rue de la Perle in the Marais, the waterlogged district on the Right Bank of the Seine that sprawls across the flood plain between the river and its ancient bed in the vicinity of Montmartre. The Marais, extending from the Bastille Prison, where criminals were incarcerated, to the Place de Grève, where they were disposed of, had not always been the most fashionable part of Paris. This damp sector to the east of the prestigious quarters around the Louvre Palace had long been peopled by merchants of mediocre prosperity, low-level civil servants like Madeleine's father, and artisans and guild workers like her mother, who was a seamstress.

But in the 1630s, during the last full decade of the tumultuous reign of Louis XIII, the area was turning into one of the most desirable neighborhoods in town. Aristocrats who had rarely ventured forth from their lands were being forced to establish secondary residences in Paris, where etiquette increasingly required them to spend much of the year dancing attendance on the King. So many noble families had built stately mansions to the north of the Rue Saint-Antoine that the Marais was becoming unrecognizable to old-timers like the Béjarts' next-door neighbor, an ancient cobbler's widow named Nicolette.

This Madeleine discovered one unseasonably mild afternoon in November of 1635, when most of the family—her parents, Joseph and Marie Hervé, along with Young Joseph, Geneviève, and little Louis—walked to the Rue de Montmartre to visit Aunt Marion Courtin, Marie Hervé's half-sister. Marion had just sent them a letter with the astounding news that although she was not yet married or even engaged, she was expecting a child. The ribbon shop where Madeleine worked as an assistant being closed for the afternoon, she was left behind to keep an eye on her favorite brother, Jacques, a rebellious thirteen-year-old who had refused to join the expedition. It was a pleasure to sit in the courtyard and listen to Nicolette's stories about olden times.

"When I was a girl," she began, "on this side of the Rue Saint-Antoine there was hardly a street. Just fields and windmills as far as the eye could reach."

"What was the point of windmills?" scoffed Jacques. "There's never a breath of fresh air around these parts."

It was a balmy afternoon without a hint of November's chilly breezes. Madeleine, the only member of the family to understand her mischievous little brother, who, she knew, worshipped her without ever showing it, observed his half-cynical, half-naïve smile with indulgence. Jacques, old enough to have a clear idea of how things were and young enough to be surprised that they had not always been so, was the member of the family most enraptured by Nicolette's tales. The quickest-witted of the Béjart boys, almost as clever as Madeleine, he'd resisted attending Jesuit school on the grounds that sitting still for long stretches of time would do damage to his *buttocks*, a word he could not pronounce without dissolving in giggles and yet managed to place in virtually every conversation. He made light of Madeleine's reassurances that the pupils being taught to read by the brothers did their lessons standing at their desks; he wouldn't even go once to see for himself. In the end Madeleine agreed to teach Jacques to read at home so as to avoid wear and tear on his *buttocks*.

Nicolette took a sip of cider and thought for a few moments. She loved spinning a yarn and wasn't above exaggerating for effect.

"Before all these houses were built there *was* wind," she replied, leaning forward to rumple Jacques's hair. "Why on some days, hens from the nearby farms would blow past the courtyard. When the wind died down we'd watch them limp back to their coops in single file." She paused to relish the invented image. "And if a storm was blowing in from downriver, your skin would be covered with flecks of salt from the sea."

Forgetting that the old lady was not the most reliable of sources, Madeleine shook her head in astonishment. Salt from the sea, here in the swampy heart of Paris? She had never in all her years set foot outside the city walls, but she'd heard that the Seine, after winding its way through Rouen in Normandy, emptied into the English Channel at Le Havre, some days' journey to the north. To her the seashore seemed like the ends of the earth. Just beyond the courtyard Madeleine spotted a peddler pushing his cart through the mud. An idealist by inclination, she tried to imagine an ocean breeze freshening sun-drenched fields where a fetid alleyway now ran between the rows of houses; a pragmatist by necessity, she could conjure neither the image nor the aroma. As fashionable a neighborhood as the Marais was becoming, most of its streets were too dark and narrow to let sunlight dry out accumulations of moisture or provide a place for sewage to flow. The eggy smell of the swampland combined with spoiled food, horse manure, and human waste to create a stench that abated only during a snowstorm or on the coldest winter days. How could a hint of the sea have blown through these muck-covered lanes?

Jacques's eyes, turquoise like his sister's, widened in response to Nicolette's fabrications, and for a moment Madeleine thought she was seeing once again the unruly boy Marie Hervé had so often left in her charge. Only four years older than he, she'd pranced about with him in tow, from time to time expending every ounce of strength to pick him up. Jacques was no longer a child, and Madeleine was proud of this little man more kind-hearted than he let on. When she was fifteen her penny-pinching grandfather, Pierre Béjart, had pressured her parents to marry her off to a rich disgusting widower named Old Man Normand; Jacques had drawn himself up with the full dignity of his eleven years to second his sister's decision to resist the match. And somehow the two siblings had persuaded Joseph and Marie Hervé to drop the matter.

Now Jacques, to disguise the fact that he wasn't quite sure Nicolette had been pulling his leg about the careening hens, countered, "You say there were no streets back then, but what about the Place Royale?" This lovely stone square featured a number of the city's most luxurious townhouses, many of them inhabited by the royal family's entourage. Jacques couldn't imagine a time when the most fashionable part of the neighborhood hadn't existed.

"There *was* no Place Royale," said Nicolette. "In those days it was a horse market, and a meeting place for men and girls at night." Nicolette dipped a finger into her cider and smoothed back a strand of hair. "If I ventured across that field in the evening I'd be black and blue from all the pinching." She looked Jacques straight in the eye. "Especially on the *buttocks*!"

He squealed, grabbed Nicolette's cider, and downed it in a single gulp before heading for the gate to stir up a bit of harmless bedlam in the interest of protecting his reputation as a young rogue. Madeleine did her best to catch hold of him but he zigzagged across the courtyard, eluding her grasp. Out of breath, she slipped and fell to the ground, then watched in amusement as he stood before the open gate and waved his rear end back and forth, as if this were the usual protocol for taking leave of one's family.

A few minutes after Madeleine watched Nicolette totter home across the courtyard, the rest of the Béjart family began to straggle in, returning from their visit to Aunt Marion. The first to arrive, the family's fastest walker but slowest thinker, was Madeleine's older brother, Young Joseph.

"How is the mother-to-be?" Madeleine inquired.

In her letter, Marion had informed the Béjarts that her pregnancy had set off a crisis. She and the child's father, Étienne L'Hermite, had met one afternoon when Marion was minding her father's shop. Étienne's wealthy family, which had aristocratic pretentions, wouldn't hear of his marrying a hatseller's daughter. As Marion explained, ending her missive on a plaintive note, the lovers were presently forbidden to communicate.

Young Joseph pondered his sister's question. Although at nineteen he was two years older than Madeleine, he hadn't been blessed with her sharp mind. He stared at the decrepit kitchen table their father had carried into the courtyard months earlier but never repaired, then stammered, "M-Marion is stout around the middle. She c-complains about having n-n-no . . ." The family did their best to ignore Young Joseph's stutter, but Madeleine couldn't stop herself from tapping a foot until he managed to conclude, ". . . no clothing to wear."

That much she could have surmised, Marion being the conceited creature she was.

"What about Étienne's parents?" she pursued. "Will they allow him to see her again?"

This time the answer floated in from just outside the gate.

"Of course they'll allow him to see her again, and to marry her as well, eventually," said a voice with a slightly flirtatious lilt. "But only once the child is born. Not that they would even consider admitting it at this point. That would be too thoughtful for the likes of them."

The voice's owner, Marie Hervé, made her appearance, struggling under the burden of five-year-old Louis, asleep on her shoulder. Her lips were parted in an engaging smile, but her eyes were glazed: Louis was getting too heavy to be toted around. Young Joseph lifted the little boy into his arms and carried him into the house.

As Marie Hervé smoothed her coiffure and caught her breath, Madeleine marveled at how fatigue and hardship only made her mother look more youthful. Although the age Marie Hervé admitted to fluctuated and never surpassed thirty-five, Madeleine suspected her to be in her forties, but she neither looked nor sounded like an aging matron. Her skin was smooth, her dark, auburn-highlighted hair free of gray. For a woman who had borne nine children and buried four of them, Marie Hervé had a trim figure and a spring in her step. Her distinguished profile, the forehead high and the nose a perfect upward curve, seemed to add to her diminutive stature.

That perfect profile had been passed down to Madeleine along with a lively imagination, but the daughter hadn't been bequeathed the mother's matter-of-fact attitude toward the truth, the rent, or the future. Madeleine couldn't remember a time when she hadn't felt mortified by Marie Hervé's willingness to lie at the drop of a hat. Still less had she inherited her mother's tendency to favor the demands of the heart over the dictates of reason, as manifested by Marie Hervé's excessive attachment to a husband who in spite of his thinness was a greater consumer of bread than winner of it. If Joseph's failings didn't escape Marie Hervé's notice they did nothing to weaken her devotion, as was proven by the babies she bore him year after year, many of whom she was destined to bury. It didn't enhance Madeleine's opinion of her mother that the noises emanating from the corner of the sleeping loft suggested just how Joseph Béjart made up for his shortcomings. Night after night Madeleine vowed that she'd never lose her head over a man.

Marie Hervé tied her hair back and headed for the scullery. There had been little to eat but at the risk of delaying supper Madeleine couldn't resist asking, "When is the baby due?"

"*Between January and March*—that was all my sister could say," sniffed Marie Hervé. "Her head is too full of grand plans for becoming a *great lady* to keep track of such details."

"At least she wishes to raise herself up," Madeleine replied.

"I wish her godspeed," said Marie Hervé with a rueful smile. "Great lady or no, I wouldn't complain about having servants to look after me." She made her way to the scullery.

Madeleine said nothing. Marie Hervé and Joseph both required more looking after than they could possibly imagine. Madeleine was not higher than her mother's waist when she realized they would demand more care than they would ever give her.

Bringing up the rear was Joseph Béjart senior, accompanied by Geneviève. Lost in a reverie, he neglected to shut the gate. Geneviève skipped over to Madeleine and planted a kiss on her cheek.

"Aunt Marion is soooo fat!" Her giggle was that of a child, although at eleven she was several inches taller than her mother. "Will you ever be fat like that, Mado?"

Madeleine deflected Geneviève's query by steering her toward the house, not letting on that the question was one she had put to herself. Did she hope to acquire a husband? To her eyes her parents' marriage resembled an endlessly renewed altercation. By day they thrashed out the time-honored question of how to make ends meet without the man of the house providing a reliable source of income, by night that of why the woman of the house put up with it all.

Madeleine's musings were interrupted by the sound of the guilty party seating himself on a chair, his knees bent at a sharp angle because of the length of his legs. Joseph Béjart was a veritable giant, over six feet in height, a portrait in pallor. He had blue-gray eyes and an impassive thin face that tended toward grimness. His once fair hair now resembled the sparse ash flakes in a cooling hearth. As a girl Madeleine had been enamored of her father and he had always held a special fondness for his willowy daughter with the copper-colored hair, one of those supremely capable girls who, born into families in which the adults behave like children, step into the breach. While Madeleine appreciated her mother's playfulness, as she matured she began to hold Marie Hervé responsible for Joseph's failings, if only to avoid blaming them on him.

Joseph Béjart sat and fidgeted. Madeleine never had the faintest idea of the reason for her father's disgruntlement. In fact no one could fathom why Joseph, the youngest son and scourge of the clan's paterfamilias, Grandfather Pierre Béjart, seemed incapable of sitting still for a quarter of an hour or holding a job for a month at a time. Whether he was employed as the bailiff of the Royal Forestry Office, the recorder of enrollments at the Place Royale Military Academy, or the personal accountant of one of his father's well-to-do friends, it would be only a matter of time before Joseph would announce that he was ill-suited to carry out the tasks the job entailed.

Why was each passing day such an ordeal for Joseph? He wrote in a legible hand and had a head for numbers. Although sullen and withdrawn, he wasn't by nature unkind. His most obvious liability was the belief that the work his father acquired for him was unworthy of his efforts, a state of affairs that infuriated Pierre more than if his son had been a simpleton.

Pierre Béjart, short, portly, dark of hair and complexion and painstaking in fulfilling every task and duty, was as different from Joseph as father and son ever were. A government lawyer who used his connections in the royal bureaucracy to get jobs for his sons, Pierre, a widower, owned a house on the Rue de Jouy, so close to Saint Paul's that the pewter plates resonated when the churchbells rang. Though constructed of stone and well appointed, the house could not hold a candle to the new aristocratic residences in the area, but it would have been impolitic to point this out to the mean-spirited miser who had the fire banked on the coldest nights and rarely kept servants for longer than a fortnight. If Pierre was universally disliked, his influence was such that the Béjarts were viewed as a family to be reckoned with, Joseph being the sole member who never amounted to anything.

A thumping noise from the scullery drew Madeleine back to attention and she espied her mother stooping to collect some onions that had rolled away. As chief provider for her family for twenty years Marie Hervé had played a difficult role, toiling long hours sewing curtains and gowns as well as cooking and keeping house. Intermittent at best in their payment of rent, she and Joseph moved the family on a regular basis, with Marie Hervé resorting to any means available to assure their survival. She lied to her aristocratic customers, substituting poor fabrics for the more expensive ones they had paid for. Once she told a bourgeois newly arrived from the provinces that she owned the house the family was renting but had lost the deed in a fire, then sold him the building in great haste. Called before a judge, she stammered that she hadn't understood the significance of the document to which she'd affixed her signature, thus prevaricating her way out of a prison sentence by the skin of her lying teeth. She sometimes lied about being Joseph Béjart's wife so as not to be harassed about his debts, especially since these had piled so high that creditors were brandishing threats of legal action against them both. Unless matters improved they'd find nowhere to escape without forsaking Paris altogether.

Madeleine turned back to her father. It distressed her to see how quickly he was aging. She barely kept her face from revealing her sadness as she poured him cider from a jug.

"How did you find Marion?" she asked. "Aside from *stout around the middle*, as Young Joseph so astutely pointed out."

Shaken from a melancholy daydream, Joseph Senior scowled and said, "Let's hope she gets herself out of this predicament. She should have thought ahead."

That Joseph called Marion feckless was equally worthy of laughter and tears. Madeleine strode to the wall separating courtyard and street. How she longed to march out the gate one last time, to see what someone of her resourcefulness might achieve once freed from her obligations! *Not now.* An exasperated voice in her head whispered the familiar refrain. Her family, without even realizing it, had her alone to rely upon.

She had never criticized her father, less from fear of questioning his authority than from an aversion to hurting this man she no longer revered but continued to love. As she prepared a retort in Marion's defense she turned back to find him still squirming in his chair and thought of Jacques's restlessness, undoubtedly inherited from Joseph. And once again her heart relented in forgiveness. It was too early to tell if little Louis would grow up to be an exception, but the three older Béjart men were delicate creatures, each in his own way.

"Yes, Marion can be a silly thing," she tossed off, "but she's young and will outgrow it."

Joseph took no notice of the irony of Madeleine's commenting on the immaturity of her aunt. He unfolded himself from the chair and made his way over to the broken kitchen table sitting in the courtyard waiting to be repaired. The decaying wood had suffered through months of exposure to rain and sun until it was now beyond hope of restoration.

"How quickly time passes," he said in a melancholy voice. "When did I bring this out to repair? It's ruined."

Madeleine ran a hand over its surface and a splinter pierced her finger. She teared up, the degraded wood embodying Joseph Béjart's obscure dreams.

He stood and shuffled toward the scullery door. His features assumed the defiant expression of a youngster staving off an imminent reproach.

"If you'd like to call on Marion tomorrow morning," he said, "I'll be free to accompany you."

Madeleine maintained her calm. "And Maître Giraud?" Joseph had been copying official documents for a lawyer friend of Grandfather's.

"I've left his employ." Joseph glanced toward the house and lowered his voice. "I wasn't suited to the work. Copying morning till evening. A mule could execute such a task."

Madeleine stared at the ground. "Does Mother not know?" she asked.

"I haven't told her," Joseph replied in a monotone.

Had things reached such an impasse between her parents that Madeleine was now expected to serve as their go-between?

"How are we to get along?" she snapped. "Will you never learn to reflect before you act? And what will Grandfather think?"

Joseph advanced toward the front gate and slammed it with such vehemence that it swung past the latch and into the street, nearly knocking over a group of priests.

"Let him think what he wishes, the old goat!" he cried out.

Accustomed to her father's tantrums, Madeleine placed a hand on his shoulder.

"Calm yourself," she said. "He's only trying to help." Joseph blinked compulsively. She waited in vain for him to speak, then added, "You know there's no love lost between Grandfather and myself." That was an understatement; she had detested Pierre Béjart long before he attempted to sell her off like a sack of grain. "But you must show him respect. He's your father."

"Silence!" It was not Joseph's voice that replied but a dry rasp, filled with scorn for everything and everyone in the world. "Respect, you say? Respect for my father? Pierre Béjart is not my father!"

CHAPTER 3

In Which a Kitchen Table and a Family Are Reduced to Ash

Madeleine stared at her father. Marie Hervé's voice wafted out from the scullery.

"Stew is ready! Be quick about it, if you want it hot. The firewood has run out."

Joseph pushed past Madeleine but she caught his arm and held him, pitting her strength against his. Her voice quaked.

"What do you mean by saying such a thing?"

Joseph answered not in his usual petulant voice but in one of regret for the forceful individual he had never become.

"It is the truth," he said.

Madeleine crossed her arms and waited. Joseph sat down and folded his hands in his lap.

"My mother, your grandmother," he began, "took a gentleman to her bed. He was a man of high birth. Pierre Béjart was never informed of it."

So it was the truth. Pierre wasn't Madeleine's flesh and blood.

"How did you discover it?" she asked.

"Shortly after your mother and I married," he continued, "your grandmother fell ill. I was the last one to see her alive. Marie Hervé had been so distraught she insisted on going in alone to be done with it. She left the room in tears before I entered to bid my mother adieu."

Marie Hervé upset over the death of Anne Béjart? It seemed improbable given the mocking terms she had always used to describe her late mother-in-law. Now that Joseph had revealed the worst, he continued in a calmer voice.

"She told me that one day a stranger approached her as she was leaving church. She was impressed by his attire and manners, flattered, I suppose, by the attentions of such a high-born gentleman. It was a fine day, and the man asked her to take a stroll. Without knowing his intentions she accepted." Joseph's tone shifted, as if so many years after the event he was still struggling to come to grips with the only sin he had ever known his beloved mother to have committed. "She was raised in the countryside," he continued slowly, "not in Paris. She was from the same village Pierre came from. She was a handsome woman, my mother was, always arrayed in the accoutrements of a prosperous man's wife. But she wasn't a woman of the world. It happened only once, and the timing was such . . ." He wrinkled his nose as if catching a whiff of spoiled meat. "Pierre never had cause to suspect."

Madeleine conjured up an image of Pierre Béjart. What she'd just heard changed nothing between herself and the person she'd long ago stopped thinking of as a beloved grandfather.

And yet she still cared deeply about the man who sat before her, for all his flaws, and her grandfather's true identity meant as much to Joseph as it meant little to her. How foolish men were, preoccupied with lineage when what really mattered was tending to those one loved!

She squeezed her father's hand and said only, "How can Grandmother have been sure which man was your father?"

"She wouldn't explain," responded Joseph after a moment's reflection. "Her strength was ebbing and I begged her to tell me his name but she was weeping too hard to reply. I asked if she could write the name down and she said nothing. By the time I found paper and quill it was too late." He shook his head. "Why did Mother not simply hold to her lie? I've never told a soul what she said, but not for one second have I forgotten. To this day I don't know who my father is. Only who he is not."

Madeleine turned toward the house and saw that now Marie Hervé was feeding little Louis from a bowl with her usual combination of patience and playfulness. And the daughter's heart broke for all the years her mother had suffered because unbeknownst to her, the life Joseph had been leading wasn't the one to which he thought himself destined. Rather than following in his brothers' footsteps and rising through the ranks of the royal bureaucracy, the youngest Béjart son had contempt for work beneath his station, disdain for the unrefined wife he increasingly treated as if she were a court jester.

Madeleine was brought back to the present by the sound of splitting wood. Joseph was reducing the kitchen table to kindling. By the time he had finished, evening was falling. As they crossed the courtyard she kissed his cheek.

"Never mind about Pierre," she said. "Strike out on your own and find a trade that pleases you. You'll be better off without him."

Before Joseph had a chance to reply, she heard the gate being lifted and put back into place and the sound of Jacques's whistling.

"What happened to the gate?" asked the boy. "And what is there to eat?"

"Stew, if the others haven't devoured it all." Jacques crowed his appreciation. "As for the gate," Madeleine went on, "it was pushed out by the wind."

"There was no wind where I was," the boy said.

She rumpled Jacques's hair and replied, "How strange. It blew up here as soon as you left. It was just as Nicolette said things used to be. It smelled of the sea."

Jacques sprinted to the house. Joseph and Madeleine crossed the courtyard arm in arm. He hadn't responded to her idea of getting along without Pierre's help but as they stepped inside the door, in the candlelight she read the answer on his face.

***

In the weeks following Madeleine's discovery of her father's secret, the household was in a state of siege. Fearful of debt collectors, Joseph insisted that knocks at the door be ignored. His only activity was casting the chopped-up table into the fire piece by piece, the burning accelerating as the mild fall gave way to one of the coldest winters in living memory. Aside from forays to the hearth Joseph spent his days lying on a straw mattress in the loft. He ate little and spoke hardly a word in response to Marie Hervé's frenzied attempts to shatter her husband's lethargy. Although she squinted over her sewing late into the night, there was barely enough money for food, and none for rent.

On the morning of January 9, 1636, the day after Madeleine's eighteenth birthday, Joseph came downstairs fully dressed for the first time in days. He threw the last remaining piece of wood into the fire and told the family thronged around the hearth that he was going out to borrow money. He kissed Marie Hervé on the forehead and was gone.

As the hours dragged on, Marie Hervé covered her growing panic by concentrating on her sewing and warming broth over the fire's dying embers. The bells of Saint Paul's seemed to be chiming away all hope of Joseph's return. As the sun set and the fire fell to soot, Marie Hervé broke into howls.

"What are we to do?" she gasped between hiccoughs.

Disbelieving her own words, Madeleine assured her mother that Joseph would be home by morning.

He was not.

Marie Hervé was too distraught to mend garments or sew curtains. She was now the one the creditors would pursue; it was her turn to fear leaving the house.

The children did what they could. In addition to Madeleine's salary from the ribbon shop, Young Joseph, who was a shoemaker's apprentice, polished boots each evening. Jacques stood in the street and offered to carry parcels or do errands for rich ladies, and Geneviève toiled as a maid in one of the splendid new mansions on the Place Royale. There was no

point turning to the Béjart uncles, who had long since broken off ties with their wayward brother, and Madeleine would
sooner have swallowed pebbles than ask for help from Pierre
Béjart. Without the generosity of Nicolette and other neighbors, there would have been no firewood at all. As it was, its
use was limited to evening, when a half-dozen carrots and a
handful of turnips tossed into a cauldron of water passed for
supper.

The Seine funneled frigid air through the city. They spent
the nights huddling for warmth on a pallet. Madeleine was
half surprised each morning to find them all breathing.

One icy evening in late January Madeleine was vainly
attempting to warm herself before the embers when someone
tickled the back of her neck. Only Jacques, aware of her particular fondness for him, was brave enough to risk such a thing.

"You little wolf, you'll pay for that," she wheezed.

It was pleasant to have a reminder of less troubled times.
She cornered Jacques and tickled him until he collapsed,
clutching his knees to his chin for protection and gasping out
between giggles, "I just wanted you to smile."

"Why?" she asked, releasing him.

He was fourteen but his face retained the mobility of a
child's. His eyes grew serious.

"Because I couldn't remember the last time you did."

Her manner was frightening him quite as much as the prospect of running out of food and firewood! The one thing
within her power was to distract him from his worries.

"Listen, Sir Jacques," she said. "Why should you be the one
to make me smile?"

In the throes of puberty, Jacques was intrigued that the discussion was turning toward affairs of the heart. Although any number of younger males in the neighborhood had attempted to keep company with her, they never seemed to get very far.

"You have a *sweetheart*?" His voice cracked on the word.

For the first time Madeleine noticed that he was crossing the line between adolescence and young manhood. "Of course I do." She kissed his forehead and drew the false words out teasingly. "Of course I have a sweetheart."

"Who?" he demanded.

"Think about it. I'll tell you tomorrow."

The matter would distract Jacques from his worries till morning, when she would say her beloved was Alain, the grocer's one-legged son, and watch her brother howl with laughter. For now she batted her eyes and puckered her cheeks into the kind of smile rich ladies wore at church.

"There, I am smiling," she said in a honeyed tone. "Are you satisfied?"

***

The plague, which made its way from the coast down to Rouen, didn't reach Paris that winter, but one morning in early February Madeleine awoke to discover Jacques burning with fever. She piled towels and a ragged tablecloth on top of him. She'd have given a year of her life for firewood and a thick piece of beef.

She lit a fire with the three remaining logs and roused Marie Hervé, who tended to the boy as best she could. The only person to whom Madeleine could turn was the one she most abhorred. Before she knew it she was sprinting through the snow-covered streets. Breathing hard, she knocked on a door of varnished oak, waited, then rapped again. The door swung open.

"Yes?" snapped a scowling maid.

"Tell Maître Béjart," said Madeleine, "that his granddaughter wishes to speak to him."

"Maître Béjart is abed," gloated the maid.

"Announce Madeleine Béjart," came the firm reply. "It's a matter of life and death."

Pierre Béjart's dressing gown and nightcap indicated the maid hadn't been lying.

"What are you doing here?" he barked.

"I need your assistance," said Madeleine. "Please, Grandfather." The word came out with surprising ease. "Can you lend me money for firewood? Jacques is very ill and Father is gone."

"Gone?" said the old man in an incredulous tone. "What do you mean, gone?"

"I believe he's left Paris," she replied. "Please. I fear Jacques may die."

Pierre showed Madeleine into the *salle*, where a fire had just been lit.

"Jacques is not my responsibility," he said brusquely, taking a seat. "If Joseph has gone off without providing for his children, let the sin be on his head."

There was an element of truth in this brutal assessment but Madeleine couldn't let it pass.

"I can't defend my father's actions, *Grandfather*," she said, this time pronouncing the word with an insolence that escaped the old man's comprehension but not his notice. "But is it not for God to judge him? My brother has done nothing wrong."

Pierre Béjart exploded.

"Nor has he or the lot of you done a thing to deserve my assistance!" he cried. "If you'd followed my advice and married Monsieur Normand you would have a warm house and plenty to eat instead of crawling to me for alms." He spat into the rising fire. "All of you combined aren't worth a sou. You need money, you say? Then walk the streets! You are no better than your aunt, that trollop who finds herself with a child to care for and no husband in sight. You're no longer my granddaughter!"

The only thing that registered amidst the barrage of insults was that Marion had delivered her baby. Perhaps one of the unanswered knocks at the door had been a message. It mattered little what Pierre thought of her, but why was her ire not raised by his scorn for those she loved? She focused on her hands, numb from exposure but tingling. She moved her fingers, welcomed the pain that marked a return of sensation, and began to laugh. The warmth of understanding spread through her veins as she roared at being disowned by one who was nothing to her.

"How dare you laugh!" he cried out. "Get out of my sight! Whore! Actress!"

It was the breaking of a spell. Joseph had spent years staging an incompetent rebellion against this man. At eighteen, with her life before her, Madeleine would make a clean break of it. Her father had never pleased Pierre Béjart. She would give herself free rein to displease him.

There was no time to lose. She could do anything, anything at all, to save her brother!

She made her way through the streets past maids laden with provisions and merchants vying for attention with beggars, more numerous since the area had become prosperous. At the Rue de la Perle, she positioned herself next to a bent old woman and held out her hand.

A gentleman on horseback pulled on his reins. The hag launched into her appeal.

"If you please, Monsieur," Madeleine said, imitating her wheedling tone. "It isn't for myself but for my little brother who is deathly ill and needs food and a warm fire."

The gentleman tossed a coin into the crone's cupped hands, then addressed Madeleine.

"Certainly, my lovely. And what do you offer in return?" He raised an eyebrow.

It took a moment to grasp his meaning. She had no experience of love besides the occasional kiss. Could she actually go with a man she didn't know? What choice did she have?

"Come into the alley with me," she said, "and you'll find out."

Pinning her against a wall, he fondled her. She closed her eyes, imagining how pleased Jacques would be to have nourishment. Suddenly, to her surprise, the man placed a gold louis in her hand and continued on his way.

Within minutes she'd stoked the fire, heated wine, and begun roasting the mutton she had bought. Hearing Jacques's banter she felt reassured but when she reached his bedside she realized it was an effect of delirium. His face was as red as a radish. Marie Hervé was using the same rag to wipe her son's forehead and the tears coursing down her cheeks.

Madeleine ordered Geneviève to run for the priest and sat on Jacques's other side.

"This is the life," he exclaimed. "Never had so much room!" Trembling from head to foot, he rolled first in one direction, then in the other. "One lady to the right, one lady to the left."

Whore! Actress! Pierre's words reverberated. Taking the first suggestion might help Jacques live. If not, perhaps following the second suggestion might help him die.

"That's right, Your Majesty," she said. "We're ladies-in-waiting, at your bidding."

"Where are the others?" asked Jacques. "Where is my court?"

"Never mind, Sire. They'll come for the evening ceremonies."

"But where are they now?" he persisted.

Madeleine thought for a moment. "Carrying out the work of the kingdom," she intoned.

"Work, shirk. Off to play, for today," he crowed in a sing-song, his teeth chattering.

"Does His Majesty desire more cover?" she asked gaily. She thought he was trying to nod and Marie Hervé slipped her shawl from her shoulders. "Does His Majesty wish to drink?" Madeleine inquired, putting a mug of cider to his lips.

He spilled it on his chest from shaking. His eyes glowing, he whispered: "Approach."

She put her ear next to his face. He mustered all his strength to pinch the nape of her neck.

And Madeleine Béjart laughed.

An explosive cough: foam poured from Jacques's mouth. With his last ounce of life he extended his hand to her lips, demanding obeisance. Madeleine held it against her cheek. She was not a demonstrative soul, but she clung to him, holding him as tightly as she could.

"Enough," he gasped. "Mustn't disturb my *buttocks*!"

She felt him tremble with a spasm of choking laughter. There was a gurgling, then silence. When she pulled away, all that her mind could take in for an eternity of seconds was that he had shut his eyes tightly, as he always did when he was having himself a good laugh.

CHAPTER 4

In Which Our Heroine Follows Her Grandfather's Wise Advice and Chooses a Profession

They sold some of their meager furniture to pay for a simple funeral. They had no way of informing Joseph of Jacques's death and it was decided not to notify Marion, who doubtless had her hands full with the new baby.

That Lent was soon upon them made little difference, the larder being so bare there was nothing to give up. In late winter they were accustomed to surviving on dark bread and boiled root vegetables seasoned with the memory of more appetizing food. By some miracle no one else fell ill and for a while Joseph's creditors, as if frightened by death, stayed away. Marie Hervé once again took in needlework, but the rent hadn't been paid for months.

On a snowy evening in late February, when supper had consisted of an unchewable galette made from flour so dark it resembled soil, Marie Hervé handed Madeleine a scroll, sighed, and kissed her daughter good night. In confusing language the scroll declared that if within a fortnight the Béjarts didn't pay the rent and other debts in arrears, Joseph and Marie Hervé would be forced to vacate the house, hand over their worldly goods, and be called before a judge.

Madeleine let herself fall onto one of the two remaining chairs. They had no news of her father. Their kindly neighbor Nicolette had barely enough to live on herself and was in poor health. Did Madeleine have no other choice than to follow Pierre Béjart's considerate professional advice and walk the streets?

Suddenly from outside she heard the thin wail of a voice calling out over the gale.

"Madeleine? Is anybody home? It's me! Open the door, I'm dead from the cold!"

Only Aunt Marion was vain enough to identify herself as "me" and assume others would understand. Madeleine hadn't seen her for months, since before the birth of her baby. The Courtins lived just inside the Porte de Montmartre, nearly an hour's walk from the Rue de la Perle even in fine weather. What was her aunt doing out on such a night?

Bracing herself against the wind, Madeleine unlocked the street gate. Her aunt, wrapped in a hooded cloak and scarf, pushed past her into the house with a shriek of misery.

"Why have you banked the fire?" she cried. "A body could freeze in here!"

Madeleine winced. Would Marion have said such a thing if she'd heard about Jacques?

"Good evening, Aunt," Madeleine said evenly, then bowed and added in a sardonic tone, "If only a messenger had informed us we would be receiving royalty, Your Majesty would have found a blazing fire."

Ignoring the remark, Marion unwrapped her scarf cocoon with a flourish, scattering snow over the straw-covered floor. A short, pretty woman in her mid-twenties with strawberry-blond curls she spent much of her time rearranging, a lovely face and a striking figure, she had aspirations of becoming an actress. Even on nights less blustery than this, she entered a room as if she had blown in.

"Madeleine, my dear," she emoted. "It's been so long! How very well you look!"

As with her sister, Marie Hervé, it was often difficult to discern whether Marion was lying or simply had a weak purchase on reality.

"I'm sorry we've been out of touch," Madeleine said. "How is the baby? Boy or girl?"

"Little Madeleine is your goddaughter, Mademoiselle, and you would have held her at her baptism if you'd received the messages I sent, but we could delay no longer. Have you been spending your days at court?"

Madeleine managed a smile. There was no point unburdening herself, so she drew the two remaining chairs to the hearth, motioned to her aunt to take a seat, and changed the subject.

"If the baptism has already taken place, why have you ventured out on such a night?"

"An excellent question! I've risked my virtue walking the streets." Marion's throaty laugh was reminiscent of the pleasures of the bedroom. "Oh, Mado, we're to be married!"

Madeleine jumped up and hugged her. At least the fates were smiling on someone.

"The wedding is March 7th," Marion went on. "It will still be Lent but we've asked for a dispensation. Shall I help you choose a dress? Turquoise, to match your eyes."

The gauntness of Madeleine's face, her frayed clothing, the denuded room: had none of it registered? And yet why spoil the moment?

"What we have all been wishing for," she said with a faint smile, "has come to pass."

"You must look your best," Marion pursued. "Father can provide a hat." Without warning she let out a yelp. "*Shoes!* I saw some of those adorable ones from Italy with satin flaps in the arcade at the Place Royale. Once you've chosen your colors you *must* buy a pair."

Madeleine smiled noncommittally and said, "Would you like soup before you go home?"

"No thank you, my darling." Marion glanced around the room with a quick, birdlike motion. "Wasn't there a table that stood before the fire? And other chairs?"

"The chairs have been sent to the joiner's to be repaired," said Madeleine after a moment's hesitation. "And Father has taken the table out to the courtyard to mend."

"In the middle of winter?"

"Months ago. You know how he is," said Madeleine, raising her eyebrows.

Marion nodded and said, "Perhaps I will take soup, while I have a word with my sister."

"She's asleep," came the swift reply. "She'll be so pleased to hear your news!"

Marion's eyebrows knit. "Your father, then. I haven't seen him in many months."

"He too has gone to bed," Madeleine said, standing and walking to the hearth. "I'm afraid the soup is no longer warm."

Marion fiddled with a thread on her sleeve. "What do you take me for?" she exclaimed. "Have I not eyes in my head? What has happened?"

Madeleine blinked hard against the tears, relieved not to carry the masquerade further. Marion pulled her chair close and said, "There, there, have a cry. You aren't very good at lying, my dear. There is an art to it. You must ask your mother to teach you."

Madeleine wiped her eyes and blurted out, "Father left town. Then Jacques ..." Her voice breaking, she continued in a whisper. "He fell ill and died a month ago. We sold the chairs to pay for his funeral. If we don't find money soon, we'll be evicted and have nowhere to go."

Marion pressed her niece to her bosom. Her cheeks streamed with tears.

"Dear little Jacques. I'll never see him again!" She wept noisily. "Can you forgive me for prattling on about my wedding? Has Marie Hervé fled Paris as well?"

"No, she is asleep." Madeleine handed over the eviction notice. "We just received this."

Marion gazed at the sheet so long it seemed having a baby had made her forget her letters. She paced the room, speaking her thoughts aloud.

"The timing couldn't be worse," she groaned. "I haven't a quarter of a sou to my name, nor has Étienne until he receives his inheritance. My father is beside himself about the cost of the wedding. The L'Hermites are giving enough to make the banquet respectable, no more."

"You needn't explain, Aunt," said Madeleine in a somber tone. "I'll manage."

Marion's face lit up. "Tristan!" she exclaimed.

Madeleine stared blankly.

"Étienne's brother, Tristan L'Hermite, the famous playwright," said Marion. "Surely you've heard of him? His tragedy of *Marianne* was the greatest hit at the Théâtre du Marais last year. Didn't you see it?"

"Of course I saw it. Mother and I attended a performance as guests of Cardinal Richelieu."

Marion blushed. "I thought you might have sneaked in, living so close to the theater."

In fact none of the Béjarts had ever had the luxury of seeing a play, but one of Paris's two theaters, the Théâtre du Marais, was indeed housed just down the street in a converted tennis court near the corner of the Rue de la Perle and the Rue Vieille du Temple. Three evenings a week, Tuesdays, Fridays, and Sundays, Madeleine observed crowds streaming through the neighborhood after the shows, reciting their favorite lines and commenting on the performances. A glimpse of a player in full regalia would scandalize her, the reputation of theater people being what it was. But she would also be mesmerized by the beauty of the actresses and the majesty of their costumes. These elegant individuals embodied a world of privilege which, although it existed practically under her nose, was as inaccessible as an invitation to dine with King Louis and Queen Anne.

"Why would this Tristan give me money?" sniffed Madeleine. "I've never met him."

"He needs someone to play Marianne's confidante in the revival planned for April," said Marion. "I'm holding out for a larger part for my début, but he might consider you."

How typical of Marion, trying to assure that she would win the race before bothering with a first step! The fact that her aunt's fiancé was the brother of a playwright as well as an aristocrat undoubtedly accounted for Étienne's appeal.

Madeleine reflected. How could she become an actress when she had never set foot in a theater? Suddenly, without warning, she doubled over and shook with laughter.

"I'm serious," said Marion. "What's so amusing?"

"Something Grandfather said about actresses," the young woman gasped.

"You fear scandal?" cried Marion with glowering eyes. "That old miser can say what he will, your reputation won't pay the rent. I'm not suggesting you walk the streets!"

More and more absurd! For someone who had been willing to pander her charms for a gold coin to help her brother, being an actress would be like entering a convent! Madeleine's laughter tapered off.

"Let's be practical," she said. "Why would Tristan L'Hermite hire me?"

"Because you're lovely," said her aunt who, though vain, was not grudging with praise.

"Thank you," Madeleine replied, "but so are hundreds of others. Why else?"

"Because you're tall," countered Marion, "and have a fine figure."

"A true rarity."

Marion reflected and said, "You have a good head and can learn lines quickly."

"And why should Tristan believe that?" snapped Madeleine.

"And why do you find an impediment to everything I say?" replied Marion, but her voice remained playful. "I'll forego the soup, my dear." She fussed with her locks. "There *is* a reason you'll interest Tristan, but you'll have to discover it for yourself at my wedding."

Madeleine accompanied her to the gate. Noticing her agitation, Marion relented.

"You're as stubborn as your mother," she said, her voice barely audible over the wind. "If there is one thing Tristan finds irresistible, it's a lovely *redhead*."

***

The next morning Marie Hervé was delighted by Marion's idea, Madeleine relieved and disappointed in equal measures that the notion she might be deemed a fallen woman did not appear to disturb her mother one bit.

As the wedding approached, they spent every spare moment producing an outfit out of thin air. A customer of Marie

Hervé's had discarded a swath of cloth which, though of wool rather than satin, velvet, damask, or silk, was of a cobalt blue that would go well with Madeleine's coloring; from this they made a gown worn over her bodice, which they dyed to match, mending the holes in the sleeves and covering the seams with ribbons. A well-to-do neighbor gave Madeleine old slippers made presentable with satin bows and lent her a fur muff and a string of pearls to set off her *garcette*, an elaborate coiffure of corkscrew curls and loops recently introduced by Queen Anne because King Louis disapproved of powdered wigs.

The trappings of elegance would have gone for naught in Madeleine Béjart's quest to become an actress if she hadn't been a woman of exceptional beauty. At five-foot seven she was as tall as most men. She had long, straight, light auburn hair that captured sun and candlelight in unpredictable ways, and a burnished complexion less delicate than most redheads. The high generous bosom, surprising in a woman so slim and set off to perfection by the low-cut bodices of the time, would be considered by many to be the loveliest of any actress of her day.

Madeleine's large blue-green eyes were mesmerizing when they exploded with merriment or anger. Though the young woman disliked her mother's flirtatiousness and wasn't often coquettish, on those rare occasions when her lips budded into a pout they demanded to be embraced. Her forehead was broad and high, the line it formed with her nose such a flaw-less curve that her profile seemed traced from an engraving of some Greek goddess. In quiet moments, when her thoughts drifted to dreams of a distant world in which she wouldn't be put in charge of fixing everything, her face resembled a thing carved.

On the morning of the wedding, with the deadline for paying the rent fast approaching, Madeleine found Marie Hervé bustling about, her cheeks glowing like a freshly peeled onion. She herself was bleary-eyed. She had spent the night fretting that if her plan didn't succeed, the entire family might soon be shivering beneath one of the city bridges.

"Goodness, Daughter, you're a sight," chirped Marie Hervé. "Didn't you sleep at all?"

As Madeleine gnawed on a rock-hard heel of bread and ran through the lines she'd use to flatter Tristan, a problem that had been lingering came suddenly to the fore. Even if he offered her work, the new season wouldn't begin until after Easter. To ward off eviction she would have to beg for an advance. Would he demand her favors?

Weary of trying to bite into the bread, she cast it onto the table. Perhaps one of the children had stronger teeth.

***

Like most fashionable marriage ceremonies, the nuptials of Étienne L'Hermite and Marion Courtin were to begin on the stroke of midnight. At half-past eleven on the evening of Thursday, March 6, 1636, Madeleine thus walked through the arched doorway of Saint Eustache Church near Les Halles accompanied by her mother and sister. A shawl fabricated from purloined silk poorly masked Marie Hervé's threadbare skirt. Geneviève wore a borrowed sepia-colored dress that set off her brown hair and hazel eyes and highlighted a figure that promised to rival Madeleine's. Marion was spectacular in a traditional red velvet bridal gown and a bonnet of burgundy and silver brocade that Simon Courtin, her father, would pass off to a rich customer as new. Madeleine followed the procession formed by Marion's entourage and made her entrance into the candlelit area of the chapel near the altar.

The ripple of admiration that greeted Madeleine augured well for the success of her stratagem. The gentleman standing next to Étienne L'Hermite bore him so close a resemblance that he had to be Tristan; when he caught sight of her, he gaped. He was thirty-five perhaps and while no one would call him handsome he was certainly fashionable. He wore an open doublet of orange silk, henna-tinted trousers tucked into low boots, a thin-brimmed hat, and a baldric, a throwback to the swashbuckling days of Henry IV that consisted of a shoulder-belt from which a sword hung at a rakish angle. Tristan and Madeleine exchanged a look and he took several steps in her direction before being drawn back into the groom's family circle. Fortunately the night was young.

After the ceremony the party made its way toward the Courtin residence. After dark this area just inside the city gates was populated by thieves and prostitutes. Winter was yielding to spring and Madeleine took care to avoid pools of muddy water that were hardly visible because of the new moon. From time to time, out of the blackness she discerned a timid voice cajoling one of the men in the wedding party.

"You won't find a more agreeable figure in all of Paris. All I ask is a place to sleep."

How soon might this be her fate as well?

At the house the candlelit *salle* held a long table covered with trays of food but no meat, milk, or eggs because of Lent.

Madeleine was so famished she couldn't imagine pheasant or a roasted pig would have tasted better than the salted fish, dolphin, and whale served with preserved fruits and vegetables. Best of all were honey-sweetened tarts and fresh bread from the whitest wheat flour spread with a special luxury, a mock-cream cheese made of boiled almonds.

The L'Hermites had compensated for their son's misalliance with colorful garments of satin and velvet trimmed with gold braid and carnation piping. Gowns were ample but graceful, wide Spanish skirts no longer in fashion because of the war with France's neighbor to the west, while men's outfits featured open doublets adorned with billowing scarves and sashes.

At the height of the banquet Marie Hervé, who had in turn been ignored, treated as a servant and chatted up, was trampled by a gentleman who pushed past as if she were a standing chandelier. Her failed attempts at catching Marion's eye suggested that her sister preferred not to socialize with someone of her ilk. Marie Hervé sashayed over to her daughter.

"The wine is good and the fire warm," she said, "but as myself and my lady-in-waiting"—here she gestured regally toward Geneviève—"have not received the regard appropriate to our rank, it's time we departed. Come, Geneviève, carry my train." Geneviève giggled, lifted the hem of her mother's tattered skirt, and ceremoniously followed her out.

Madeleine spied Tristan bantering with the groom. She was taking a bite of trout fried in walnut oil when she felt a hand brush against her hair. She wheeled about to find a plump homely face featuring a bulbous nose, weak chin, and scraggly salt-and-pepper moustache. Dark liquid eyes, staring intently, were focused slightly above her forehead.

"You're Marion's niece, Madeleine Something," said Tristan. She nodded, chewing discreetly. He went on. "I believe it's customary for guests to embrace on festive occasions?" He clasped her hands and gave them a squeeze, kneaded her forearms, and planted a kiss on her lips. She forced herself to return it, thankful she had resisted the onions marinated in ginger vinegar.

"Pleased to make your acquaintance, Monsieur," she said with a curtsy.

Tristan gazed wordlessly at her *garcette*. She didn't know what to say. To her relief the ball was about to begin.

Through double doors flung open onto the courtyard a bonfire blazed. The bride and groom danced a traditional number reenacting their courtship and then, to the accompaniment of lute, recorder, and drum, the other guests were invited to join in. Madeleine and Tristan watched the throngs, faces framed for an instant by firelight before disappearing into the darkness. Lulled by the spectacle, Madeleine was startled when Tristan, his hand sticky with food, seized hers.

The music continued after the first line dance and they swayed along with it. He reeked of ambergris; only the most affected men wore scent, and she found it distasteful. Tristan's hand wandered toward the more intimate regions of her anatomy, finally reaching her buttocks.

Without warning Madeleine found herself fighting back tears as she remembered how Jacques used to place his favorite word in the most unlikely contexts. She hadn't been able to save him, but if, by giving herself to this vain, foolish man, she could prevent the prospect of Louis begging in the street or Geneviève offering herself to strangers, how could she refuse?

"Monsieur," she said with a pout, "Marion didn't tell me you were such a fine dancer."

The words, though technically true, were false by omission: Tristan danced like a sow in heat. Passing the point of no return, Madeleine had sealed her surrender with a lie.

Tristan beamed with self-adoration. "There are many things Marion didn't tell you," he leered, pressing against her to make her feel what he was referring to. "With that figure and that hair, why are you not an actress?"

"I'll answer your question with another," she replied. "How can I become one?"

Tristan murmured, "I can help you, but not here. We must arrange for an audition."

She nodded. "When and where?"

"Tomorrow, that is, today. Midday at the Théâtre du Marais. We'll see if one of the costumes suits you."

"I'll be there." He would help her into an outfit, or out of one, and that would be that.

The music suddenly stopped and the crowd parted to make way for the bride, propelled forward by a trio of girls who turned her round and round, chanting a traditional wedding song:

> Here you are, married at last, our lady the bride,
> Here you are, married at last, to your good husband tied
> With a long golden thread that won't break till you've died.

Tonight the words took on new meaning. The golden thread was not love, but money.

A tall figure approached Tristan but his words indicated he was addressing Madeleine.

"As I've been introduced to this gentleman, Mademoiselle," he said, "I am obliged to greet him first. My only hope of making amends for this oversight is to join him in the pleasure of your acquaintance."

He was a decade younger than the playwright, perhaps twenty-five; his shallow bow was so perfunctory that it was clear he was from the uppermost reaches of society. His face was striking, with a prominent nose, wavy jet-black hair, bushy moustache, and full lips. The closed doublet of crimson brocade, inlaid with a silver weaving of a sunray penetrating clouds above the sea, bespoke privilege. Tristan introduced Madeleine as if yielding a newly acquired trinket to a bully.

"Monsieur le Comte de Modène, allow me to present Madeleine Béjart. Mademoiselle, Monsieur is Chamberlain to His Highness the Duc d'Orléans and a generous patron of the arts."

Madeleine knew that writers were often supported by patrons, but a chamberlain of Gaston d'Orléans, the King's only brother and the heir apparent to the throne?

Out of nowhere the bride, who hadn't addressed a word to Madeleine since leaving the church, swooped down on the threesome like a hawk on a nest of bunnies.

"Madeleine, where have you been?" she gushed before turning to Tristan. "Dear Brother, I'll introduce you to my niece if you present me to this distinguished gentleman." Marion gazed at the Comte de Modène, her eyelashes fluttering in a way customarily reserved for the groom.

"Too late, dear Sister," retorted Tristan, fuming at being outranked. "Mademoiselle and I have already met."

Suddenly the music started up and with forced gaiety the bride called out to her husband and disappeared into the crowd. Madeleine's hand was grasped, but this time she felt cool fingers and the light touch of a respectful kiss. She looked up to discover not Tristan but the Comte.

"Mademoiselle, will you do me the honor?" he asked, bowing deeply. The final word was pronounced without irony, though a hint of playfulness had made its way into his sober gaze.

Tristan bristled. Madeleine was wondering how she would make amends when she found herself being whisked back into the dance.

The Comte guided her so skillfully that no onlooker would have believed that she had never danced a minuet. Marion pranced about the courtyard but at odd moments, when she thought herself unobserved, she cast covetous glances in Madeleine's direction.

After a while the pressure of the Comte's hand became more insistent and Madeleine found herself responding to his touch without having decided to do so. Soon he made his wishes known. In whispered words that she couldn't later recall she informed him of her conditions. Tristan stood along the edge of the dance, guzzling wine and trying to catch her eye.

It occurred to her that even if her plans for him were damaged beyond repair, perhaps that didn't matter. If the Comte gave her the full sum he had just promised, she wouldn't have to wait and see if she was well suited to a theatrical career. Pierre Béjart would be proud of her. Faced with a choice between the two professions he'd suggested, she'd opted for the more reliable.

She wouldn't be an actress. She would be a whore.

CHAPTER 5

In Which Our Heroine Loses Something of Great Value and Finds a Person of Great Importance

In none of the scenarios Madeleine Béjart had imagined for her deflowering was the setting a storage shed. The Comte was surprisingly patient but the episode left her drained. Afterward he pressed a leather pouch into her hand, opened the door of the shed, and was gone.

She adjusted her clothing. It was too dark to count the money and she couldn't leave until the guests departed. She wrapped herself in a burlap bag. It was out of expediency that she had agreed to go with the Comte, but her practical façade covered a heart tenderer than she allowed others to see. She watched the stars through a hole in the roof, envying their obliviousness.

Daylight awakened her. In the purse she found twenty gold coins, twice what the Comte had agreed to and a sufficient sum to pay the overdue rent and live on for months. She stowed the pouch in the lining of a sleeve and made her escape.

Somewhat the worse for wear, she proceeded home at a gingerly pace. How would Marie Hervé greet the news that her virtue had been traded for the family's security? Perhaps it would be simpler to say she had danced with Tristan until dawn to coax an audition out of him. The audition was no lie, but with twenty gold coins in her pocket, should she keep the appointment?

Before long Madeleine found herself in the district of Les Halles, not far from Saint Eustache, where the wedding ceremony had taken place a lifetime ago. In the murky light the streets were desolate. Here and there an early rising merchant was visible through open shutters, the upper one used as an awning, the lower one a countertop to display wares. The colorful rolls of velvet and satin raised her spirits. She had money enough to buy cloth, but would such a luxury not make her feel as if she had sold herself for a new dress? On the other hand, since she had in fact sold herself, why not have the dress for consolation?

As she reflected on the matter a mounted soldier cantered toward her. He examined her from head to toe and in an intoxicated voice bellowed, "Leaving for the front today and the old lady don't love me no more. You with the red hair. How much for an hour?"

"I beg your pardon?" asked Madeleine, stiffening.

"How much for an hour?" he repeated. "Got a place we can go."

Fury rose within her and she opened her mouth to declare she was not that type of woman but the words stuck in her throat. After her activities in the shed she resembled nothing so much as a streetwalker, the seams on her bodice ripped open and ribbons and bows askew. Above all, her elegant coiffure, the focus of her efforts at attracting Tristan's attention, was in a deplorable state, strands of auburn hair flowing in every direction and the pile of curls that had been its shining crown now falling into her eyes as if she were possessed.

Madeleine prepared to face down her suitor. Such a man, however pathetic, could be a real threat with so few people about. She smiled and tossed off an airy rejoinder.

"Sorry, Monsieur," she said. "I wish you godspeed, but I must return to my family."

She walked briskly down the street. There was a pounding of hooves and before she knew what was happening she had been seized from behind and found herself on horseback, the soldier's breath hot on her neck, one hand covering her mouth and the other clutching her bosom.

"All right then, you trollop," he cried, "we'll have it for free!"

Suddenly, for no apparent reason, he shrieked and loosened his grip. Nothing was holding Madeleine in place on the rearing horse. When she came to her senses she was sitting on the Rue Saint-Honoré in the middle of what was surely the deepest pile of muck in the whole of Paris.

***

It happened so quickly that it seemed the start of a nightmare cut short by a welcome awakening. Madeleine was getting her bearings when a voice spoke to her from another world.

"Are you injured, Mademoiselle? Please, may I assist you?"

Peering at her anxiously was a young man dressed in black and more formally than the hour warranted, an effect made incongruous by his uncombed hair. A brown lock had fallen into his eyes. Of an ambiguous hue, these expressed the kind of concern young men rarely feel for a stranger and some-times feign to make a good impression, but the knitting of his brows, bushy for one his age, was more evocative of a sincere individual of mature disposition than a callow youth out to inveigle her.

He helped her to her feet. She stretched her limbs and walked a few steps. As was her custom when something had frightened her, she hid her fear by assuming a superior tone.

"I am not hurt, Monsieur," she said. It dawned on her that her attacker hadn't fallen but had been pulled from his horse. This young man with his proper attire was an unlikely defender, but none other was to be seen. "Was it you who saved me?"

"Anyone would have done as much, Mademoiselle." He sounded relieved, but Madeleine was uncertain whether that was because she was uninjured or had recognized his part in her rescue. "That scoundrel!" he exclaimed. "I'd have liked to teach him a lesson for treating a lady in such a fashion. I dismounted him but he fought clear of me and escaped." The young man removed his vest and placed it around Madeleine's shoulders. "You're shivering. Come sit by the fire in my father's store." He gestured toward a draper's shop a few yards away manned by a middle-aged merchant, who, also attired in black, was unloading bolts of cloth into a bin.

"You're kind, but I must go." He blinked, taken down a peg. To soften the rebuff she added, "Does your father rise at dawn to offer a place by the hearth to perfect strangers?"

"The best that can be said of my father is that he has a heart as generous as any miser's."

Madeleine made a motion to slip off the young man's vest and depart.

"Don't go, please don't go," he said in such a doleful tone that she wondered if he was teasing. He pondered for a few moments and his face brightened. "We can tell Father you're shopping for fabric. For a gown." He inspected her attire, that of an overdressed chambermaid. "Not exactly a customer, but a potential one, since you're most likely carrying little money on your, uh, person." Suddenly aware that he was pointing directly at her bosom, he blushed.

Did her dishevelment give him an inkling of the events of the previous night?

"You're mistaken," pronounced Madeleine, imitating the speech of one of her aristocratic neighbors. "I wore this ludicrous garb to a masquerade. Imagine my dismay when the festivities went on so late that I couldn't locate a chair to take me home!"

"How awful, Mademoiselle," replied the young man. He examined his fingernails. "Your servants, no doubt, were unable to accompany you?"

"There was only my valet, who was taken ill. An excess of drink."

"Quite." He pulled a long face, whether compassionate or mocking she couldn't say.

Did he believe her story? She thought not. She took the purse from her pocket and let the twenty gold coins run through her fingers. His eyes bulged. It occurred to her that the gesture proved nothing, for large sums were rarely carried by honest women of any estate.

He bowed and said, "Please do me the honor of resting a while at my father's house."

Why was he going along with her lie? Was he imagining a tender reward for rescuing her?

She was about to dismiss him when his features assumed a catlike expression, the eyes wide and a faint moustache passing for whiskers. Yes, she mused, he did somehow know all that had transpired. In spite of his timidity he, too, longed to enjoy her favors. And yet the last thing in the world he would ever do was to treat her with disrespect.

**

He guided her toward a stone building with a carved façade and iron gates before an arched entryway and soon a valet was ushering them into a reception room. The manservant said nothing about the state of Madeleine's clothing but showed her to an alcove, poured water into a basin, and set out a towel. She wiped mud from her face, neck, and clothing, then returned to the reception room where, beside a crackling fire, the kitchen maid was setting down a silver tray bearing two porcelain cups and a tankard filled to the brim with mulled wine.

The young man poured out the wine and gestured to a seat across from his. The sweet aroma of cinnamon and cloves permeated the room. Madeleine drained her cup and refilled it without asking permission, drank again. She looked around the room, not bothering to hide her curiosity. Black velvet draped the entryway. So that explained the austere clothing. "Oh, who died?" she blurted out. His features contracted like those of a child who has taken a spill. "Was it your mother?" Madeleine inquired more gently.

"My stepmother," he said, "but I loved her dearly."

"And your own mother?" she asked. "When did you lose her?"

He said nothing. She followed his eyes to a portrait of a chestnut-haired lady with a gracious smile. She wore a turquoise gown, the richness of the fabric and strands of amber in her coiffure signs of wealth. Her eyes, matching the jewels, shone with a vitality tinged with sadness.

The young man turned away, unable to withstand this image of paradise lost. Madeleine reached across the table, lifted his chin, and tidied his hair.

"What's your name, young man?" she asked.

"Jean-Baptiste," he replied, his voice constricted with grief.

"Pleased to meet you." To cheer him up she stood and executed an exaggerated curtsy.

His features remained grave. "And yours?" he asked.

"Madeleine," she said, bowing again in a still more absurd manner.

He smiled out of politeness. He walked over to her side of the table and raised her hand to his lips. Against her fingers she felt the soft growth of his cat moustache. His eyes, widening at his own audacity, suggested he was as untried in love as she had lately been.

What strange destiny had taken charge of Madeleine's existence? Her meeting with Tristan could hardly be attributed to fate, but she had taken no steps to cross paths with the Comte de Modène, the drunken soldier who had assailed her, and now the irresistible Jean-Baptiste.

That was the word. She longed to have met him a day earlier, to offer him a pure heart.

She guided him onto the bench close beside her. Whether by coincidence or discretion, the servants were nowhere to be seen and the two young people gazed into each other's eyes. Jean-Baptiste's, which in the sun had been of a bluish-gray reminiscent of an April sky, were now the indefinable color of mushrooms under a canopy of dense foliage.

Without a word of explanation Madeleine pulled his head against her shoulder and he shook with sobs. She held him close, feeling as if she would do anything in her power to console him. When at last Jean-Baptiste lifted his head, as if by chance their lips met and he held her in a long embrace. His soft tickling whiskers brought her to her senses. She pulled away.

"I don't know what's come over me," she said, standing so abruptly she felt the room spinning. "I suppose I'm not accustomed to drinking wine so early in the day."

Also reeling from the kiss, he seemed unsure of where he was.

"Would you like some more?" he asked, lifting the tankard.

"I've had quite enough. Maître Jean-Baptiste, how do you keep yourself occupied when you aren't saving people on the street?"

"I assist my father," he replied. He strutted about the room, his confidence boosted by the intimate moment they had shared. "One day I too will be a draper. How I shall survive in so dull a trade I have no idea. I am to leave for Orléans any day now to study law. And you, how do you spend your days? What is your trade?"

Caught off guard, Madeleine went pale.

"How foolish of me," Jean-Baptiste continued quickly. "As a noblewoman you're supported by your family fortune. I beg your pardon." He bowed his head.

"I lied," she blurted out. "I am not a lady." She collected herself. "Actually, I'm an actress."

"You're an actress?"

She nodded. Again his eyes widened. For all she knew Jean-Baptiste, like many bourgeois, considered actresses no less depraved than prostitutes.

"What have you played in?"

"My latest role was in *Marianne*, by Monsieur Tristan L'Hermite, at the Théâtre du Marais."

"Really? Which part did you play?"

"The title character," she said, not knowing other names. "I don't suppose you saw it?"

"Five or six times," he said. "Grandfather adored the play."

He sat down. They exchanged a look.

Popular tragedies often drew repeat spectators, but it could only be called bad luck that Jean-Baptiste probably knew the play by heart and would catch her out.

"Ah yes, it's coming back to me," he said. "I didn't recognize you without make-up."

Now *he* was lying! Without knowing why she needed comforting, he was trying to console her. Madeleine had spent years listening to her mother's lies but couldn't recall a single one of such a generous nature. For the first time she understood that just as bread is not merely bread but is also coarse, fine, salty, or sweet, a lie always tastes of the ingredients that go into it.

Resolving now to tell the whole truth, she seized the tankard of wine and drained its contents. She walked to the fireplace and took a deep breath.

"I thank you for accepting my lies," she began, "but that's what they are." She turned to face him. "I am not an actress. It's true I intended to become one. I was to audition for Monsieur L'Hermite this morning, but last night . . ." She looked at the floor. "My father left us. My brother died. We're about to be cast out. Last night I gave myself to a stranger for the coins I showed you. He paid me twice what we agreed upon so I would be foolish to complain." She didn't immediately recognize her own laughter. "What then is my profession?"

He stood and applauded. Tears covered his cheeks.

"Magnificent! To improvise like the Italians, but on a tragic theme!" He embraced her. "I've never heard of such a conceit. We must develop the story and the characters. The title will be *Marie-Madeleine, Sinner and Savior*. We'll take inspiration from your portrayal of the doomed Marianne." He snatched the mourning cloth from the wall and tossed it over his shoulders like a shawl, then spoke in the voice of doom. "Marianne is falsely accused of infidelity by King Herod, her husband. Accepting her lot, she goes to her death thinking only of the innocent children made motherless by her fate." In shaky falsetto Jean-Baptiste then launched into Marianne's final recitation, as if catastrophe were hanging low over the brow of a eunuch:

> *Herod desires my death, I fear it not,*
> *But feel only sadness for the children he begot*
> *Who, dragged through the mud because of me,*
> *How unworthily treated are bound to be!*
> *They are helpless, O God. Please hear my plea*

That You might help them, a Father to them be.
And if, observing Your laws, they are made to suffer,
May they die without reproach, like their blameless mother!

His oration drawing to a close, Jean-Baptiste leaned forward with arms extended as if hovering over an abyss. He tumbled to the ground and lay motionless. Madeleine rushed to his side. He looked up at her, smiled, and asked, "Was I good?"

She planted a kiss on his cheek. "Very good," she said.

He attempted to pull her down but she resisted. Like a cat licking himself after being refused a request, he smoothed his clothing.

"Shall we retire to the sitting room?" he asked. "I'll have the hearth lit. If Father calls me to task about having two fires going at once, I'll say it's for the illustrious actress Madeleine!"

The illustrious actress Madeleine! As if under the effect of a magic spell the humiliations of the previous day vanished. In an hour's time this strange boy had transformed her from a bedraggled courtesan-in-training into a distinguished woman of the theater.

The two were standing close and anything might have happened, but the bells of Saint Eustache chimed terces, putting Madeleine in mind of her audition. And suddenly she knew that finding success as an actress wasn't just a way of protecting her family from hardship, but an ambition she herself wished to realize.

"You've helped me more than you know," she said, pulling away from him. "I have an urgent engagement to attend to. Goodbye."

"Please stay," pleaded Jean-Baptiste, seizing her hand.

"I can't," she insisted. "As I told you, I have a meeting with Tristan."

"Will I ever see you again?" he asked. The orphan face returned and it was all Madeleine could do to refrain from soothing his melancholy once again.

"If God wills it," she responded brusquely, kissing his cheek. "But now I must go."

She feared he would make a fuss but he said, "Wait a moment."

He disappeared for so long that Madeleine wondered if he would return but then there he was, carrying a carefully folded garment.

"My mother was shorter than you," he said, handing her the turquoise gown his mother had been wearing in her portrait, "but the color will bring out your eyes."

"You are most generous," she said in bewilderment, "but I can't accept such a gift."

"It would have pleased her greatly."

She took the garment from him and said, "Thank you for everything."

"Remember our collaboration," he said playfully, accompanying her to the door. "*Marie-Madeleine, Sinner and Savior*. I count on you to tell me when you're ready to begin."

"Of course," she said in haste, her mind on her audition. She threw her arms about Jean-Baptiste's neck and kissed him on the lips. At the front door, turning back for a final look, she discovered he'd lain down on the hearthrug and was waving his legs in the air like a baby.

And that was how Madeleine Béjart met the man who'd one day be known as Molière.

CHAPTER 6

In Which a Speech About the Birthing of a Foal Proves Astonishingly Effective

---

It was late morning when Madeleine opened the door of the *salle* and called out. She heaved a sigh of relief when there was no reply; at least she could change her muddied clothes before facing the challenge of informing Marie Hervé of the night's unexpected turn of events.

The gown belonging to Jean-Baptiste's mother struck Madeleine's legs at midcalf but the material was so fine and the bodice such a perfect fit that she deemed it more suitable for an audition than her own tatters. She was peering at her reflection in a copper pan and attempting to arrange her hair when a noise behind her made her drop the utensil with a shriek.

"Calm yourself," said Marie Hervé with a yawn, still in her nightgown and bleary-eyed from drinking wine and staying out late. She dissolved in giggles at the sight of Madeleine's abbreviated finery. "Marion is generous with her hand-me-downs, but it must have looked better on her."

Madeleine collected the pan and said, "It doesn't come from Marion. Let me explain."

She started with the easy parts, the audition Tristan had arranged and her meeting with Jean-Baptiste. Then, her eyes tightly shut, she told of her encounter with the Comte.

"Twenty gold coins!" squealed Marie Hervé. "You're a liar! Give me that purse!"

Having inspected its contents she made the sign of the cross and gave herself over to sobs of relief.

Snatching it back, Madeleine said, "This is not for you. God knows how long we'll have to live on this money, and we also have Father's debts to think of. Someone in this family must make a decent living. My audition is at noon."

Marie Hervé's expression suggested a grave matter on her mind. Was she about to reprimand or thank her daughter for her sacrifice?

"This Comte de Modène," she finally said. "When will you see him again?"

***

Far from deciding to shun Madeleine after watching her disappear into a storage shed with the Comte de Modène, Tristan was engulfed by ardor. He vowed to take full advantage of the audition he had arranged for the young beauty with the astounding red hair.

He arose at eleven to primp. Given that the girl was unknown she would respond favorably to his advances. He smiled at his taste in women; the image in the mirror smiled back. Despite an inkling that his reputation as a lady's man owed more to fame than allure, he saw himself as an irresistible promoter of aspiring actresses. If this one played her cards right he would introduce her to Mondory, the director of the Théâtre du Marais. He finished his toilette by anointing his earlobes with the ambergris the girl had found so irresistible at the wedding dance.

The bells of Saint Paul's chimed sexts as Tristan stood waiting for Madeleine in front of the Théâtre du Marais. He expected her still to be dressed like a bedecked kitchen maid and licked his lips at the thought of helping her change. A majestic young lady approached, her hair pulled back in a chignon, her gown outmoded but impressive. He took her for an aristocrat inquiring about tickets and was about to offer his services when he recognized Madeleine Béjart.

She nodded. Dumbfounded by her transformation, Tristan fumbled with his keys, then unlocked and held the theater door. She receded into the building with a queen's gait. Would she be difficult, her liaison with the Comte having gone to her head? Noticing that her gown was a foot too short, Tristan felt reassured. He relocked the door with a smirk.

The Friday matinée wouldn't begin until three and the building was deserted. Two plays were scheduled for the day, both by the fashionable playwright Pierre Corneille. The matinée would be his new work, *The Comic Illusion*, the evening performance a revival of his tragedy, *Medea*.

Tristan led Madeleine toward the stage. She had never been inside a theater and gaped at the long and narrow room illuminated by sunlight pouring through high windows. Rows of benches abutted the parterre, a pit reserved for standees. Seating galleries were built into the walls. The stage itself was square and only slightly elevated, with huge wooden props depicting a vague sort of landscape strewn along its back edge.

"Climb up, my dear," said Tristan from the stage. He helped her onto the low platform. When she noticed he was pulling her toward him she broke away and inspected the props.

"What are these strange shapes?" she asked from the far end of the stage.

He glanced at them and said, "A magician's grotto for the matinée and mountains along the seashore for the tragedy of Medea this evening."

He took a step toward her. Madeleine backed up without turning around.

"May I please begin, Monsieur?" she asked. "Shall I read something from *Marianne*?"

Tristan struck his forehead with the palm of a hand and said: "I've forgotten the script."

"From this *Medea* then?" she countered.

"That script is backstage," he said, reaching out a hand to escort her.

"Thank you, Monsieur," she replied. "I'll wait here and prepare myself to read."

"The players will be arriving," he said. "How shall we use these moments alone?"

They were maneuvering about the stage for position. When Tristan had offered Madeleine an audition, this was precisely how she had imagined it would be, and she had resigned herself to the inevitability of surrender. But since then, the Comte had alleviated her immediate need, Jean-Baptiste allowed her to glimpse the glory of becoming *the illustrious actress Madeleine*. Did such a goal, no longer tainted by desperation, require that she give herself yet again?

"Please, Monsieur," she said, "bring me the script and I'll show you how strong my voice is and how quickly I learn lines. My mind is excellent."

"The mind isn't everything," Tristan responded. "An actress must also use her body."

"Medea is the woman who murdered her children, is she not?" inquired Madeleine with a grimace. "If you please, tell me what sort of voice I must use to play such a monster." Brushing against a painted wall of rock, she said, "Please answer my question, Monsieur. What voice shall I use to recite the part? If I am to become an actress, I must find out what to do."

"What the theater is really about," said Tristan, inching toward her, "is passion. Medea is a tempestuous woman. She kills her children out of hatred for the husband who has spurned her."

"How could the wife forget she's a mother?"

"Desire for the husband is stronger than love for the children."

An image of her own mother flashed across Madeleine's mind but she shook it away. "Begging your pardon, Monsieur," she said, "but that trait escapes my comprehension."

"An actress must explore passions she doesn't understand," he insisted.

"But I can't imagine such a thing," she rejoined.

Tristan came toward her; she had nowhere to escape. Once again the nauseating smell of ambergris swept over her. He kissed her cheek and said, "Release your hair, let it hang loose over your shoulders." He stroked it; she recoiled. "I won't devour you. It's part of the work. An actress must learn to embody passion so that she might convey it to the public."

Draping herself in the curtain, Madeleine declared, "Monsieur, I cannot play such a role."

He lunged. She flung the curtain at him, sending him tumbling. The shortness of her gown allowed her to scuttle to the front of the stage. With Tristan still crouching on the floor preparing for a fresh offensive, she addressed her appeal to the empty hall.

"How can I embody a passion I do not feel?"

Tristan came to his feet.

"A difficult task indeed," he concurred, "but one that must be undertaken. Heroes and heroines must suffer. What can be known of suffering if one has not loved?"

The kind of suffering to which Tristan alluded Madeleine had not experienced. She recalled a shepherdess's speech from a book in the arcades of the Place Royale, fell to her knees, and raised her face toward the ceiling.

"What knows a man of suffering?" she exclaimed. "Is the honeybee pricked by the rose, the stallion chastised for his lust by the pangs of his foal's birthing?" That was as much as she remembered, so she now improvised. "Woman, too, has passions, but they are, above all, of the soul. What is it but passion when the mother protects her child, the daughter tends to her parents or the sister cares for her ailing brother?" Jacques's sweet defenseless face in his final moments came before her eyes; she realized that a sob would add to the effect and allowed her voice to go ragged. "These are the passions I know. These I would ask to play."

"Bravo, Mademoiselle!"

A figure materialized out of the obscurity of the seating area. Tristan saved face by pretending that the arrival of the director of the Théâtre du Marais was part of his plan.

"Monsieur Mondory," he said, "you're just in time. Please allow me to introduce you to Mademoiselle Madeleine Béjart. She has been auditioning for that role in *Marianne*."

Mondory, accustomed to Tristan's auditions, said, "A thousand pardons for interrupting, Monsieur." He inspected Madeleine with a practiced eye. Aside from the absurd gown, she was a picture of womanly perfection. "Are you really finished?" he asked drily, turning back to Tristan.

Tristan replied breezily, "She was to read from *Medea* but preferred to improvise. Yes, we're through with the audition, are we not, Mademoiselle?"

Madeleine found herself exchanging a look of complicity with Tristan. And as she was reflecting that the theater must indeed be an enchanted place for them to have so quickly become allies of a sort, without further ado Monsieur Mondory offered her a job.

She left the theater in a state of exaltation. Without having realized where her feet were leading her she found herself knocking at Jean-Baptiste's door.

"Mademoiselle?" asked the valet she had met earlier that day.

"Is Monsieur Jean-Baptiste at home?" said Madeleine, finally catching her breath.

"I'm sorry, Mademoiselle," he said. "He has left for Orléans to study law."

"Orléans?" she echoed. "But this morning he said nothing about leaving today."

"Monsieur didn't inform the young master until dinner, Mademoiselle," the valet replied.

"Will he return soon?" she asked.

"I cannot say, Mademoiselle," said the servant. "Soon he is also to begin traveling with the court as assistant draper to the King. He may not be in Paris again until the new year."

***

Late that evening, as Madeleine was about to bank the fire and go to bed, she heard a pounding. At the courtyard gate she was astonished to see, hat in hand, the Comte de Modène.

"Please excuse my audacity in calling so late, Mademoiselle," he said, bowing as deeply as if she were his equal. "It was difficult to wrest your whereabouts from Monsieur L'Hermite."

She led him across the courtyard and seated him by the hearth. He raised his eyebrows at the room's paltry furnishings but at least she had purchased kindling with the money he'd given her and a fire blazed. In the barely heightened tone that signified emotion in a man of his rank, he said, "I had to see you again, Mademoiselle."

"And so you have, Monsieur."

"I should like to see more of you."

She twisted her hair into a knot. "You're welcome to return," she said to stall for time. She had not expected ever to see the Comte again, let alone so soon. "Thank you for your generosity," she continued slowly. "I'm grateful to you for adding to the sum we agreed upon. You've saved us from ruin."

"A trifle, Mademoiselle," the Comte tossed off, but his eyes expressed a silent entreaty. Madeleine mused that they were his most arresting feature, black flames ready to erupt.

She sat down in the other chair and sighed.

"What do you expect of me, Monsieur?" she asked. "Shall we return to my aunt's shed? Or enjoy a night of passion in the loft, where my mother and the other children lie asleep?"

He pulled her hand to his lips, then clasped it in his own.

"I expect nothing of you, Mademoiselle. I simply ask you to accompany me to my residence in the Hôtel de Lavardin." Madeleine had heard of this townhouse on the Place Royale inhabited by the entourage of the King's brother. "I'll see you home afterwards," continued the Comte, "and provide you with whatever further assistance your family may require. I would be pleased to explain to your parents the advantages of such an arrangement."

Madeleine stood and circled the room. Was she suffering from an ailment of the ears? No, the dark gaze that followed her every movement told her that she had taken the Comte's declaration precisely as it was intended.

She murmured that she would have to think it over and left him to await her reply. Passing through the scullery she stooped to pick up an onion black with rot that had fallen into a corner. As recently as yesterday it would have been a precious object, but now it had little value. Why did the sight of it sadden her so? She strode into the courtyard, the early smells of spring calming her spirit. She found a dry spot beneath a poplar and settled down to consider her decision.

There was good reason to accede to the Comte's request. Having a connection to the court could be useful even if her career as an actress flourished. Wasn't it safer to establish this liaison than leave her family dependent on her success? To save them she'd been prepared to sell herself. What could be simpler than becoming the consort of a rich and prominent man?

Perhaps, in spite of the idealistic notions that had filled her mind that morning thanks to Jean-Baptiste, Pierre Béjart was right. The world was tit for tat. Marie Hervé had reacted to her selling her virginity with tacit approval. When Marion learned that Madeleine's liaison was developing into an affair she would be green with envy. Pierre Béjart himself would welcome this development as confirmation of Madeleine's debased nature. As for Joseph, if he returned to Paris, it was possible he would disown her, but wasn't it equally likely that he might interpret the relationship as evidence of his own noble origins?

There was, in fact, no one to raise objections to the Comte's proposition. Young Joseph might stammer out his disapproval but prosperity would soon silence him. Geneviève, a hopeless romantic, would protest that such a nobleman would never ask for Madeleine's hand, but it was merely a matter of time before she understood that she herself would need money for a dowry if she wished to make a good match; that such was the way of the world.

Out of nowhere arose an image of Jean-Baptiste's face. Madeleine couldn't tell whether it was sad or amused but felt drawn to it in the way a sick woman longs for a remedy without being aware of the nature of her affliction. And yet however noble Jean-Baptiste had seemed in accepting her lies, what proved he hadn't been flattering her for his own purposes? If she hadn't insisted on leaving, how long would he have contented himself with demonstrating his talent for oratory? The only thing separating Jean-Baptiste from the Comte was that the latter, accustomed to the rules of the game of love for pure pleasure, had made his proposal with a directness that might inspire disgust in a sensitive soul but had the virtue of honesty. And sensitivity was a luxury she could not afford.

Madeleine stood and brushed herself off. She walked into the house, having come to her decision about the Comte's proposition. If her heart said no, her head said yes.

"I accept, Monsieur," she said. "My father is away on business. My mother is asleep. Will you allow me time to write her a note in the event that she awakens before my return?"

"Certainly, Mademoiselle."

When Madeleine let herself back into the house a few hours before dawn, she saw by the dying embers that her note sat on the chair exactly where she'd left it. She was not surprised; Marie Hervé was a sound sleeper. Before mounting the steps to her bed, she threw the paper into the hearth and stood watching it fuel a final outburst of light that sent the fire to ashes.

CHAPTER 7

In Which a Revenant Warrior Distinguishes Himself with Beard and Sword

———

Each evening the Comte called for Madeleine at the house or, if it was Tuesday, Friday, or Sunday, at the theater. Playing the role of Marianne's confidante onstage was less challenging than masking her indifference to their trysts. She wondered about his intentions; aside from short bursts of passion he was as effusive as a turnip. Once, when he asked her to stay the night, she called the question.

"Why?" she blurted out.

His hands behind his head, the Comte stared at the bed's satin canopy.

"Have you reason to be discontented?" he inquired in the voice of a merchant preparing to defend his goods.

"No, Monsieur le Comte. I am most grateful for your assistance." She paused. "I just wondered why."

He stretched his limbs. "Interpret my invitation as you wish," he said with a yawn. "If you prefer to return home as usual, I am pleased to escort you."

"Thank you. My mother would fret," she lied, reaching for her bodice. "Never mind about my question."

He lifted his doublet from a chair. "Perhaps it was your way of asking me for a jeweled mirror," he said, "to see your lovely face at every moment. I'll attend to it tomorrow."

If Madeleine's relationship with the Comte was remunerated in gold, she would have gladly worked at the theater for the sheer pleasure of it: the rustle of brocades; the enraptured faces of the audience; the actors' voices whispering unveiled secrets or ringing out with shocking affirmations of desire or fury; and more than all else, the magical aroma—a fusion of perspiration, make-up, and melted wax from the chandeliers above her head—more potent than incense at church. Her only source of dissatisfaction was that she was not a permanent member of the troupe. With Marie Hervé and Geneviève now sewing costumes and her brothers hired as scenery and prop assistants, she could only hope that Mondory would call on her again for another role when *Marianne* closed. Waiting for that call became excruciating once all of Paris began clamoring to see Monsieur Pierre Corneille's tragicomedy of *Le Cid*, which opened at the Théâtre du Marais on New Year's Day of 1637 and was selling out every performance.

***

Madeleine was wondering if she'd ever see the play, let alone act in it, when one afternoon in early February there was a knock at the gate. A boy handed her a note in her father's hand stating that if she wished to have news of him, Young Joseph should accompany her to a tavern called the Seine-et-Bièvre that stood under the sign of the two blue pitchers in the Faubourg Saint-Victor. By the time she lifted her eyes to question the boy, he had disappeared.

She cried out with joy. Joseph was alive!

Ignoring her father's instructions about an escort, Madeleine donned her warmest cloak and set off for the malodorous district at the confluence of Paris's two rivers, the Seine and the Bièvre. It was an unsavory area of clothdyers, tanneries, and slaughter-houses where putrid water was discharged into the Bièvre before it flowed into the Seine not far from Notre-Dame Cathedral.

Bracing herself against the wind, she strode across the Pont Marie, a new stone bridge leading onto the Île Saint-Louis, a recently established area almost as desirable as the Marais for nobles building Parisian residences. Halfway across the Pont de la Tournelle, a smaller bridge linking the Île to the Left Bank, a sudden thought stopped her in her tracks. If her father was well enough to send tidings to his family, he would expect to receive news of them as well!

Madeleine stood on the bridge and reminisced about the day thirteen months earlier when Joseph had vanished. Jacques had spent the afternoon trying to coax a smile out of their panic-stricken mother, playing the fool to distract her and the others. Back then the Seine had been a block of ice but this winter was less severe and Madeleine watched the river course ahead toward the Île du Palais, its waters parting as if out of respect for the grand cathedral. She mused that just as rivers were destined to thaw, freeze, and melt again, much had changed since her father's departure; everything in fact. Which news would more resoundingly gladden his heart, his son's death or his daughter's transformation into a courtesan? Whomever Joseph was sending to meet her would report back on her appearance: the scarlet gown of delicate weave, embroidered grey cloak, and red velvet hat set off by the ruby earrings and necklace the Comte had given her for her nineteenth birthday. Were these the garments of an impoverished young woman struggling to keep her family fed and housed in straitened circumstances?

The wind gave a mighty gust that interrupted her meditation; she scampered the rest of the way across the Pont Marie and onto the Left Bank of the Seine. When she spotted the Seine-et-Bièvre beneath the sign of the blue pitchers, she came to a halt, took a deep breath to clear her mind, and smiled. Had becoming an actress not only saved her family from ruin but also taught her how to embroider upon the truth?

***

The Seine-et-Bièvre was a hovel. Night was falling as Madeleine peered into the dim tavern through a small window in the door and caught a glimpse of primitive tables occupied by men dressed with varying degrees of shabbiness. An unaccompanied young female festooned in the latest fashions would attract unwelcome attention, but if she returned home without entering she might never have word of her father again.

Inside, the floor was strewn with filthy straw, the stench of ale and vomit overpowering that of the rivers. Several of the customers shouted obscenities as soon as they caught sight of her. A young man with a scar on his forehead appeared ready to pounce when a voice from the far end of the room issued a call to order and a middle-aged individual gestured to her to approach his table. Though she couldn't make out his face until she drew nearer, something about the restlessness of his stance told her he was Joseph Béjart.

"Father, Father," she cried, clinging to him. "I've missed you so! I never dreamed it would be you." She waited for him to speak but he remained silent, so she said, "This place . . . Please come back to the house with me. Mother will be beside herself with joy."

He pulled away and winced. "Will she?" he asked in a hoarse voice. "And why have you come alone? You were foolish to take the risk."

He was quite presentable, dressed in a tunic and leggings and a black doublet and shod in decent-looking boots, but he had aged, his hair now white. He wore a beard, also white, and by his side hung a sword sheathed in a bronze scabbard. She had never seen him carry a weapon. It gave him a dignified mien.

He put his arm around her shoulder and led her toward the door. Basking in his presence, she was oblivious to catcalls from the customers until the man with the scar gave her back-side a slap and was sent crashing to the floor by Joseph Béjart's free fist. The others cheered as father and daughter left the inn.

The wind made it difficult to converse. Soon they found themselves crossing the Rue Saint-Antoine, not a quarter-hour's walk from the house. If Madeleine further postponed informing her father of Jacques's death and her own circumstances, the ordeal would take place amidst Marie Hervé's histrionics. Without explanation Madeleine guided Joseph toward the Place Royale.

Houses on all four sides offered shelter from the wind. Elegantly dressed gentlemen and ladies milled about the arcades or strolled along the edge of the green that formed the heart of the square. She led her father to a quiet spot at the very center of this wooded area. The King had plans for landscaping it but for the moment it remained overgrown. They sat side by side on a broad low tree stump, illuminated only by the distant lights of the arcades. The moon had not yet risen.

Joseph pulled a crust of bread from his doublet and offered it to her but she shook her head. After he'd finished chewing he said, "Why have we stopped? I don't share your opinion about how Marie Hervé will greet me, but what's the point of further delay?"

"It's better to discuss things here than at the house," said Madeleine.

"What is there to discuss?" he countered. "I've come back."

"Why didn't you send word?" she asked. "We were sick with worry."

Looking down, Joseph replied, "I thought of you each day. Your mother, the children. You especially, Mado." She squeezed his hand. It had been years since he called her that. "I would have liked to put your minds at ease," he continued. "But I couldn't take the risk."

"What risk?" she queried.

"Having my whereabouts discovered," he said, lowering his voice.

"By your family?"

"A letter, once sent, may go astray."

"Why then," she demanded, "did you not warn us of your departure?"

He sighed and said, "You must believe me, Daughter. I had no intention of leaving Paris that day. I went out so that I could borrow money, as I said I would. But no one, not even François or Nicolas, would give a sou to the likes of me."

So Joseph had begged for assistance from his miserly brothers.

"My poor little Father," Madeleine said, stroking his hair. "Why didn't you return home?"

"It was too dangerous," Joseph replied. "My creditors would have had me arrested."

"We would have found a way."

His face contorted, he fought back tears. "I was ashamed."

She waited for him to regain control. He continued in a monotone.

"I walked south to escape the cold but the weather worsened. I took shelter in barns and drank snow but there was no food. A dozen times I was ready to be done with it. But each time, I would remind myself that, once dead, I could be of no assistance to my family.

"One day I begged food at a manor house to avoid starving. The mistress, a marquise, saw that my manners were not those of a vagabond and took me on as a valet. I worked there for over a year, until a few days ago."

"I'm so happy you've returned," said Madeleine. "But why now?"

"A year has passed," he said, his voice weary. "My creditors must think I am dead. I've saved some money. I'll pay them when I can. Just imagine, reparation from a ghost!"

Joseph's laughter was unsettling. Was he fully of sound mind?

"If Marie Hervé takes me back," he continued, "there is much to make up to her. I'll find employment with the help of your grandfather. And this time I shall keep it."

Madeleine kissed her father's cheek. It was infuriating that Pierre Béjart would congratulate himself on finding the prodigal son returning with his tail between his legs, but who was she to give him lessons about holding to one's principles?

As if reading his daughter's mind, Joseph inspected her for the first time and said, "You look well, Daughter. How did you acquire such finery?"

"It has been a year since you left, Father," she said, "and much has changed. We were about to be turned out. It was freezing cold. We—I—had to do something to survive."

Joseph raised an eyebrow. He fingered her necklace.

"Obviously you've survived," he observed. "What was it that you did?"

Madeleine muttered a prayer to St. Genesius, the patron saint of actors. She assumed a prim voice.

"I found employment at the Théâtre du Marais. Aunt Marion has married Étienne L'Hermite. His brother is a playwright. He introduced me to the director, who hired me."

Joseph nodded. "I am glad to hear your mother has finally taken the time to teach you how to sew properly."

"It's true that Mother and Geneviève have been sewing costumes. I have also befriended an aristocrat, the Comte de Modène. He works for the King's brother." She feigned a coughing spell, then smiled weakly. "It's getting cold. Perhaps we should wait until we're home to discuss this more fully. You must be cold and hungry."

"I won't deny that, Daughter." Joseph pondered. "But this count, why in the world did you befriend him?"

"We'll get to that in a moment, but the truth is that I have been playing a small role in a play. I have become an actress." Joseph's face revealed nothing, so she continued. "I'm presently out of work awaiting a new role." Joseph stared but remained silent. In a neutral tone of voice she added, "As for the Comte de Modène, . . . I am actually his mistress."

The blank gaze persisted. All at once there was an explosion.

"You have become an actress and you're the mistress of a count!" sputtered Joseph. "Shall I soon have the privilege of being grandfather to the latest bastard at court?"

Madeleine closed her eyes and waited for his rant to trail off. She looked up to find her father kneeling with his head on the tree stump like a nobleman awaiting the axe.

"I'm sorry, Father," she whispered. "I had no choice. We were about to be cast out and it was winter. We might have died."

"You should have," he cried. "Death is better than a loss of honor."

"I would have died willingly," she said, "but would you have had me stand by and watch the others perish one by one?"

Joseph raised his head. His cheeks were streaked with tears and mud. "It is I who ask your forgiveness, Daughter," he said. "The fault is mine."

She kissed his forehead. She was meditating on how to break the news about Jacques's death when Joseph stood abruptly and asked, "This Comte de Modène, where does he reside?"

"Just here, at the Hôtel de Lavardin," she answered, pointing to a brick residence. "Why?" She pulled her cloak close. "Father, before we go home I must tell you about Jacques."

"I'm afraid your news will have to wait," Joseph said. "Run along and prepare Marie Hervé for my arrival while I pay a visit to the Hôtel de Lavardin before it's too late."

"Too late for what?" asked Madeleine.

"Why, to challenge the Comte de Modène to a duel," responded her father. "Before another sun rises, he shall pay with his blood for what he has done or he will shed my own."

***

Madeleine scrutinized Joseph's features. Had her announcement, added to the long months of hardship, rendered him lunatic? His eyes bugged out and his lower lip worked in rage. In the center of the Place Royale, a favored dueling ground in spite of the King's prohibition of the practice, Madeleine pleaded with her father to abandon his mad intentions.

The compromise they reached was that if they found the Comte at home, she would introduce the two men. Otherwise, father and daughter would return to the Rue de la Perle, and the matter would be dropped for now.

Access to the Hôtel de Lavardin was gained through a locked entry flanked by high walls; while Joseph wore out his fists on the door Madeleine applauded the obstacle. A final kick injured his foot and he hastened off, hopping and gesticulating. She was about to follow when she heard the courtyard door swing open behind her. She turned to discover the Comte himself.

"Good evening, Mademoiselle," he said, kissing her hand. "I had an errand to see to before calling on you but as you're already here it can wait, especially since it concerns you. Enter, if you please."

Madeleine glanced over her shoulder to check on Joseph, who, held up by a wagon unloading goods, was shifting his weight as if standing on hot coals. Again facing the Comte, she said, "Good evening, Monsieur. My father has returned to Paris and insists on paying you a visit." She pointed to Joseph and said, "He's the one twitching in front of that cart." The Comte spotted him. "He hopes to kill you by morning," she added drily.

"Ah, your venerable father," said the Comte, raising an eyebrow. He stroked his moustache. "I can only pray that he will not take offense if I am not eager to kill *him*."

That as a nobleman of high standing the Comte would not duel with a mere bourgeois was in equal parts insulting and reassuring. Joseph would do his utmost to provoke the Comte, who might have little choice but to deal him a good thrashing, and Madeleine feared the poor soul would die of mortification.

"I thank you for your understanding, Monsieur," she said in an even tone. "You're wise to grasp that my father's intent is the result of a sickened heart. You have been most generous and I regret asking for your help once again."

"Are you in need of money?" asked the Comte. "Is your father burdened by debts?"

"He is, Monsieur," she replied, "although that's not . . ."

"Consider them paid," snapped the Comte.

"Thank you, Monsieur," she said humbly, "but he's too proud to accept. He thinks himself of noble birth. I can't vouch for it but he himself believes it. If you engage in combat, he would be killed in an instant." She found herself tearing up.

"What is it that you wish of me?" asked the Comte with unaccustomed gentleness.

Madeleine wiped her cheeks and said, "First, when my father challenges you, say anything, anything at all to assuage him. Forgetting who you are, treat him as if he were the fool in a comedy."

The Comte said nothing but looked amused.

"Second," she went on, "if he insists, please accept his challenge but don't hurt him."

The Comte's smile vanished and he said, "A man of my standing cannot cross swords with a commoner." He glimpsed Madeleine's disappointment and reflected. He stared at the sky before going on. "The evening is cloudy and cold and the moon hasn't risen. There will be few people about. If we found an isolated spot . . ." Resigning himself, he nodded. "All right then, I'll flatter your father to placate him. If forced to fight I'll parry his thrusts and exhaust him."

Madeleine bowed her head and said, "I am most grateful to you, Monsieur le Comte. At the risk of straining your indulgence, I have one last entreaty. It is by far the most important."

"I preferred your father when he was away," said the Comte wryly. "Well?"

"In spite of your scruples I beg of you to behave in such a way as to make him conclude that his wish to kill you is reciprocated."

CHAPTER 8

In Which the Moon Illuminates the Butt of No Joke

It was only once the cart blocking Joseph's path went on its way that he noticed his daughter hadn't followed him. He retraced his steps and found her conversing with a young man of noble dress and bearing.

"Father," she exclaimed, "here is the Comte! Let me introduce you."

Joseph looked the Comte up and down.

"It is no pleasure to make your acquaintance, Monsieur, for you have established a shameful liaison with my daughter. You have offended my name and my honor."

If Joseph's words had been in rhyme they would have been suitable for a tragedy! He must have acquired this flowery language at the manor house where he was employed.

The Comte bowed deeply and said, "May the pleasure I feel in making your acquaintance, Monsieur, compensate for your displeasure in making mine. I intended no offense. No man or woman in the kingdom do I respect more greatly than your esteemed daughter."

"If you respect her," snapped Joseph, "redress your infraction. Marry her."

The Chamberlain to the King's brother wed a Béjart? Madeleine stared at the ground, praying the Comte would not believe the idea had been hers.

"A pleasant notion, Monsieur," he replied. "I regret that I am not in a position to ask for her hand. But please allow me to pay your debts and offer compensation for the match your daughter would have made had we not become acquainted."

"How dare you put a price on my family's honor!" Joseph declared.

"It is not a price but a token of my consideration." The Comte pulled a scroll from his doublet. "Mademoiselle has not yet been informed that I have purchased a house in her name. It stands in Bagnolet, to the north and east of the city walls. If you don't wish to live there it will yield a tidy income. What I hold in my hands is the contract. I was on my way to collect the deed when I discovered Mademoiselle outside my door."

Madeleine absorbed the shock, speechless.

"I suppose your intentions were good," Joseph said after a silence. "And you acquired this residence in my absence. But now I have returned. My daughter cannot accept such a gift."

"What do you mean?" asked a voice that to Madeleine's surprise turned out to be hers.

"Silence!" said Joseph. "This is not your concern." He turned back to the Comte. "It is not compensation I request but retribution."

"Of course, Monsieur," said the Comte coolly. "In what form?"

Before Madeleine knew what was happening, Joseph Béjart delivered a resounding slap across the Comte's face. Caught unawares, the younger man drew himself up, protocol determining his behavior in this most consecrated of situations.

"Very well," he replied. "What is your weapon of choice?"

Joseph pulled his sword from its scabbard and brandished it with a cry. "Here's my weapon, Monsieur le Comte. And yours?"

"My sword is not on my person," the Comte responded. "I'll meet you here in half an hour's time. Choose a suitable area of the Place Royale for us to resolve this matter. See to it that it's hidden from sight." He opened the courtyard door and was gone.

Without a word Joseph began striding across the green. Drawing alongside him with difficulty, Madeleine grasped the scabbard swinging at his side and pulled him to a halt as if he were a frothing stallion.

"Father, I must speak to you," she panted, clasping his two hands in her own and kneeling before him on the grass. "I beg of you, put a stop to this madness. Shall I stand by and lose you for a second time? The Comte has more victories than he can tally. You stand not the slightest chance of defeating him."

"You have nothing to fear," said Joseph, his face glowing like that of a fresh convert expounding on his faith. "I assisted the young master at the manor house and learned more from his fencing lessons than he did. If I die, I forbid you to pity me. It is a privilege to defend one's honor. Noble blood flows through these veins, and through yours as well."

He pulled his sword from its sheath and drew the point against his wrist, raising a trickle of blood which he flaunted. He then executed a set of graceful thrusts and parries and in the torchlight of the nearby arcades his eyes flickered, now crazed, now lucid. He disappeared into the darkness of the green.

Madeleine awaited the two men's return as if bracing for Act Five of a tragedy. Only if the Comte played his role to perfection could her father's pride and life both be saved. As the courtyard door swung open and the Comte called out, Madeleine spied her father returning from his reconnoitering expedition, an expression of ecstasy on his face. He led Madeleine and the Comte to a thicket of junipers.

In the hidden clearing chosen for the battle, Joseph fought with such savagery that his adversary was forced to counterattack with ever increasing strength in order to survive. The Comte dodged his thrusts but Joseph fought like a hellion, leaving the younger man no choice but to disable him before he himself lost his life. When Madeleine saw that the Comte had unintentionally punctured her father's heart, she felt as if her life's blood were pouring from her veins. But as Joseph's strength ebbed and death approached, his pride remained intact. She held his head in her lap and stroked his beard, the white fleece thick with blood.

"Can you ever forgive me, Daughter?" he croaked.

"For what?" she asked, holding back sobs.

"Leaving," he said haltingly. "Making things difficult. Putting you through this."

"There is nothing to forgive, Father," Madeleine said, kissing his forehead.

The breaths came more slowly, the words harder to make out. "Do you recall what I told you about my father?" he whispered. "I lied. My mother did explain how she knew why the gentleman, not Pierre, was my father. But it was humiliating, so I didn't repeat it."

"Hush, Father," she said, "save your strength."

Joseph attempted to sit up but couldn't. "My father had a birthmark. She saw it that day they were together and on me when I was born. It was . . . on the backside and I could not see it myself. Before I'm buried, I ask you to do so."

"What can that matter now?" she cried out.

"Perhaps one day you'll see it on another." Joseph's eyes fluttered like the wings of a fledgling and he gasped out, "Then you might discover who you really are."

Only a man would harbor the ludicrous notion that the identity of her grandmother's seducer might determine who she really was, but it was her father's final request. She raised his bloodied hand to her lips.

"I'll do as you ask."

His head had become a dead weight in her lap. He could hardly speak.

"You said there was news of Jacques," he managed to say. "I would like to know."

"Jacques has been apprenticed to a draper," Madeleine responded after a moment's thought. "I never would have believed it, but he has skill and patience for the work."

"Thank you, Daughter," Joseph wheezed. "After you he was my favorite. In death I am proud of my children. Especially you."

He closed his eyes. This time they did not reopen.

***

The Comte comforted Madeleine as best he could. Eventually they had to decide what was to be done. He preferred that news of the event not be leaked. The King might have him arrested for his infraction of the law, and at any rate his reputation would be compromised if news of his duel with a commoner were to make the rounds. And how would they put it to Marie Hervé that after a year's absence, Joseph had perished a quarter-hour's walk from home?

When the strange idea came to Madeleine, she acceded to it. She would tell her mother nothing: neither that Joseph had died, nor that he'd ever returned. However much Marie Hervé missed him, he was no longer expected. Were she informed of the duel, even after being sworn to secrecy, the news might spread, the Comte be arrested and Joseph viewed as an upstart.

While Madeleine kept watch, the Comte called on a cleric at Saint Paul's who owed him a favor. The mild winter had left the ground unfrozen. Within two hours Joseph Béjart had received the last rites and been buried beneath an oak in the center of the Place Royale.

It was late when Madeleine arrived home and all was still. Drifting into slumber, she recalled the dénouement of her father's noble end. After the Comte had left to fetch the priest, she'd lit a small branch from one of the torches that lined the arcades, returned to Joseph, and undone his leggings. She was obeying his last request but her hand trembled as she illuminated his backside, sweeping from head to toe and back again. It was only on the third try that she thought she discerned a birthmark on the left buttock. At that moment a gust of wind extinguished her torch and she feared she wouldn't have the stamina to light it again. She was despairing of following Joseph's orders when a crescent moon suddenly appeared from behind the clouds and she saw it, flawless and unmistakable. She gazed in gratitude for this perfectly timed conjunction, which she herself could not have better contrived.

***

Madeleine admired her father's pride in refusing the house in Bagnolet and shunning the Comte's offer to repay his debts, but was it not easier to die with such ideals than to live with them? It would be madness to refuse such a gift: though the family's financial situation was now less dire, there was no word from Mondory about a part, and any day the Comte might take up with one of the countless females who made themselves available to members of the royal circle.

As Madeleine spent her days with Marie Hervé and Geneviève sewing by the fire, it was a form of torture to pretend nothing had happened. One morning Geneviève went out to collect a bolt of cloth, leaving Madeleine to listen to Marie Hervé's reminiscences.

"When your father asked for my hand I thought I'd sing with joy. I never expected someone so tall and attractive to give me a second look."

Madeleine tried to block out the agonizing words but heard herself screaming, "Will you never stop talking about him?"

Marie Hervé stared in silence.

"Forgive me, Mother," Madeleine stammered. "But Father is gone, don't you see? What is the point of nostalgia? We must learn to get along without him."

For once there was no hint of teasing in Marie Hervé's voice. "Would you have me behave as if he had never existed?" she asked.

"You speak as if you were happy together," Madeleine countered. "That's not how it appeared to me."

Marie Hervé sighed. "I suppose you're right, Daughter. We were happy for a while, before you were born. But I soon learned he was not the man he appeared!"

"What do you mean?"

Marie Hervé shook her head. "Years ago it was, and now another has passed, and Joseph . . ." She pulled a square of cotton from her apron to wipe her eyes. "I haven't dared say it aloud but we must speak of it one day and now is as good a time as any. Your father is dead."

Madeleine gazed at the gold embroidery on the costume she held, counting the seconds.

"You think it's my usual foolishness," her mother continued, "but it's the truth."

"How do you know?" Madeleine asked in a detached tone.

Marie Hervé drew her chair closer. "Joseph came to me in a dream not a fortnight ago." "He asked forgiveness for the sorrow he'd caused, kissed me goodbye, and vanished."

Madeleine had ceased putting stock in dreams, whether formed in sleep or in wakefulness, but her mother's vision was true: Joseph had asked forgiveness, then vanished.

"We're in agreement, then," she said, kissing her mother and squeezing her hand. "However much we may wish it, Father will never return."

The two women resumed their sewing. After a few minutes Madeleine said, "What did you mean that Father wasn't the man he appeared? Did he have a secret?"

Marie Hervé stared into the fire, and as they heard the front door open and Geneviève call out a greeting she said hastily, "All I can say is I did what I thought best. I'll go to my grave wondering whether it helped or hindered in the end."

CHAPTER 9

In Which Stage Fright Is No Match for Love

On the Sunday before Lent, Mondory, the director of the Théâtre du Marais, knocked on the door of the Béjart residence and offered Madeleine the role of Chimène, the female lead in *Le Cid*, for the remainder of the season.

At the Friday performance two days earlier, Mademoiselle de Bellemaison, the actress who had been playing the role and was equally renowned for her captivating contralto voice and her tendency to tipple before each performance, fell off the stage in Act Five and broke her leg. A stool on wheels was hastily constructed to fit underneath her gown for Sunday's matinee, but in Act Two, during an impassioned speech about the death of Chimène's father, she lost her balance, fell forward and exposed her rump. Whoops of laughter from the audience and eventually the players greeted the remainder of the play's grave events. Only Mondory was not amused. La Bellemaison's understudy having fallen seriously ill, the director decided to offer the role to Madeleine Béjart, starting with the Tuesday performance, which happened to be Mardi Gras.

"How long do I have until the first rehearsal?" Madeleine asked shakily after the first excitement had worn off.

The Béjarts were crowded onto a bench beside the fire while the Comte de Modène shared a sofa with Aunt Marion, who was visiting with little Mado. Mondory was seated in the grand chestnut armchair the family had recently purchased with money from the Comte.

"Rehearsal?" roared Mondory. "What rehearsal? The première was a month ago."

Madeleine went to the hearth and stirred the remnants of stew in the cauldron. "I can learn the lines," she said, "but I haven't even seen *Le Cid*. How shall I play the role?"

Putting an arm around her shoulder, Young Joseph said, "We'll see it together. If seats can't be found we'll stand in the p-p-pit."

Madeleine kissed him on the cheek. Mondory was less tactful.

"Until she learns the part there's no play to be seen, you moron," he thundered. Young Joseph slunk back to the bench like a kicked dog. It was all Madeleine could do not to send the director packing. "You have two days to work out how the role is to be played," he snapped. He stood abruptly. "Can you be ready? If you say yes and are unable to do it, you'll never act in my theater again."

Without warning Marion cried out, "See how she hesitates! Offer the role to me!"

Mondory sent Marion a withering look and said, "You've married into wealth, Madame, but you'll not marry into my theater."

Marion sobbed into the Comte's shoulder. He picked up little Mado and promised to return after accompanying mother and daughter home.

The diversion gave Madeleine time to reflect. "I can learn my part," she said, "but where shall I stand as I speak my lines? And will the costume fit me?"

"You're chestier than La Bellemaison," said Mondory after a long stare. "Never mind, the bodice will keep the audience's mind off your acting." He deposited the script. "Be at the theater by Tuesday noon, and bring the script. We haven't had a chance to have a copy made."

That night Madeleine was so absorbed reading *Le Cid* that only in the morning did she realize the Comte had not returned from seeing Marion home. Marriage had apparently done nothing to diminish her aunt's ambition to become a *great lady*.

***

In the two days that followed, Geneviève devoted every free moment to helping Madeleine learn her lines. It was a daunting task that normally required a week, but an even more serious challenge to confront would be how to portray the enigmatic character of Chimène.

The play was set in Spain in the days of yore when Christians battled Moors. Chimène was in love with Rodrigue and the pair hoped to marry until Rodrigue's father received an insult from Chimène's father, the Comte de Gormas. Against Chimène's wishes, this led to a duel between Rodrigue and the Comte, and when Rodrigue killed his adversary, Chimène found herself torn between avenging her father's death by having his murderer killed and marrying the murderer, the man she loved. Rodrigue having defended the city against the Moors, the King silenced Chimène's demands for revenge by pronouncing that she would do no dishonor to her father's memory by marrying Rodrigue.

In Monsieur Corneille's heroine Madeleine saw a sister under the skin, subject to the whims of men and left to her own devices to face the problems they created. Like Madeleine's own father, the Comte de Gormas caused no end of trouble, and yet Madeleine, thinking of Joseph Senior, understood Chimène's insistence on upholding her father's honor after his death. The King, who claimed Chimène was like a daughter, still ordered her to marry Rodrigue in spite of her protestations. The men made the decisions and the women suffered the consequences.

Portraying Chimène's adoration for Rodrigue presented the greatest obstacle. Chimène's passion made her swoon several times for fear that Rodrigue had come to harm. How could a lady be smitten with one who had enhanced his reputation by killing her father? In Madeleine's opinion Rodrigue compared unfavorably to the Comte de Modène, who had respected Madeleine's wishes and gone against his own interests by agreeing not only to duel with Joseph Béjart but also to do his best to protect him from harm. If Madeleine felt gratitude but not love for the Comte in spite of his consideration, how could Chimène be so deluded about a man who prized his reputation above his love for her?

The answer came to Madeleine as she mulled over the quandary the night before her debut. Chimène was in love; Madeleine never had been. The words Tristan pronounced at her audition rang strangely true: it was difficult to personify an ardor she had never felt. At this moment she would have welcomed true love, if only for the experience. But if in nineteen years she had not lost her heart, she was unlikely to do so before the curtain rose tomorrow.

***

When Madeleine put on Chimène's gown that afternoon she found that Mondory's observation about the size of her costume had been an understatement. It would be tricky not to pop out of the bodice. In spite of its snugness from the waist up, the dress, designed to imitate the Spanish-style hoopskirts that had been all the rage before the war, was as wide in the hips as the Rue de la Perle. Once Madeleine had been made up by an assistant and a black comb inserted atop her pile of light auburn braids, a mirror was brought. The assistant assured her she was the very embodiment of Chimène. To her own eyes she resembled a Spanish wetnurse.

Ten minutes before the performance was to begin Mondory strode toward her with a bearded man of thirty on his arm. The man's finely tailored silk doublet and rich accessories suggested he was a personage of some importance.

"My dear," said Mondory," we are graced by the presence of the playwright!"

Pierre Corneille, the most famous writer in France, sitting in judgment the day of her debut! He didn't even live in Paris but in Rouen. What had brought him here on this very day?

A panicked curtsy left Madeleine scrambling to collect her comb from the floor. In a twinkling her coiffure came undone and her glorious braids drooped over her bare shoulders.

Pierre Corneille kissed her hand. "Pleased to meet you, Mademoiselle," he said. "I see that my friend hasn't exaggerated in saying that all eyes will be on you."

Was he complimenting her beauty or jesting about her disheveled state? Either way she needed to attend to her hair before her entrance in Act One, Scene Two.

"I'm most honored, Monsieur," she said, inching toward the dressing room.

"How kind of you to say so," he replied. "The plague has reached Rouen and we have taken refuge in Paris until the danger passes. My youngest brother, Thomas, insisted on accompanying me this evening. I'll introduce you after the performance. He's an utter devotee of the theater!"

Madeleine said weakly, "A thousand pardons, Monsieur, but my coiffure . . ."

"Leave it as is," he bantered. "Perhaps it was the fashion six centuries ago!"

Laughing at his quip he slipped into the wings. As Madeleine arranged her hair before the mirror she found her eyes wide with fright: she could not recall her opening line to save her life. Normally she could have relied on the *souffleur*, who prompted the actors, but she'd neglected to bring the only script from home. Just as she was shoving her accursed Spanish comb into her hair, she heard the three blows struck by a staff against the floor to announce curtain time. And Madeleine Béjart, scorner of swooning ladies, had all she could do not to pass out.

***

So preoccupied was Madeleine trying to recall her first lines that she hardly registered the play's opening words, spoken by Chimène's maid to the father of Rodrigue, Chimène's favored suitor:

> *Among Chimène's suitors whose youthful ardor*
> *Worships your daughter and curries my favor,*
> *Don Rodrigue and Don Sanche most admirably show*
> *The flame that her beauty in their hearts has made grow.*
> *It is not that Chimène pays heed to their sighs,*
> *Or quickens their desire with approving eyes.*
> *A true lady, she shows indifference to them all,*
> *Neither dashing their hopes nor holding them in thrall,*
> *Receiving them politely, not displaying what she feels,*
> *In the choice of a groom to you, her father, she yields.*

Now it was Chimène's father, the Comte de Gormas, replying to Chimène's maid:

> *The King must choose a tutor for his son,*
> *He'll surely raise me to this rank I've won.*
> *What my valor and courage do for him every day*
> *Makes me certain no other can wrest this prize away.*

There it was: her cue. The Comte de Gormas exited, nodding to Madeleine as she made her way onstage. A deep breath compromised the decency of her décolletage, and she turned her back to the audience to adjust her bodice and walked toward the stage. Chimène's maid was exclaiming:

> How happy for Chimène that her father approves
> Of Rodrigue, that his blessing her heart's choice behooves!

Madeleine recalled the substance of her lines but not the words. If only the play hadn't been in rhymed couplets she might have improvised. The actress playing her maid shot her a look. As if she wasn't aware that it was her turn to speak!

She could not accept defeat until she'd looked the spectators in the eyes. She would make a dignified speech of apology and march out with her head held high, as Chimène would have done.

Such a moment warps time and it took an eternity to survey the hall. At the very back she could make out the fair hair and sweet smile of Young Joseph. Mondory, at the rear of the seating area where he could observe the weaknesses of the production, was also smiling his encouragement. Further up sat the Comte de Modène, for once his features betraying agitation. She'd turned down his amorous demands for the first time the previous evening to study her lines even though she realized she was probably sending him into Marion's arms, but the knitting of his brows made her suspect he truly cared for her more than he'd ever say. Next to him Tristan beamed with pride over the quick rise of his unwitting protégée. In the first row of high boxes she caught sight of the dashing Pierre Corneille who, far from sitting in judgment, sent a heartening wave in her direction. And suddenly a tall slender boy, presumably Thomas Corneille, leaned forward out of his brother's shadow to gaze at her with an attentiveness in which politeness was heightened by an inexplicable widening of the eyes.

So many males waiting to see whether she would sink or swim but wishing her well. Someone was missing, someone who should also be there. Her father, or dear Jacques? Tears gathered beneath her lids. How she yearned for them both, but the theater was not where they belonged.

She closed her eyes, imagined being seated in the audience and watching herself. And in her fantasy, seated next to her, materialized the young man who more than a year earlier had shown her the power of theater and been her strange inspiration. Were he present today he would cheer her on like the others, but while her success merely suited them, he would want her to achieve greatness for her own sake, and for the sake of the theater.

Stirrings from the audience brought Madeleine back to the present. Just as she was about to announce her capitulation, she was distracted by two eyes staring at her from near the front of the parterre, dead center. The person's body was largely blocked by other spectators but she watched with fascination as two hands gestured to capture her attention. The mouth opened wide and she realized that with exaggerated enunciation, it was offering her Chimène's opening line.

An instant before her mind was able to attach a name to the individual, her heart understood how she'd play the role of Chimène. As clearly as if the scene were being illuminated not by flickering candles but by a blazing sun, Madeleine Béjart knew that the eyes, the hands, and the gesticulating lips belonged to the man she adored, Jean-Baptiste.

CHAPTER 10

In Which Pees and Cues Are Minded and Two Colliding Phalluses Do Not Amuse a Great Lord

———————

During the lengthy heartstop just before Jean-Baptiste saved Madeleine yet again, she could imagine the motivations of all the various males observing her, except for one.

When Pierre Corneille blocked his brother's view, forcing him to lean forward to gaze at the striking newcomer playing Chimène, it was the first time in all of Thomas's twelve years that he'd emerged from Pierre's shadow. Old enough to be Thomas's father, the playwright had been famous for as long as the boy could remember, and until recently Thomas had basked in his aura. But in the past year, as the colt overtook the stallion in height and began to attract attentive glances from young ladies, he had been seized by self-consciousness. Tonight, forgetting his shyness, he sat with his eyes fixed upon

Madeleine's spellbinding form. By the obscure logic of pubescence, it no longer seemed enough to be the youngest brother of the illustrious Pierre. It was time for Thomas to become someone all on his own.

In the course of the performance he realized just what it was that would set him apart from his brother and all other males. He alone would be capable of appreciating Madeleine Béjart at her worth and devoting himself entirely to her happiness.

The one snag in this thrilling fantasy was that Pierre too was clearly under her spell. The boy suspected his brother's collaborations with actresses were not purely professional; Madeleine would simply have to be an exception. Pierre could take a new mistress every week for all Thomas cared. Madeleine Béjart would belong to him and him alone.

***

Your Highness, whatever fate you decide for me today
About this sad wedding, what will people say
If my grief for my father lasts only twelve hours,
Rodrigue in my bed while the grave's decked with flowers?

After uttering Chimène's final words, Madeleine struck a pose and awaited her fate. Thankfully that single prompt from Jean-Baptiste had been all she needed to recall her lines, but had the public been moved? And while Jean-Baptiste could not know that when she swooned she was picturing him as her injured suitor, what did he think of her acting?

As the crowd erupted and Madeleine prepared for her first curtain call, Pierre Corneille allowed himself to be led onstage. The actors did their best to smile as he took bow after bow. Only after a quarter of an hour did he doff his hat and disappear.

It was then that Madeleine Béjart experienced for the first time the adulation of strangers, more satisfying, she mused, than the kiss of a man one doesn't love. She basked in the acclaim. Jean-Baptiste applauded like one possessed. Not knowing how to express her newfound passion she cast her eyes in his direction while clasping her hands over her heart.

She made her way backstage and was relieved to find the dressing room deserted. Used by both men and women, it contained a couch, mirrored tables, and a privy behind a screen. The others were dancing attendance on Monsieur Corneille. Surely Jean-Baptiste would not be long in coming.

She was mistaken.

After what seemed like an eternity she had little choice but to remove her make-up, change, and face the Comte de Modène, who would be waiting for her in front of the theater. She began swabbing her forehead, but glimpsing the sadness in her eyes, she laid down her cloth. Was Jean-Baptiste not as eager to see her as she him? A tear meandered across her egg-white make-up, leaving a vale of naked skin. She gave herself over to sobs.

A noise alarmed her. She turned to discover a tall ungainly youth standing in the middle of the dressing room. He removed his hat and fell to his knees.

"Mademoiselle," he said, his face flushed, "I am Pierre Corneille's brother. I came in to use . . . Please allow me to express my admiration. You were the very essence of Chimène. The role will forever be yours. You are a true wonder of the stage."

They were stock phrases the boy must have heard in the circles he and Pierre frequented, but the pubescent voice, now manly, now timorous, gave them poignancy.

"Why are you here?" snapped Madeleine. "This room is reserved for the actors. And you might have announced your presence. You gave me a fright!"

Still kneeling, Thomas bowed his head and stammered, "I had need of ... that is to say I had to relieve myself." His blush deepened. "My brother told me to go outside but I don't care for that and thought I would not be noticed. When the door opened I hid. I heard you weeping and came out to see what was wrong." He looked up. "It was then that I realized it was *you*."

The register of his voice lowered on the word, as if his infatuation had suddenly turned him into a grown man. He was so sweet and strange, his eyes so earnest, that Madeleine relented.

"All right then," she said. "Please rise. This is not a church."

Thomas was tall, his gangling legs making him appear even larger than he was and his precociousness exaggerated by adult attire, black except for a doublet of dark-blue velvet. His ash-blond hair was long and flowing. A snow-white strand rose from the center of his forehead such as one sometimes sees in a youth whom nature thus marks out as an old soul. His eyes were the color of wet sand.

"Perhaps I am in church," he said gravely. "If so, the divinity I worship is you."

Madeleine stifled a laugh. She had only heard such phrases recited by actors ridiculing amorous gentlemen but was wary of hurting this boy who struck an unidentifiable chord within her. She took him to be sixteen or so, old enough to go courting.

"You are generous, Monsieur," she said, wiping make-up from one side of her face to play the clown and put him at ease. He remained somber. "As for worshipping an actress," she went on, "given that we are not permitted to worship in church, perhaps we should be allowed to be worshipped in the theater."

Thomas emitted a high giggle and in that single moment his apparent age was halved from sixteen to eight and Madeleine correctly surmised that the truth was somewhere in the middle. She took him by the hand to escort him back to Pierre.

"Come along, then," she said. "I'll see if the way is clear. Your secret is safe with me. We needn't share what happened with anyone, not even your brother."

Caught unawares by the soft feel of Madeleine's hand against his, Thomas threw his arms about her just as the door swung open and in walked Pierre Corneille.

"A thousand pardons, Mademoiselle," said Pierre Corneille. "I had no idea my brother was in here." He sent a fierce look in Thomas's direction.

"Why then have you come?" asked Madeleine drily.

Pierre Corneille laughed and said, "A pointed question, Mademoiselle. I hoped I might congratulate you in a manner similar to the one my brother has apparently discovered."

"I assure you, Monsieur," replied Madeleine with dignity, "that what your brother was doing here he was doing for his own benefit, not mine. He was visiting the place where kings can't send their servants to go for them!"

Thomas, who had never heard the euphemism, looked ready for the earth to swallow him up. He threw himself onto a chair in the far corner of the dressing room.

"Since I'm here," Pierre pursued, "please allow me to assure you that you were the very spirit of Chimène. You've changed the character forever. You're destined for greatness, a true marvel of the stage." He pressed her hand to his lips.

She stifled her amusement at how similar the brothers sounded. She picked up Chimène's fan and vented her face so as to inspect the great playwright at her leisure.

Monsieur Corneille cut an impressive figure. A sword hung at his side. The stout fingers that curled around his plumed hat were more like a soldier's than a writer's and suggested the sheathed weapon was not mere decoration. He was shorter than Madeleine, with broad shoulders and a thick neck. His wavy brown hair framed a conventionally handsome face, with bright hazel eyes and smile lines warning those who met him that he would be difficult to dislike.

"It is your play that is remarkable," she finally replied, "not I, as the public also thought. Weren't you convinced of it by their show of appreciation?"

"I could only think what a shame it was," Pierre rejoined, "that they made such poor use of their judgment, when you alone were worthy of admiration."

"Ah, that explains why you cut short your bows."

Pierre smiled and said, "*Touché*, Mademoiselle. I won't deny it is satisfying to feel adored. Surely that's something you can understand?"

"Indeed I can," she said. "It is a poor actress who cannot imagine being loved."

"Quite true," he replied, "but some actresses may imagine it more easily than others."

"Oh? And the reason, Monsieur?"

"Why, from a greater experience."

"Monsieur, the audience proved that you're in a better position to know about being adored than I."

"But as for you, Mademoiselle," Pierre quipped, "I'd like to be in a better position to prove to you that you are adored."

Thomas shot out of his seat and charged his brother. He came to a halt, wavering over Pierre like a steeple struck by lightning about to topple onto the church below.

Pierre gave his brother's curls a yank; Thomas blushed and smiled.

"Thomas my boy," Pierre said, "Mademoiselle Béjart has had a long day." He turned toward her and said, "I gather you've made the acquaintance of this young hothead?" She nodded. "These days," Pierre continued, "he fancies himself questing for the Holy Grail in some medieval romance." He clapped Thomas on the back. "He's sworn me to secrecy about his age, but it appears he's old enough to have been as taken by you as all other men."

Thomas's solemn expression couldn't have contrasted more strongly with his brother's mirth, but in spite of the differences in age and temperament, the two faces were similar and Madeleine found the twinning effect of this leggy colt next to a seasoned stallion comical; a giggle escaped her lips. When Pierre Corneille realized that he and his brother were the cause of the laughter he too was overcome. The contagion spread to Thomas, who whinnied and neighed.

Light-headed from fatigue, Madeleine doubled over, then stood to give her belly room for the rising spasms. A cramp took hold of her gut, leaving her breathless. Concern crossed the brothers' faces but the pain passed quickly and she attributed it to exhaustion. The image of two worried steeds fed her hilarity, hers in turn fueling theirs. Madeleine laughed until her legs would no longer hold her. She fell back onto her chair and roared and roared.

***

When Madeleine exited the theater she found the Comte de Modène wedged between two goats with enormous phalluses that knocked against each other in time to a pulsating drumbeat. It had slipped her mind that it was Mardi Gras. He disengaged himself without a smile and made his way through the press of revelers as if running a gauntlet.

As he led her in the direction of the Place Royale, masks and costumes appeared only to vanish again into the blackness. Bulls, mules, griffins, and unicorns paraded amidst demons and divinities. Singing erupted from all sides, and from everywhere and nowhere emanated a pungent aroma of bonfires.

Madeleine welcomed the hubbub as an excuse not to talk and to reflect on how she might be free of the Comte for the night, to go home alone and take only her dreams of Jean-Baptiste to bed to console her for his absence. The Comte stepped aside to observe a fistfight more to his taste than the festivities. A voice nearby chanted in time to a tune being wailed by a group of drunkards.

"Ma-d'moi-*selle*! Ma-d'moi-*selle*! Ma-de-*leine*!"

Who was addressing her? She turned to look. The man wore a devil's costume and brandished a trident. She was about to be swept forward when he pulled off his mask.

"Jean-Baptiste!" she cried.

Without so much as a look over her shoulder to see if the Comte was watching Madeleine flung herself at Jean-Baptiste and kissed him passionately. She pulled back from the embrace and they gazed at each other. Backlit by a bonfire, his eyes shone with the thrill of the moment. The fuzz on his upper lip, which had sprouted into a proper moustache, lent his smile a devil-may-care allure. As befitted his costume, his hair curled up on either side of his head like the soft horns of a charming Lucifer about to propose an enticement.

"You were magnificent," he gasped, catching his breath. "I saw *Le Cid* three times with Grandfather and sneaked in twice before on my own. When I walked past the theater today and saw the name Madeleine on the billboard I thought it might be you, so I stole in again. I tried to come backstage but they wouldn't let me through."

"How long have you been back?" she asked. "Why didn't you call on me?"

"I returned a month ago," he replied, "but you never told me your surname."

Suddenly she felt her arm being grabbed. The Comte was at her side, eyes afire.

"Who is this boy and how do you know him?" he barked.

"I am not a boy," interjected Jean-Baptiste.

The Comte's lips curdled into a smirk. "I beg your pardon, *Monsieur*," he said. "I'll rephrase my question. Who is this rude young man and how do you know him?"

At that moment a drunken celebrant dressed as the Roman goddess Venus pitched himself in Madeleine's general direction. He fell to the ground and lay on his back like an overturned beetle. Madeleine picked up the Venus mask and placed it before her eyes.

"His Excellency Esprit de Rémond, Monsieur le Comte de Modène, please allow me to introduce Jean-Baptiste . . . I beg your pardon, I don't know the young man's family name."

"Poquelin," said Jean-Baptiste.

"Coquauvin?" she screamed over the tumult.

"Poquelin," he shouted back, fairly exploding the P and the Q.

Madeleine repeated the name. "He is merely an acquaintance," she murmured.

"All right then," said the Comte. "We've no time to converse." He took her hand.

Madeleine pulled away with a cry. It was high time for her to make the Comte aware of her true feelings. As of this evening she was a successful actress and had no excuse to deceive him further. Just as she opened her mouth to explain, her midsection was gripped by pain. Staggering through the smoky air, she fell to the ground.

The Comte, still glaring at his rival, remained oblivious to what had happened. Jean-Baptiste split the crowd and crouched next to a recumbent masked figure whom the Comte didn't recognize as Madeleine.

"The lady is ill, give her room to breathe," shouted Jean-Baptiste, driving away the curious. "Yes, you two. Are you deaf or merely rude?"

Neither of the men he was addressing, mercenaries about to leave for the Spanish front, looked like the cooperative sort, but the uniforms receded and soon there was room for Jean-Baptiste to spread his devil cape underneath Madeleine. When the Comte finally grasped who the woman was, he strode over and yanked his rival from her side.

"I'll see to her needs," he said in an ominous tone. "I require no assistance from the likes of you."

"I beg your pardon, Monsieur, I intended no offense," said Jean-Baptiste. "Her well-being is my only concern."

Doubt flashed across the Comte's face. The words were respectful but the tone was not. This young bourgeois could hardly think himself a worthy opponent for a duel. Why was he not groveling as he ought to be?

Madeleine stirred and lifted her head and the two men helped her to her feet. She smiled weakly and took a few steps. Jean-Baptiste made a move to depart, but the Comte pinned his arms, turned to his mistress and said, "Why you have such acquaintances I cannot understand. This man has insulted us both. Give me one reason not to give him a thrashing."

Nausea swept over her. The Comte had taken her father's life and was now poised to kill Jean-Baptiste in a jealous rage, her love for her savior the cause of his death.

She shook off her queasiness, faced the Comte, and declared, "I met this young man once, Monsieur, by chance, long ago. He means nothing to me." She allowed her heart's indignation at the lies to creep into her voice. "I fainted from fatigue. You've slept these past nights, but not I! He was doing his best to assist me." The Comte was wavering. "He meant no harm, Monsieur," she concluded. "He's just a boy."

"Not according to him," said the Comte, loosening his grasp on one of Jean-Baptiste's arms to run a hand over his upper lip. "What have we here, some sort of moustache?" His voice softened; even the most humorless of souls has lapses. "All right then. We'll call it an error of youth. But if I see you near this lady . . ."

"You won't, Monsieur. There's nothing to fear," Madeleine hastily assured him.

"That's right, Monsieur. There's nothing to fear, nothing to fear, nothing to fear," echoed a shrill voice, which added, "Or is there?"

Madeleine glanced about to see if some strange woman was mocking her. As Jean-Baptiste blended into the safety of the crowd, it sank in that the voice had been his.

Thus it was that Madeleine Béjart came to understand that she bore a most inconvenient passion for Jean-Baptiste Poquelin shortly after realizing she was carrying the child of the Comte de Modène.

CHAPTER 11

In Which Love Pangs of Various Sorts Rain down on Our Heroine

When the bodice of Chimène's gown became so tight that Madeleine could scarcely breathe, she smuggled her mother backstage to let it out. Marie Hervé raised an eyebrow but said nothing. By a stroke of luck Madeleine's involuntary swoons onstage always seemed timed to match the demands of the script. Hecklers hired by the rival Hôtel de Bourgogne troupe had to be endured but didn't dampen the general acclaim. Day after day Madeleine dazzled the public without anyone's guessing her secret.

As the days turned to weeks without a word from Jean-Baptiste he himself became a man of mystery. Had he been frightened off by the Comte's warning in spite of his bravado, returned to his studies in Orléans, commenced traveling with the court? A final possibility was too painful to consider: that she alone lay awake nights wondering if they would ever be together.

From time to time she considered paying Jean-Baptiste a visit, but were she to find him in town, what would she say? The day they met she had lied twice, posing first as a noblewoman, then as an actress. Later, to save him from the Comte's wrath, she had claimed he meant nothing to her. After a third round of lies he would never believe her again. And yet how could she reveal the truth—that she was pregnant by another but loved only him?

The Comte was less attentive by the day; either her indifference was becoming more apparent or his interests increasingly lay elsewhere. She would have broken with him as she had intended, but eventually she would have to rely on his support for the child of whose very existence he presently remained unaware.

***

As if in consolation for Madeleine's plight, on the day *Le Cid* closed before Easter, the members of the Théâtre du Marais voted to offer her a contract. Only La Bellemaison dissented, unable to forgive her rival's success. Madeleine prayed that the thickening of her girth might slow, as sometimes happened, or that as the pregnancy progressed she could play in tragedies with a Roman theme featuring loose-fitting gowns with high waists.

On Palm Sunday spring flowers peeked through the Parisian muck and her queasiness miraculously disappeared as she now approached her fourth month. A surge of euphoria inspired the idea of a stroll to the Rue Saint-Honoré, but whether or not she would have told Jean-Baptiste the truth she would never discover. Shooting pains in her abdomen forced her to knock at the door of a strange house on the Rue de la Verrerie where she was invited to rest. On her way home she visited Margot, the neighborhood midwife, who pronounced that any activity beyond walking from mattress to chair or chair to mattress might be fatal to the child.

Her secret had already been guessed by Marie Hervé, delighted to have a closer connection to a rich and prominent man. The Comte received the news without comment but began stopping by daily with gifts of food and novels. That Marion did not visit even once confirmed that he had moved on to greener pastures.

The one person who took the news badly was Mondory. Informed of Madeleine's condition, he exclaimed that the public was fickle and there was no telling if the troupe would welcome her at a later date, then stormed out.

For the next six months Madeleine was a captive in her own home. She bedded down in the *salle*, the coolest room in summer, when the Dutch-style door could remain half-open. Mondory, remorseful over his harshness, sent over a fan discarded from the set of *Le Cid*, and Madeleine whiled away her days contemplating the joys and sorrows of impending motherhood.

Of course she desired a child some day, but why now, just short of having her fortune and her future assured? If only the child could wait a year! Her reputation would then be established, Joseph's debts paid off. No longer would she have to depend on a man except to ease her loneliness. Her last wish before drifting off to sleep each night was that Jean-Baptiste might be gazing at her when she awoke.

***

One morning in July, Madeleine was roused just after dawn by a knock at the door. Pulling herself upright was a challenge. She found the Comte dressed in traveling clothes, riding boots and a long cape, holding the reins of his sturdiest stallion and flanked by an entourage of servants, also on horseback.

"Esprit, where are you going?" she inquired. He had allowed her to call him by his Christian name since learning about the child.

The Comte wiped a speck of mud off his boot.

"I have affairs to attend to. Back home."

"Affairs?"

"The grape harvest last year was poor. My father needs help. You understand."

Madeleine eased herself onto a bench. The Comte had never been expansive, but to take his leave with no warning and such a paltry explanation?

"Yes, I understand," she said. She did not, but she had learned that that was what people said by way of accepting each other's lies.

The Comte snapped his fingers. His valet, without dismounting, handed over a coffer that had been resting on his horse's withers.

"This will tide you over," said the Comte, directing the valet to deposit the box on the kitchen table. He kissed Madeleine's forehead and said, "I shall return for the birth."

"Of course. I wish you a safe journey."

The cortège set off, and for a long while Madeleine listened to the horses' hooves recede into the din of a Parisian morning. Then she made her way to the kitchen to see what the strongbox contained.

Added to the monthly rent received from the house in Bagnolet that the Comte had given her, the sum would be sufficient for the family to live on for a year while continuing to pay off their debts. His generosity was not to be impugned. Madeleine stowed the box at the back of an armoire. She lay down but sleep was out of the question.

There was more to the Comte's story than met the eye. Did a fiancée, perhaps even a wife await his return? Or was he involved in the machinations of the man he served, Gaston d'Orléans, King Louis's younger brother? There were rumors that with the blessings of the Queen Mother, herself a Spaniard, Gaston had made a separate peace with the Spanish and was plotting to overthrow his brother the King. After twenty-two years of marriage Anne and the sickly Louis had not produced an heir. Gaston, who had, was next in line. If Gaston's plot had been discovered, perhaps the Comte de Modène's sudden decision to flee Paris had stemmed from his role as Gaston's chamberlain.

Madeleine pulled the covers close and yawned. To her mind politics was something men invented to waste their time arguing while women were busy working. She reflected that in spite of her dismay, an effect of surprise, the Comte's departure did not greatly disturb her. If the birth went well she would be able to return to the Théâtre du Marais in time for the holiday season. Should the Comte never return, she wondered whether she would miss him at all.

His very reality seemed to dissipate in the balmy breezes of late summer, and Madeleine's thoughts turned once again to Jean-Baptiste. Disheartened by his silence, she composed scenes in her head, to be played out if he should reappear. How would he react, seeing her belly? With jealousy? With laughter, as she was sure he sometimes did to cover emotions he did not wish to reveal?

By September her days and nights became unbearable, the discomfort silencing all desire but the wish for a child to look after. She was praying for a girl, a daughter who, unlike the men in her life, would not vanish into thin air.

***

The Comte did not return. One night in October, at midnight, Madeleine went into labor.

The midwife Margot was sent for but could do nothing to shorten the ordeal. The endless agony erased all sense of time. Marie Hervé refused to leave Madeleine's side, swearing the pain would soon be over. For once Madeleine found her mother's lies reassuring.

Françoise was born at dawn on the second morning. Inattentive to Margot's tone and the absence of a cry, Madeleine rejoiced at the words "It's a girl." Margot searched for a way to break the news. "It's a girl," she repeated, "but . . ."

But.

Madeleine squeezed her eyes tightly shut. Whether the weeping was coming from Marie Hervé or Margot she couldn't tell. A hand stroked her forehead. She heard her mother's voice saying, "Would you like to hold her until the priest arrives?"

"Take her away," rasped Madeleine. "I cannot look at her."

"You must," said her mother. "You will never cease to regret it."

Marie Hervé, who had suffered two stillbirths and buried three other children, had learned to mask her sorrow in the presence of others, but Madeleine knew that beneath her mother's good cheer the losses had taken their toll. Marie Hervé kissed her first granddaughter and placed her in Madeleine's arms.

Françoise was tiny, with a head of downy black hair. Except for the blue tinge of her skin everything about her was perfect: the bud of a mouth, the curve of the elbows and knees, the little fingers. Madeleine pressed her lips against her daughter's belly and quietly rocked her, reduced to silence by this child who would never shriek in protest or gurgle with joy.

She heard Marie Hervé talking to a man and then murmuring to her, "The priest is here. Would you like him to say a blessing over you as well?"

Priests. Sometimes it seemed all they ever did was arrive too late and talk too much. Madeleine shook her head. She would pray for her baby and allow the priest to, but that was all.

It was beyond her capacity to hand Françoise back of her own accord. Her mother gently pried away this child who, like Jacques, seemed almost to be smiling in death, as if to ease

Madeleine's suffering. Try as she might, Madeleine could not smile in return. She knew she had failed her little girl, though she didn't understand how.

***

As was frequent after a stillbirth Madeleine caught a fever and nearly died herself. She was physically out of danger within a month, but the death of Françoise quickened memories of Jacques and Joseph. For weeks she lay in bed, eating only when her mother insisted.

In late November the chill of winter roused her and she forced herself to venture outdoors. The wind and snow battering her face lifted her spirits more than Marie Hervé's motherly ministrations. At first she had little strength but on a mid-December day, without intending to go there, she found herself in front of the house of Jean-Baptiste.

"Mademoiselle?" asked the same elderly valet she had already met twice.

"Yes, I . . . if you please . . ." She was more winded than she realized.

"Are you ill, Mademoiselle?" he asked politely. "Shall I bring you a chair?"

She shook her head.

"Very well," he said. "What name shall I announce?"

She finally caught her breath and replied, "Madeleine Béjart. I've come to call on Jean-Baptiste."

"Master Jean-Baptiste is presently in Orléans, completing his studies," replied the valet in a neutral tone.

"Did he return for the summer?" she inquired.

An almost imperceptible pause. "He did, Mademoiselle," responded the valet.

So Jean-Baptiste had spent months in town without coming to see her. He couldn't bother to discover her whereabouts when the Comte had forced the information out of Tristan, his own rival. Why had she made such outlandish assumptions? Only a fool would believe that this dream of a boy she had met on the street and embraced at Carnival was destined to be part of her life.

The earth rose up; Madeleine gripped the gate. The valet rushed forward.

"Mademoiselle, please allow me to . . ."

"No, I tell you," Madeleine snapped, brushing him aside. "I must be on my way."

She turned and walked a few feet, then leaned against a wall, waiting for her strength to return. Behind her she heard the valet clear his throat.

"Is there a message, Mademoiselle?" he asked discreetly.

For the first time since the death of Françoise, Madeleine felt a surge of clarity. What had she expected would result from losing her head over a man?

"No message," she declared.

"Very well, Mademoiselle," the valet replied. He stared at his feet, embarrassed by the breach of decorum he was about to commit. "If you care to call again it's likely the young master will come home for the holidays."

"Thank you for your kindness," said Madeleine. "Good day."

And with that, she set out in the direction of the Théâtre du Marais.

CHAPTER 12

In Which Our Heroine Flees Paris While Pursued by a Manly Eve

————

It was not a performance day but Madeleine found the theater door unlocked. Standing at the back she observed that Mondory was holding a rehearsal of *Le Cid* even though the play had been in the repertoire for nearly a year. The reason soon became clear: La Bellemaison's preposterous performance as Chimène. Her voice had grown increasingly strident in the past months, as if in compensation for her fading splendor. Her wildly gesticulating swoons were evocative of a gravely ill woman subject to seizures rather than a dignified and heartbroken princess.

"How can she shriek out her lines one moment and faint the next?" Madeleine blurted out.

"Madeleine Béjart!" exclaimed Mondory. "What are you doing here?"

"You thief!" screeched La Bellemaison. "Get out!"

Madeleine was charging the stage when Mondory stepped between the two actresses and ordered Madeleine to wait in front of the theater. He soon joined her and they strolled down the Rue Saint-Louis, a thoroughfare that ran along the city walls toward the Place Royale.

"I am sorry for your misfortune, my dear," Mondory said simply. "But it has been two months since your confinement. I sent word several times asking when you could work but never heard back. The holidays were upon us. I could wait no longer."

Messages from Mondory? Madeleine recalled none. Possibly Marie Hervé had kept them from her for fear of slowing her convalescence. Just as likely Madeleine had paid them no heed.

"La Bellemaison isn't as good as you, my dear," he continued, "but she has a contract, and I can't—"

"What about the Infanta?" Madeleine replied, interrupting him. This second-most important female role in the play was that of the King's daughter, also in love with Rodrigue.

"The Infanta is taken as well," said Mondory. "All of my actors have contracts. As much as I'd like to, I can't pay two people for a single role."

Madeleine felt tears welling up. "After Easter, surely?" she asked in a tremulous voice. The coming season was four months away but the Béjarts could survive for that long on the money the Comte had given her.

"It won't be possible," muttered Mondory. "The public's memory is short. You played in only a dozen or so performances and La Bellemaison will move heaven and earth to dissuade the others from voting for you."

They approached the arcades that had sprung up to the north and west of the Place Royale. A few short months ago Madeleine had thought that if her career continued to flourish and she could pay Joseph's debts quickly, she might consider moving her family into a townhouse in this area. She had imagined Geneviève, dressed in the latest fashions, catching the eye of a prosperous bourgeois who could offer her the kind of secure existence none of them had ever known. Just as she was about to thank Mondory for his time, he came to a halt.

"There might be one possibility," he said, "if you're willing to travel. An acquaintance of mine, Philippe des Rosiers, is in town looking for a lead actress to replace one that unexpectedly left his troupe. They perform mostly in the South. He is not much of a judge of talent, but with a word from me he would probably hire you. I won't pretend the productions would be comparable but at least you'd be earning a salary and perhaps in a year or two . . . La Bellemaison is no youngster."

Suddenly it all made sense. The Comte's disappearance and the money he'd left her; the death of Françoise; Jean-Baptiste's vanishing act; and now La Bellemaison's repossession of the role that Madeleine felt belonged to her. It was as if all these events had mysteriously conspired to encourage her to leave Paris.

But was that what she desired?

"Thank you, Monsieur," she said. "I'll let you know." And she wandered toward the green of the Place Royale to ponder her decision.

***

The first problem to be faced was how her mother would react. Madeleine was the mainstay of the household; if a crisis arose, Marie Hervé would have no one to call upon, especially since Marion's carryings on with the Comte before his departure had become public knowledge and strained the relationship between the two sisters. On the other hand, unbeknownst to Marie Hervé, a good half of the Comte's money remained. Madeleine could set aside a small sum for her own needs and present the remainder of the coffer's contents to her mother with some invented explanation. Financial considerations might not be the only objections Marie Hervé would raise. Traveling across France with a theatrical troupe, especially for a young woman, was not a secure profession. There were the dangers associated with being lodged among strangers or in barns or sheds exposed to the elements and at the mercy of thieves. Nevertheless, the sight of the remaining portion of the Comte's gift would soften the blow.

As for Madeleine's siblings, Geneviève would dissolve in tears, Young Joseph sputter to hide his sadness, and little Louis beg to be taken along. Could so many reasons to stay in Paris be countered by a single one to leave, her passion for the theater?

Lost in thought, Madeleine happened upon the stand of oaks beneath which Joseph Béjart had been laid to rest. What would her father have advised? He clearly had seen acting as a wicked profession, and in many ways he had not been a man of sound judgment; giving his life in defense of her already lost honor was ample evidence of that. And yet his strange sacrifice had forged a noble and enduring image of him that would remain with his eldest daughter always. Joseph had died reaffirming who he thought himself to be. Even if living in the world meant accepting that most dreams were little more than pleasant fantasies, should she not pursue one that might, if she chose wisely, come to pass?

***

For Madeleine's audition Mondory lent her a low-cut gown of saffron-colored taffeta being used for a revival of one of Corneille's comedies. She let down her hair so that it hung provocatively beneath a pale-yellow hat she trimmed with turquoise ribbon. She reserved the Théâtre du Marais for the entire morning; twenty minutes would have been sufficient. Philippe des Rosiers, the fat, bald, fifty-year-old director of the Troupe du Vent who because of his name was known as Old Rosebush, stared at her chest while she delivered one of Chimène's speeches from *Le Cid*. He then stood, applauded, and offered her the position.

Madeleine gathered the family in the *salle* that evening. She began with a story about a bag filled with money that she had just received from the Comte, then announced the news of her decision to leave Paris. Marie Hervé listened quietly, busied herself with calming the children, and tucked them into bed. Madeleine was sorting through her clothing when Marie Hervé returned and clasped her to her bosom.

"I beg you not to leave, my darling," she said with a sob. "Anything can happen to a young woman without the protection of her mother. Is there no other way?"

What had Marie Hervé ever shielded her from? Madeleine swallowed an ironic retort, wiped her mother's tears with a bodice she'd been folding, and said, "You needn't worry. Monsieur des Rosiers will protect me."

"He will not," snapped the older woman.

"What do you mean?"

"He'll be part of the problem. You're young and beautiful. You've signed a contract. He'll take advantage of you at every turn."

"Why don't you ever encourage me?" cried Madeleine. "Don't you think I know I'll have to defend myself from Monsieur des Rosiers?" Her misery loosened her tongue. "And when did you ever defend me from anyone?" She fell onto a chair, laid her head on the table, and wept.

She felt a hand stroking her hair.

"You're right," said Marie Hervé. "Perhaps I was wrong to encourage your liaison with the Comte. Your father's faults were considerable but in circumstances such as these, he would have done everything he could to protect you, as I cannot."

Madeleine's sobs escalated at this observation much truer than Marie Hervé could have guessed. When she had cried herself out, she lifted her head. Marie Hervé was standing in silence, her eyes pleading.

"There's no point chastising yourself on my account," Madeleine said at last. "You did what you could. And why bring Father into it? I thought we were in agreement. Father isn't here to protect me, or you, or anyone else. What purpose is served by imagining what might have been? What good has such a thing ever done anyone?"

Marie Hervé smiled, though her eyes remained sad. She pecked Madeleine on the cheek.

"These are questions of youth. The years will bring understanding to you." As she turned her attention to tidying the kitchen, she added, "But here's a word of advice for your travels. Never underestimate the power of a well-turned tale!"

***

The Troupe du Vent was presently housed in Arles; to arrive in time to rehearse for the New Year's performances, Madeleine and Old Rosebush set out in mid-December. The morning was cold but as their carriage clattered across the Place de Grève the sun came out and Paris, its filth masked by a layer of fresh snow, looked its best. Madeleine dabbed at her eyes with one of the muslin handkerchiefs Marie Hervé had embroidered for her. In another few weeks she would be twenty, but she had never before been separated from her family.

As their carriage approached the Pont Notre-Dame an influx of carts slowed traffic and Madeleine dozed off to the swaying of the carriage. The Pont au Change to the west also being congested, the driver called back that they would cross the Seine on the Pont Neuf. Usually this lively bridge with its minstrels, charlatans, and mountebanks was a poor option for a carriage, but the Pont Rouge, the next crossing to the west, would take them too far out of their way.

They crept across the Pont Neuf with Madeleine drifting in and out of sleep. The holiday season had begun and groups of singers, hoping for a few coins, offered up variously harmonized renditions of traditional tunes. Images of hilarity merged in Madeleine's mind with half-waking dreams. Suddenly Marie Hervé was there, dressed in black, her face drawn and her palm extended. "Come along then, Mademoiselle, give us a coin," she begged her, eyes deadened. "Surely a great lady can spare a gold louis for her brother's funeral." So now not only Jacques and Joseph but also Louis was dead? It must be Louis because of the coin her mother demanded.

The carriage jerked forward and Madeleine awoke to see the traffic had eased and they were about to drive onto the Left Bank. Three buskers disguised as a serpent, a hairy-chested Eve, and a puny Adam reenacted the Fall in a bawdy manner. Madeleine laughed at the manly temptress offering an apple to her mate. She was nodding off again when she heard a pounding.

"Madeleine, come back! Don't leave me!"

She couldn't see the man running beside the carriage, but surely the voice was Jean-Baptiste's! The valet had said he might return for the holidays. He'd waited for her all this time!

How could she have misjudged him so? And why had he suddenly reappeared?

Had he believed the lie she had recited—that he meant nothing to her—to protect him from the Comte's threats? That must be it. When Jean-Baptiste returned to Paris and the valet informed him of her visit, he must have seen the truth and realized she had been acting.

Madeleine tried to stand and speak to the driver but was thrown off balance. She fell into Old Rosebush's lap and felt him groping her with eager hands, then sprang to the other side of the seat, as far away as possible from his grasp.

"Driver, stop!" she cried out with all her might over the commotion. "Just for a moment. I must have a word with this young man. Stop I tell you, I must alight!"

Old Rosebush, his eyes burning, grabbed hold of her arm.

"Stay where you are," he cried out. "You belong to me now. Driver, on the double!"

As they headed toward the Rue Saint-Jacques, the main artery leading out of Paris to the South, Old Rosebush loosened his grip and Madeleine leaned out, straining to catch a glimpse of Jean-Baptiste. But he had disappeared; and as she felt the shock of cold air rushing against her skin, she couldn't be certain he'd been there at all. It was clear he had vanished yet again. But whether he had receded into the crowd or into the world of her dreams she could not ascertain.

CHAPTER 13

In Which, Amidst Bleating, a Woman Half-Opens Her Heart to a Man Who Half-Closes His

---

The Troupe du Vent performed in the reception rooms of country estates and the courtyards of towns scattered throughout Provence and Languedoc. The hours onstage were brief in comparison with days of jolting along rutted roads. If Madeleine soon learned that Old Rosebush's declarations were harmless, unwelcome advances from spectators and men in taverns were not. The troupe often spent nights in barns where the danger of marauders made sleep all but impossible. She grew accustomed to catnaps but was sad to lose access to her dreams.

That of a reunion with Jean-Baptiste faded more quickly than the others. She spent her first journey to the South wondering whether his voice calling out to her had been real, but when she met the downtrodden members of the troupe in Arles and Old Rosebush proclaimed her mildewed pallet their finest, the crudeness of her new life chased her exalted love for Jean-Baptiste into the innermost recesses of her heart. During the troupe's annual spring visits to Paris to recruit actors, purchase supplies, and procure new plays, she never once sought news of him.

Madeleine ceased expecting to hear from the Comte de Modène once it became known that, as she had suspected when he so abruptly left Paris, he was implicated in Gaston's failed plot against the King and had taken refuge on his family's lands. To the astonishment and jubilation of the realm Queen Anne, approaching forty, gave birth to two sons in quick succession, but even after Gaston, no longer the heir apparent, became less of a threat, the Comte de Modène stayed away from court. Upon returning to Paris after her first year away Madeleine was touched to find a letter from him expressing sorrow over Françoise's death, news of which had only just reached him. Unaware that she was traveling with a troupe, he expressed the wish to see her again when he could safely return to Paris.

The family was thriving. Each spring Madeleine marveled at the changes in Louis, soon as adept at building scenery as Joseph. Geneviève was content to sew costumes while awaiting a chance to become an actress, oblivious to Madeleine's insistence she would be far more secure if she did what her older sister had not done: found herself a prosperous husband.

In 1642 the Théâtre du Marais fell on hard times: the King, who favored Paris's other troupe, the Hôtel de Bourgogne, issued a decree allowing the troupe to hire any Marais actors they pleased. The first chosen was Madeleine's archrival, La Bellemaison.

Madeleine, who happened to be in Paris, pounded on the door of the Théâtre du Marais as soon as the news reached her ears, praying that Mondory would finally be in a position to offer her a contract. But this fresh slight from the King had been too much for the aged thespian who, upon learning of the defection of four of his players, suffered a fatal stroke. Floridor, the Marais's new director, a man of questionable talent, said he would keep Madeleine in mind for the future, but that was all.

Shortly thereafter Marie Hervé fell gravely ill and was sent to the country to recuperate for some months. Madeleine was tempted to stay in Paris and look after the family, but for all his foolishness she couldn't forget that Old Rosebush had offered her a job when she desperately needed one; she refused to leave him in the lurch. Geneviève, now seventeen, could manage until Marie Hervé recovered. Moreover, with some advanced planning and even from a distance, Madeleine could establish connections in Paris during the Troupe du Vent's road season. So, vowing it would be her last, she resigned herself to one final year of the perils of the road.

***

She was never sure of the exact date of the interlude in Nîmes but it was in the late spring or early summer of that year and remained in her mind forever associated with the smell of roses.

It had been difficult for the troupe to receive permission to play in Nîmes, where the numerous Protestants were as distrustful of actors as were the Catholics elsewhere. Farce and certain tragedies were out of the question, so Old Rosebush settled on Monsieur Corneille's somber Roman war tragedy, *Horace*. Madeleine played the title character's sister, Camille, accused of being a traitor to Rome and dispatched by her brother, the soldier Horace, to the other world because she insisted on weeping for her beloved, an enemy of Rome whom Horace had slain in battle. Although it was sobering being killed by one's own brother, the climactic confrontation with Horace in Act Four allowed Madeleine the rare opportunity of lashing out at an oppressor as well as capping her performance with an exciting death scene that brought down the house. On a purely practical level, her demise also allowed her to spend Act Five freshening up for her curtain call. But not on this particular occasion.

The afternoon was heavy with an approaching storm. Early in the play Madeleine glimpsed a dark-haired man at the very rear of the seating area following her every move with sultry eyes. He wasn't close enough for her to judge whether he was handsome, but life on the road being harsh and lonely, after a while she allowed herself to send noncommittal glances in his direction. In Act Three she met his gaze from afar and raised a brow.

After Camille's death scene, Madeleine spent the beginning of Act Five peering at the man from behind one of the pillars that held up the curtain. His clothing suggested that he was in the King's entourage. Louis, plagued by enemies and in failing health, was crisscrossing the South of France in an attempt to muster support. That morning he had set up camp in the vicinity of Nîmes.

Just before the final scene, Horace's trial for the murder of Camille, Old Rosebush pulled Madeleine aside and insisted that to rouse the somnolent audience she must be carried onstage so that Camille's corpse would remain visible during the trial. The two of them exchanged furious whispers about this strange conceit not to Madeleine's liking. A gust of wind could expose parts of her anatomy that would infuriate the city fathers. Her protestations having gone unheeded, she prepared to be dead yet again.

For the next half-hour she lay on the ground praying the public would not notice that their slain heroine was bathed in sweat. At least she stayed mute, unlike her colleagues who, stricken by the heat and the numb audience, recited their lines as if at death's door. When the curtain was unrolled to light applause mixed with jeers, she was so thirsty that her admirer in the audience had slipped her mind. After a perfunctory bow she beat a hasty retreat to the changing tent.

She was revived by a clap of thunder and a freshening of the air. She was adjusting the neckline of a cotton dress when she saw an image of steamy eyes projected in her mirror. It was her new devotee. She pulled a handkerchief from her bosom and wiped her brow.

"Yes?" she said without turning, addressing his reflection.

"How kind of you to answer my request before I put it to you," he replied. "Please grant me a moment to modify my question now that I know you intend to accept."

The attack was cleverer than most. The voice and smile seemed vaguely familiar.

"In my travels with the King," he continued, "the one pleasure I didn't anticipate was seeing *the illustrious Madeleine* laid out in all her splendor on a country stage!"

She wheeled about and threw herself into his arms.

***

Images of Jean-Baptiste had drifted through Madeleine's memory in the past five years, but she had sometimes had difficulty convincing herself they were inspired by an actual human being. When she pulled back from the embrace and observed him standing before her, what became unreal was the time she had spent thinking she could live the rest of her life without him.

He was now a distinguished servant of the King. The close-fitting jerkin trimmed in burgundy emphasized his manly shoulders. His gray stockings were molded onto shapely calves. A feathered hat perched atop his tidy hair and the gold-buckled black shoes bore gray and red lace to echo the colors of the ensemble. His eyes were still full of mischief but appeared less inclined to reveal the sadness of a motherless boy; Madeleine found herself longing for the soulful lad she'd comforted. She vowed not to show how hurt she had been by his disappearance.

"Illustrious Madeleine, indeed!" she said, gesturing wryly toward the squalid surroundings while what was really on her mind was why, given that Jean-Baptiste had dropped out of her life in the twinkling of an eye, he still recalled the affectionate and respectful name he coined for her on the day they first met six years earlier.

"I grant you it isn't the Théâtre du Marais," he conceded, "but the setting matters little. I saw La Bellemaison in the role of Camille two years ago. I gave her my compliments but her interpretation doesn't hold a candle to yours."

"You're too kind," said Madeleine. "What a fine gentleman you've become!"

"How else might I hope to escort such a fair lady on a stroll?" he said, offering his arm. "As you said yes before hearing what I'd ask, you may not now refuse."

Beneath his teasing a hint of the old forlornment emerged, like a pallid full moon rising at sunset. Just then a cool breeze smelling of the mountains emerged through the tent flap, signaling that the wind had shifted, the storm passed through. And suddenly the best thing Madeleine could imagine was to stroll through the cleansed town with Jean-Baptiste, then find a quiet spot to lie beside him and show him that she had not forgotten him.

And yet were these sentiments she could reveal? The simple fact that their paths had crossed was apparently a good enough reason for him to speak in a tender voice that lured her into offering her heart without presenting his own in return. She chose her words with care.

"What a courteous request, given that I accepted in advance!"

***

Night was falling. The cloudburst had cleared the streets around the Roman Arena and they walked arm in arm through the magical light. Madeleine would have been content to bask forever in Jean-Baptiste's presence, but the past five years cried out to be accounted for, so she said, "I see from your attire that you're traveling with His Majesty."

"My title is *valet de chambre du Roi*," Jean-Baptiste replied with barely masked irony, "but I'm a glorified bedroom attendant. I have the urgent task of making certain His Majesty's chambers are properly made up. He's a poor sleeper and is disturbed by the slightest fold in his sheets. If I hadn't inherited the function from my father, it is the last thing I'd have chosen."

"At least you're certain of food and shelter and have time to do as you please."

"Perhaps," he conceded. "As His Majesty's sleeplessness attests, my job is less troublesome than his." He brushed away a persistent bee. "But it isn't as enthralling as yours."

They made their way around the Arena, the starkness of its ancient stones softened by the twilight. Musing aloud, Madeleine said, "Sunset is the saddest time of day, and the loveliest."

"I wonder," replied Jean-Baptiste in a contemplative tone she had never heard, "if it is beauty that makes it sad or sadness that makes it beautiful."

How could a man be capable of such a thought? "Must I be sad then, if I hope to be beautiful?"

They came to a halt.

"How can you speak of hoping to be beautiful?" His eyes glistened.

"I see," she said lightly. "Shall I give up all hope of it, then?"

He fell to his knees and cried, *O miracle of love!*

She recognized the allusion to Rodrigue's declaration to Chimène in *Le Cid*, but rather than quoting Chimène's glum reply, *O pinnacle of woe!*, she guided Jean-Baptiste's lips to hers.

***

A sudden embrace in the shadow of the Roman Arena made for a lovely moment but raised the problem of where to go if they wished to carry things further. The sun was setting and Jean-Baptiste would have to make his way back to camp before long to prepare for the King's bedtime ceremony, the *coucher du Roi*, so he suggested he and Madeleine stroll to the outskirts of town and find a barn.

She frowned. She hadn't expected the King's chambers, but a *barn*?

They ended up in a barn.

The sun had set by the time they reached the edge of town. The moon cast enough light for them to spy a boxlike building in the distance. They picked their way silently across a grazing field to avoid startling the recumbent animal forms along the edge of the field, from their smell sheep rather than goats; the murmuring of lambs was barely audible beneath the wind's rustling through high grass. The mountain breeze, bracing at first, turned chilly as they crossed the field. With the barn looming she flung her arms around Jean-Baptiste's chest, rested her cheek against the wool of his jerkin, and welcomed the feel of his arm encircling her shoulders.

Just inside the barn lay a pile of hay illuminated by a renegade moonbeam. Madeleine shook her hair free and pulled her gown over her head; he too disrobed in silence. Then, his chest pressed against hers, they kissed and she closed her eyes, lost in the aroma of his hand which she brought to her lips and the sound of his quickening breath. Her eyes still shut, she delighted in the animal senses, touch, taste, odor, and sound, which unlike vision do not deceive or betray. At the final moment his laugh, arising from his pleasure, startled a rooster who fluttered his wings. But while Madeleine and the animal had both been set aquiver by Jean-Baptiste, the sigh of contentment that followed came from her alone.

She awoke to find him fully dressed, standing beside her. He crouched, kissed her forehead and said, "There is much to prepare at the encampment. I'm sorry I won't be able to escort you back to town."

She propped herself up on an elbow and brushed hay from her face. "When will we see each other again, Jean-Baptiste?" she asked, holding her voice steady.

"The King has announced we'll be leaving first thing in the morning."

Her heart sank. She wished he would say her name but asking him to would spoil it. She dressed quickly and said, "Perhaps our paths will cross in Paris."

He kissed her hand and held it against his cheek. His voice was somber. "Do you suppose?"

Paris was the kind of place where the only acquaintances one happened upon were those one was avoiding. Anger welled up in Madeleine at the thought that she alone had taken the trouble to call on Jean-Baptiste while he was apparently content to leave things up to chance. Most of the males she encountered persisted in their demands far longer than was reasonable. Was Jean-Baptiste incapable of expressing his desires?

And yet once at least he had done so, the day she left Paris in Old Rosebush's carriage. That meeting too had been unplanned, but Jean-Baptiste had spoken from the heart, voicing the words she had longed to hear: that she must wait for him, that he couldn't live without her.

"I believe our paths did once cross," she began cautiously. "On the Pont Neuf, the day I left Paris. Or at least someone with a voice like yours knocked against the side of the carriage I was in and cried out my name."

"Is that so?" he replied.

He gazed at her, unperturbed, and waited for her to go on. Only a fool would fail to see she was asking him a question.

"Yes," she continued, "he made a terrible ruckus and ran alongside the coach shouting at the top of his lungs. Was that you?"

Jean-Baptiste pulled away. "What was he saying?" he inquired coolly.

To avoid uttering the words, he was waiting for her to repeat them! Her patience worn thin, she was about to bid him a curt adieu when suddenly the moon emerged from behind a cloud and out of nowhere appeared the bereft orphan's face to which her heart had once yielded. The wary features revealed a secret, one of which the brash young man was clearly unaware: if falling in love meant risking heartbreak yet again, he would struggle against it like death itself.

She put her arms around his neck, kissed him on the lips, and said, "Never mind about Paris. If it's meant to be, we shall meet again. This is my final season of traveling. My family lives on the Rue de la Perle, up the street from the Théâtre du Marais. If you care to, pay us a visit once I've returned."

Hand in hand they crossed the field. When they reached the road, just as they were about to separate, Madeleine pulled Jean-Baptiste close one last time.

"It would be a lie to say you were my first," she whispered into his ear, "but it's the God's truth that I wish you had been."

Clouds had again covered the moon so she couldn't gauge his reaction. Without uttering a word he bowed, and before she knew it he had disappeared into the darkness.

CHAPTER 14

In Which a Paternity Is Mockingly Invented, Earnestly Falsified, Then Tearfully Revealed

---

If in the months following Madeleine's discovery of true love in a barn she only gradually began to fathom the ways her heart would be transformed by the event, before the heat broke in September she clearly knew its effect upon her body. She stood alone in a field and welcomed the rain that mingled with her tears of joy. In late winter or early spring, shortly before she returned to Paris, she would receive a living and breathing token of her passion for Jean-Baptiste.

She had three obsessions: keeping the waists of her gowns adjusted to mask her girth; never being observed in a state of undress; and holding her head high to conceal the double chin that lent her a passing resemblance to the late Queen Mother. By November she felt as large as the barn where her child had been conceived. Was she carrying twins? Or, as was recounted in one of the troupe's comedies, had some pagan divinity taken the shape of a bull while she was asleep and left her carrying a heifer? If only her life were composed of such whimsy!

One day during the busy Christmas season, when the troupe was performing in a covered market in Arles, Madeleine spent the matinée cavorting across the stage in a farce. She scarcely made it through her curtain call before she found herself crouching in an alley, vomiting uncontrollably. That evening she was to play the title role in Monsieur de Rotrou's tragedy, *Antigone*. She had no choice but to inform Old Rosebush that she couldn't perform.

If she simply said she was indisposed he could fall back on her understudy, who had recently been recruited for her fresh face, yellow hair, and pleasing curves. Though talentless as far as Madeleine could judge, Anne des Forêts would presently look more fetching in Antigone's gown than she herself did. On the other hand, if Madeleine admitted the truth, Old Rosebush would terminate her contract and she would risk forfeiting an entire year's salary.

She mulled over the dilemma while removing her make-up. Perhaps it was only fair to speak to Old Rosebush with complete candor. Since realizing that his demands posed no threat she'd found him pitiful; he wasn't the worst type of man she had ever encountered. She would state with dignity that she was expecting a baby; that she could no longer fulfill her obligations; that nonetheless she desperately needed money for her unborn child; and that it was her fervent hope that he'd pay her as much of her annual salary as was humanly possible.

She imagined the furrowed brow, the peevishness in Old Rosebush's voice as his lips formed a rejoinder. "My pretty *demoiselle*," he'd say, "can you give me a single reason why I should pay you salary to which you aren't entitled by the terms of your contract?"

Her reply came to her out of thin air and she spoke it aloud to the mirror: "Of course, Monsieur. Because you are the father of my child."

***

It was child's play convincing Old Rosebush that one moonlit night some months earlier, after consuming a great deal of wine, he and Madeleine had lain together. His astonishment quickly yielded to pride. He approached her with a tender look; before he could open his mouth, she proclaimed that she wouldn't dream of asking him to recognize a child conceived in a moment of intoxication, when he had vainly resisted her bold advances before finally surrendering. All she asked was to be released from her contract and given a year's pay. Was that too much to hope, she concluded, when she would spend the rest of her days caring for the product of their union?

Old Rosebush stammered that he'd inform the others she'd been taken ill and returned to Paris. Could she use a few extra *livres* for the baby? In reply she offered her most alluring smile.

The state of the roads made the journey to Paris a nightmare. Swaying to and fro along frozen highways was a poor remedy for queasiness. She prayed her child wouldn't be harmed.

She arrived in Paris on the evening of January 3, 1643. She needed to recover before facing her mother and directed the driver to a nearby inn. After a night's rest she'd decide how to put the matter to Marie Hervé. A thornier question was what, if anything, to tell Jean-Baptiste.

After an eighteen-hour sleep Madeleine devoured a loaf of bread and a round of cheese and primped before the mirror. At least her face now looked presentable. It was Saturday, not a theater day. For fear of being recognized in the neighborhood, she waited until dark. A billowing shawl was used to mask her condition. As she walked, she went over her story in her mind.

At the house she would explain to Marie Hervé that her pregnancy was the result of a chance encounter. If her mother demanded details she'd invent an unforeseen reunion with the Comte de Modène. Once things had settled down, Madeleine would send word to Jean-Baptiste and, if he was in town, find some excuse to summon him to the house. If he seemed disinterested in her news, she would wish him godspeed. If he led her to believe he loved her, perhaps they would wed. However alluring a union with him might appear, she wouldn't marry him unless she was convinced that that was what he too desired. She had already been in one loveless relationship and that was enough.

She was relieved to find the Rue de la Perle deserted. She tapped cautiously at the door of the *salle*. Suddenly Marie Hervé was there, sweeping Madeleine into her arms.

"My beloved daughter!" she exclaimed. She made a motion to clutch her to her breast but Madeleine hurried into the house and Marie Hervé took no notice of her daughter's midsection.

"Madeleine, my darling, I couldn't be happier," she said, dabbing at her eyes with a kitchen rag. "But why have you come home in January? Has the troupe disbanded?"

"I'll explain in a moment, but first come sit across from me. Geneviève wrote that you recovered well from your ailment but let me judge with my own two eyes."

Marie Hervé's illness had left few visible effects. There were now wrinkles at the corners of her eyes and lips but her skin was otherwise smooth. Her hair had but a few gray strands. All in all her ongoing claim of being not a day over forty was compromised less by her looks than by the fact that Young Joseph would soon be twenty-seven.

"I'm pleased to find you well," said Madeleine. "Where are the others?"

"Louis is asleep," said Marie Hervé. "Joseph and Geneviève are at the theater."

"At the theater?" asked Madeleine. "On a Saturday?"

"Not in the audience," said Marie Hervé. "They were engaged for the holiday season and are rehearsing a new tragedy by Monsieur Corneille about some Christian martyr. I forget the name. They're small roles but we need the money. They should be home soon."

So Geneviève was being granted her wish to become an actress, but Joseph, whose stutter was incomprehensible when he spoke before a group? Marie Hervé guessed her thoughts and added, "Your brother has studied *elocution*. He is able to speak normally."

Madeleine nodded and said, "There's something I must tell you while we're alone."

Suddenly seized with apprehension Marie Hervé cried, "Is it bad news? Are you ill? Is that why you've returned before the end of the season?"

"I'm not ill and it's not bad news," Madeleine began slowly. "For one thing, Monsieur des Rosiers gave me my entire salary in spite of it." She pulled a bag of coins from her pocket.

Marie Hervé didn't inspect its contents, proof of her anxiety. "In spite of what?"

Madeleine undid her shawl. As she was removing her bodice the door opened, allowing in the voices of Joseph and Geneviève, in high spirits after their rehearsal. And the image they happened upon was the mainstay of the family, all belly, wearing nothing but a shimmy.

***

After a long moment of frozen silence, Joseph's face became that of a cackling ape while Geneviève dissolved in tears. Marie Hervé sent the masks of comedy and tragedy to bed, brought Madeleine a cup of steaming wine, and placed a folding chair across from her daughter.

"Who is it?" asked Marie Hervé without further ado.

"A man," Madeleine replied in a neutral tone.

"Fancy that," Marie Hervé shot back. "I had assumed it was the Holy Ghost."

"It's someone you don't know," Madeleine said primly. "I hardly know him myself."

"That was wise of you," countered Marie Hervé. She sighed. "You aren't a girl of eighteen. In a few days you'll be twenty-five. This may be your last chance. Will he marry you?"

"I suppose he could," Madeleine began slowly. "He knows nothing about the child."

"We must speak to him then," said Marie Hervé. "Where does he live?"

"I met him while he was traveling with the court."

"The court?" Marie Hervé's interest was piqued. "What is his station? Is he a nobleman?"

"I'm sorry to dash your hopes of my marrying into the royal family," Madeleine replied, "but he is not. He is the son of a draper."

"Has he anything to recommend him? Is he well off at least?"

The question of whether the Poquelins were wealthy hadn't crossed Madeleine's mind since the day she met Jean-Baptiste. Thinking back to his father's grand residence on the Rue Saint-Honoré she surmised the family was prosperous.

"Perhaps. I hardly know."

"Since you learned nothing before inviting him to become the father of your child," said Marie Hervé in a voice edged with impatience, "it falls to me to find out. Surely you must know something about him. Were you not planning on informing him?"

"That's my affair. I'm not sure of his whereabouts." Madeleine fought back tears. "I'm sorry if I didn't ask him for an account of his fortune when he said I was beautiful."

Marie Hervé caressed her daughter's cheek. Allowing her eyes to rest on Madeleine's lovely face, which she had missed so terribly, she stroked her hair.

"Forgive me," she went on in a reflective tone. "It's only of your well-being I'm thinking." She sighed. "I see now that's something I haven't often done. What would have become of us without you? You must think me a foolish woman, but now it's my turn to care for you, or find someone who will."

"You're not foolish, Mother. And you needn't worry. I can care for myself."

"If you're like every other woman," Marie Hervé responded, standing and walking to the hearth, "you can and you can't. Your father did little to look after us, but when he left . . ." She cleared her throat and in a businesslike tone returned to the matter at hand. "Perhaps this man has a greater fortune than you realize. I'll make inquiries. My child, you must tell me who he is."

Marie Hervé had a knack for obtaining what she sought. If she insisted on forcing Jean-Baptiste to marry her daughter, she might succeed. And yet the surest way to ruin whatever chance for happiness Madeleine might have would be to allow her mother to impose the union.

"The truth is that the father of my child isn't a stranger but the Comte de Modène."

"The Comte de Modène!" cried Marie Hervé.

Something in her tone made Madeleine uneasy and words flew from her lips.

"Imagine how astonished I was when he attended a performance in Avignon! It seems a coincidence but his family lands are very near. I didn't recognize him in the audience but afterwards he paid his respects." The doubt lines on Marie Hervé's forehead were creasing. "The Comte is losing his hair but still as handsome as ever. He asked after you and Geneviève. I never knew he had a young sister the same age as she."

"And what happened," inquired Marie Hervé, "after he *paid his respects*?"

"What do you think? One thing led to another. I grant you it was imprudent."

Marie Hervé crossed her arms.

"So you're under the spell of the Comte de Modène. Some things never change."

"I'm not under his spell, I just—"

"Hush, Daughter." Marie Hervé put a finger to Madeleine's lips. "There's no need to go further. What I meant isn't that you still love him. I know you never did. What I meant is that you're still a wretched liar, and the poorest one ever to bring shame on this family!"

Madeleine looked down and mumbled, "How could you tell?"

"A mother always knows," declared Marie Hervé. "One lie deserves another and I could keep the truth to myself, but I hope you will feel as foolish as you are when I inform you that the Comte de Modène has been in Paris most of this past year."

"The Comte de Modène in Paris?" exclaimed Madeleine.

"He arrived in town shortly after Monsieur de Richelieu's passing made it safe for him to return," explained Marie Hervé. "He wasted little time before frequenting the theater again and it's there . . ." She broke off, then continued. "You're bound to find out sooner or later. Marion has been hired to replace La Bellemaison. She's the lead actress at the Théâtre du Marais!"

The blood drained from Madeleine's face and she heard a buzzing noise. To avoid a swoon she laid her head on the table. Marie Hervé's voice droned on.

"I have broken off ties with Marion, that scheming tart! If she was unable to wheedle a single role out of poor Monsieur Mondory it wasn't for lack of trying and she must have thrown herself at Floridor in a similar manner. The reason he hired her was not her gift for oratory! The Comte paid her a visit after seeing her perform, and I'm sorry to say Étienne L'Hermite stood by without a murmur while the Comte took up with his wife once again."

Madeleine wept. Why should the news upset her so? Marie Hervé was right that she'd never loved the Comte and it was years since she'd harbored illusions about Marion's dependability. Why did Jean-Baptiste's face suddenly loom up?

Marie Hervé put an arm around her daughter's shoulders.

"Calm yourself. It's not about the Comte you're crying, or Marion, may the devil take her." She spat. "It's for the father of your child. You fear what will become of him in this cesspool of a world of which he understands nothing. He's barely more than a boy, isn't he?"

"How can you know?" Madeleine said between sniffles. "I've told you nothing."

"As I said, a mother always knows," intoned Marie Hervé. "You might as well give me his name. We'll both sleep better if you get it off your chest rather than waiting until tomorrow."

Madeleine opened her mouth but no sound issued forth. Saying the name would be delivering Jean-Baptiste up to the world of arranged marriages, painful duties, and other cruel expediencies; to the same mistreatment she had suffered at its hands.

"You're in love with him, aren't you?" asked Marie Hervé.

Madeleine nodded, then rested her head in her mother's lap and sobbed her heart out.

CHAPTER 15

In Which Our Heroine Is Knocked Out by a Flying Fish, Then Rescued by a Passing Tortoise

The following morning Madeleine awoke with a feeling of dread at the decision that lay ahead. Should she inform Jean-Baptiste of her return? How would she face him if he visited? How would she face the future if he didn't?

Marie Hervé chased the other children from the house by insisting they buy a goose for a celebratory meal. No sooner had the door shut than she said, her face aglow, "God has blessed us, my darling. I've spent all night thinking, and I have a *plan*."

Madeleine folded her hands in what remained of her lap. The elaboration of one of her mother's plans was guaranteed to be unsettling even if the strategy proposed was legal.

"The way I see it," Marie Hervé began, "we must bide our time."

"The child is due in two months. Shall we pass it off as my dowry?" "No, as mine!" cried Marie Hervé. Perceiving her daughter's confusion she elaborated. "Not as my dowry, foolish girl. As my child!"

Madeleine cradled her head in her hands and stared at the floor as she listened in silence to the details of the plan. Her pregnancy would be kept secret and she would await the delivery on the farm where Marie Hervé had recuperated from her illness. After the birth, the child would stay with a nurse in the country, as was the custom, and would eventually come to live with Marie Hervé, to be raised as her own son or daughter.

The plan was utterly implausible, but it was best to open on a constructive note.

"Your offer is most generous," Madeleine began slowly. "It is no small undertaking to raise another's child. However, there are points you have not taken into consideration."

"What points? I've thought of everything."

Madeleine counted them out on her fingers. "One: your age." Marie Hervé started to object and Madeleine quickly added, "I know, but the neighbors may not believe, as do I, that you're not a day over forty. Two: who and where is the father? Three: how did the baby happen to be born on a farm while you were in Paris darning socks?"

Marie Hervé raised her thumb and said, "One: I'll swear on my mother's soul I'm capable of bearing a child." She stuck out her tongue to support her claim of youthfulness. Her index finger shot up. "Two: only you and I know that Joseph is dead. Suppose I received news of him, met him in secret, then changed my mind about a reconciliation?" Her middle finger joined the others. "Three: the child was born last spring while I was in the country recuperating."

"Last spring!" exclaimed Madeleine. "But you didn't have a child last spring!"

"Of course not," came the serene reply, "but I could have."

Monsieur Corneille could not have hit upon a cleverer conceit! Marie Hervé had spent six months in the country, ample time to have hidden a pregnancy, given birth, and recovered. As unlikely as it was that a middle-aged woman might bear her husband a child six years after he was last heard from, it was not outside the realm of possibility.

To postpone her surrender Madeleine said, "The child will be almost a year too young."

Marie Hervé replied blithely, "He'll be three or four when he comes to Paris and by then the difference won't be so noticeable. We can say he's small because of my age. Everyone will believe what we tell them. What choice will they have?"

There was no denying the plan's cleverness. The baby would benefit from a semblance of respectability. Madeleine could spend as much time with the child as she wished. True, there would no longer be any excuse to see Jean-Baptiste now and give him an opportunity to ask for her hand, but perhaps their chance for happiness would come at a later time.

What was holding her back? Could she explain to Marie Hervé how desperately she wished to care for this child of a man she loved and might never see again?

Marie Hervé observed Madeleine struggling with herself. She reached over and squeezed her daughter's knee.

"You needn't explain, my dear. I know how much this little one means to you." She paused. "There are women born to be lovers and women born to be mothers. It's surely not news to you that I am not of the second sort. Mind you, I love my children dearly. But your father's well-being always came first. Everything I did was to make his life easier and at that too I've been a failure." Madeleine started to speak but Marie Hervé placed a hand on her lips. "Not a word. I've made my peace with it. What's important now isn't my life, but yours. You say you love this young man, but if ever a woman was born to be a mother it was you, Mado. Love for a man will always come second."

"But I *do* love him," cried Madeleine, "more than I can say. Why does a woman have to choose? Why can't she be both?"

Marie Hervé shrugged. "Of course you can have both, up to a point," she said. "It's just that somehow one always manages to get in the way of the other. I know you love him, my darling. But those born to be mothers are rarely loved in return by those they lose their hearts to. Perhaps it's because maternal types care for their men so much that they never have to be pursued, I don't know. But that's how it is, and that's how it will be with your young man."

Marie Hervé was giving voice to Madeleine's own doubts about Jean-Baptiste. As much as she loved him, the wellbeing of their unborn child mattered even more.

And so, with a knot in her heart, she nodded her consent.

***

Marie Hervé's plan was carried out to the letter, almost. Catherine, the peasant woman who had nursed her back to health, agreed to attend to the birth and care for the child as long as an allowance was paid. Madeleine was to set forth on January 8, her twenty-fifth birthday.

On the eve of her departure, Young Joseph and Geneviève having left for their rehearsal and Marie Hervé and Louis gone out to buy firewood, Madeleine found herself alone with her thoughts. Her trunk was packed. Nothing remained to be done but await a journey she had no desire to take and a child she wouldn't be able to call her own.

There was a tap at the door. To avoid being seen by the neighbors she'd been instructed to ignore any callers, but Marie Hervé and Louis had just left and she assumed her mother had forgotten the bag that held money and the key.

Madeleine gasped at the sight of Jean-Baptiste, he at the sight of her belly. She clapped a hand over his mouth and yanked him inside.

They stood face to face in an uneasy silence. Jean-Baptiste's appearance was more ordinary than Madeleine remembered and it came to her that this was the first time she was seeing him in street clothes. He was dressed in a long brown cloak thrown over a dingy tunic and shapeless leggings. His boots were respectable but his hair disheveled. He lacked a hat.

He opened his mouth to speak but, staving him off, Madeleine blurted out, "It's yours."

He carried her hand to his lips. "How wonderful!" he exclaimed. "When did you return?"

"A few days ago," she replied.

His forehead creased. "Don't tell me you've been dragging our child on the heels of the Troupe du Vent all these months!"

"I wanted to work for as long as I could."

"Why didn't you write to me?"

Because I was afraid to, she thought. "What would have been the point?" she said.

"You saw no reason to inform me that you were carrying my child?" he cried.

"Please, Jean-Baptiste," she said, "I'm pregnant, not deaf." She sat down and leaned against the chairback. "We spent a few hours in a barn," she said carefully. "Why should I assume it would be of importance to you? Can you honestly say you would have joined me?"

"I'd have flown to your side," he said.

"I see," said Madeleine drily. "And now you have. But why? Did you expect to find me?"

"I wanted news," he said. "To write you a letter, if your family knew where to send one."

"I see," she repeated more gently. "Well, here I am. What would you have written?"

Jean-Baptiste stood and turned away. His back still toward her he mumbled, "That I hadn't stopped thinking about you."

It wasn't the most ardent declaration she'd received, and he might feel obliged to speak in this way, knowing her plight. And yet without being aware of it, he'd taken the trouble to make inquiries. Surely that counted for something.

"It's been the same for me," she conceded. "What else?"

They gazed into each other's eyes and she prepared for an embrace but he took her hand and kissed it instead. He took a turn about the room. "Madeleine, I have so much to tell you!"

How could she feel discontent hearing him say the words he'd so often uttered in her dreams? Perhaps it was his voice, its exaltation difficult to confuse with the ecstasy of love.

For the first time since her arrival in Paris she felt a spasm of nausea.

"I've sold my titles to my father and he will transfer them to my younger brother. I received six hundred and thirty *livres*. I am no longer a draper. I signed the papers yesterday."

"Why sell your titles for money when they are your best means of earning money?"

"Madeleine, my . . . beloved," he said clumsily. "I've decided to become an actor. I'll use the money to start a troupe."

"You've decided to become an actor? That is your news?"

He nodded vehemently, oblivious to her tone.

"Will you join my troupe?"

Fury rose within her. In a slow crescendo she said, "After all this time you find me carrying your child and that is all you have to say to me?"

Falling to his knees, Jean-Baptiste clutched both her hands.

"It is not. Will you marry me?"

***

There it was, the question Madeleine had longed for and feared in equal measures, for if she knew her own heart she could give no answer until she knew his. She raised him from his kneeling position and asked, "Is that one of the things you intended to write in your letter?"

Taken aback he said, "If I had known . . ."

"Assume you didn't. If your only reason to choose a wife was the desire for one, would you wish to marry me?"

"Of course," he said. "With the baby and the troupe, think how much easier it would be."

"I haven't said I would join your troupe, nor am I speaking of ease."

He fell silent. How could she make him understand? Her eyes alit on a paper crown that had been used for Twelfth Night. It was in Louis's cake the charm had been found, granting him the right to crown a queen, and he'd placed it on Madeleine's head in a manner that brought tears to her eyes, for it reminded her of Jacques. She handed the crown to Jean-Baptiste.

"Imagine this is yours to bestow on any woman in the world. Who would receive it?"

As she had sensed, he loved games. He affected a look of indecision. Finally he reached over and solemnly placed the crown on her head.

"Marie-Madeleine," he intoned, venturing a little smile, "I dub thee Queen of Sinners and Saviors. Will you be my bride?"

His voice told her nothing. It was foolish to expect a serious reply from him in response to a fanciful conceit any more than to a direct question. She lifted the crown from her head.

"I'll join your troupe, Jean-Baptiste, but I cannot marry you."

The tiny smile collapsed. "I thought perhaps you loved me," he said.

"You've asked me to marry you, not told me you loved me."

"But haven't I shown you . . . ?" Jean-Baptiste sputtered. He struck his fist against the brick hearth. "May the devil take us both. You know what I mean."

She stood next to him and waited.

"All right then," he said. "I do. Are you happy?"

"Yes, I am," she said. "I love you, too, but I can't marry you. Not now."

In few words Madeleine explained her mother's plan and swore Jean-Baptiste to secrecy. If he felt disappointment he showed none. They agreed that after the birth Madeleine would return to Paris to help him hire actors, find a building, have the stage constructed, and procure costumes and scenery. With luck they would open by the end of the year.

"My mother will soon be home," she said, "I'll see you in a few months."

She hoped for a final word of tenderness or a passionate embrace, but he kissed her cheek and departed.

***

The baby, another girl, was born on a snowy day in late February. A thin wail allayed fears of another stillbirth. The child drew shallow breaths and her cheeks soon had a faint blush. Weak and sickly though she was, she was the loveliest creature Madeleine had ever beheld.

For a fortnight Madeleine spent every moment with her. The idea of leaving her daughter filled her with anguish but in mid-March actors flocked to Paris to seek contracts and there was no time to spare. As soon as new troupe members had been hired, she'd go back to the country with Marie Hervé, the putative mother, for the baptism. Joseph Béjart, whereabouts unknown, would be inscribed as the father, Madeleine the godmother. If there should be any danger to the child before their return, Catherine was to call for the priest and have the child baptized in haste.

Within a week of Madeleine's return to Paris the troupe members had been selected. Young Joseph and Geneviève expressed their enthusiasm for the opportunity and six other young people, none with acting experience, were also engaged. The baptism was set for the week following Easter. Madeleine felt a great weight lifting from her shoulders at the thought that her child would soon have a respectable name.

March had been wintry but April 1st dawned with blue skies overhead and a southerly breeze. Jean-Baptiste was performing with traveling comedians on the Pont Neuf and had asked Madeleine to visit an abandoned tennis court on the other side of the Seine that had recently become available and might be a suitable home for their troupe.

The house was empty by the time Madeleine ventured forth. At the street gate she found a young man standing with a folded piece of paper in his hand.

"Is this the residence of Madeleine Béjart?" he asked.

"Yes," she said.

"Please receive this letter, Mademoiselle," he said, extending it to her.

The address was written in Catherine's painstaking hand. Undoubtedly she was confirming the date of the baptism. Madeleine went inside and unfolded the paper.

Her baby had caught a fever. Catherine had done her best to have the child baptized when she realized her life was in danger but the priest had arrived too late.

She was dead.

***

Beyond tears, Madeleine was driven from the house to wander the streets. The air was springlike. She let herself be led by the wind, not keeping it at her back as one tends to do on a stroll but heading into it. She had never had the wind at her back and never would.

A sudden gust from the left beckoned her toward the Pont Neuf.

April Fool's Day. She had forgotten. The pandemonium had reached its height; paper and wooden fish, material pranks symbolizing Lent, went hurtling in all directions. The flow carried her along, the crowd so dense she had trouble breathing, and though she had no particular desire to continue doing so, instinct sent her struggling to the side of the bridge for air, grateful that unlike the other bridges in Paris this one had no houses built along its margins. Grasping a pillar for support she crouched, glimpsed the water. The wave of April Fool's deviltry swept over her. A wooden April fish struck her forehead.

"Madeleine, here I am!" said a voice. "Are you hurt?"

In her torpor she recognized it vaguely but couldn't recall the name of its owner. The back of her neck hit the ground just as she caught sight of a giant tortoise rushing to her side.

The first thing she was aware of was a hand gripping hers. She was lying on a straw mattress in a dark room. Two eyes peered at her with an intensity not associated with tortoises.

The blows to her head had been such that she had no memory of what had transpired. She thought there was some unfinished business between herself and the tortoise but couldn't remember what, so she said, "Why are you dressed as a tortoise?"

He smiled in relief, mistakenly assuming she had come to her senses.

"How can I play human roles, Mademoiselle," he said gravely, "when so clearly I am a tortoise?"

He fell to the floor and began crawling around in a perfectly ridiculous way. He rolled on his back, waved his legs, then, righting himself, withdrew his head into his costume. Finally he collapsed on his belly underneath the tent of his green sackcloth shell, with only his grinning face peeking out.

She tried to smile, still not quite sure of who he was or what he was to her. He scrambled to his feet and from a shabby armoire took a blanket that he wrapped around her shoulders.

"I'm sorry there's no fire," he said. "As you know, tortoises are not well paid and my cave is, well, as it is. I must complain to the Tortoise Guild."

He puttered around in the far corner of the room, then returned with a cracked board that held a slab of salted fish, an onion, and a small pitcher of cider. They ate in silence.

"Madeleine, my dear, never mind about that errand I asked you to run. You're still exhausted from the birth. Perhaps you should postpone the baptism until you've rested up."

She gasped at the return of memory.

"Darling," he said, "what is it?"

She pretended to cough and held her belly. How could she tell him the truth? Would it not be tantamount to giving their little girl permission to die? With her child would perish the only evidence that what bound them together was more than a series of chance encounters magnified out of all proportion by her desire that his feelings might one day match her own. Might he not come to love her in the same way she loved him, if only their little girl was kept alive?

Madeleine heard herself speak in an ordinary voice.

"I'm sorry to have frightened you," the voice was saying. "Fainting and cramps can occur long after a birth." She paused, her mind thrashing about for a serviceable lie. "The journey to have the baby baptized is unnecessary. The priest prevailed upon Catherine to have the child christened. There's so much to do here, it's probably for the best."

"Of course it is," Jean-Baptiste said earnestly. "You've been working too hard. You're recuperating from bringing our daughter into the world!" He went on in his more usual bantering tone. "I must return to the bridge; my public awaits. It's true that tortoises are slow but we are reliable! Slow and steady wins the race." He pulled his head into the turtleneck, then popped it out with a flourish.

Madeleine lay back, grateful for the prospect of solitude. At the door Jean-Baptiste turned on his heels and said, "Sleep, my darling, dream of me! By the way, if our daughter has been baptized she must have a name. What did you call her?"

To Madeleine's lips leapt a name that for no particular reason she had always loved. If Jean-Baptiste demanded an explanation for the decision, she would invent one. He would have to believe whatever she said. As Marie Hervé had taught her, what choice would he have?

"Her name is Armande."

PART TWO

THE PROMISES OF
CHANCE

CHAPTER 16

In Which a Father Forgets His Recently Delivered Daughter but Himself Delivers Good News

––––––––––

The most immediate consequence of Madeleine's resurrection of her beloved daughter was the cornucopia of falsehoods designed to thwart Marie Hervé's wish to visit her granddaughter, ranging from the expense of a needless journey to the potential risk to Marie Hervé's still delicate health after her illness. There was no need to produce lies for Jean-Baptiste: Armande, it seemed, had slipped his mind!

In the dark of night Madeleine sometimes closed her eyes and confided to her deceased child's spirit the feelings she couldn't reveal to the man who inspired them. Neither did she receive a vision of her child's face nor could she hear the infant's gurgles, but thoughts and answers would come to her mind that she imagined to have been sent by Armande.

"Why doesn't your father show greater concern for you?" she'd murmur so as not to be overheard by Geneviève sleeping on the other side of the mattress. She fell silent, awaiting Armande's response. "I suppose so," Madeleine whispered back. "Men do prize their accomplishments above matters of the heart. But will he ever learn that success means little without love?" Another silence. "Yes, I must be patient, but he knows himself so poorly!" A final pause before Madeleine concluded the strange conversation. "You're right. I understand him better than he understands himself. If only he could be made to see that a heart as tender as his needs to be protected from the world but not hidden from the woman who adores him!"

However comforting it was to share her secret thoughts with her departed daughter, convincing others of the baby's existence without allowing them to see her would soon become challenging. Madeleine's dearest hope was to become pregnant once again, but each month her time came, bringing a fresh disappointment. She vowed that if she were only given a second chance, she would never allow her baby out of her sight.

***

Madeleine was touched that Jean-Baptiste named the troupe the Illustre Théâtre in honor of *the illustrious Madeleine* he had invented to lift her spirits on the day they met, but she fretted that the destinies of nine novices, including Joseph and Geneviève and Jean-Baptiste himself, were in her hands. In

June of 1643, shortly after Louis XIII's death and the naming of Queen Anne as Regent for the four-year-old Louis XIV, the troupe's contract of incorporation was drawn up and signed. In August an abandoned tennis court was procured. It stood in the unfashionable district of Saint-Germain-des-Prés, far from the areas north of the Seine in which most of the theater-going public resided, but it was all they could afford. Soon Jean-Baptiste and Madeleine were having spats reminiscent of her childhood.

It came to a head one night in early September, when they lay side by side in Marie Hervé's courtyard, gazing at the stars. Jean-Baptiste had been feeling romantic but Madeleine was too preoccupied with all that had to be attended to before the opening: costumes, repertory, rehearsals, and publicity. Only gradually did she notice that he was snoring.

"Wake up!" she called out, shaking him by the shoulders.

"Who's that, who's that?"

"I'm sorry," Madeleine lied. "I didn't mean to startle you."

Jean-Baptiste wiped his eyes. "What then?"

Madeleine sat upright. "I've given the question a great deal of thought," she began in an even tone. "We've got no choice but to postpone the opening." He frowned but said nothing. "The actors will need several months of rehearsals before they're ready to appear before a public. What's the point of selling tickets to spectators who will be dissatisfied and tell their friends not to come?"

Jean-Baptiste's face brightened.

"How could anyone be dissatisfied at the theater? Why, the simple privilege of gazing on your lovely form will guarantee us a public."

"You're very gallant," said Madeleine, "but if the Queen Regent herself sat onstage and the spectators weren't given a show to their liking, we would close on opening day."

"But the longer we wait to open, the more money we'll need, my darling," came the amiable retort, "and in the meanwhile we've nothing to live on but love." He blew her a kiss.

"Enough of your jesting. There are important matters we've never discussed. What plays will we perform?"

"How good of you to ask, Mademoiselle. I have a plan."

"A plan? What plan?"

"Patience, patience!" He too sat up. "It has been bruited about," he began grandly, "that Pierre Corneille is composing his first comedy in years, set in present-day Paris. What could be better suited to actors plucked fresh from the streets of the capital?"

The news took Madeleine by surprise. In the six years since she'd met Pierre Corneille on the set of *Le Cid* he'd enjoyed a series of triumphs, but they had all been tragedies.

"One of Monsieur Corneille's plays could guarantee the success of almost any troupe," she conceded. "But I fail to see what his new comedy has to do with us."

"It must be admitted," replied Jean-Baptiste, "that my connections aren't as intimate as one might wish. But I have a friend, actually a friend of a friend, who knows someone who knows Monsieur Corneille. I shall have myself introduced and convince him to give us his play!"

His exuberance only made matters worse. Why would Monsieur Corneille give a play to a group of unknowns? The Théâtre du Marais had premièred his works for years.

"Has it ever occurred to you, my dear boy," she said, brushing away an oak leaf that had come to rest on Jean-Baptiste's head, "that a famous playwright doesn't hand his works over to any obscure troupe that asks for them? If Monsieur Corneille agreed to meet with you, which he won't, and to give you his play, which he won't, how would you pay him?"

"I'll cross that bridge when I get to it," he said, using one of Marie Hervé's favorite expressions. "But as of today, at least I know where it is."

"Where what is?"

"The bridge." He drew a deep breath. "I have been saving my good news for the right time," he said, "and this is it! The bridge to be crossed is in Rouen. My dear, we have struck gold!"

"What do you mean?"

"I've been making inquiries. Today I received a response. The Illustre Théâtre will perform in October at the Saint Romain Fair in Rouen!"

Rouen, the city of Pierre Corneille! While Monsieur Corneille would not grant an audience to a complete unknown like Jean-Baptiste, might the Great Master not agree to hear out an actress in whom he had once voiced a certain interest?

"That *is* good news," Madeleine said, lying back and pulling Jean-Baptiste down with her. She put her arms around his neck. "I have always wanted to visit Normandy."

***

The troupe set out on the morning of October 10th. The fair was to begin on the 23rd but they'd need time to settle in and rehearse their comedies, both loosely adapted by Jean-Baptiste from Spanish farces. Costumes sewn by Marie Hervé and Geneviève and simple props built by Joseph and Louis were piled into four carriages for the long, slow journey to Rouen.

As the carriage Madeleine and Jean-Baptiste were sharing made its way past Les Halles, Madeleine drew a deep breath for the first time, it seemed, in months. She was looking forward to the journey, with nothing to occupy her but gazing at autumn leaves and contemplating strategies for capturing Pierre Corneille's attention. She would send him a letter, try to arrange a private meeting, and hope for the best. And once they were alone . . .

She shook her head vehemently as the coaches exited the city through the Porte de Montmartre. Monsieur Corneille's support would not be obtained at the price of infidelity. If the troupe's best chance for success was his new comedy, Madeleine would have to acquire it without compromising her love for Jean-Baptiste. The only question was how.

Suddenly Jean-Baptiste exclaimed, "Wasn't I clever to cram us all into four vehicles? The owner wanted to use five, but I refused!"

"Four is bad enough," observed Madeleine. "How did you pay for them?"

He craned his neck over a painted board with a picture of a house and kissed the tip of her nose. "Why must you worry about everything?" he asked. "Do you doubt my competence?" She smiled and said nothing. He went on. "I promised the drivers double the usual rate once the fair is under way. With our receipts the coffers will soon be restocked."

"Will they?"

"Of course, my sweet naysayer," he replied. "Why do you always assume the worst? How can we do poorly with talent such as ours?"

"Talent can't compensate for inexperience," Madeleine observed. "And I don't always assume the worst. The worst is simply what usually happens."

Jean-Baptiste shrugged his shoulders. "Until the experience has taken place and the question been decided," he said, "we are as likely to succeed as to fail."

She sighed. She loved his good cheer but it could be maddening.

"The fact that the event has not yet occurred," she said slowly, as if addressing a child, "does not make the two possible outcomes equally probable."

His brows knit. "What's your point?"

"My point is that it's no use congratulating ourselves prematurely, since we're actually more likely to fail than to succeed."

"And if we don't succeed, the prospect of success will have compensated for its failure to materialize."

He grinned from ear to ear; she fought the impulse to cover his face with kisses. He poked his head out the window to take the sun, leaving Madeleine to pursue her reflections.

Although she was wary of discouraging Jean-Baptiste, now that she'd seen the troupe rehearse she deemed that without a drawing card like Monsieur Corneille's new comedy, success in the capital would be impossible. At provincial fairs the crowds were easy to please; Paris was quite a different matter. Everything hinged on her scheme. She must write Monsieur

Corneille a letter and suggest a rendezvous. What she'd say if he came to the meeting she had yet to decide; Jean-Baptiste must not be allowed to suspect a thing. To make matters worse, after a delay of two weeks that had raised her hopes, her time of month had just begun. The whole troupe was to be lodged in a single large room of an inn; the lack of privacy would not be conducive to lovemaking. Would she ever become pregnant again?

Jean-Baptiste was dozing off. She felt a swell of affection and reached for his hand.

"I too would prefer to look on the bright side, my love," she said in a pensive tone. "I was merely trying to assess our situation with open eyes."

"Don't open your eyes," he mumbled. "Rest now, sleep. You're in safe hands."

Safe hands; had she known any but her own? She laid her head on his chest. He must have climbed over a bed of late roses in bloom before their departure; his scent reminded her of their enchanted evening in Nîmes. Perhaps there was truth to what he'd said. Perhaps the only aspect of the future upon which one could rely was one's dreams about it. Still, of one thing she was certain: she would always love him. Would she ever be able to tell him?

Perhaps, now that they had left Paris behind, it was worth a try.

"Whatever happens," she murmured, "one thing will never change."

He looked up. "Something that will never change? What's that?"

She could hear it in his voice: her words had put him on his guard.

"Oh, nothing."

"You take me for a fool, don't you?" he replied in a congenial tone. "What you're trying to tell me is that so long as we have success in Rouen, we shall refuse to change our stockings. I too know of the outlandish superstitions harbored by comedians!"

***

Troupes from all over France flocked to the Saint Romain Fair. The Illustre Théâtre was housed in the Red Bull Inn, a dilapidated hostel on the outskirts of the Beauvoisine quarter. Their rehearsals were held in a secluded corner of the courtyard. In one of the comedies Jean-Baptiste was a mild-mannered husband with a domineering wife played by Madeleine; in the other Madeleine had the role of a strict mother whose daughter, played by Geneviève, was engaged to a dullard played by Joseph but also courted by a livelier suitor portrayed by Jean-Baptiste. The troupe was performing with only slightly more animation in Rouen than they had in Paris.

Discreet inquiries revealed that Pierre and Thomas Corneille resided on the Rue de la Pie and that Pierre rarely granted requests for meetings. The day before the fair was to begin, Madeleine crept out of the Red Bull at dawn holding a sheet of paper, a quill, a bottle of ink, sealing wax, and a candle that she lit on the dying embers of the hearth.

In the early morning chill she sat beneath a tree in the courtyard and wrote.

> *Rouen, 22 October 1643*
> *Monsieur,*
> *Many are the reasons I have to remember you; have you a single one to remember me? Six years ago you led me to believe that my performance as Chimène had touched your heart. It now transpires that I have an urgent affair that I must discuss with you. It is a matter of life and death for ten individuals and I pray that you will agree to meet me tonight at nine o'clock on the banks of the Seine just beyond the Cloth Market. I implore you to come alone. You have surely forgotten my face, according to some passably fair, but you will recognize me by my red hair. There is not a soul in the kingdom who would not recognize you.*
>
> > *Your humble servant,*
> > *Madeleine Béjart*

She reread the letter by the flickering light, sealed it, and placed it in the pocket of her gown. It was the best she could do, but was it good enough? There was only one way to find out.

CHAPTER 17

In Which a River's Waters, Which Flow Past Only Once, Witness a Tender Scene

The rising sun revealed that the Corneille residence was an imposing three-story structure in the Norman style, with a steeply pitched roof and dark wooden strips decorating the façade.

A gnarled old woman flung open the door and cried, "You're late!"

"I beg your pardon?" stammered Madeleine.

"I beg *your* pardon, Your Highness!" came the riposte as the hag inspected her from head to foot. "The regular milkmaid don't put on such airs."

"I am not the milkmaid," said Madeleine sedately. "Please give this letter to Monsieur Pierre Corneille."

"Why should I?" squawked the old woman. "What's it worth to you?"

"I'm only asking you to hand it to him. It will cost you neither time nor effort."

"You try giving a letter to Monsieur on a chilly morning, and the milk en route!"

Madeleine reached into her pocket to discover a single coin, all she had left. She handed it over. "All right then, but give him the letter when he's alone, as the matter is confidential."

"We'll see about that," said the servant, dropping the coin and the letter into her apron.

***

Madeleine excused herself from rehearsal that evening by instructing Jean-Baptiste that the scenes in which she didn't appear needed attention, not technically a lie because it was true of every scene in both plays. At half-past eight, with the rehearsal in full swing, she slipped out and made her way toward the Seine. She ignored pleas for money from beggars and lewd calls from drunkards. As she passed the cathedral she felt a moment of serenity cut short by the thought that the priests believed all actors and actresses destined to burn in hell. It was a blustery evening and she drew her cloak closer. At least she would not spend all of eternity shivering.

At this hour when in Paris the banks of the Seine would be bustling, here few people were about and the river looked broad and forbidding. With the adjoining Grain Market and Linen Market, the Cloth Market stretched from the Seine to the chapel that held Saint Romain's bones. A large open area was thus formed, connected to the river by a passageway.

During the day it was the busiest district in town but on a windswept evening it held a certain menace.

The cathedral bells rang compline. A man abruptly emerged from behind a column.

"Mademoiselle Béjart?" he called out.

He was barely at arm's length and the moon was nearly full, but his face was in shadow and it was difficult to discern his features. Still, who could he be besides Pierre Corneille?

"I am Madeleine Béjart," she answered. "Do I have the honor of addressing Monsieur Corneille?" He nodded wordlessly and she felt a surge of relief. "How can I ever thank you for coming?"

She curtsied and waited for him to approach. Suddenly she became aware that he'd kneeled in front of her. Why in the world would such a man be paying her obeisance?

"Monsieur," she said, grasping his hands and pulling him to his feet. "It is wrong for you to abase yourself. I should be paying my respects to you."

"Never!" he exclaimed, carrying her hands to his lips. "I humbly await your pleasure."

She scrutinized his face. Why was she craning her neck to look him in the eye?

He was not the Monsieur Corneille she'd been expecting.

***

Thomas Corneille, the gawky lad of twelve she'd met six years earlier, was this strapping young man! Nearly as tall as Joseph Béjart, he had wide-set expressive eyes, a hooked nose, and full lips. Thomas had not been blessed with his brother's debonair manliness, but his height and long slender neck lent him an air of nobility. One white strand was still visible in the tawny hair that flowed gracefully to his shoulders.

"You expected my brother," he said in a dejected voice. "I am sorry to disappoint you. As his secretary I open his correspondence so that he may be spared reading letters that are of lesser importance. I did not inform him of your request."

"A fine remark!" she replied sharply. "Did my letter not deserve his attention?"

"Without a doubt, Mademoiselle! If I had told my brother of your message, he would have come himself. Of that I am certain."

Madeleine felt her temper rise. Spending her last pistole on a bribe had gone for naught.

"I have no time for chatter. Why have you come here in your brother's place?"

Again Thomas fell to his knees. She resisted the urge to yank him up and shake some sense into him. Would this maddening individual never put a halt to his histrionics?

He lifted his eyes to peer into her own. "You know the answer."

"I do not."

"I have lost my heart. The moment I set eyes on you at the Théâtre du Marais six years ago I swore I would never love another."

"You have not lost your heart, young man," sputtered Madeleine, "but your mind!"

"So it would seem," he continued, his gaze unwavering. "And yet in spite of my madness, I understand you. Has a single one of your countless suitors ever understood you?"

The question gave Madeleine pause. Thomas's instincts were fine and sharp. She was put in mind of the affinity she had felt for him in the dressing room of the Théâtre du Marais.

"Whether or not my suitors understand me is not your affair." She pulled him to his feet.

"Why is everything for Pierre?" Thomas lamented. "Why don't ladies write *me* letters?"

"I'm sure that if ladies knew you desired such a thing, they would write you letters finer than the one I sent your brother. Mine was a letter not of adulation but of self-interest."

"Now that you know I want a letter, would you write me one?"

Madeleine hesitated.

"Not a love letter."

"Why not? Do you love another?"

She nodded.

"Is it my brother?" Dread crept into his voice.

"No."

Thomas's face relaxed. "This man, does he love you as well?"

"He claims he does." Madeleine sighed. "At least he said so, once."

"Once? If you gave me your heart I would say it every minute."

She smiled and stroked his cheek.

"Men always believe such pledges. As have you, when you've made them to others."

"Others? There have never been others. How could there be others?"

Across from them a cargo ship made its way up the Seine toward Paris, its sails hissing. From a nearby street wafted the ruckus of a wine-fueled fistfight. The moon was still in its usual place. These external signs suggested to Madeleine that things were as they'd always been, but they were not. Thomas Corneille, untainted by the world, loved her and her alone and claimed that he always would. What would she not have given to hear Jean-Baptiste utter those words?

She turned away to collect her thoughts. She had spent her whole life putting the needs of others before her own. Just once, might it be possible to let another give proof of his devotion?

"Monsieur," she said, facing Thomas, "would you be willing to perform a service that would require going against your better judgment?" He began falling to his knees yet again and she added, "Please remain standing."

"I would be honored, Mademoiselle," he replied. "I would do anything in the world."

A gust of wind sent Thomas's hat flying. He gave chase and returned clutching it.

"I fear you'll take ill, Mademoiselle," he said breathlessly. "I know of a warmer place where we can speak at our ease."

Soon they were climbing a spiral staircase at the back of a sleepy tavern. The owner had pressed a key and a candle into Thomas's hand and gestured toward the rear of the drinking area. At the top of the staircase they found a room furnished with chairs, an armoire, a lamp, and a pallet. A small window, its pane shattered, opened onto the Seine, which could be heard rushing past. No fire had been laid but for now they were protected from the wind. They sat face to face.

"As you may be aware," Madeleine began, "my success in Paris was short-lived. For five years I traveled with a troupe but now I have returned and formed a new one. We hope to open in Paris as soon as possible. We're in Rouen for the fair." Thomas said nothing and she continued. "Your brother is presently composing a play, is he not?"

"Yes, a comedy. He has nearly finished."

"Our only chance for success," she said quickly, "is to open in Paris with that play."

He blinked. "Of course it is," he replied. "And so you shall."

***

Madeleine stared. "You'll get us the play?" she asked. "But how?"

Thomas reflected. "I'll use his admiration for your beauty to persuade him."

"And if you're unsuccessful?"

"Love will find a way!"

She stood and paced the room.

"I am most grateful for your help," she said quietly, "but I cannot pretend to love you."

"Oh." His voice was ragged.

"If you wish to change your mind . . ."

"No! Love must be freely given. It is a gift, not a service repaid." He walked to the window and sighed. "I have never loved anyone but you. Here we are, alone in this room, as we may never be again. This water of the Seine that I can see in the moonlight courses past only on this night. And I have seen enough of the world to wonder how long I can offer you a pure heart." He brushed away a tear. "Whatever you decide, I shall always love you."

Madeleine pondered her dilemma. How could she better prove her devotion to Jean-Baptiste than by obtaining Pierre's play with Thomas's assistance? But could she exploit the love of this strange, sweet boy purely to advance her love for another? Could she offer him nothing in exchange and treat him with the same harsh self-interest he already recognized as the world's dismal emblem?

On the other hand, would thanking him with her charms truly be an act of betrayal? However deserving Thomas might be, she would never love him, such matters being beyond the power of reason. What she was contemplating doing with Thomas would be of greater benefit than harm to Jean-Baptiste, who need never know.

Yes, that was it. If it was in her power to give Thomas Corneille a night of happiness in exchange for his gift, she could not refuse.

There remained the question of how she'd explain to Jean-Baptiste her acquisition of the treasure that Thomas offered to procure. "I'll cross that bridge when I come to it," she said under her breath. She giggled aloud, amused at her borrowing of her mother's maddening refrain.

Thomas blushed and looked crestfallen.

"It's not at you I was laughing, but at myself," Madeleine said, sitting back down across from him.

"You needn't lie. People always find me ridiculous. I am accustomed to it."

"I was not lying. You are not ridiculous."

"I am. I am too sensitive, too soft. I do not like fights. There is always a reason." His face was a mask of anxiety. "Do I remind you of Pierre?"

"No," she replied. "Only of yourself."

He smiled sadly. "I am weary of being compared to him. People don't say it but they never consider me as handsome or as clever as Pierre. My only advantage is that I'm taller."

They both laughed. Madeleine stepped carefully to stand behind Thomas and put her hand on his shoulder. "You're also more mature than Pierre," she said, "at least in spirit."

It dawned on Thomas that she was praising him. Was the miracle he'd scarcely allowed himself to hope for about to take place? He stared at his feet. How was it meant to begin?

She took his hand. He had no experience of love. She helped him off with his clothing, removed her own. For a long while they lay side by side on the pallet, gazing at each other in the candlelight as if fearing to shatter the perfection of the moment. And afterward it seemed to her that it was she who, rather than offering herself to Thomas, had taken him, nor could she imagine giving herself to Jean-Baptiste more completely than Thomas gave himself to her.

CHAPTER 18

In Which a Stolen Kiss Inspires a More Portentous Theft

———

After their love, nestled under a blanket, Madeleine and Thomas listened to the Seine flowing beneath their window toward the sea.

"My darling," he said hesitantly, as if testing to see whether his lips could utter the endearment, "how can I ever thank you?"

"If there are thanks to be given," she replied, "it is for me to give them."

"How can you say that?" cried Thomas, sitting bolt upright. "My brother's play is nothing. You have made me happier than a man should ever be."

He cleared his throat and started to speak again, then stopped.

"What is it, my boy?" asked Madeleine, sweeping his long hair into his eyes.

"I was thinking, that is, wondering . . ."

She parted his hair. "Are all men born to be praised? Yes, it was good."

"How good?"

"Very."

"As good as . . . ?"

Madeleine faced away. "Such things are not to be compared. Now I must go. It's late and he'll be wondering where I am."

"You're returning to him now, tonight?"

"He's a member of the troupe. Is there a reason I shouldn't?"

Thomas stood and walked to the window. The wind changed direction and a sudden gust set his bare shoulders to trembling. "I didn't know he was in Rouen." He gathered his clothing, went into a corner and began to dress.

"If you must know," said Madeleine, "we're sharing a room with the other members of the troupe. We'll have little privacy in Rouen."

Thomas's face lit up. "Then you'll be free to meet me here from time to time?"

"I cannot meet you—in this way—ever again."

"Even though he doesn't love you as I do? You said he told you he loved you only once."

Madeleine drew the cover close about herself. "What I said was true," she mused, "but even if he doesn't say it, he thinks it."

"If he says nothing, how can you know?"

"By his actions. He helped me when I was in need. Several times."

"How did you meet?"

"By chance. That first day, he saved me from a drunken soldier."

"You can hardly say that proved his affection," reasoned Thomas, "since he didn't know you. Perhaps he did it in order to make your acquaintance and be in your good graces."

"But why would he wish to be in my good graces? Is that not a proof of affection?"

"No, only of desire."

She blushed. Her words had been more naïve than anything Thomas had said. Had she herself not wondered about Jean-Baptiste's motivations on the day they first met?

"Of course it may be the beginning of affection as well," Thomas went on. "Passion may begin with a chance encounter, but to become affection it must be transformed into a commitment. This man, has he ever pledged to love you alone?"

The finer points of love that this young innocent reasoned about with such finesse were not even in Jean-Baptiste's vocabulary! To cover her disarray Madeleine burst out laughing.

"He's not the type for declarations," she tossed off. "He jests whenever serious matters like love arise. He's embarrassed, I suppose, fearful of being hurt."

"Did you become his mistress the first day you met, when he rescued you?"

"No, we parted as friends. Then later a second time as well, at the theater, although the assistance he gave me was of a different sort. We met again last year and that's when it really began."

"How did you meet again? Did he seek you out?"

"Not really. That time too it was more or less by chance. And eventually . . ."

What had happened—or would happen—between Jean-Baptiste and herself *eventually*? Did the story of how their affair began and developed amount to more than a series of chance meetings set in motion when a perfect stranger came to the rescue of a damsel in distress?

"This man," Thomas asked, "have you ever told him how much you love him?"

"I have wanted to, but . . ." After a pause she assumed a playful tone. "Perhaps he is no more inclined to receive declarations than to make them."

Thomas took Madeleine's hand.

"You have not revealed your heart to this man because you fear that he will never return your love in kind. You are awaiting a moment that will never come."

"All I know," she replied, withdrawing her hand, "is that I cannot love you as I love him."

Thomas swung his legs over the side of the bed and pulled on his boots in silence.

"My fine Thomas," said Madeleine, again assuming a bantering tone, "what about water passing this way just once?"

"I am not water." He finished fastening his buckles. "Are we never to be together again?"

"No."

The moon broke through the clouds. Pale light flooded the room.

"If it is of any consolation," Madeleine said, "I have never before felt so loved. You have reminded me that loving someone is one thing and being loved quite another."

"But if it gave you pleasure once, wouldn't it again?"

She leaned on the windowsill, struggling against the truth. "Yes."

"Then why can't we ... ?"

"Precisely for that reason."

She expected him to demand an explanation but he nodded, gathered his cloak and made his way to the door. "Will you leave for Paris as soon as the fair is over?" he asked, turning back.

"On November 17th. Thomas, I wish there were something ..."

"Meet me here on the evening of November 16th, at ten o'clock. If there are problems regarding my brother's play we can make further arrangements at that time."

As the door was swinging shut she called out, "By the way, what is the title?"

The muffled reply came to her through the closed door: "It is called *The Liar.*"

***

Madeleine crossed the threshold of the Red Bull Inn past midnight and hoped to find everyone asleep, but Jean-Baptiste and Geneviève, still in costume, sat in a corner of the tavern discussing the evening's rehearsal with animated voices. Jean-Baptiste, dressed as a prosperous bourgeois, was holding forth about the accolades the troupe would garnish when the fair began the following day. Arrayed in the low-cut bodice of a voluptuous kitchen maid and would-be seductress, Geneviève was the first to notice her sister's arrival.

"Hail to thee, O sister! So the captain has decided not to abandon ship after all!"

"There she is!" bellowed Jean-Baptiste, "our guardian angel, our inspiration, our muse!"

To the delight of the few remaining tipplers he removed his wig and prostrated himself at Madeleine's feet.

"Oh wise one," he continued, lifting his head from the floor, his hair decorated with dustballs, "without you we are like unto the children of Israel lost in the wilderness! You have led us close to the Promised Land but without your succor we cannot enter therein. Command, and ye shall be obeyed!"

A drunk at the next table applauded, knocking over a pitcher of ale that splashed onto Madeleine's skirt. She felt as if she was waking up from a lovely dream.

"How was the rehearsal?" she asked mildly.

"The best one yet," exclaimed Jean-Baptiste. "Every scene sparkles!"

"Now that our savior has reappeared," Geneviève piped up, "where has she been?"

"I undressed and got into bed some time ago," Madeleine said after a short pause, "but was unable to sleep." She chuckled at the literal truth of her explanation. "I took a stroll to clear my head."

"For four hours? Something on your conscience?" Now that she was nineteen Geneviève was becoming a handful, most likely because she bore a striking resemblance to her older sister but had not been endowed with the power of fascination Madeleine wielded over men. "I for one," pursued Geneviève, "have no need to *clear my head* and hence no difficulty sleeping. Good night." She flounced out of the room.

The other drinkers took their leave and a hush fell over the tavern. Madeleine and Jean-Baptiste, who hadn't had an opportunity to be intimate since arriving in Rouen, gazed at each other across the table. His eyes, slate blue in the candlelight, exuded that particular charm, at once kindly and boisterous, that was his alone. His chin dimple deepened as it always did when he was having difficulty containing his enthusiasm.

Even when, such as tonight, his good cheer was founded on questionable judgment, was there in the entire world a face more entrancing?

"By tomorrow at this time," he declared, the world will be a different place." He leaned forward and lowered his voice to a whisper. "Tell me the truth. Are we ready?"

Madeleine averted her eyes. Back in the little room, with Thomas, the right course of action had seemed obvious: without her intervention, Jean-Baptiste's life would not hew to his hopes and expectations; not now and not ever. It was in that spirit that she had gone with Thomas. Wouldn't the greatest act of love be to make Jean-Baptiste's dreams come true without hurting his pride; without, in fact, his realizing that she was doing anything at all to assist him? She had vowed that to the extent that it was in her power, she would spend the rest of her days shielding from harm this heart more fragile than her own.

If only she could blot out Thomas's worshipful gaze, or observe a similar one in her lover's eyes!

"I suppose we are ready, or will be soon," she said, smiling without meeting his gaze. "We'll soon find out."

Arm in arm they walked slowly, their steps matching. At the door of the sleeping room, a veritable wall of snoring broke their tender mood. They both laughed and crept separately into the beds they were sharing, Madeleine with Geneviève and Jean-Baptiste with Joseph. Their intimacy would have to wait.

***

On the day of their debut, Jean-Baptiste cavorted through both comedies in a bacchanalian frenzy that complemented Madeleine's perfectly executed grimaces and understated punchlines. Geneviève incited hilarity with her doomed attempts at seducing her master in the first play and the mixture of coquettishness and aloofness with which she treated her clandestine suitor in the second. In slow moments Joseph used his stutter to elicit laughter and took full advantage of his scarecrow-like frame. Each play concluded with a dozen curtain calls.

To celebrate, Jean-Baptiste ordered a lavish supper from the innkeeper. Spurred on by wine, he harangued the troupe with predictions of the triumphs that awaited them in Paris. As her mood darkened Madeleine said nothing.

"Check out my dear sister, the party-pooper!" Geneviève called out after Madeleine had scowled at several of her lover's *bons mots*. "Pay her no mind! She is wrong and you are right, JB," Geneviève added, chucking her newly abbreviated common-law brother-in-law under the chin.

"Obviously I'm right!" roared *JB*, in his cups. "I'm always right. Name a single occasion when I've been wrong!" He wagged a finger at Geneviève. She dissolved in giggles and fell into the lap of another actress; they tumbled to the floor. Joseph hung from the rafters, allowing his dangling feet to be pushed back and forth by the revelers below. Madeleine frowned but said little until, at the height of the festivities, she stood abruptly.

"Enough, you morons!" she cried. "Have you any idea how ridiculous you are, believing a day's worth of laughs at a country fair will guarantee our success in Paris?"

There was a moment of silence. Geneviève picked herself up off the floor while Joseph hopped down from the ceiling.

Jean-Baptiste strutted over to where his mistress stood and faced her down.

"*In vino veritas*, my dear, so I shall allow this nectar of the gods I have been consuming to speak the truth. I have long suspected that comedy is not the strong suit of our dear Mado, but now all doubt on the matter is banished! My *darling* Madeleine, is it humanly possible for you to forget your woeful visions and baneful predictions for the space of a single hour? Never fear, tomorrow morning you can scoop them right back up where you left them!"

"Comedy may not be my strong suit," said Madeleine in an ominous voice, "but your gift for it is not limited to the theater! Have you the slightest idea of how ridiculous your boasting is after a handful of bawdy guffaws offered by a drunken assemblage of country bumpkins?"

"You can't stand being wrong! You'd be happier to see us fail and be right yourself than have us succeed and be wrong! It's written all over your face."

"Has it slipped your mind that you are the one who begged for my assistance? Apparently so, because now you have all the answers. Then answer me this: what plays will we perform in Paris? The kind of gibberish that drew applause today from drunken farmers?"

"Mind your own beeswax!" howled Jean-Baptiste. "I'll attend to that in due time!"

"That's what you said two months ago! What about Monsieur Corneille?" She was certain Jean-Baptiste's story about having connections to the great writer was invented.

He opened his mouth for a counterattack, then sat abruptly, nearly missing the chair. "About Monsieur Corneille," he said, "I . . . I was mistaken." He assumed an expression of wounded dignity. "When I'm wrong, I for one admit it! I'm afraid my old friend cannot help us."

"Of course he can't," Madeleine cried. "Because he never existed!"

Jean-Baptiste examined his fingernails and sighed.

"You're speaking in anger, so I forgive what you've just said. My friend passed away."

"Please accept my condolences." Several of the other actors tittered. "What, then, were you planning on using for plays?"

Jean-Baptiste came to his feet.

"I have given it much thought. I shall compose our plays myself. If I've learned nothing from the lines we've recited, I'm no better than an ape!" He set to chattering and leaping about, his long arms trailing along the ground, his ire forgotten.

It was like arguing with smoke. At the door Madeleine felt a pang of remorse at having ruined the celebration and turned to add a conciliatory word. But what met her eyes was Geneviève pitching herself into Jean-Baptiste's arms and planting a kiss on his lips.

***

After the battle between Madeleine and Jean-Baptiste on the night of the troupe's debut, she mused that lack of privacy became the least of their woes. For the remainder of their stay in Rouen they barely spoke except onstage, where the jubilant crowds little suspected that the two lead actors' repartees were fueled by sincere irritation.

To all appearances something was going on between Jean-Baptiste and Geneviève. They sat together at meals and from time to time whispered conspicuously into each other's ears. No doubt they were flaunting their flirtation, whether or not they had actually carried matters further.

On the evening before the troupe's return to Paris Madeleine and Thomas once again found themselves sitting across from each other in the room overlooking the river. The night was brisk and she thought fondly of the broad fireplace on the Rue de la Perle and sighed. Even though Jean-Baptiste was about to move in with the Béjarts to save money, in the wake of their dispute they were unlikely to sit by it together any time soon.

Thomas was clutching a large wooden box.

"I'm sorry I couldn't come to see you perform," he began. "Every moment was taken."

"Of course," she said, staring at the box. Her heart pounded.

"How was your troupe received?"

"If the audiences in Paris are half as appreciative, we shall have no cause for complaint."

Thomas went to the window and gazed down at the Seine.

"Just think," he said, "this water has flowed here effortlessly from Paris but only a miracle would allow it to return there. Why is it easier to leave the place you wish to be than to reach it?"

"Would you like to move to Paris?"

"I would like to live anywhere but here."

She was reminded of herself at his age. With difficulty she refrained from stroking his hair. "Are you so unhappy?" she asked. "Is your brother not good to you?"

"My brother has always treated me like a son," Thomas replied, "but now his wife has given him one of his own. How handsomely I am repaying him for all he's done for me!"

"I beg your pardon?"

"I'll explain in a moment." His jaw set. "At least now I'll be forced to become something other than Pierre Corneille's bumbling brother."

"That's hardly how I would describe you."

"How would you then?"

"I would say that you're kind, clever, resourceful . . ."

"Am I as handsome as my brother?"

Madeleine reflected. "You have a kind of charm he lacks."

"And yet . . . you don't love me."

"Have you forgotten that I love another?"

Thomas flung himself onto his knees and clutched her waist.

"Take me with you!" he cried. "I know you don't love me, but I too can write you plays!" He clung to her and wept. When his sobs abated, she sat down on the floor beside him.

"You know I cannot take you with me." She smiled. "Now what have you brought me?"

Thomas removed the cover of the box. The top page read *The Liar, Comedy.*

Madeleine gasped. "How did you manage to persuade him?"

"I made no attempt to. It was only to assuage you that I said I would convince him. Pierre can be generous when the spirit moves him, but not where fame and money are concerned. He never would have agreed. Asking him about it would only have put him on his guard."

She browsed through the manuscript. Lines of dialogue jumped from the pages; it was Pierre Corneille at his best. Finally she looked up in utter bewilderment and said, "But here it is nevertheless. How did it fall into your possession?"

"I stole it!" Thomas declared.

CHAPTER 19

In Which Our Heroine Is Given and Refused the Title of Most Beautiful Woman Who Ever Lived

———

"You did what?" stammered Madeleine.

"I crept into the library each night," said Thomas, "and copied the play word for word."

She said nothing, hardly believing that the miracle she had hoped for had come to pass.

"How can I ever thank you?" Thomas started to reply, his eyes aglow, but she put a hand on his lips. "You have shown great courage and devotion. I will be eternally grateful to you."

"I hoped you'd be content," he replied in a modest tone to underscore his bravura.

"I cannot help but wonder, however," Madeleine said carefully, "what will transpire when your brother finds out we've performed the play without his permission."

"I've got it all planned," Thomas replied with relish. "He will never find out."

"I beg your pardon?"

"You'll perform the play only once, on opening night, to catch the public's interest. In the theater first impressions are everything. You'll invent a different title and announce that the author chooses to remain anonymous. I overheard that the Théâtre du Marais is to première *The Liar* in mid-January, so as long as you open before then, you'll be off to a fine start without Pierre's being any the wiser."

Madeleine leafed through the pages of the manuscript to stall for time, clearly hesitating.

"I owe you my life," she said slowly, "and the last thing I would ever do would be to make light of what you have accomplished." She paused. "But what is the point of attracting the attention of the public if the play we present for our second performance is not by Monsieur Corneille but by an untried author with little chance for success?"

"An untried author? Who?"

"My . . . our director," she said.

Thomas shot Madeleine a meaningful look.

"Ah, your . . . director. Surely he has written something in the past?"

"He adapted two Spanish comedies for the fair and has composed two other plays."

Thomas stroked his smooth chin thoughtfully, as if to encourage a beard to grow there. "If I myself gave you a second play, would that put your mind at ease?"

Madeleine was still taking the words in when he reached deep into the box containing the manuscript of *The Liar*, extracted a separate sheaf of papers, and thrust it into her hands.

"Here is my first play," he announced. "A comedy about love and secrets. Once you've whetted the public's appetite with my brother's work, you may invite them to feast on this." He reddened, mortified by the boastful image.

Madeleine brought the top sheet close to the candlelight and read the title: *The Promises of Chance*. She glanced at the first page, lines of dialogue catching her eye.

> Cél.:   *You are more than annoyed at the secret I keep.*
>
> Clar.:   *My word, you're not a girl if you don't breathe a peep.*
>
> Cél.:   *If not a girl what am I? Tell me, or out of my sight!*
>
> Clar.:   *I forget what they call it—a hermaphrodite.*
>   *To hold the tongue of the yacking girl inside you*
>   *The man in you must hold his fist close beside you!*
>
> Cél.:   *Is that so?*
>
> Clar.:   *Yes! A girl finds it harder to hide*
>   *A secret than a judge to discern who has lied.*

"You're a fine turner of phrases," Madeleine began. "But do you actually believe women incapable of keeping secrets?"

Thomas blinked. "I don't, but all the other men I know seem to. It's believable on my character's lips."

Again she had underestimated him.

"A play about love and secrets," she said breezily, as if the subject was of little consequence. "I don't see what the one has to do with the other."

Thomas stood and paced the room, his hands behind his back.

"True love is always a secret," he began, "to be revealed only to those who have proven themselves worthy of trust. In my play the heroine, Elvire, has a great love for her suitor, Don Fadrique, but fears revealing it to him until she's convinced he returns her love in kind."

Madeleine stared. She had barely alluded to her feelings for Jean-Baptiste a few weeks earlier, and yet the story was her own.

"I suppose you began the play some time ago," she said in an offhand manner.

"I started it the day after we were together," he said.

"But how is it possible?" asked Madeleine in astonishment. "You said you spent every night copying your brother's play."

"And every day," he declared, "composing my own to offer as an additional token of my devotion. I told you I have slept little in the past month," he added with a charming laugh.

Dedication of this kind with no hope of recompense she could hardly fathom. Undaunted by her rejection, Thomas had spent every waking moment since their sad parting in her service! Why search for the words to thank him when to all appearances he was able to discern her thoughts and feelings?

"This heroine of yours, what does she do to discover if she's truly loved?"

Thomas sat down across from Madeleine. "First she disguises herself as a mysterious stranger." His voice brimmed with pride, as if the conceit had never before occurred to the mind of man. "Then she gives Don Fadrique an assignation and begins meeting him, taking care to cover her face and disguise her voice. In that way," he concluded grandly, "she can speak from within her soul without revealing she is the very same woman he has been courting!"

"But isn't she lying to him?" asked Madeleine.

"The lies are in the name of a greater truth. That's why I chose my subject. My brother's play is about the lies men tell to women when they're in love, or simply desire them. Men inflate their feelings and say anything to lure their ladies into returning their love, which is why they're not to be trusted. Women lie about their feelings in quite the opposite way. When they are actually in love they're inclined to act as if they are not, out of pride and caution. You know better than I how often women are forced to protect themselves in that way."

"How does your play end?" Madeleine inquired to cover her amazement. "Does the man truly love her?"

He nodded and gave her a knowing glance, then looked down. "Yes, he does."

"And *The Promises of Chance*?" she asked to change the topic. "What is the meaning of your title?"

"When a man is first drawn to a woman's beauty, it's largely a matter of chance. Why do their paths cross? How is she dressed? What is his mood, her disposition to receive attention? What makes him prefer a dark woman to a fair one, a woman of slight build to an Amazon? But for infatuation to become love it must turn into a commitment, a promise. That's what I meant. Have I got it right?" he asked, again meeting her gaze, his gold-colored eyes placid but sad.

"How is it," Madeleine asked, "that one so young understands so much?"

"It's a kind of curse, really," replied Thomas with a smile. "Would that I understood less." He stood and bowed. "I must return. If you use my play you mustn't reveal my name, not even to the other troupe members, except your, uh, director." He blushed. So he had guessed the truth. "It would upset Pierre," he concluded, "for me to try my luck without his consent. I wish you every success. Write to me if you'd like."

She kissed his forehead. She ran to the window and watched him depart from above. As the tall figure receded, she felt grateful to him not only for the miraculous gifts he'd just placed in her hands, but also for containing his distress at leaving her with no prospect of a reunion.

***

Madeleine was relieved that the troupe arrived back in Paris so late that Marie Hervé was asleep. Jean-Baptiste would spend the night gathering up his affairs for the move, leaving her free to read the manuscripts she had brought from Rouen.

The brilliance of Pierre's comedy was indisputable. A man's play, with great artistry it delighted in the posing and boasting that made gentlemen courting ladies resemble large strutting peacocks. Though Thomas's play could be called immature, that was to be expected, and it was filled with delicate sentiments that would, she felt, be especially pleasing to the female members of the audience. With works like these the Illustre Théâtre's Parisian debut might be a success.

Just before dawn she lay down on her pallet and spilled her heart to Armande.

"What shall I tell your father?" she whispered. "If I say we've been given Monsieur Corneille's new comedy but for only one performance, he'll demand to know why, and he will refuse to perform a stolen play. How can I tell him the truth about what happened between Thomas and me and make him understand that I did it for him, that it remains my dearest hope that he can love me as much as I love him—and as much as Thomas loves me?" She waited for one of those solutions that came to her out of the air when she addressed her problems to her daughter's spirit. It did this time as well and she smiled at Armande's wise words. "Thank you, my darling," she sighed. "I'll do as you say. And you're right, asking Jean-Baptiste to love me as much as Thomas does is not a good way of currying his favor."

In the morning Madeleine awoke to discover that in the previous month work on the theater had come to a standstill. The carpenters having refused to pay for lumber in the troupe's absence, the stage had not yet been built nor the area in front of the building paved so that patrons alighting from their carriages wouldn't sink into the notorious muck that covered the streets of Paris. Father Olier of nearby Saint Sulpice, a notorious opponent of the theater, would have to be mollified somehow. But the most pressing matter for Madeleine was convincing Jean-Baptiste the troupe should perform the two plays that had unexpectedly fallen into her possession.

By the end of their month in Rouen the troupe's success at the fair had soothed his wounded pride, thus easing the strain between them. As the return to Paris approached, now and again they exchanged a teasing phrase that suggested a truce might be imminent, but they hadn't yet renewed their intimacy. Whatever it was that had taken place between Jean-Baptiste and Geneviève had run its course, the fact that they now treated each other with courtesy rather than acrimony suggesting that the dalliance had been staged purely for Madeleine's benefit. As she proceeded toward Jean-Baptiste's lodgings a stone's throw from the Pont Neuf, she mused that if her tender reunion with him didn't take place that very day it would likely have to be postponed, for her time of month, several weeks overdue, was about to begin.

The room Jean-Baptiste was vacating was in an ancient wooden dwelling that looked as though it wouldn't withstand a gust of wind. A half-loaded wagon stood before the open gate. His room showed scarcely more disorder than usual.

"Hallo," he called out. His head appeared above a precarious tower of miscellaneous items. "Oh, it's you. Are you here to give me a hand? How very thoughtful!"

No chairs remained so Madeleine, fatigued from her walk, leaned against a beam. It shifted slightly and gave off an ominous groan.

"I'm happy to lend you a hand," she said, "but first there's something we must discuss."

"Why so serious, my lovely?" he replied, kissing her on the lips for the first time in weeks. "Rouen was a great success, as I predicted. Our treasury is bursting and our glorious opening but six weeks away. What could be wrong?"

"Have you given further thought to the plays we'll be performing?" she asked.

"Oh, that," he said, waving a hand. "Now that we're home, I'll devote myself to writing a play that will make you proud!"

He tweaked her nose. It was going to be more difficult than she'd imagined.

"We'll need a month to rehearse," she said flatly, "so I assume your comedy will be ready in a fortnight. Have you chosen the subject?"

"Have I said it would be a comedy?" asked Jean-Baptiste. "Such humble fare would not do justice to the solemnity of the occasion."

"What then?"

"A tragedy," he replied, his eyes aglow. "The greatest love story in all of history! Cleopatra, the most beautiful woman who ever lived!"

Suddenly it was all too much. Madeleine fell onto a crate and sobbed. If she failed to persuade Jean-Baptiste to stage the two new plays in her possession, the Illustre Théâtre was as likely to succeed with a tragedy written and performed by novices in six weeks' time as the troupe was to sprout wings and nest in the rafters of the Louvre Palace!

"How can I be such a fool?" cried Jean-Baptiste, crouching beside her. "Don't you see it was poetic license? It goes without saying that the most beautiful woman who ever lived is you!"

She allowed him to fuss, enjoying the attention. How she had missed being held by this brash, fragile young man! A hint of success had sufficed to make him feel capable of conquering the world; a whisper of doubt would send him into a tailspin. In their altercation the night of the opening he'd said she couldn't stand ever to be wrong; more to the point, he couldn't stand for her always to be right. If they failed in Paris or he came to believe that they succeeded only thanks to her intercession, her reward would be an estrangement that might be irreversible.

And yet did his limited discernment where she was concerned not suggest how she could lead him, without liability, to do her bidding? From their very first meeting he had proven eager to view her as a frail creature in need of his protection. It was time for her to start learning how to play the woman he wished her to be.

"You are far too kind," she said with a sniffle, "and I'm grateful that you've once again closed your eyes to my imperfections." She pulled a rag from her sleeve to wipe her cheeks, then conjured up a blush by remembering what she'd done with Thomas in Rouen. "It is my hope, however misguided is your assessment of my beauty, that I'll have contributed in some small way to the success of the Illustre Théâtre."

"Needless to say," said Jean-Baptiste in a soothing voice, "you'll play the title role."

"Thank you, *mon ami*," she said, bowing her head graciously. "It will be an honor. As for this matter we must discuss . . ." She bit her lower lip to signify her reticence to continue.

"What is it?" asked Jean-Baptiste gently.

"Something happened in Rouen," she said, "something that may be quite wonderful, but I don't know how you'll receive the news of what I did and what was the outcome."

"You did something in Rouen that I don't know about?" he asked, intrigued but without agitation.

"It's not exactly that I did something," she answered slowly, "but rather that something was done to me."

This time Jean-Baptiste lifted an eyebrow. Madeleine's fit of coughing poorly covered her giggle at her wretched choice of words.

"What I meant to say," she went on, "is that after one of the performances, on a day when I stayed behind to help Joseph tally up the take, I was approached by a man I knew, really no more than an acquaintance. He proposed something that might be of use to us."

"Who, pray tell, was this mysterious stranger?" emoted Jean-Baptiste, "and what manner of suggestion can he have offered? Quickly! I am devoured by curiosity, nay, jealousy!"

"If I say it was Monsieur Corneille," Madeleine responded with deliberate understatement, "you mustn't draw hasty conclusions. It will take time to explain."

"Monsieur Corneille!" he shrieked. "You met Pierre Corneille in Rouen?"

She shook her head. "Not Pierre, his young brother, Thomas."

"Pierre Corneille's brother is an acquaintance of yours and he approached you in Rouen?" asked Jean-Baptiste incredulously.

Madeleine nodded. She reviewed in her mind the main points of the tale Armande's spirit had suggested to her.

"Perhaps you recall," she began, "that Pierre Corneille attended my debut in *Le Cid*."

"How could I forget?"

"That evening," she went on, "I met him before the curtain and saw him again backstage after the performance."

The news sank in. "All this time you knew Monsieur Corneille," Jean-Baptiste said with a trace of indignation, "but made no mention of it?"

"There was no reason to," rejoined Madeleine. "I didn't know him well enough at that time for us to approach him now about his new play. But back then he was accompanied by his brother, Thomas, who was just a boy. Now he is a young man."

"And he's the person who approached you," reiterated Jean-Baptiste.

She nodded. "I didn't recognize him at first but he introduced himself and said there was something he wanted to discuss, and would I come to a tavern with him so that we could be alone. I thought he might provide a means of being in contact with his brother, so I did indeed meet with him," she concluded, galloping over the euphemism.

"What was it he wished to discuss?" asked Jean-Baptiste eagerly.

"It so happens," she responded, "that Master Thomas Corneille wants to follow in Pierre's footsteps and has written two comedies. He attended the fair to see if there were promising troupes he might approach about staging them. I am pleased to report that he was most impressed by ours."

Jean-Baptiste took a turn around the room. "Are you telling me," he asked slowly, "that the Illustre Théâtre is being offered the premières of Thomas Corneille's first two plays?"

Madeleine smiled. "I've brought two manuscripts from Rouen, both of them from his pen!" she stated truthfully.

"But surely the Marais or the Bourgogne troupe would snatch them up if given the chance," Jean-Baptiste pursued. "The crowds would flock to see them, if only from curiosity."

"Without a doubt," concurred Madeleine, "but Master Corneille fears ridicule if his plays are poorly received. He will not let his ambitions be made public until he has proven himself. I have read both plays and they'll suit us well. He insists that the first one has flaws that must be remedied but that it would be helpful to see how it might be received if staged once—but only once, for now. The second play could be performed for as long as we wished but would have to be presented anonymously as well, at least until he gave us permission to reveal his name to the public. With such exacting conditions he has no choice but to bypass the established troupes."

After a short silence, Jean-Baptiste lifted Madeleine into the air and spun her around.

"But this is miraculous!" he said. "If Thomas Corneille hasn't got theater in his blood I don't know who has. The first play will be an instant success and he'll relent. We can alternate the two for months and months, using his name. That will give me time to make my tragedy into the masterpiece the subject deserves!"

Madeleine took a moment to let her stomach settle after her unexpected flight.

"May God grant that it happens as you predict," she said. "But you must bear in mind that it is far more likely that we will be able to perform the first play only once, however successful it might be."

"But . . ."

"No arguments, Jean-Baptiste," insisted Madeleine. "Master Corneille was quite emphatic and we mustn't vex him. There's no dearth of ambitious actors in Paris who would commit murder to have the chance of launching a new troupe with the first two plays written by Pierre Corneille's brother, whatever the conditions. We need Master Thomas Corneille far more than he needs us."

"I suppose," sighed Jean-Baptiste, "but a more peculiar conceit for the première of a play I can't imagine." He brightened and went on in a more buoyant tone. "What are the plays called? What are they about?"

Having foreseen the questions Madeleine had prepared her answers carefully and invented a new title for *The Liar*. "The second one, which will be our mainstay," she said, "is called *The Promises of Chance*. A woman is desperately in love and disguises herself in order to find out if the man she loves feels the same way about her." She did her best to keep her voice even; Jean-Baptiste opened his mouth to interject a comment but she rushed on. "The first one, the more amusing of the two, is called *The Teller of Tales*. A man, Dorante, arrives in Paris and begins spouting lies. He falls in love with one woman and lies to her to impress her, but his father wishes him to marry another. To avoid marrying the second one he lies about a third one to whom he claims to be married already and who he says is expecting a baby."

"A role made for you, my dear," said Jean-Baptiste expansively.

"Dorante?" Madeleine replied. "But he's a man."

"I'll play the man, of course. I meant the liar's pregnant wife. You played that part when you gave birth to our Armande!"

It was as if stormclouds were passing overhead. Jean-Baptiste had not alluded to Armande for weeks and he did so now only to illustrate how Madeleine might portray a character in a comedy! Something else about his words stirred up an ill-defined anxiety in her but she forced a smile and said, "I didn't say his wife was expecting a child. The liar's wife doesn't even exist. She's one of his lies, completely invented by him."

"If you protest that you are *not* in such a blessed state," pursued Jean-Baptiste, as inattentive to her words as ever, "that's one matter easily remedied!"

This time she smiled her approval. He seized her waist and pulled her toward himself. It was over a month since they had last been together. They undressed and fell into each other's arms.

After their love, they dozed off. When Madeleine opened her eyes, she found Jean-Baptiste, his eyes still shut, curled up in contentment like a child.

"Even if Dorante were a woman," he murmured, "the part would be wrong for you. You haven't a dishonest bone in your lovely body."

She sat up and began to dress. She had to do something, however slight, to ease her conscience. "Jean-Baptiste," she said tentatively, "I haven't *always*, that is, there are things I've said and done . . ."

"Of course, my angel," he said, cutting her off, "we all indulge in little fibs from time to time. No need to worry your pretty head." He pulled up his leggings, then snatched his doublet and his shoes. "Let's make haste," he said. "We've got no time to lose."

"That much is true," said Madeleine, gesturing at the pile of items to be packed.

They had been working in silence for some time when Jean-Baptiste's voice wafted over a high chest of drawers. "This Thomas Corneille," he said, "you must introduce me to him one day. I can't possibly repay his generosity at the present time, but the least I can do is to express my gratitude for the precious gift he's given you!"

CHAPTER 20

In Which "A Liar Is Trapped in His Web of Deceit"

For the next six weeks Madeleine struggled with a sense of foreboding set off by Jean-Baptiste's notion that the role of the liar's invented pregnant wife was suited to her. She fought against the mounting evidence but upon reaching the theater on opening day—Friday, January 8, 1644, her twenty-sixth birthday—she could fight no longer. Fastening her gown made her feel as if she had been caught between doors and was being compressed from two directions at once.

She slumped onto a chair. Her time of month had not come since early October, before the troupe's arrival in Rouen. She was plagued by nausea. And now her dress was too small. The dreadful conclusion could no longer be evaded. If Thomas Corneille had left her with a *precious gift*, it was not only the two plays she had reported to Jean-Baptiste, but also another gift of which Thomas himself was unaware.

Why was God singling her out? While her prayers for another child with Jean-Baptiste had gone unheeded, a moment of passion with Thomas had born unintended fruit. She and Jean-Baptiste had not been intimate during their stay in Rouen in October. If the baby arrived on time in July he might harbor suspicions but that was the least of her woes: an ill-timed birth could always be dismissed as early or late. Far more troubling was whether or not she was willing to pass off Thomas's child as Jean-Baptiste's.

Soon the other actors began arriving; the baby issue would have to be tabled. She calmed their stage fright and reminded them of the play's trickier spots. Jean-Baptiste had adored *The Teller of Tales* but not *The Promises of Chance*, which would première two days later, on January 10. She had more than enough to keep her mind from dwelling on her offstage *ennuis*.

***

Curtain time was three o'clock and at half-past two the hall was deserted, but soon spectators began filing in, first in dribs and drabs and then in an accelerating stream. It was bad form to raise the curtain less than an hour after the announced starting time; by four o'clock the house was three-quarters full. As Jean-Baptiste picked up a baton, struck the three blows against the floor that by tradition signaled the start of a performance, and strode onstage, Madeleine held her breath, actually something of a relief given the tightness of her gown.

She had suggested that Jean-Baptiste elongate a phrase in Dorante's opening speech to elicit a quick laugh. His voice rang out.

> *I have finally traded my books for a sword,*
> *What joy to be in Paris! In class I was soooo boooored!*

The hall erupted. Madeleine readied herself for the entry of her character, Clarice. As the script required, she stumbled and was helped to her feet by Dorante, delighted at being allowed to take this lovely stranger's hand but also disappointed that such a favor was granted by mere circumstance. Madeleine launched into Clarice's opening speech.

> *I hold dearer a gift than a payment that's made,*
> *For a giver gives more than a service repaid,*
> *And good fortune that comes to the one who deserves it*
> *Is no more than a debt owed the lender who serves it.*
> *A favor that's earned is like something that's bought,*
> *One brings greater joy if it never was sought.*
> *Its benefits grow if it's freely accorded*
> *And not as a debt to the worthy rewarded.*

For the first time it came to her that the lines echoed Thomas's words in the little room in Rouen about the generosity of love, and yet he could not have borrowed the notion that love must be freely given from his brother's play, which he had not yet begun to copy.

There was no time to delve into the mystery; the play moved swiftly. The public roared at Dorante's first falsehoods: a law student freshly arrived in Paris, he claimed to be a soldier who had seen Clarice a year earlier and had deserted the army and been trailing her ever since, waiting to declare his passion. His lies then escalated, reaching ridiculous heights until he received his comeuppance in the end. Joseph was hilarious as Dorante's indignant valet, Geneviève perfection in the role of Clarice's friend and rival for Dorante's heart. The troupe outdid itself, the crowd's constant uproar egging them on.

Before Madeleine knew it the final scene was upon them. She swelled with pride as Joseph recited the moral of the story without a single stutter.

> *How a liar is trapped in his web of deceit!*
> *And yet few could escape in a manner so fleet.*
> *For you who had doubts he would find his way clear,*
> *Follow his rare example and hold lying dear!*

The acclaim was instantaneous, the curtain calls thunderous and prolonged. Backstage a fresh wave of elation swept over the troupe. Jean-Baptiste threw his arms around Madeleine while Geneviève and Joseph danced a parodic minuet. It was a cold evening and kegs of wine and cider were brought from the storage area.

As if reluctant to shed their success, the others had not removed their costumes, but Madeleine, her nausea worsening, disappeared behind a screen.

"Is something wrong, my beauty?" exclaimed Jean-Baptiste in a raucous voice upon seeing her reappear in street clothes.

"Nothing," she protested. "Why do you ask?"

"I was wondering why our dear Clarice has left us so soon," he said expansively.

"I . . . the fabric of my costume is pale," Madeleine said. "I was afraid someone might spill wine on it." She managed a sickly smile. "Never fear, Clarice is still here in spirit."

He took her hand and kissed it. "Dorante, however, is not," he teased, "for I am not lying when I express my love for you."

A hint of color returned to her cheeks. "The reason being, I suppose," she blurted out, "that you so rarely do?"

His forehead creased and for once the playfulness disappeared from his eyes. "Is that how you see things, my darling?" he asked.

She pressed her lips together, fearful that she might weep if she opened her mouth to reply. After the anxious months of preparation, her unwelcome realization that morning, and now the relief of the troupe's success, this moment of tenderness had caught her off guard.

Jean-Baptiste pulled her gently into a corner, sat her on his lap, and rocked her. This small island of consolation went unnoticed amidst the hubbub, but eventually the revelers caught sight of the somber looks on the couple's faces. For no apparent reason the fun had gone out of the celebration. Without a word, one by one they took their leave.

As Jean-Baptiste and Madeleine prepared to lock up for the night, he kissed her on the cheek. "Have I told you," he managed to get out with visible effort, "that I could never have done this without you? There, I have said it."

Yes, he had said the words he undoubtedly thought she wished to hear, but there was the problem in a nutshell. She loved Jean-Baptiste not for his actions but for himself: for his secret tenderness and fragile, magnanimous heart; for his mad aspirations, his dreams of heroism, and his boyish enthusiasm flying in the face of reason; and, finally, for the way he could bring the gift of uncontrollable laughter to perfect strangers and also relished others' attempts at humor, howling even when he found them dull as a parent might praise a child's heartfelt but clumsy attempts at a cartwheel. Jean-Baptiste loved Madeleine for her beauty, certainly, but also, she reckoned, for her assistance in realizing his dreams. But how could he love her for herself unless he understood her well enough to discover the secrets of her heart, as Thomas had?

***

Back at the house they agreed to stay up late and reread *The Promises of Chance* in preparation for their dress rehearsal the following day. Jean-Baptiste had made no bones about disliking the play; Madeleine was nonetheless caught off guard when after barely half an hour he pitched the script to the floor.

"We simply must continue with *The Teller of Tales*," he declared. "I know all about Thomas's conditions, but if he'd seen the public's reaction he'd agree."

"I understand your frustration," Madeleine said, collecting the pages, "but I assure you we would bring ruin down upon our heads. It is out of the question."

"But why?" he raged, kicking the table, which rocked back and forth. "He has no reason to fear humiliation. The play is a sensation."

"I don't understand it any better than you do, but Master Corneille must have his reasons." Jean-Baptiste fumed but said nothing. "And anyway," she continued in a conciliatory tone, "there's no need. We've got *The Promises of Chance* to fall back on."

"*Fall* is the word," he snapped. "That's what will happen if we present this nonsense!"

"You spoke otherwise in November," she said mildly.

"In November," he riposted, "I hadn't read the plays and spent over a month rehearsing them. In November I didn't know that we would be teased by a work of genius, have it snatched away, and be offered sentimental rubbish in its place."

"I consider the second play most agreeable," Madeleine ventured, "if not a work of genius like the first. The ladies will find it charming."

"A whole play about love and secrets!" sputtered Jean-Baptiste. "What's secret about love? It's the simplest, noblest thing on earth. That's why the most effective way of treating the subject is tragedy." He struck a pose and began to orate. "The tragic hero's love is doomed but dignified. He speaks his mind, accepts his suffering, and stares destiny in the face. That's the sort of love a man understands." He went on in less pompous tones. "Mind you, my character, Don Fadrique, is a reasonable man at heart who doesn't see what all the fuss is about any more than I do. But he plays along, nattering away to please this woman, this, this . . ."

"Elvire," Madeleine interjected.

"Yes, that's it, *Elvire*," he said with spite, as if the name itself were an infraction of common sense. "Why should Elvire go around in disguise and keep her love secret? There's not a shred of dignity in such behavior. If she has deep feelings she should be truthful and say so."

"I congratulate you on how sure you are about a character you're not playing, but has it occurred to you that women don't view these matters as men do? We don't always . . ."

"Never mind what you women don't always do," said Jean-Baptiste. "Speaking up about your feelings is what any rational person, man or woman, would do. Why not speak the truth about something as straightforward as love?"

"We've no time to debate the matter now." Madeleine turned her back to him before proceeding. "But it might be pointed out that I have not heard a barrage of such declarations issuing from your lips. Shall I conclude you have no *deep feelings* for me? Look sharp, or you will break my heart, O Callous One!" She placed one hand next to her breast and made a thumping sound while with the other hand she brushed away imaginary tears from her cheek.

"I don't deny it," muttered Jean-Baptiste. "But that's different."

"Oh? And the reason?"

"Because I have already expressed my fondness for you," he said. "Why repeat myself? What has changed since I told you about it the first time?"

***

With *The Promises of Chance* to première on Tuesday, Monday would be devoted to a final day of rehearsal. Madeleine was to wear the same slender-waisted gown as in *The Teller of Tales*. She couldn't ask Marie Hervé to let it out without raising suspicion but feared for the safety of her child; the only solution was to do the job herself. She rose at dawn, fetched a small bag of supplies she had prepared, and set out for the theater.

It was raining and chilly as she hurried through the streets. The south bank of the Seine, which lacked the bustle of the

Marais and the crowds thronging the Halles, was peaceful this early in the morning, especially in inclement weather, and she welcomed the quiet, which allowed her to review the lines her character of Elvire would recite. The dressing room was gloomy in the January light and from time to time she warmed her fingers next to the candle.

Suddenly there was a knock at the dressing-room door and she recalled with a start that she'd neglected to lock the main entrance. Arming herself with a cardboard sword used as a prop, she quietly pushed a table against the door. In a deep voice she called out, "Who's there?"

"I beg your pardon," came the muffled reply, "I'm looking for Mademoiselle Béjart."

The voice sounded familiar but she couldn't place it.

"No actresses here at this hour!" boomed the buxom baritone. "I'm the carpenter."

"May I wait for Mademoiselle Béjart inside?" came the timid voice, barely audible through the oak door. "She said I could call on her if I was in Paris. I'm very cold."

Madeleine heaved the table aside and flung open the door. A bedraggled Thomas Corneille, sopping wet from head to toe, had the astonishing presence of mind to fall to his knees.

"I see you haven't lost your taste for genuflecting," Madeleine said with amusement.

"Nor you the beauty that inspires it," he intoned. He took her hand, kissed it, and pressed it against his cheek.

"How can you tell?" she teased. "You haven't even looked at me."

He gazed up at her. "It's not upon the evidence of my eyes that I rely," he said, "but on the knowledge of my heart."

She led him into the dressing room and closed the door.

"I'm here early repairing a seam," she asked. "What are you doing here?" She offered Thomas a seat. "I didn't expect to see you in Paris quite so soon."

"Nor did I," Thomas admitted, clapping his arms for warmth. "The première of *The Liar* at the Théâtre du Marais is this Friday. As my brother is indisposed he asked me to pass along certain instructions to Floridor and attend the final rehearsals in his place. I see by the signboards that you've already given your performance of his play. Was it well received?"

"A great success," Madeleine replied. "I must thank you once again. Tomorrow afternoon we open with *The Promises of Chance.*"

"So the play pleased you?" he asked after an awkward silence.

"Yes," she replied shortly. She feared Thomas might read too much into greater words of praise.

He blushed. "I'm glad to hear it," he said quietly. "Of course I wish you every success," he went on in a stronger voice, "but we must face facts. In four days the Marais is opening with my brother's first comedy in ten years. They can't hold a candle to what the troupe was under Mondory and I'm sorry to say that Marion L'Hermite, who is, I believe, your aunt, is an exceedingly poor choice for the role of Clarice. But they'll draw more spectators than a fledgling troupe presenting an anonymous play. As long as I'm in town," he concluded, "perhaps I could attend your rehearsal tonight, incognito, and offer you advice for the première."

Already in Rouen Thomas had told Madeleine that the Théâtre du Marais was to open with *The Liar* on January 15th, but it had slipped her mind that soon they would have to contend with these formidable rivals.

"Yet again, please accept my thanks," Madeleine said warmly. "I'll leave the gate open and you may come in at any time. The director of our troupe has heard all about you and will be pleased to make your acquaintance. The others will be kept in the dark about your identity."

Thomas blanched. Did he recall having suspected the director was her lover?

The bells of Saint Sulpice chimed and Madeleine said, "I must finish my task and return home before I'm missed." Suddenly it seemed to her that Thomas's eyes were boring into her and she summarily sat down and draped the gown on the dressing table over her midsection.

"I've heard that on the morning following a performance," he joked, "actresses refuse to rise with the sun, not wishing to compete with the golden orb till they've regained their own luster. Are you an exception to the rule or have you forsaken acting in favor of costumes?"

"Perhaps you're unaware that I'm a seamstress's daughter," said Madeleine, pulling in her waist before displaying the gown to be repaired and grateful that she hadn't yet inserted the extra fabric. "Just imagine, this tore during the performance last night. I had quite a task avoiding indecency! My mother has been working on costumes night and day and was so exhausted that I thought I would let her sleep and mend it myself."

"Couldn't it have waited until tomorrow?" asked Thomas. "May I be frank?"

"Of course," she replied.

"Your color is bad and your face bloated. Are you ill?"

Leave it to Thomas to notice what had escaped even Marie Hervé's keen eye!

"No, merely tired," Madeleine replied. "Another reason to be quick, so I can nap before rehearsal."

Thomas stood. "The man you love, he's the director of your troupe, is he not?"

She nodded, hoping he would drop the matter.

"And he's playing the role of Don Fadrique to your Elvire?"

"Yes," she answered curtly.

He turned to face her. "Is he well suited to the role?" he queried.

"He's quite proficient," she said after a moment's reflection, "and draws laughter whenever he wishes. He received great acclaim from the audience as the liar in your brother's play."

"And yet the role of Don Fadrique is not only comic," ventured Thomas, "but also the role of a deeply devoted lover. And you're not quite pleased with him in that role, are you?"

She pretended to be absorbed in her mending. "He does the best he can," she said lightly. "In truth he is not especially fond of your play, particularly the character of Elvire."

"Then he can't make a suitable lover," murmured Thomas.

"I'm not sure I know what you mean," Madeleine replied.

"Simply this," he elaborated. "Like the liar, he hides behind a wall of laughter rather than proving himself to be truly devoted to his lady and worthy of her in the end."

"He tries to do what I suggest," Madeleine said in the voice one might use in an argument with oneself. "He has made progress in the role. But you may see for yourself this evening," she concluded, looking up from her work. "Perhaps he'll heed your advice. He certainly doesn't listen to mine."

CHAPTER 21

In Which Life Imitates Art and a Seam Is Concealed from a Peeping Thomas

---

In the course of the tumultuous day that culminated in Madeleine's introducing her lover to the father of her unborn child, countless concerns crossed her mind. Given Jean-Baptiste's lukewarm discussion of love the previous night, was there any real likelihood that he was in love with her in his heart of hearts? Were there no limits to the devotion of young Thomas Corneille? Could a play about the secret nature of love succeed when the male lead considered the subject absurd? The only thing that seemed certain was that revealing the truth of her condition to either man would doom the première of *The Promises of Chance* to failure, a destiny that it already seemed well on its way to fulfilling.

Altering her gown so that she could actually breathe took longer than anticipated since care had to be taken to leave not a trace of evidence. However inattentive Jean-Baptiste was where she was concerned, Marie Hervé and Geneviève had sharper eyes, and a haphazard seam around the midsection would give them dangerous food for thought. By the time Madeleine's sewing was complete it seemed foolish to drag herself back to the Rue de la Perle only to turn right around. Nearing the end of its third month, the pregnancy was beginning to tire her. She fell onto the pallet in the corner of the dressing room and dozed off.

"How sweet you look," a voice came to her in her dreams and she awoke to discover Jean-Baptiste's eyes dancing with mischief. "It is my opinion," he continued, "that we should devote this day to pleasure rather than rehearsing the poor excuse for a play we're condemned to present tomorrow afternoon." A dour expression overspread his features.

Madeleine sat up. "O ye of little faith," she said, "your savior is nigh."

"Saint Mary Magdalen," Jean-Baptiste intoned, "you are sinner and savior in one. Why would I have need of any other to save me?"

"Or to sin with?" Madeleine chimed in, kissing him and beginning to change her clothes.

"Precisely," concurred Jean-Baptiste. "If only we had time . . ." He picked up the script of *The Promises of Chance* lying on a shelf. "Confound this drivel!" he cried.

Madeleine pulled her gown over her head, keeping the alteration out of sight. "For today you'd best keep your opinion of this *drivel* to yourself," she scolded, "because the savior I mentioned is its author." She shook the hair from her eyes and added in an offhand manner, "Thomas Corneille is in Paris and called at the theater this morning to inquire about his plays."

"What splendid news!" cried Jean-Baptiste. "When he heard of our success, he must have said we could continue with *The Teller of Tales*. Am I wrong, or am I right?"

"Wrong, wrong, wrong!" Madeleine exclaimed, pounding the wall in a display of anger exaggerated to cover the fact that it was not actually feigned. Were Jean-Baptiste to raise the issue with Thomas, both men would discover her lie about the play's authorship. She continued in a calmer voice. "I have informed him of the warm reception his comedy received, but he's adamant. If any of us so much as mentions its title," she embroidered as she did up the buttons on her bodice, "he'll withdraw both plays. And don't forget, we alone know that he's our author. The others are not to suspect. He was very definite about that as well."

Jean-Baptiste pouted. Suddenly he grinned and pinched Madeleine's backside. He gave chase as she scuttled to the other side of the room. "However peculiar his ideas," he puffed, out of breath, "I am eager to meet this boy-wonder. When will he be here?"

"Not until evening," Madeleine replied, carefully adjusting her sleeves like a halfheartedly prim lady distracting onlookers from her swooping décolleté. "Thomas will spend the day assisting the Théâtre du Marais with their rehearsal of his brother's new comedy, which is to open Friday."

"It's just as well that Thomas won't be here until late," remarked Jean-Baptiste, ignoring the dire implications of the news about Pierre. "Between now and then, Dionysos and

Apollo and all the muses of comedy will have to inspire us to find a way to enliven his dreary lines!"

***

The rehearsal went even more disastrously than Madeleine had expected. Because the performance of *The Teller of Tales* had intervened since the previous run-through of *The Promises of Chance*, entire lines from the first play made renegade appearances in the second one, muddling cues and bewildering the cast. The love story between Elvire and Don Fadrique was all the more difficult to follow as it was based on a confusion of identity between Elvire and the veiled lady she posed as to hide her true feelings until Don Fadrique's trustworthiness could be ascertained. The convoluted plot combined with the periodic botching of lines were such that Madeleine herself could not always keep track of the play's twists and turns.

By late afternoon the more comical scenes were competent and after supper it was decided they would work exclusively on the serious ones involving Elvire and Don Fadrique. While the women found this delicately evolving relationship the most captivating part of the play, the men had been stifling guffaws during the love scenes. The most worrisome offender was Don Fadrique, né Jean-Baptiste Poquelin.

To refresh the cast's memory about the intricacies of the lovers' situation they began with an early scene in which Elvire, in love with Don Fadrique but engaged against her will to another man, admitted to her confidante that she was not yet ready to reveal the truth to Don Fadrique: that she was not only Elvire—a family friend he considered unavailable because of her engagement—but also the mysterious masked lady he had been secretly courting.

With the scene reaching its climax, Geneviève, playing Elvire's confidante, prostrated herself before her mistress and cried out:

> *Don Fadrique's the secret object of your desire*
> *And all you do with him is play the liar?*

Madeleine clenched her hands to her breast before giving Elvire's anguished reply:

> *To let others beside you see how weak I am*
> *And disgracefully confess that my pride is a sham*
> *Before I know if he loves me? No, I'll not reveal*
> *That secret until I'm sure his love is real!*
> *Until I can trust him with my naked soul*
> *I'll clothe my feelings in the same impenetrable role.*
> *Shall my heart show its secrets to the man I adore*
> *Until I can be sure what he will use them for?*

The scene's final lines echoed through the cavernous seating area. As if in response to a prearranged signal, the other actors and actresses reacted at precisely the same moment, but in opposite ways.

"This play could not have been written by a man," gushed one of the women. Another actress climbed onstage and embraced Madeleine. "Elvire is like me, like you, like all women," she sobbed, wiping her tears with a sleeve. "Intelligent, refined, and yet utterly misunderstood."

In counterpoint to this tender female encomium several of the men, including Jean-Baptiste, had fallen to the floor of the standees' pit and were rolling about in hysterics. All at once he leapt onstage, turned his back to the theater's seating area, and bent over, yelling between his legs in a falsetto shriek:

> *Until I can trust him with my naked derrière*
> *I'll clothe my buttocks and cover my hair!*

He now faced forward and lifted high his doublet to reveal his chest.

> *Shall I show off my bosom to the man I adore*
> *Until I can be sure what he will use it for?*

Aside from Joseph, loathe to mock his sister, Jean-Baptiste's satire sent the other men into apoplectic fits. The women, horrified, said nothing.

Madeleine observed the scene with a detached expression. She walked toward the wings, turning as she reached the curtain, and addressed the men as a group. "I'm delighted to have entertained you, *messieurs*," she said in a pinched voice. "Relish it, for it's the last time."

Drawn to attention by her somber tone, the entire troupe fell silent. "What do you mean?" asked Jean-Baptiste, the merriment drained from his voice.

"Elvire fears revealing the truth," said Madeleine, addressing him directly, "but I don't." That wasn't so, but it sounded good. "You claim to love the theater," she went on, "but there's one important lesson you have yet to learn. You may forget your lines, recite them poorly, or trip onstage, even fall flat on your face. Any of those errors an audience can forgive. But if you're not moved by what you're presenting, the public will know it in an instant." She surveyed the troupe. "If we perform this play tomorrow," she went on ominously, "it will be a debacle. With Pierre Corneille's new comedy opening on Friday we won't be given another chance. When we make fools of ourselves, which we will, the Illustre Théâtre will be finished."

One could hear a pin drop. Rather than protesting, as she expected him to, Jean-Baptiste stared miserably into space. "What do you propose we do?" he asked in a monotone.

"Close our doors, at least for now," Madeleine said. "We'll lose momentum but our reputation will remain intact. We can try again in a few months' time."

The men hung their heads. The women looked angry and sullen.

"Be that as it may," came a resounding voice from the back of the theater, giving them all a start, "perhaps I might be able to offer a more agreeable alternative."

A majestic figure advanced rapidly toward the stage, hoisted himself up, and kissed Madeleine's hand. For all she knew Thomas had been waiting in the shadows for the perfect instant to make his entrance. He whispered for a long time into her ear. She nodded, her face a blank slate, then smiled and spoke to the troupe in a sugary tone of voice.

"My friends," she said, "please allow me to present Monsieur Charles de Grandgarçon, a young actor of great renown from Rouen. I had hoped to introduce him when we were in that fair city but he . . ." She faltered and glanced over at the man, who murmured something under his breath. "Unfortunately he fell ill and remained bedridden for the entire month of the fair. Now he's recovered, and as he's visiting Paris he's agreed to assist us in our final rehearsal before the première tomorrow." An excited twitter permeated the theater. "I refrained from announcing this windfall until now because I was uncertain if he'd be able to fit us into his schedule." She thought for a moment before concluding, "Monsieur is a close friend of the author's and knows our play exceedingly well. He'll observe us and offer his advice."

Nine pairs of eyes turned to scrutinize this imposing young *deus ex machina*. Jean-Baptiste rushed forward and pulled him into a corner. After some animated whispering between the two men, Madeleine was asked to confer with them; more gesticulations from Monsieur de Grandgarçon and dismayed head-shaking by Madeleine suggested an idea not to her liking, but finally she acquiesced.

Now Jean-Baptiste addressed the troupe.

"Monsieur de Grandgarçon has suggested that since he knows the script well and time is short, he can best demonstrate the spirit of the play by rehearsing the role of Don Fadrique himself." A murmur went through the troupe. "Hush, we've no time to lose," Jean-Baptiste continued brusquely. He picked up the script and called out in the voice of a town crier, "Act Four, Scene Three, Don Fadrique and Elvire. After learning that Elvire's fiancé has been killed and that she is now free to consider other suitors, Don Fadrique admits to her that his feelings for the mysterious disguised lady about whom he's told her have taught him the value of loving another without hope of being loved in return. He then reveals it is Elvire alone whom he loves."

He turned to Madeleine and Thomas. "Are you ready?" he called out. Thomas nodded vehemently; Madeleine's only response was to lift her eyebrows. She was so preoccupied by the perplexing situation that she recited her opening lines in a dreary manner:

> *What surprises me most, Don Fadrique, is to observe*
> *That your love for this lady, whose love you deserve,*
> *Has continued without your having love from her received,*
> *Which in the past, of you, I would never have believed.*

Thomas launched into his declaration in a voice that fused the intensity of youth and the pathos of embattled experience:

> *It is true that nothing stings as much as scorn,*
> *But how often one receives it once love is born!*
> *Love's blindfold must keep my lady's name obscure,*
> *But, loving without reward, my heart remains pure.*
> *One sometimes falls prey to a desperate love,*
> *And now my dueling heart has taken off the glove.*
> *The object of my love, she whose power I revere,*
> *Forbids me all hope, though my love keeps me near.*
> *Yes, I love you!*

He fell to his knees. Suddenly Madeleine realized he was nose-to-nose with her dress alteration! In a panic she spun away from him. It must have appeared that she was recoiling from his declaration, the effect being so dramatic that several of the actresses gasped.

Now Thomas stood abruptly and gazed into Madeleine's eyes for what seemed an eternity before facing the audience and resuming his declaration.

> *Yes, I love you! but with a love so pure*
> *That in silence I've suffered this illness without cure.*
> *Burning with desire, my beleaguered spirit*
> *Told my virtue to ignore my love and not to hear it.*
> *Controlling my passions, I thought all I could do*
> *Was be pleasing in your sight if I couldn't be loved by you.*
> *Finally today, from heaven's firmament,*
> *Came a whisper of hope to calm my lament.*
> *Your fiancé is lifeless, yet I don't dare avow*
> *That I love you, unless my love you'll allow.*

Here Thomas turned toward Jean-Baptiste and stared at him. Petrified, Madeleine glanced up to gauge her lover's reaction and was so taken aback by his unperturbed expression that only after a long silence did she recall that the next line, a question, was hers:

> *With implausible confessions you continue to mock?*

Without warning Thomas, genuflecting again, seized her about the waist. She struggled to loosen his grasp so that he wouldn't feel her abdomen but he held on for dear life and cried:

> *You disbelieve my love is solid as a rock?*
> *To assuage your doubts and make you realize*
> *The strength of my love, must I resort to sighs?*
> *Must I cast languid dying looks your way*
> *To tell you all the things my heart can't say?*

He heaved a sigh, looked up, and fixed his eyes on hers, his features suffused with suffering. Then in a single smooth motion he released her, turned his back, and concluded with a flourish:

> *I find such frivolous strategies absurd,*
> *All that true love requires is a single word*
> *To give voice to love's most exalted desires*
> *And show that all one's previous words were liars.*

The scene was supposed to continue but wild applause from the audience kept Madeleine from giving Elvire's reply. Thomas bowed graciously. Jean-Baptiste came forward and clapped him on the shoulder.

"Congratulations, Monsieur," he said heartily. "You've recited Don Fadrique's lines not lightheartedly, as I've been doing, but with the grandeur of tragedy, as if you truly meant what you were saying. It was quite effective."

"Your praise is unjustified," Thomas said. He looked his rival in the eye. "When I declared my love for this lady, I was not acting." He gestured toward Madeleine, who counted the seconds. Seeing her waver Thomas offered her a chair. "What I meant," he said to Jean-Baptiste to calm her agitation, "is that I was speaking from the heart."

"Yes, I understand," said Jean-Baptiste. "However foolish the words of your play sound when read in a normal voice, if one imagines being desperately in love it's altogether different."

Rather than taking offense at the backhanded compliment Thomas nodded politely. Jean-Baptiste squatted down on the stage and held his head in his hands, deep in thought. "There's only one solution," he finally said, turning to Thomas, "but will you agree to it?"

"I am prepared to do whatever I can to be of assistance," said Thomas.

"I appeal to you all," said Jean-Baptiste, executing a clumsy half-circle to address the entire troupe. "We must avail ourselves of Monsieur's generosity and ask him to play Don Fadrique at tomorrow's première." Silence. Madeleine felt nausea rising in her gorge. "I can learn quickly," Jean-Baptiste continued, "but I must see the role from start to finish. Tonight there's no time. Tomorrow I'll observe Monsieur and his every gesture and intonation will be etched in my memory. By Friday I'll play the part exactly as he does." He faced Thomas. "If you wish you may wear a mask throughout the play to disguise your true identity from the audience so that you won't be seen onstage with a troupe beneath your standing. Your answer, Monsieur? Are you willing to go to such extremes to help us?"

Thomas glanced at Madeleine. Almost imperceptibly she shook her head. With Jean-Baptiste hanging on Don Fadrique's every word she feared he might begin to suspect that Thomas's passions weren't feigned. And given the close scrutiny she too would be subjected to from both men, would her own secret not also be at risk?

"You flatter me," said Thomas, "far above my worth. I must, however, decline."

The three of them looked ill at ease, as if they had suddenly lost track of why they found themselves together onstage. "Once more I entreat you, Monsieur," persisted Jean-Baptiste, "for our future hangs in the balance! I know we've done nothing to deserve your favor," he concluded, "but as a great man recently wrote, *A favor that's earned is like something that's bought, One brings greater joy if it never was sought.*"

It was from Clarice's opening speech in *The Liar*. Though Jean-Baptiste mistakenly believed that Thomas rather than Pierre had written the play, by chance he'd struck upon the very lines that Madeleine had noticed unaccountably echoed Thomas's own way of thinking. The passage having struck precisely the right chord to please the young man, he beamed and looked at Madeleine again.

What good was it to struggle against fate? This time she nodded.

***

The opening performance of *The Promises of Chance*, which a matter of hours before the curtain rose promised to be an unmitigated catastrophe, was another triumph for the Illustre Théâtre. Afterwards Thomas declined to join in the celebration, expressing regret that he'd be unable to attend the Friday performance because of the première of his brother's play. He wished them all the best of luck and bade them farewell.

A few moments after his departure Madeleine excused herself. She ran into the street. Thomas was disappearing around a corner. "Monsieur!" she cried.

He turned and waited. When she reached him he kissed her hand.

"Mademoiselle," he said, "you're scantily attired." She hadn't changed out of Elvire's gown or thought to bring her shawl.

He undid his cloak and placed it around her shoulders. She pulled him into a nearby arcade illuminated by chandeliers hanging from a vaulted ceiling.

"As always, Monsieur," she said, "I am overwhelmed by your kindness. You've shown Jean-Baptiste not only how to play the role of Don Fadrique, but also . . ."

In the candlelight the sadness Thomas had kept hidden for the past two days welled up and her voice trailed off. "Go on," he said, mastering his grief. "What else?"

"Now that he claims to understand your play," she said, "perhaps it will teach him something about love."

"If in helping him I've helped you," Thomas responded with a sigh of resignation, "my time has been well spent. You if anyone must understand that I was serious in saying I was speaking from the heart." He pondered something. "I hesitate to raise the subject but it's best that you know. It's not simply the idea of love that your Jean-Baptiste must come to understand, but the nature of your love. I can't find it in my heart to wish him success in unlocking the secrets of yours, but until he does he'll play my role poorly, for each man expresses true love in his own particular way. The audience will sense that the gestures and intonations he's using aren't his own. He must respond to your love from the depths of his heart. Otherwise your hall will soon be empty. Unless . . ."

"Unless what?" demanded Madeleine.

"Unless we prevent *The Liar* from opening on Friday," Thomas replied.

"Prevent it from opening?" she exclaimed. "It's your brother's play. It's his right to have it performed by anyone he pleases."

"Of course it's his play," he said soberly, "but . . ." He paused. "The male characters pose no problem for him," he continued, "but sometimes he has difficulty imagining a lady's thoughts and feelings, so we discuss it." His expression resembled that of a disapproving matron. "I love my brother but he doesn't understand much about women, so we talk about his heroines. His words are always his own, of course, but he says he sometimes keeps my observations in mind."

So that explained it. When in the little room in Rouen Thomas had said true love doesn't expect to be repaid, his words were echoing not *The Liar*, the final version of which he hadn't yet read, but rather the ideas he himself had discussed with his brother to assist him in understanding the female characters in his play.

"But when you spoke of preventing the Marais troupe from performing *The Liar*," Madeleine pursued, "what did you mean?"

His eyes grew large and round, like those of a cat about to pounce. "There may be another way," he said, turning to depart. "You'll just have to trust me."

And in spite of her entreaties, he refused to elaborate.

***

Thomas was right: however proficient Jean-Baptiste was at mimicking his performance, something was missing. Friday's show, the first one with Jean-Baptiste playing Don Fadrique, was received with polite applause and two rather perfunctory curtain calls. Madeleine put a bright face on it, praising

Jean-Baptiste for his improvement. At least he no longer snickered while declaring Don Fadrique's devotion.

It was Jean-Baptiste's birthday and after the performance he and Madeleine marked the occasion at a tavern on the Rue Vieille du Temple. Despite feeling unwell Madeleine told Jean-Baptiste amusing stories about her days traveling with the Troupe du Vent. It was lovely to sip mulled wine and listen to the howling wind from beside the hearth, but just when the memory of the disappointing show was beginning to dissipate, the Théâtre du Marais next door let out after its evening performance of *The Liar*. Soon the tavern was filled with theatergoers who could speak of nothing but this fresh proof of Monsieur Pierre Corneille's genius. The two lovers fell silent.

Madeleine sipped her wine and reflected. With *The Promises of Chance* certain to close quickly in competition with *The Liar*, perhaps it was time to stop inventing stories to protect Jean-Baptiste and tell him the simple truth.

About everything?

It occurred to her that she too could learn from Thomas's willingness to reveal his deepest emotions. If she wanted Jean-Baptiste to see into her heart, why did she continue to go to such lengths to conceal it? Should she make a clean breast of it, tell him the truth about Armande, and what happened in Rouen, and the baby she was expecting—the baby that wasn't his?

An expression of chagrin crossed Jean-Baptiste's face when he grasped that Pierre Corneille's new play was a triumph but it was quickly replaced by determination. "I say we press on!" he exclaimed. "Those windbags at the Marais are passable at tragedy, but if the public is pleased by their attempts at comedy, it's sheer novelty. By this time next week they'll be paying passersby to fill the hall." He gulped wine and wiped his mouth on the sleeve of his doublet. "With all due respect to your theatrical aunt, my dear," he concluded, squeezing Madeleine's knee, "I've heard that the only way Marion can get a laugh is if she forgets her lines, a gift that apparently comes to her naturally!"

Glad of the distraction, Madeleine chimed in. "I still can't believe that Floridor was so foolish as to hire Marion," she asserted. "If he simply bedded her I would wish him godspeed, for she's never refused her charms to anyone who could be of use to her. But to make her a member of his troupe? My aunt may be a courtesan, but is she worth so high a price?"

"Judge for yourself!" came the furious reply out of nowhere, and Madeleine looked up to find none other than Marion L'Hermite! She charged Madeleine before continuing her rant. "I would look in the mirror before calling someone else a whore!" she cried.

Marion was a vision from a bad dream. Although she was just past thirty, her once lovely skin was sallow, her hair dyed the color of overripe strawberries. Marion's figure remained pleasing but her excessively low-cut gown was better suited to an ingénue half her age.

Madeleine could think of nothing to reply. She had no wish to feud with her aunt but was saddened by what Marion had become. To make her astonishment complete, Marion was being restrained from attacking her by the gentleman accompanying her, the Comte de Modène.

As dashing as ever, he bowed and kissed Madeleine's hand. His eyes simmered but he said only, "How nice to see you again, Mademoiselle," as if they had once been introduced at church.

Jean-Baptiste yanked Madeleine backward by the hand, placing himself in front of her.

"Madame," he said, turning toward Marion, "I beg your forgiveness. It was the wine speaking, nothing else. Your dear niece intended no offense." He turned to the Comte before continuing. "Monsieur, I believe we met under similar circumstance some years ago. But today Mademoiselle is with me, and it is I who am asking you to leave us in peace."

Marion seemed somewhat mollified. The Comte bowed and led her out of the tavern without another word.

Hardly had Madeleine and Jean-Baptiste seated themselves again and recovered from the strange interlude when two men at a nearby table began recounting their favorite scenes from *The Liar*. If she did nothing to prevent it he'd soon realize that in spite of the different title, the play the men had seen was the same as the one the Illustre Théâtre had put on for its debut. She hadn't the strength to find an excuse to leave. This, then, was where the revelations would begin.

What other lies might come to light? If Madeleine explained that the play hadn't been written by Thomas Corneille but stolen by him for her benefit, what questions about their involvement would arise? Sooner or later she would have to decide what to tell Jean-Baptiste about the child she was carrying. And in explaining why she'd hidden the pregnancy from him, would she not have to reveal the most agonizing truth of all, the death of Armande? She shut her eyes, almost relieved the masquerade would soon be over.

The drinkers' voices became louder and although Madeleine's eyes remained closed, she imagined Jean-Baptiste's expression of dawning alarm as he grasped the implications of what he was hearing. The tissue of lies she had woven to nurse along his love was about to be torn apart. She covered her face with her hands and waited for the explosion.

A clamor erupted. Patrons began pouring out into the Rue Vieille du Temple.

"What's happening?" cried Jean-Baptiste, grasping a customer by the shoulders.

"Haven't you heard?" the man replied. "The Théâtre du Marais is on fire!"

CHAPTER 22

In Which a Suitor's Burning Love Takes a Fair Lady's Breath Away

Madeleine cried out that she would run home to verify that the family was safe, but she was turned aside momentarily by the conflagration and stood riveted by the dreadful spectacle. Amidst showers of sparks and spasms of orange light, the stun of falling beams marked the rhythms of the disaster. Wheeling through her mind was an explanation for this astounding reversal of fortune, but it strained belief.

A lone figure appeared out of the gray cloud enveloping the street. He approached and bowed deeply.

"Is your family safe?" asked Thomas in a somber voice.

For a few moments Madeleine stared at him in silence.

"I don't know. I must find out. But . . ."

Suddenly a gust of wind sent smoke in her direction and she raced toward the house.

Marie Hervé and the children stood in the courtyard with a group of terrified neighbors, unharmed. Thomas remained at a discreet distance.

"Thank the Lord!" cried Madeleine, clasping her mother to her breast. The uproar was dying down. "Go inside and put Louis to bed," she said to Geneviève, "he's trembling from the cold. When Jean-Baptiste arrives tell him I'm with Monsieur de Grandgarçon. He'll know who I mean."

She and Thomas walked in silence as they made their way toward the Place Royale through streets so musky with the aroma of charred wood that even breathing was difficult. By the time they reached the Place Royale, the air had cleared; Thomas was lodged in a room belonging to a friend of Pierre's who was a marquis, in the same building where the Comte de Modène had once received Madeleine's nightly visits.

They took seats across from each other at a small table. The room was faintly illuminated by a small chandelier that gave a glimpse of luxurious furnishings, but in size and arrangement it reminded her of the humble tavern lodgings overlooking the Seine in Rouen where she and Thomas had come together. In spite of the turbulence of the evening's events, Thomas's eyes gazing across the table remained placid.

"I attended your play today," he said. "Your performance was exemplary."

"I didn't see you," Madeleine replied.

"I stood in the shadows," he said. "There was so much excitement at the Marais about the première of *The Liar* that no one noticed I'd slipped out."

"Why did you?" she asked.

Thomas looked down at the table.

"I wished to confirm that this Jean-Baptiste of yours is not without talent. Not only that he could make the audience laugh, but also that he'd be able to play a love scene convincingly."

"And?"

"If he loses his fear of showing his true feelings, he will make a good lover. Onstage, I mean," Thomas added with a blush, lifting his eyes to meet her gaze.

"I am pleased that you approve," said Madeleine. "As for the fire . . ."

"Yes?" said Thomas evenly after a long silence.

She hesitated.

"I was wondering how Pierre will react when he hears the news?"

"Naturally he'll make a fuss. He'll yell and thrash about as he does in the wake of anything that doesn't suit him. Then he'll do what he can to have the play performed elsewhere."

"But how?" she inquired. "Hasn't the Théâtre du Marais got exclusive rights?"

"Yes," said Thomas, "but only as long as they can guarantee at least two performances a week."

"I suppose," Madeleine said reflectively, "that he'll have no choice but to approach the Hôtel de Bourgogne. They're between shows and would take a play of his, sight unseen."

"They would," Thomas concurred, "if Pierre could give them the script."

Madeleine stared blankly. "Why couldn't he?"

"For the simple reason that he hasn't got it," replied Thomas. "Floridor was so eager to begin rehearsals that he convinced Pierre to give him the script before having it copied. A copy was made in Paris as soon as the actors had learned their roles, but I know for a fact that both the original manuscript and the copy were being stored at the theater."

"Do you mean to say," said Madeleine in disbelief, "that the only remaining copy of *The Liar* sits on the table at the Rue de la Perle?"

"I won't be certain until I've spoken to Floridor," Thomas said, "but I believe so."

Madeleine leaned back in her chair, staggered by this turn of events. An idea crossed her mind.

"In the end it means little," she said pensively. "All your brother will have to do is hire a scribe and have the Marais actors recite their memorized speeches for him. He'll soon have a fresh copy of the play in hand."

"Not likely," replied Thomas, shaking his head. "If Pierre is desperate to have a new copy of the script written down, they'll understand that it can't be for them. They can't stage the play again until their theater is rebuilt. They'll realize he intends to give the play to the Hôtel de Bourgogne. They will refuse."

Madeleine nodded. "What will you say to your brother?"

"When I admit I have a copy of the play," he replied, "he'll be so relieved that he'll be well disposed toward my suggestion that the Illustre Théâtre should present it until the Théâtre du Marais has been rebuilt."

Madeleine stood abruptly, knocking over her chair in the process.

"The Illustre Théâtre?" she exclaimed. "The Illustre Théâtre might stage *The Liar*? For several months?"

Thomas stood, picked up Madeleine's chair, and held it for her as she reseated herself.

"In any event," he continued in a matter-of-fact tone of voice, "a comedy of this sort is not well suited to the Bourgogne troupe."

"But once he finds out how you came into possession of the play," countered Madeleine, still in disbelief, "he won't be so amenable. Won't you be forced to tell him you copied it behind his back?"

"I'll give him a close enough approximation of the truth to assuage my conscience," said Thomas, "while flattering his pride. My brother is not immune to adulation and I've got long experience of appeasing him. I'll say I copied the manuscript because I planned to try my hand at writing and wanted to study the work of a master. I did indeed write a comedy, then chanced upon you at the fair and discovered you were the lead actress of a new troupe."

"Imagine he still says no," she insisted.

"My brother has nothing to lose by giving a promising new troupe a chance for a few months, just to prove themselves. I'll emphasize the gratitude that you in particular would feel toward him, Mademoiselle. In matters of gallantry my brother can be an exceedingly generous man, especially with a person of your talent, poise, and . . . beauty."

"His generosity pales next to yours," exclaimed Madeleine, placing her hand gently on Thomas's. "You have saved me and those I love, including your own rival. I have never before encountered goodness of that ilk."

Thomas's face caught fire, as if an inner spark long dormant had kindled. He carried her hand to his lips.

"One last time I must ask you," he cried. "Marry me! Let me devote myself to your happiness. I bear Jean-Baptiste no ill will, but are you secure in your choice? I am not incomparable in goodness, only in my love for you. All I ask you to do is listen to your heart."

Her heart. It had caused her little but grief, it seemed, since she began listening to it that evening in Nîmes with Jean-Baptiste nearly two years ago. Perhaps it was time for her head to take over; Thomas's fine qualities were so numerous that her mind could hardly encompass them. He was perceptive, kind, attentive, and courageous. One could not imagine a more ferocious devotion than he had shown her. Jean-Baptiste might never develop feelings of the sort for her. He was fond of her, of that she was sure. But she was gradually coming to understand that he needed to prove himself more than he needed her. Until he did so, their feelings for each other would be askew, her adoration eclipsing his affection and his occasional bouts of manly protectiveness poorly compensating her willingness to sacrifice everything to help him succeed.

Yet even her head had to recognize that the very success Jean-Baptiste so desperately needed if their love was ever to become equal now seemed within reach. Was it not reasonable to pursue her dream of being truly loved by helping him to pursue his dream of fame and glory?

One thing was clear: she would do all she could to free Thomas from his doomed passion. Dreams often remained elusive, as well she knew, and Thomas would ask nothing better than to wait for her. But she would not hold him hostage.

"It pains me to hurt you once again," she said, "but I cannot marry you. My heart will allow me no other reply."

Thomas stood and bowed. "In that case there is nothing more to be added," he said in a monotone. "When I return to Rouen, if my brother agrees to offer *The Liar* to the Illustre Théâtre, I'll send word to you immediately. Our paths may not cross again soon," he went on, his voice breaking. He extracted a small object from his doublet and handed it to her. "This will remind you that you are always in my thoughts."

She brought it close to the chandelier. It was a silver signet ring, the seal on its face composed of a heart pierced by two arrows with the letters *TC* appearing in the two drops of blood that flowed from the double wound.

She examined it. "I cannot accept this," she murmured.

"Please reconsider, Mademoiselle," said Thomas in a whisper. "If you fear your lover's jealousy, the ring need not be worn, but only kept within reach. If you require my assistance, now or in the future, have it sent to me. Wherever I am, I'll follow the messenger to your side."

Madeleine placed the ring carefully into a pocket. Later she would thread it onto one of the laces of her bodice for safe keeping, but for now it would be ill advised to draw attention to the shape of her midsection.

"It seems I am destined to spend my life thanking you," she said. "I'll do my utmost never to avail myself of this gift. One day you'll take a wife, Monsieur, and have obligations to her that will take precedence. And that is as it should be."

"However impossible it seems," said Thomas ruefully, "to deny it at my age would be foolhardy. But if one day you discover I've married or taken a mistress, please don't ever assume that I've forgotten you. Think only of Don Fadrique's words in my play:

> *If I seem to love another you must never think,*
> *Into whatever blind confusion you might sink,*
> *That my motivation is other than to show*
> *That loving in silence is a skill that I well know.*

He bowed again and was gone.

***

The days crawled by in anticipation of news from Rouen. With the Théâtre du Marais in ruins and the Bourgogne troupe in rehearsals, audiences crowded into the Illustre Théâtre, but Madeleine was keenly aware that their success was unlikely to last unless Thomas's plan succeeded and Pierre gave them permission to stage *The Liar*. In spite of her worries, at least she slept soundly, increasingly fatigued by her pregnancy, which was entering its fourth month.

One morning she was awakened by a voice calling out from the gate. The others had left for the theater early to brush costumes and spruce up props.

"Good morning," a young valet in livery said crisply when she opened the door. "I have a message for Mademoiselle Béjart."

"I am Madeleine Béjart," she replied, pulling her shawl closer about her shoulders.

"Please receive this letter," he said, bowing and extending an envelope.

She lit a fire, drew up an armchair. The seal was identical to the one on Thomas's ring.

> *Rouen, 20 January 1644*
> *Most Esteemed Mademoiselle,*
>
> *I pray that this letter finds you well. I arrived home yesterday to discover my brother in a pitiful state. News of the conflagration had reached Rouen by King's messenger. Pierre had sent an urgent message to Floridor to inquire about the safety of the manuscripts only to discover what I myself had ascertained before leaving Paris: that they had both been destroyed.*
>
> *I told Pierre of the additional manuscript and the Illustre Théâtre. He agreed with my suggestion that until the Marais troupe reopens its doors,* The Liar *should be yours. If you wish, you may also continue with* The Promises of Chance *and make my name public. I did not anticipate how pleased my brother would be to hear I've taken up the pen. He assures me he'll help me however he can, just as I have, in my own small way, done my best to be of assistance to you.*
>
> *Your faithful servant,*
> *Thomas Corneille*

They would perform *The Liar* with Pierre Corneille's blessing! Jean-Baptiste, a mediocre lover when spewing forth Thomas's sentimental notions, would shine as Pierre's conniving suitor. Madeleine would invent some justification for having lied about the authorship of the play but Jean-Baptiste, ecstatic at this godsend, would hardly even register what she said.

Her elation was interrupted by a twinge of discomfort from deep within her belly. Such occurrences were now fairly regular when she was seated for too long. She stood and paced the room, collecting her thoughts.

A watershed had been reached with the wonderful news about *The Liar*, but what about Thomas's child? She could not hide the pregnancy indefinitely. How would Jean-Baptiste react to discovering that she was expecting a child whose father he would believe himself to be?

In terms of the future of the Illustre Théâtre, continuing to conceal her condition might not actually benefit the troupe in the long run, for if she worked for as long as possible, she might be forced to step aside at a moment's notice. Unless Geneviève was carefully coached and able to rehearse the roles she'd be taking over in the two plays she would be a poor replacement. Madeleine's child would have been endangered without benefit to anyone.

No, there was only one solution: to find an excuse to leave Paris without revealing the true cause of her departure. She must step aside and give Jean-Baptiste freedom to seal his success.

But what reason could she give for a sudden departure? More than half a year after Armande's death Madeleine was still haunted by the question of why this child, who unlike the stillborn daughter of the Comte de Modène had been the product of Madeleine's true love for the baby's father, had not survived. Had her death been a sign from God that Jean-Baptiste was not prepared to devote himself to either Madeleine or the child? The child she was now carrying was the product of the love of both parents, though not for each other: Thomas's love for her and her love for Jean-Baptiste. If it was God's will, perhaps this child would live and, while never making up for the loss of Armande, provide some measure of consolation.

Why, if the baby was a girl, she too could be named Armande. Not another soul besides Madeleine herself and Catherine, who had tended to Armande, knew that the child had died.

The baby she was carrying could be raised in Armande's place!

The daring conceit left her in a stupor. She racked her brain for obstacles to the plan but found none. Neither her family nor her friends had ever seen Armande, so there would not have to be any resemblance between the two half-sisters, the deceased Armande and the living one.

As for finding a reason to leave Paris without revealing her pregnancy, she'd use the very fiction of Armande's survival as an excuse. She'd say that Armande was ill and needed her!

The door swung open. As if conjured up by her ruminations, in walked Jean-Baptiste.

"Good morning, or is it afternoon?" he said, sounding besieged and rubbing his eyes. "Are you just out of bed? I wish I could say the same for myself. I'm a walking shipwreck!"

"You look like one," agreed Madeleine. "Where are the others?"

"They'll be along," he replied. "They're finishing up at the theater. My head is splitting!" He slumped onto a chair and rested his elbows on the table.

Madeleine sat down across from him, rumpled his hair and spoke in a teasing voice.

"Oh? Perhaps you're not going to bed early enough for a growing boy."

He grumbled something inarticulate and let his head fall onto his folded arms. "I wish I *were* still growing," he moaned.

"Perhaps life would be easier if I could see it from higher up, like Master Thomas Corneille, or even you."

It had been a long while since he'd alluded to her one-inch height advantage. Madeleine walked over and lifted his chin from his knuckles. His eyes were dreary.

"I've just received a letter this morning," she said, "a letter with thrilling news, and I won't find a better time to deliver it. It's so exciting," she added, trying to get a rise out of him, "that you'll have trouble believing your ears."

"All right, get it over with," he muttered.

"A letter has come," she said, "just this morning. From Thomas."

"Oh, him," said Jean-Baptiste with a pout. "The author of our *masterpiece*, the one who tricked us by briefly giving us one play worth putting on before leaving us with . . ." He sat up straight and shook his head. "Forgive me, my sweet. We all observed that *The Promises of Chance* is quite serviceable if Don Fadrique is played by one who believes in *true love*, like Master Corneille himself. But I'll never be very good at it, will I?"

"Help has arrived," said Madeleine quickly to avoid giving him or herself an answer to his damnable question. "*The play worth putting on*, as you dubbed it, is ours!"

His jaw dropped. He stared blankly into space.

"Just imagine," she ran on, "it turns out *The Teller of Tales* isn't actually entitled *The Teller of Tales* and Thomas Corneille is not the play's author."

"He's not? Who is?"

"Pierre Corneille." She paused to leave time for a burst of enthusiasm but none was forthcoming. "*The Teller of Tales* is none other than *The Liar*. Thomas acquired a copy of the manuscript before it was to open at the Marais. He wanted to help us get off the ground but realized it would have to be performed anonymously, under a different title, and only once, or else Pierre would get wind of it. So he told me it was his own creation. The rest you know."

"Why are we being offered it now?" asked Jean-Baptiste in a rising tone.

"That's all Thomas told me," Madeleine answered breezily. "The choice was between the Hôtel de Bourgogne and us and Pierre decided to give us a chance. We have been granted permission to perform the play until the Théâtre du Marais reopens." There was still no clear reaction from Jean-Baptiste. "Are you not pleased?"

"Certainly," he said, patting her hand. His features and his voice brightened. "This is excellent news." He stood and, stretching across the table, gave Madeleine a firm but brusque kiss on the lips.

There was a pause. On the spur of the moment Madeleine blurted out: "I received another letter this morning. From Catherine."

"You're certainly popular," teased Jean-Baptiste, his good humor finally restored. "Who is this Catherine?"

He had forgotten the name of the woman purportedly looking after their child!

"Armande's nurse," Madeleine replied. "She's expecting another child herself and fears that with Armande's being so small and sickly, and without the attention of her own mother . . ." She turned away to hide her anguish. "I must go to her," she whispered.

"But with you away, who will play Clarice?"

"Geneviève can replace me. I mustn't delay my departure for more than a few days. I didn't want to upset you, but Catherine says in her letter that the girl is ill."

"Perhaps you should leave today," said Jean-Baptiste frostily. "Why not?"

"She didn't say the child's life was in danger," said Madeleine, masking her pain at his tone. "I'd ask nothing better than to leave immediately but Geneviève will need help with her rehearsals if she's to take over quickly."

"Fine. I'll manage nicely without you," he said in a monotone that cut her to the quick. "You must leave tomorrow at the latest. We have not only ourselves to consider but Armande. I'm surprised you could be so selfish as to risk our daughter's life!"

CHAPTER 23

In Which Our Heroine Is Admitted by Her Mother to the Female Liars' Guild

The family greeted with jubilation the announcement that they had permission to stage *The Teller of Tales*, which was none other than Pierre Corneille's new comedy. More sobering was word of Armande's illness and Madeleine's departure, set for the following day.

After supper, as Madeleine was arranging clothing and other items in a trunk, she looked up to find Marie Hervé, having spent the entire day sniveling, standing and staring at her with her most implacable gaze.

"I don't need your help," said the younger woman, though Marie Hervé had offered none. "I've nearly finished." No reply. "For goodness' sake, Mother, go to bed," she snapped.

Marie Hervé sat down heavily. Her mouth set. "Not till we've discussed your trip."

"Armande needs me and I must go to her," said Madeleine. "What is there to discuss?" She rearranged shawls and woolen stockings to make room for a large beribboned hat, purchased out of the generous sum that Jean-Baptiste had given her for her stay now that the troupe's prospects had improved. The hat was a gift for Catherine, who wasn't expecting her.

"Of course you must," Marie Hervé retorted, "but I'm going with you."

Madeleine scowled. "No you're not. You're needed in Paris. The others will be busy night and day with the new production. Who will cook and look after Louis?" The youngest of the Béjarts, now fourteen, fell into mischief when left to his own devices.

"Then bring Armande here," retorted Marie Hervé, crossing her arms.

Madeleine peered at her, then averted her eyes. Marie Hervé was no longer the force of nature she'd been, but when backed into a corner she could still stare down a charging bull. "Travel in winter with a sick child," said Madeleine with faux indignation, "to breathe filthy city air?"

"I didn't mean immediately," sniffed Marie Hervé, "but as soon as she's well enough to make the journey. I'll take better care of her than any country nurse!"

"It's difficult to predict when that might be," said Madeleine less forcefully. "She's not a year old and has been small and sickly from birth."

"What exactly did Catherine say in her letter?" asked Marie Hervé in a disquieting tone.

"Why, just that she feared for Armande's health and I should come as soon as possible," Madeleine replied, reddening. She'd grown accustomed to lying when the need arose, but it was disconcerting having a true connoisseur observing her technique.

"I see," said Marie Hervé. Her eyes narrowed as she stood and extended a hand. "Show me the letter."

Madeleine rearranged items in the trunk. "I'm sorry, Mother," she said. "It was a cold morning and I lit a fire. A draft blew it into the hearth after I read it."

She looked up to find her mother's face aglow. "Forgive me," the older woman said, "now I understand, fool that I am!"

"What do you mean?" protested Madeleine. "I tried to catch hold of it but . . ."

"Not another word," interrupted Marie Hervé. "I don't know what you're hiding but I trust you. A woman who lies always has her reasons." She whispered in her daughter's ear. "You're better at it than you used to be!" she added, kissing her good night.

After closing her trunk Madeleine fell onto her pallet, oddly exhilarated by the day's topsy-turvy events. The thought of the beloved baby she had lost brought her down to earth.

"What matters is that there's to be another Armande," she whispered, addressing the girl's spirit. "She'll never replace you, my dearest, but I do hope that in some small measure your spirit can reside in her body."

Suddenly a worrisome thought popped into Madeleine's head.

What if her baby was a boy?

A slow smile spread over her face. Being welcomed into the liars' guild by Marie Hervé had been strangely heartening.

She would cross that bridge when she got to it.

***

The Liar was a hit; a second show was scheduled on Sundays for the overflow. That in his monthly letters Jean-Baptiste suggested Madeleine's absence was causing no hardship brought her both relief and disappointment. He would include a word of inquiry about Armande's health but never gave a hint of a tender sentiment for Madeleine. Soon Marie Hervé started adding a few words, increasingly desperate in tone, begging Madeleine to return. Doubtless she wanted to make it sound as if someone at least missed her.

Madeleine's replies were brief: Armande was stronger but still needed her. Spring brought the greening of trees and fields and Madeleine thrilled to the miracles of the season. Unlike Françoise born in the fall and the first Armande in the dead of winter, this baby would arrive in the most beautiful part of the summer. That alone boded well for the child's survival.

Madeleine's third daughter came into the world on July 15, 1644, just before supper, as if this child of voracious appetites had timed the event. Something about her eyes was vaguely reminiscent of her namesake but one could hardly miss the sharp contrast between the first Armande and this stout squawking girl. The red-faced newborn clamored for nourishment and was constantly in motion. She was an unusually large child, especially promising in that it would facilitate passing her off as older than she was.

In mid-August, with Madeleine's return imminent, it was time to bring Catherine in on her plan. It wouldn't be easy explaining things. Catherine wasn't aware that Madeleine had kept the first Armande's death a secret, and now Marie Hervé's original plan of being taken for the first Armande's mother would have to be combined with the substitution of the living Armande for the dead one. Moreover, in spite of Catherine's skills and talents, this kindly peasant woman seemed disinterested in stringing two thoughts together in a logical manner.

Each morning for a week as she did her chores, Catherine listened to Madeleine repeat the story point by point, but her bewilderment showed it was to no avail. Finally Madeleine vowed to sit down with her when there were no distractions and explain it all in the clearest way possible.

The next afternoon, after finishing with the cows, Catherine looked up to find Madeleine standing before her. The peasant woman smiled to see this beautiful lady with her fine clothing and city ways holding her baby in the doorway of a homely barn. She gestured for Madeleine to enter and pulled two milking stools close together. Madeleine seated herself, bounced the baby on her lap, and said, "If you've got a moment I'd like to go over it one more time."

Catherine nodded. She was a portly woman of about thirty with long blond hair and a broad cheerful face animated by lovely hazel eyes. Spending all of her waking hours hard at work, at any moment of the day or night she was game for a laugh.

Madeleine took a deep breath. "As you remember," she began, "I gave birth to the first Armande last February. Mother wanted people to believe the child was hers and told them she'd given birth the previous spring, while she was with you, recuperating from her illness."

"I see," said Catherine, "but I forget why."

"If people believed I was childless, I would have a better chance of marrying one day."

"That was only good sense," rejoined Catherine. "So everyone thinks the child who died was your mother's?"

"Not quite. As I've told you, no one else knows that the child died."

"Not even your mother or Jean-Baptiste?" Catherine asked. "Why not, Mademoiselle?"

"I've already explained," Madeleine replied abruptly, "that that is not your concern."

"Please forgive me," said Catherine in a humble tone. "I didn't mean to pry."

"There's nothing to forgive," Madeleine reassured her. "But now you understand that everyone, including my mother and Jean-Baptiste, believes that the first Armande is still alive."

"Yes, I understand, Mademoiselle," intoned Catherine, nodding vehemently.

"Now they also believe," Madeleine said, "that I've come to the country to care for Armande, who's been ill."

"That much is true, in a way," said Catherine. "She was so ill that she died, poor thing."

"What I mean to say," said Madeleine, regrouping, "is that you and I are the only ones to know I've had another baby. When I left Paris nobody knew I was expecting a child."

"Just think how happy they'll be!" cried Catherine.

"The point is," Madeleine persisted, "that we're going to tell my family that *this* child is the other one, the one born last February, a year-and-a-half ago."

Catherine gave her a look. "But Mademoiselle," she started to object, then thought better of it. After a short pause she said, "So everyone will believe she was born last February?"

"Almost," said Madeleine encouragingly, "you're getting the gist of it. Jean-Baptiste and my family will believe she was born last February, but no one else will."

"And what will the others believe?" asked Catherine.

"That she was born when Marie Hervé was recuperating with you, two years ago," said Madeleine. "Don't you remember? That's the story we told them last February, when the first Armande was born."

Catherine nodded again, this time more convincingly. She counted something out on her fingers and looked up.

"So from February of last year, when the other Armande was born, to July of this year, when this Armande was born, your family and Jean-Baptiste will believe this Armande is nearly a year-and-a-half older than she is." Catherine paused. "And from the time when Marie Hervé was with us recovering two summers ago," she went on, "to this summer when you gave birth to the child you're holding, everybody else will believe she's two years older than she is?"

"You have it at last!" cried Madeleine. She stood and embraced Catherine, then grasped her hands for a celebratory roundelay which ended in a fit of giggles from both women.

Back at the house Catherine asked, "And the christening? What will we tell the priest?"

"Nothing for now," said Madeleine. "We'll wait until she's much bigger, when a priest will believe she's two years older than she really is. Thankfully she's large for her age."

"That she is," laughed Catherine, taking the child and cradling her. A dark thought crossed her mind and she asked, "Do you mean to say that we'll have to lie to the priest?"

"Never you mind about that," Madeleine replied soothingly. "If there's any lying to be done, I'll be the one doing it."

When Madeleine departed for Paris in late August it was almost more than she could bear to leave Armande behind, but at least the child was thriving in a way the first Armande never had. The next evening a carriage deposited Madeleine at the entrance to the Rue de la Perle. She collected her thoughts and prepared to face Jean-Baptiste.

She found Marie Hervé staring into space, her chair the lone piece of furniture in sight.

"Mother, what's wrong?" cried Madeleine, rushing to her side. "What's happened?"

Marie Hervé threw herself into Madeleine's arms. "They've seized the house in Bagnolet," she said, "and now they're threatening to put us out on the street!"

"Why?" asked Madeleine, unable to believe her ears. "And who would do such a thing?"

"His creditors!" Marie Hervé said with a moan. "They come round day after day."

"Father's creditors?" Madeleine cried. "But we finished paying off his debts long ago."

"Not Joseph's," wailed Marie Hervé, "Jean-Baptiste's. The Illustre Théâtre is bankrupt!"

***

Bankrupt! Madeleine had left the troupe on the verge of success. What had gone wrong?

Nothing at first, apparently. Geneviève and Jean-Baptiste spent every spare moment at the theater, allegedly rehearsing. She did well in both roles and the two comedies often sold out.

It gradually emerged, however, that Jean-Baptiste had been hard at work on a tragedy with Geneviève assisting him. In March he announced that his *Cleopatra* was ready to perform. After the Easter break, over the objections of the entire troupe except for Geneviève, he insisted they put the comedies aside and première his tragedy, with her in the title role.

The story of ill-fated passion, chock-a-block with diatribes about duty and destiny, lacked a discernible plot. Geneviève as the fabled queen and Jean-Baptiste as Mark Anthony alternated these speeches with fondling sessions to signify their devotion in spite of Egypt's and Rome's political divisions. By Act Five the actors couldn't be heard over the public's laughter and hoots.

Jean-Baptiste stayed up every night modifying the script and the following day would have the actors rehearse the changes, which he vowed would turn the play into a sensation.

The public never stopped laughing; they only stopped coming. The nail on the coffin was pounded in by Father Olier at Saint Sulpice who categorically forbade his parishioners to go to see the roiling tale of sin being staged in their midst. Soon the troupe was performing to an empty hall.

Refusing to concede defeat, a panicky Jean-Baptiste borrowed a substantial sum of money to refurbish a theater close to the Louvre, where they would enjoy a larger public and greater tolerance for the royal family's weakness for theater from the local priests. Marie Hervé gave in and offered as collateral Madeleine's house in Bagnolet, but the opening had been repeatedly delayed and Jean-Baptiste, unable to repay his debts, couldn't prevent it from being repossessed. The new theater was now ready but the nightmare far from over, concluded Marie Hervé: other creditors clamored for their money. To whom could they turn?

The two women were sitting together and weeping when the others arrived. Madeleine embraced them, handed Joseph and Louis some coins to buy food, and settled Marie Hervé down as best she could. Finally she pulled Geneviève into the courtyard.

The two sisters sat beneath the poplar. It was a warm evening and Madeleine welcomed the pungent aroma of Paris the memory of which had left her strangely bereft in the country.

"Do I dare ask where Jean-Baptiste is?" Madeleine began in a dispassionate tone.

"I believe he's resting in the loft," said Geneviève uneasily. "He's not been himself."

"He must have heard me arrive," Madeleine observed. "Is there any reason you know of that he hasn't come to greet me?"

"Oh Madeleine," Geneviève suddenly cried, falling into her sister's arms, "we've been such fools! Can you ever forgive us?"

Madeleine stroked her hair, noticing she'd dyed it red in imitation of her own. She was touched by the gesture and said lightly, "It might be easier for me to forgive you if I knew what there was to forgive." To hide her anxiety she forced a laugh. "Or perhaps more difficult."

Geneviève tore a leaf from the poplar and used it as a handkerchief. "Flirting when we were all in Rouen, just to make you angry," she began. "Writing the tragedy in secret. We wanted to do it all without you. We knew better, but in the end you were right. You're always right!" The final words were less self-accusatory in tone and bore a hint of reproach.

"I forgive you," said Madeleine. She hesitated. "Are you and Jean-Baptiste in love?"

With a look of mortification Geneviève shook her head. "I never thought I was in love with him," she said, "and I'm sure he never thought he was in love with me."

"Are you certain?" Madeleine demanded.

Geneviève covered her face and nodded.

"Don't cry, my big girl," said Madeleine, pulling Geneviève's hands away from her face and kissing them. "If I'd had a big sister like myself I'd have done the same." The two sisters laughed. "Just one more question," she went on, "and I want the truth. Does he speak about me?"

"Sometimes," Geneviève replied, "but only good things."

"Has he said what his feelings for me are?" demanded Madeleine.

"He doesn't have to," said Geneviève. "It's clear he worships the ground you walk on."

"I don't believe you!" exclaimed Madeleine.

Geneviève's face set. "Perhaps it was an exaggeration," she said, "but not a lie. He looks up to you. There's nothing more important to him than having your admiration."

"He's never hinted as much to me. Why should he doubt that I admire him?"

"Do you?" asked Geneviève bluntly.

"Of course," Madeleine snapped. "In a way. I certainly love him just as he is."

"I don't question your love," countered Geneviève, "but your esteem. You told him he didn't have the experience to write a tragedy, which was true. Do you think he's a good actor?"

"What's that got to do with it?" Madeleine burst out. She frowned. "His energy and acrobatics please audiences but he's not yet terribly good in other ways. He will be in time."

"If that's what you mean by admiring a man," remarked Geneviève, "I'd hate to hear what you would say about one you looked down upon."

"You asked for my opinion and I gave it. Would you prefer that I lie?" She went on more gently. "Naturally I would never say such a thing to him."

"He feels it anyway," observed Geneviève. "Every man has his pride. I grant you, Jean-Baptiste acts like a buffoon," she concluded philosophically, "but he's no exception to the rule."

Madeleine stared at her. In the past months Geneviève's face had lost all vestiges of youth; though it retained its beauty, it was now the countenance she'd show the world until the onslaught of graying and wrinkles. And it held more wisdom than a big sister is wont to notice.

"How have you become such a connoisseur of men?" Madeleine asked with amusement.

"That is something I'm afraid I'll never be," said Geneviève, standing and stretching like a cat. "What complicated creatures they are! Are they worth all the bother?"

"That's for each woman to determine," Madeleine said. She made her way toward the ladder. "For now, pray for this Christian martyr about to face the lion cub in his den!"

***

A single candle was burning on the other side of the room from where Jean-Baptiste lay. It flickered with Madeleine's passage and she watched her shadow, cast onto his recumbent form, shrink and grow to the rhythm of her movement. He had his back toward her but the tenseness of his position suggested he was awake. She sat beside him on the pallet and rested a hand on his shoulder.

"I'm home," she announced simply.

He began to sob, though he continued to face the wall. After a while his breathing became regular once again. He turned toward her and pulled her close.

"How I've missed you," he said. "I didn't believe you and we're all paying the price for my obstinacy."

"There, there," Madeleine said, rocking him. "We weren't prepared for all we had to face. What was surprising was that we had a real taste of success, not that it was short-lived."

"That was what you were trying to tell me that evening in the courtyard," he intoned, "and then in Rouen and again in Paris. That we needed more time. That I wasn't ready to write a tragedy and we weren't prepared to perform one. I should have listened to you." He sat up and regained his composure. "The new theater is ready. Do we stand a chance of success this time? You may consider yourself our director. Hide nothing, I beg of you."

What good would the truth do him? Caution had already been thrown to the winds. There was no point scurrying after it.

"Perhaps," Madeleine said slowly, "if we work together."

Jean-Baptiste's lips broadened into a smile that deepened his chin dimple and would have made her fall in love with him again if she hadn't remained so.

"That's all I ask," he said. Suddenly brightening, he exclaimed, "I've forgotten to ask you for news. Has Armande recovered?"

"She is well and flourishing," said Madeleine.

"I hope I can meet her soon," said Jean-Baptiste.

Finally he had spoken of their daughter with real interest, but too late.

"Of course, my darling," Madeleine said, "but not now. When the time is right."

CHAPTER 24

In Which Two Buttocks Land on a Prison Bench and Two Others Solve a Mystery

---

The rebuilt Théâtre du Marais had just opened with *The Liar*; Madeleine and Jean-Baptiste could only hope that their new digs would put the Illustre Théâtre back on its feet. By the time it reopened they deemed their revival of *The Promises of Chance* worth seeing—if only there had been people in the audience to share their opinion.

The new theater failed more spectacularly than the old one. By the end of the season it was clear that they would not reopen after Easter and had no way of paying off their debts.

As in the weeks preceding Joseph Béjart's flight from Paris nine years earlier, there again came a time when the family stopped answering the door. In July a visitor arrived whose knock was accompanied by the cry, "Open in the name of Her Majesty, the Queen Regent!" Despite Marie Hervé's frantic whispers, Madeleine answered the door.

There stood a royal bailiff who read from a scroll. "I am under orders to arrest one Jean-Baptiste Poquelin," he proclaimed, "for delinquency of debts. He is to remain in prison until such time as he pays the sum of three hundred *livres*. The Béjart family is hereby given notice that they must vacate this house one month from today. Does the individual I've named reside here?"

"He did, Monsieur," stammered Madeleine, "but he's moved, I don't know where."

"Your name?" demanded the bailiff.

"Madeleine Béjart."

He consulted his scroll and said, "I am also authorized to arrest you. All the members of the Illustre Théâtre are listed on the complaint. I won't leave empty-handed!"

"Nor will you leave this house with Mademoiselle Béjart!" came a cry accompanied by the sound of frenzied footsteps. "I am Jean-Baptiste Poquelin. Arrest me."

Madeleine threw her arms around him. She whispered into his ear, "You fool! You should have run when you had the chance. He never would have arrested me."

Before Jean-Baptiste could reply the bailiff clamped his wrists and dragged him away. As they reached the gate Jean-Baptiste produced a series of absurd grimaces to prove that he considered the situation laughable. Since he preferred it that way, Madeleine shrugged her shoulders, assumed a clownish expression of doom, and waved goodbye.

***

With each passing day Madeleine felt greater distress at what Jean-Baptiste must be suffering. One night toward the end of the summer of 1645 when the house was stuffy and smelled of mold, she rose from her pallet and tiptoed out. She crept into the courtyard and spread a blanket amidst fallen leaves; it was her favorite place to speak to the first Armande. The fragrance of wildflowers wafted on a cool breeze. She gazed at the stars.

"What shall I do?" she whispered. "I've never felt so helpless."

Jacques's feverish face flitted through her mind, reminding her of a day when she'd felt even more powerless. "It's not the same," she murmured, taking the image as a sign from her beloved daughter. "Jacques was beyond assistance. Jean-Baptiste is not." Another image came to her. "Yes, I remember what I did for Jacques. I went to see Grandfather, and for my trouble I was rewarded with insults!"

Why had Armande sent her the memory? Madeleine had not seen Pierre Béjart in nine years and it seemed impossible anything would be gained from seeking him out. And yet however unkind he had been, perhaps he would welcome reconciliation with someone he thought to be his granddaughter. Even misers could feel lonely.

"All right," Madeleine said, "I'll visit him first thing in the morning. But he's unlikely to receive me. What if he doesn't?"

Out of nowhere came strains of music and she relived the night she'd danced with the Comte de Modène at Marion's wedding and disappeared with him into a shed.

"But what of my love for Jean-Baptiste?" she said. "I've already been unfaithful to him once. If I am again, there will be no end to it."

No further wisdom was imparted to her but she vowed not to let another day go by without taking action. In the morning she would approach Pierre Béjart. If he turned down her plea for assistance, she would pay a visit on the Comte de Modène.

***

The sun had scarcely risen when Madeleine knocked on Pierre Béjart's door. A young scullery maid opened it and said in a breathless voice, "Yes, Mademoiselle? May I help you?"

"I'd like a word with Maître Béjart," Madeleine said. "I'm his granddaughter."

"How did you learn of it?" exclaimed the girl.

"Learn of what?"

"Never mind, you've come just in time. The doctor said Monsieur wouldn't pass the night. The priest has come and gone. It won't be long now. May God have mercy on him!"

"But where are his sons, his other grandchildren?" asked Madeleine.

"They abandoned him long ago, Mademoiselle," the maid responded, "saying he had a heart of iron. I can't say it's untrue but no man should die alone. Come, follow quickly!"

At the end of a dark corridor a door was pushed open.

"Grandfather?" Madeleine said, approaching the bed.

The movement of his chest was barely perceptible. She sat at his bedside and waited, for what she couldn't say. She'd believed she felt nothing for Pierre Béjart, but as she observed the ravaged face, she pitied this wretched individual as solitary in death as in life.

The breathing slowed. Suddenly Pierre's eyes flew open. In a final moment of lucidity, he recognized his granddaughter.

"Why are you here, my child?" he said.

To ask you for money. Her motive for approaching Pierre today was no more ignoble than in the past; he, not she, had lived a life in which wealth was all. He might find it in his heart to make a last gesture of generosity but, faced with this once arrogant countenance humbled by death, Madeleine couldn't bring herself to utter the words.

"To care for you," she said.

Pierre looked perplexed but pleased.

"Will I see your father before I die?" he asked in a hoarse whisper.

"He's ailing," she replied, "but he's sent me in his place."

"I treated him poorly," mused the old man. "He was the only one who didn't court me for my fortune." She stroked his hair and he smiled at this unexpected human contact *in extremis.* He mustered his dwindling strength to focus his failing eyes on her. "You too, Granddaughter," he croaked. "The last time I saw you . . ." He paused to draw a breath. "I can't remember why I cursed you but I'm sorry. I give you my blessing."

He reached for her hand. His was cold in spite of the heat of the morning. She put it to her lips. And it was with tranquility on his face that he drew his final breath.

She sat alone with him until the scullery maid entered and emitted a cry.

"Are you able to prepare him for the priests?" Madeleine asked.

"I've never touched a dead man," the girl moaned. "I beg of you, don't ask it of me."

"Are there no other servants?" Madeleine inquired.

"I'm the last, Mademoiselle," responded the maid. "One by one the others left."

"Go to Saint Paul's," Madeleine said wearily, "and ask the priest to come in two hours."

The maid departed. Madeleine hauled fresh water from the well and gathered clean rags. She washed Pierre's body with care, imagining herself elsewhere so as to be able to execute the unbearable task. After she'd finished the front of the body, she turned him over.

On Pierre's left buttock appeared a birthmark in the shape of a crescent moon. It was identical to the one she had seen on Joseph Béjart the day he died.

***

By the time the priest had come and gone it was mid-afternoon. Back at the Rue de la Perle the family had just finished a sparse meal and Madeleine, after refusing what little remained, chased the others away to speak to Marie Hervé alone in the scullery.

"Where have you been, Daughter?" asked the older woman, who was rinsing out a pot.

"You won't believe me," replied Madeleine. "I come from the deathbed of Pierre Béjart."

The pot clattered to the floor. Marie Hervé sat abruptly, anointed her forehead with the brown washwater to revive herself and said, "That miserable wretch is still infesting this earth?"

"He was this morning, but no longer," responded Madeleine.

Marie Hervé spat on the floor and said, "May God not change His mind! I'd like to replace Saint Peter for a single hour to turn him away!"

"So I thought myself," said Madeleine, "until this morning."

"Why were you visiting Pierre Béjart?" demanded Marie Hervé.

"Never mind why. There's something I must ask. It has to do with Father."

A smile hovered on Marie Hervé's lips and her eyes focused on a distant vision, as if what separated her from the man she continued to long for was not time but space.

In few words Madeleine told her mother of Anne Béjart's deathbed confession to Joseph and the shocking revelation that Pierre was not his father. She held back the circumstances of her learning of it eight years earlier, after Joseph was mortally wounded by the Comte de Modène, and Joseph's story of the birthmark Anne had told him he shared with his real father.

"Well?" asked Marie Hervé. "What is it you're asking of me?"

"Isn't it obvious?" Madeleine burst out. "Why must the simple truth be pried from your lips? Was Pierre Joseph's father, and if he was, why did Grandmother Anne say otherwise?"

"There's a reason I'm stingy with the truth," said Marie Hervé, lifting her chin with dignity, "and I'll explain it in a moment. As for your other questions, they're not as simple as you seem to believe. Yes, Pierre Béjart was Joseph's father. Anne told him otherwise because I asked her to, just before she died."

No reaction from Madeleine. Marie Hervé pecked her cheek and said, "Why do you stand there like a statue of the Virgin? As you might suspect I had my reasons. Come sit and listen."

She led Madeleine into the *salle* and took the one remaining chair; Madeleine, standing, crossed her arms. Marie Hervé gathered her thoughts. It occurred to Madeleine that her mother lied spontaneously but required time to present the truth.

"Your father." Marie Hervé sighed, as if the words were a statement. "I lost my heart to him in the time it takes to sneeze or I never would have married him, for a simpleton could see he'd never be prosperous enough to buy two loaves of bread at a time." Her voice became firmer. "But I *did* marry him, and all too soon I saw that if we were to survive, it was up to me.

"One thing was on Joseph's mind night and day: his father. All Pierre cared about was gold. He considered Joseph worthless because he had other ideas. Joseph would sooner have died than be like him. And yet he remained in thrall to Pierre. He depended on his father to find him work but carried out his duties poorly, and time after time he was dismissed or quit. The children started coming. I was at wits' end! I worked day and night and still we had nothing.

"Once when Joseph had lost another position I prayed to the Virgin Mary and she heeded my prayer by reminding me of a tale my mother used to tell. It was of a farmer's son who hated his father and the hard life that was theirs until a vision came to him and said he was the son of a prince who'd fallen in love with a peasant girl and left her with child. From that day forward the man was content, for he knew he was better than the life he was forced to lead."

"A fine lesson your mother's tale gave you!" Madeleine interjected. "The man should have moved heaven and earth to regain his rightful station."

"You're Joseph all over again," cried Marie Hervé, "prideful and haughty!" She went on in a quieter voice. "Haven't you learned that pride can be a curse as well as a blessing? You're strong, so for you it's a blessing. Joseph was not, so for him it was a curse." She shook her head. "I understood him so poorly! I had no idea what effect my plan would have."

So at the root of it all was one of Marie Hervé's *plans*. And Madeleine had felt bad about not telling her mother of Joseph's death! "All right, out with it," she ordered.

Marie Hervé sat back in her chair and closed her eyes.

"Joseph's mother, Anne, was deathly ill," she began. "He was beside himself when we went to bid her adieu. Even Pierre wept, for Anne was the only creature he loved as much as money. I wondered how I might spare Joseph from continuing to be tormented by the father he detested now that he was about to lose the mother he adored. All at once it came to me.

"I begged to see Anne alone. I revealed my plan. I wasn't fond of your grandmother nor she of me but she knew Joseph well and loved him dearly. She agreed to tell him his real father was a fine nobleman whose name she couldn't reveal. It would hurt nobody and free Joseph from his anger, allow him to rise above it. I added a few details to make it more believable."

"What details?" Madeleine asked.

"What can it matter now?" replied her mother. "Something to do with a birthmark I had noticed on Joseph that Anne would say matched one that his true father had."

"But what if Pierre had the same one instead?" Madeleine asked carelessly.

"No one would find out," said Marie Hervé. "The mark was in a place, that is . . . It was somewhere no one was likely to see it."

Madeleine pretended to have a coughing fit. Her mother handed her a rag to wipe her face, then concluded her story.

"The rest of it you know, alas!" said Marie Hervé. "My plan only made things worse. Joseph despised Pierre more than ever but couldn't find the strength to strike out on his own. I should have understood his despair and comforted him, God rest his soul! I was blind to it all and have paid for it ever since. Not a day goes by that I don't wish he were with us again!"

Marie Hervé's eyes filled with tears. She had done her best for the man she loved; she too had suffered greatly. What could be said to ease her sadness?

"Forgive me, Mother," Madeleine began. "I said you were stingy with the truth, but you're generous with lies. You've got no reason to blame yourself. You did what you thought best. Father would no more have thrived with the truth than he did with your lies." She embraced her mother, holding her cheek against Marie Hervé's and hugging her tightly as she'd done so often as a little girl.

"Thank you, Daughter," said Marie Hervé. "It's the truth that's stingy, not those who offer or refuse it. What man receives sufficient nourishment from the truth to be content

with his lot? Your father didn't, nor does your Jean-Baptiste."
She stood and collected herself. "Don't be discouraged, my
darling," she said. "The Comte de Modène is far more likely
to give you the money you're about to ask him for than was
Pierre Béjart!"

***

Fortunately it happened to be a performance day;
Madeleine could approach the Comte as he waited for
Marion in front of the Théâtre du Marais. An outfit squir-
reled away when the assets of the Illustre Théâtre were
being auctioned off, a blue taffeta gown and velvet bodice with billowing sleeves, lifted Madeleine's spirits. She
braided her hair and made use of a box of unused makeup.
Night was falling when she saw the Comte arrive. She pretended not to notice him.

"Good evening, Mademoiselle," he said and she looked up,
as if startled. He took her hand, kissed it, and held it for longer
than etiquette allowed.

"Good evening, Monsieur le Comte," she said with a curtsy.
"Are you waiting for my aunt? Have you seen her perform in
The Liar?"

"I have," said the Comte without elaboration. "I can safely
say it's not for Marion that you're waiting. Yet I was given to
believe your Jean-Baptiste was not in this troupe."

"Quite true, Monsieur," she replied shortly.

"Please forgive me," he rejoined, "if I've happened upon an
indiscretion."

Had the Comte de Modène acquired a sense of humor? She thought from his manner that he still desired her but he'd said nothing to that effect and yet joked about an imaginary rival!

"I've been meaning to call on you," he said less ambiguously. "Shall we go for a stroll?"

"If Marion should arrive and you're not here," Madeleine observed, "she'll be furious."

"Yes, she will," he answered, "but she will wait for me nevertheless."

It was the time of the Dog Star, the indolent summer days when aristocratic patrons took refuge on their country estates; for once the arcades of the Place Royale were quiet. A garden had been planted since the time of the Comte's and Joseph Béjart's combat, a statue of Louis XIII erected as a warning against duelers. Might it have preserved her father's life, as she could not?

"I hope you'll forgive my brashness, Monsieur le Comte," she said, "but I'm no longer a timid girl. It was for you I was waiting. My situation is desperate. I have none other to turn to."

The Comte nodded, indicating that she was to continue.

"I'm sure you've heard," she began, "that our troupe has failed and we're heavily in debt. Jean-Baptiste is in prison, my family destitute. My tale must seem familiar." In spite of her desperation she laughed and shook her head. "It comes to me, Monsieur le Comte, that I have made little progress in my life since the day we met."

"I beg to differ," replied the Comte in a voice she'd never heard. "It is I who have made little progress, since it's still of you that I think."

"And Marion?" Madeleine asked wryly.

"She amuses me," he responded, reverting to his usual flat tone. "She once offered me consolation, and when I returned to Paris three years ago I found her charming."

"Consolation for what?" Madeleine asked.

"Mademoiselle," he cautioned, "there are matters one does not discuss."

"Please forgive me, Monsieur," she said. "All I meant to say was, why choose Marion when a hundred others could have offered you comfort just as well?"

"Because when I made her acquaintance," he said, "she reminded me of you."

"Of me?" cried Madeleine. "But you left me for her before you departed for your lands!"

"I didn't abandon you," the Comte replied stiffly. "It was you who were indifferent, grateful for my help but nothing else. I didn't have your heart any more than my wife had mine."

"Your wife?" she exclaimed.

"Yes, Mademoiselle," he went on, ill at ease to speak of intimate matters even to a former mistress. "When I met you I was already married. My father had forced me to wed. My wife, Marguerite, refused to accompany me to Paris, for she never felt more than friendship for me, nor I for her. She died bearing me a son," he said, his voice barely wavering. "My father succumbed to the coughing sickness shortly thereafter, just before I came back to the city."

"Please accept my condolences," Madeleine said. "Why didn't you tell me?"

"By then you had left Paris," he responded, "so I took up again with Marion even though she'd feuded with your family.

Her dolt of a husband, Étienne L'Hermite, who imagines himself a *grand seigneur*, was so impressed with the circles I traveled in that he considered it a veritable honor that I was bedding his wife. After you returned I discovered that another man had captured your heart."

"And still possesses it," she interjected, "as you yourself are aware."

"But tonight," he rushed on, "seeing you again, I can resist no longer. Had I been unmarried at that time and free to choose a wife without my father's permission, I'd have asked for your hand. Though I dare not expect your indulgence, in all humility I ask you for it now."

Was there no second way to interpret his words? How was it possible that in spite of the difference in their stations, this man who had rarely expressed stronger feelings for her than a statue was announcing after eight years' absence that he wished to make her his bride?

"I'm unworthy of such an honor, Monsieur," she said, "and cannot be your wife."

In spite of his claim of humility his eyes flashed. "And the reason?" he asked.

"Because I love another," she replied simply.

"This Jean-Baptiste," the Comte pursued, "what does he offer you beside his heart?"

"Nothing," she said, turning away. "His heart is all I wish for. Although if I'm honest with myself," she added, "I cannot say he's truly offered it to me, or accepted mine."

"That foolish boy from Carnival," the Comte went on, "has been refusing you his heart?"

"Not refusing it, Monsieur," she said slowly, "but not offering it either. He needs me, that much I know. And right now, it must be enough."

Why was she confiding in the Comte? Was it because, against his custom, he had offered a halting confession of his own feelings? She turned back to face him, expecting to find anger at her refusal. Instead he pulled a bag from the inner pocket of his doublet.

"What is the price of liberating your foolish boy?"

"Three hundred *livres*. His debt is far greater, but with that sum he can be freed for now."

The Comte placed the bag in the palm of her hand and closed her fingers around it.

"You'll find five hundred *livres* in this purse," he said. "They were to be given to Marion this evening in recognition of her indulgences, but you have greater need of the money than she and are far more worthy of receiving it."

"How can I thank you, Monsieur?" Madeleine cried, pressing the bag to her breast.

"There's no need, Mademoiselle," said he, "not even in the usual manner, although you were intending to do so if necessary, were you not?" She said nothing, not certain whether it was true. "I am surely a fool to pass up what you might have offered," he continued with a sardonic smile, "but your thoughts would have been elsewhere, and that would not have been pleasing."

He walked her home. At the gate she said, "Come in. Mother will be happy to see you."

"Forgive me, Mademoiselle, but I must return to face Marion's wrath." His face assumed a hapless expression of which Madeleine would not have thought him capable when she first knew him. He took a few steps, then turned and said, "You may expect two letters of introduction from me tomorrow. One to the Duc d'Épernon, an old friend, the patron of a traveling troupe, and the other to Charles Dufresne, director of the troupe. I wish you godspeed."

He bowed deeply. Before she could say a word he was gone.

CHAPTER 25

In Which a Gentleman Belatedly—and Mistakenly—Loses His Heart

Madeleine was touched by her brother Joseph's offer to accompany her to bail out Jean-Baptiste but preferred to go alone; Joseph was a poor liar and likely to compromise the tale she had concocted to spare Jean-Baptiste the further humiliation of being rescued by his mistress's former lover. The recently deceased Pierre Béjart, she would say, had left her a sum sufficient to cover Jean-Baptiste's bail, while an acquaintance from the Troupe du Vent had provided letters of introduction for a traveling company in the South with whom they could join forces. Freshly liberated from his prison cell, Jean-Baptiste listened to Madeleine and nodded without a word. Had she ordered him to pitch himself headfirst into the Seine from the Pont Neuf, she felt he would have reacted in a similar fashion.

The entire family would follow Madeleine and Jean-Baptiste to the South. The reprieve from the debts incurred by the Illustre Théâtre being temporary, they might make another attempt at performing in the capital if at a later time they scraped together the money to repay them all. In the middle of the night they boarded a carriage for Bordeaux, where they would meet up with the new troupe.

Madeleine shed a tear as they crossed the city walls at the Porte Saint-Jacques. She knew the hardships of the life they'd be leading; she had withstood them before and could do so again. What saddened her the most was that she would be far from Armande. The little one would have to stay with Catherine in the country until she was old enough to look the age she was purported to be.

In Bordeaux Charles Dufresne welcomed them into his troupe with open arms. He had recently lost his main actress and was pleased to have a new leading lady in the lovely Madeleine Béjart. For the time being Jean-Baptiste would have to content himself with smaller parts; he received the information with the same listless expression that never seemed to leave his face.

How Madeleine missed the exuberant dreamer she had occasionally belittled but always adored! To all appearances he had ceased to exist. In comedies his acrobatics were frenetic but his lines delivered in an enervated fashion, as if the energy he expended to leap about the stage should earn him a dispensation from communicating in language. In tragedies he recited the most exalted soliloquies with a hint of cynicism. And yet Monsieur Dufresne was not displeased with this melancholy young man whose unsettling techniques captured the public's attention.

That Jean-Baptiste had not insisted on meeting Armande simplified matters. Marie Hervé, despite having cottoned on to some sort of deception regarding Armande, insisted that the little girl would be better off with them, an idea Madeleine sadly vetoed. And yet she longed for the time when she could introduce Marie Hervé to the girl the world would believe to be her daughter, Jean-Baptiste to the child he thought was his.

***

The troupe returned to Paris at Easter each year to replenish their supplies and replace departing actors; Madeleine's yearly trips to Catherine's farm to visit Armande were a source of both delight and torment. The little girl would shriek with excitement at the sight of the beautiful lady who brought gifts and coddled her as Catherine never seemed to have time to do, while the lady's departure some days later elicited cries of fury. At Easter of 1649, when Armande was going on five and the family thought she was six, it was agreed that she was precocious enough to pass for seven, which would be her legal age, all the more so as Madeleine had continuously harped on how small her tall daughter was. A priest in Catherine's village was told that due to a family crisis the child had not been christened as an infant and that no one could recall her precise date of birth. The baptismal certificate thus read that Armande Béjart, the tenth child and fifth surviving child of

Marie Hervé and Joseph Béjart, was born in 1642, exact date unknown. The child's godmother was listed as her oldest sister, Madeleine Béjart.

Madeleine's intention had been to take Armande on the road with the troupe, but political turmoil foiled her plan. Five years after Louis XIII's death in 1643, France was rent by a civil war pitting the nobles against the boy-king Louis XIV and his mother, the Queen Regent, Anne of Austria. By 1649 the Parisian revolt had been squashed, the conflict displaced to the provinces; it was safer to have Armande living in the capital than to expose her to the vagaries of the road. The family's debts had been repaid and a long stay in Paris presented no legal problems. Marie Hervé, weary of traveling, welcomed the prospect of settling down with Louis, her youngest son, and her putative daughter, Armande. One last time Madeleine left for the country, this time to bring her daughter to Paris, where Marie Hervé's new lodgings on the Rue de la Lune would soon be available.

Armande had never been further from home than Catherine and her husband could take her in their oxcart; the news of her trip to Paris was met with squeals of joy. One fine day in late April, with the smell of early flowers in the air and a bright sky to guide them on their way, Madeleine and Armande boarded a carriage and waved goodbye to the weeping Catherine.

Madeleine had told Armande accurate stories about Paris but the girl imagined the Seine flowed through the streets and stone towers reached the sun. Her gaze fixed on the horizon.

"You'll wear out your eyes before we approach the city walls," Madeleine remarked.

"There are walls around Paris?" asked Armande in wonderment. "Walls are for houses!"

"For cities as well," Madeleine replied, pulling her close. "You'll see, you and Louis and Mother will be living near them. Come out of the wind. I want you to look your best for her."

The girl scowled; was she about to question for the hundredth time if Marie Hervé was really her mother? Instead she asked in a timid voice, "Why don't I have a father?"

"I told you," responded Madeleine, "you had the same father I had. He was a tall and handsome man who loved you dearly. But he went away."

"Why?" queried the child.

"Because men do," Madeleine said after a pause. "I'll explain it when you're older."

"How many other people will there be with us in Paris?" asked Armande anxiously.

"Our brother Louis will be living with you and Mother. Our other brother and sister, Joseph and Geneviève, will be there for a few days before the three of us leave Paris to go on the road." She paused. "Also our friend Jean-Baptiste. Soon you and Mother and Louis will live in a fine house. Until you can move in, we'll all stay in a big room at an inn with soft feather beds."

"I'll have one all to myself!" declared the girl.

"My little Menou says that now," teased Madeleine, using the girl's nickname, "but wouldn't she be lonely in a bed all alone?" She chucked her daughter under the chin. "No, for the time being you'll share my bed or Geneviève's."

Armande was silent and after a while it seemed she was dozing. But she took Madeleine's hand and murmured, "Is Geneviève as beautiful as you are?"

***

It was after nine o'clock in the evening when they arrived at the Fleur-de-Lys, a boarding house near the Palais Royal frequented by actors, but in spite of her yawns Armande insisted on meeting all of the family members before bed-time. Madeleine asked the stable boy to track them down. She dressed her daughter in a light-blue cotton nightgown Marie Hervé had made for her. The girl's curly brown hair was brushed until it glowed, pulled back and gathered in a blue ribbon to reveal the high forehead shared by all of the Béjarts. Thus arrayed, sitting on a chair with her plump legs dangling, Armande was an enchanting sight.

Joseph and Louis were out on the town but Marie Hervé, Geneviève, and Jean-Baptiste soon appeared. Marie Hervé, known to weep at a moment's notice, was the first to greet the child. Between sobs she clasped her tightly and smothered her with kisses. Armande shrank from the old woman. "Come now," said Madeleine, "kiss your mother." The child adhered to Madeleine's neck with the ferocity of a lion cub.

Geneviève, whose resemblance to Madeleine was a point in her favor, anticipated Armande's shyness and kissed her lightly on the cheek, then stood back to gauge her reaction. This discretion was rewarded with a tentative smile. Geneviève and Madeleine gently pulled the little girl off of her chair and flanked her, each holding one of her hands. Madeleine introduced her to Jean-Baptiste, who had been looking on, anxiously awaiting his turn.

He approached the girl standing between the two tall Béjart women and for a long moment stood motionless at the sight of this diminutive version of Madeleine and Geneviève, neither as fair as the one nor as dark as the other but blessed with the same perfect features the sisters shared, only in a rounded, more childish form. He had been instructed to introduce himself as a family friend, but no one had thought to mention that the niceties of adult etiquette would be lost on a young child coming from the countryside. Therefore he bowed deeply and in a solemn voice said, "I am enchanted to make your acquaintance. You have often been spoken of to me by your sister, one of my most cherished and illustrious friends, but it is a veritable privilege to meet you in person at long last, my lovely demoiselle."

Armande giggled at the incomprehensible language and the grown-up title accorded her, emitting a delicate tinkly sound more refined than what one would expect from a small child. Jean-Baptiste stood shifting his weight from side to side, not knowing where to put himself. It didn't occur to him that all four females present, including Armande herself, expected him to bend over and give the girl a kiss.

"It's late," said Madeleine to break the uneasy silence. "There will be plenty of time to get better acquainted in the morning. Come along now, my darling, it's been a long day. You must choose a bed. You others, out!" She shooed them away with a smile.

Armande, who had never seen a feather bed, hurled herself into the very center of the one Madeleine had chosen, then stood and jumped up and down. Madeleine took her firmly by the shoulders and tucked her in. On her first night in a strange place Armande couldn't be expected to fall asleep without someone by her side; Madeleine sat on the edge of the bed and stroked her daughter's hair. The joys of motherhood that flooded her as she lulled her to sleep were tempered this evening by grave cogitations.

Only now that she had seen Jean-Baptiste with Armande did she grasp the full implications of her deception. She had not changed her opinion that what she had done with Thomas nearly six years ago had at the time appeared to be to Jean-Baptiste's advantage. But had her attempts at realizing her lover's ambitions led thus far to a life of glory for him in Paris? Moreover the obscure itinerant existence that had instead been thrust upon him paled in comparison with a much more important dilemma that she could no longer avoid facing. No amount of rationalization could make the child born of Madeleine's night of passion with Thomas Corneille into the daughter of Jean-Baptiste Poquelin.

He had never expressed the wish to have a child nor made any real attempt, once one had been born, to meet her. For that matter, if Madeleine faced the truth, he had never convincingly expressed a desire to spend his life with her. She must tell him the truth about Armande; if he left her, so be it. How she would face life without him was her problem alone.

Once Armande was asleep, Madeleine stepped outside to look for Jean-Baptiste, who was waiting for her in the corridor. She prepared to plunge into the void.

"Jean-Baptiste," she said, clenching her fists as if to defend against the pain she was about to unleash on herself. "We must have a talk."

"My darling," he said in the tender voice he normally used only in moments of intimacy, "why didn't you tell me how beautiful she is? I ought to have made her acquaintance long ago. She's exactly like you, but so small and helpless! She's my little girl. What a pity we can't take her on the road until she's a little older. We must do everything in our powers to get established in Paris and be close to our little Armande!"

After years of agonizing over the right thing to tell her lover about Armande—the right story, the right time and the right way—now it was as simple as a few utterances she'd never expected to hear! It had been so long since Madeleine had allowed herself to weep in her lover's arms! Her careful reasoning, her resolution to reveal everything, her firm intention to set him free once and for all dissolved in her flowing tears. Whatever else happened now, all other considerations remained in the shadow of Jean-Baptiste's new obsession: to establish a troupe in Paris so that Armande could be raised by her parents, whose passion would be rekindled by the child's presence in their lives—or so Madeleine hoped.

At times, after their love, Jean-Baptiste would gaze at Madeleine in a way that led her to believe he was thinking of how much she resembled Armande. She would find herself feeling a hint of resentment. Though she would laugh at her own foolishness, the sentiment recurred whenever Jean-Baptiste waxed poetic about his love for his little daughter. Might matters improve if Madeleine bore a child who would actually be his, perhaps a boy who might resemble him and distract him from his fixation? One night she mentioned the possibility. Horror flashed across his face, as if she'd suggested flinging Armande from the heights of Montmartre. No one, it seemed, could ever dare to vie with the child for Jean-Baptiste's heart.

How could Madeleine not be happy? Never before had Jean-Baptiste seemed so firmly anchored in her life. Gone were her fears of losing him to another actress or some rich patroness. His ambition had returned with a vengeance, this time tempered by a healthy dose of skepticism of the most useful sort, acquired not through advice from others but through his own failures. This new Jean-Baptiste was neither the impetuous boy she had first met nor the melancholy young man who had pined over the downfall of the Illustre Théâtre. Now, at last, he had a good chance of realizing his goals and loving her as her equal.

But would this remarkable transformation have come about without Armande?

The Promises of Chance: that was how Thomas had characterized the development of true love, the metamorphosis of a more or less arbitrary spark of passion into a steadfast affection that would stand the test of time. While it was difficult to dispute that the series of fortuitous encounters that had brought Jean-Baptiste and Madeleine together had long ago gone far beyond coincidence, this new Jean-Baptiste was not the transformed lover that Thomas had described to her, the one she had longed for. The deepening of his love had come not from his looking inward to understand the profundity of his feelings but from yet another fortuitous event he had done nothing to bring about: his relationship with Armande, whom Madeleine herself had arranged to be taken for his daughter. Though it had been her plan, would his renewed love for Madeleine ever have blossomed—indeed, could it possibly persist—without Armande?

That he decided at this time to take a stage name marking his newly discovered passion for life was in itself a good sign, but did it too not encompass Madeleine only incidentally?

"Why *Molière*?" she demanded after he announced his strange choice of a *nom de plume* during a stay in Montpellier.

"Because it's a beautiful name that rolls softly off the tongue," he rejoined, "like *Armande Molière*, for example, and unlike *Armande Poquelin*!"

"Are you imagining then," asked Madeleine, "that Armande might one day be moved to take the name as well?"

"There will never be an Armande Molière," he replied, "because she is not my daughter."

Panic seized Madeleine. How had he discovered it, and what did that disclosure augur for her future with him?

"Don't forget," continued the newly dubbed Molière in a teasing voice, "she is your parents' daughter, not ours." Madeleine managed a smile of relief. "My dear, can such an important fact have slipped your mind?"

She burst into the dark laughter of the absurd, the type that barely differs from tears.

"If you have another moment of uncertainty in the future," he pursued, "take a fresh look at the baptismal certificate of our darling Armande. Are we given as her parents?"

"Certainly not," she replied, her face growing somber once again.

"And how could such a sacred document ever perpetrate a lie?" tossed off Molière with a snicker.

PART THREE

ARMANDE

CHAPTER 26

In Which a So-Called Father Approves a Request from His So-Called Daughter

Who Armande's parents were supposed to be did occasionally slip Madeleine's mind once the maddening but irresistible Jean-Baptiste morphed into the strutting Molière. Though he spoke of the girl as tenderly as a father, that honor had been legally bestowed upon the late Joseph Béjart and rightfully belonged to Thomas Corneille. While Madeleine herself was the girl's mother, Marie Hervé, with whom Armande lived in rooms on the Rue de la Lune, was her legal mother and guardian. It seemed to Madeleine that the girl belonged to everyone but her.

Once Molière took over direction of the troupe from Monsieur Dufresne he tried his hand at writing comedies. As an actor he enchanted audiences with his bold gestures, wry intonations, and hilarious banter, but despite the troupe's rising fortunes his ambition of conquering the capital remained elusive. He continued to dream of being a great tragedian but was ill equipped to portray the all-consuming passions of tragic heroes. Madeleine was reminded of Tristan's observation that actors could not do justice to passions they themselves had never experienced, first illustrated for her when she was struck by Cupid's arrows while gazing at Jean-Baptiste in the audience the night of her début as Chimène in *Le Cid*. If only Molière could truly lose his heart to her, even after so many years, as she had lost hers to him!

Meanwhile, back in Paris Marie Hervé and Armande spent four stormy years in their little flat on the Rue de la Lune without ever seeing eye to eye. Each Easter when the troupe returned to the capital Marie Hervé was given money to live on, but she also took in sewing to supplement their income. Armande, first required to manage fabrics and hand Marie Hervé her supplies, then taught how to sew buttons and simple seams, despised spending her days sitting beside her mother, who rambled on endlessly about people and things that held no interest for the child. While Armande begrudgingly learned her letters at the Jesuit school, a constant source of conflict was her dream of going onstage like her sisters and brothers and her beloved Molière.

Beloved of Armande Molière had certainly become. At Easter, no sooner would the two lay eyes on each other than they became indifferent to all else around them. In the first few years, when Armande was small, he would lift her high into the air and parade her on his shoulders. Around and around the room the two of them would go until they were dizzy and breathless. He would set her down as suddenly as he'd scooped her up and she would hold out her little arms to receive a hug and a kiss. Later, when she was too big for such games, they would greet each other by doing a dance, Armande crowing with delight and Molière glowing with love for this girl who from year to year grew taller and lovelier and more like her mother. As for Madeleine, she would wait patiently in a corner until Armande and Molière were done with their ceremony. The child would run to welcome her as well, but not half so warmly.

Madeleine continued to be dissatisfied with this state of affairs. Was some demon intent on refusing her a moment's peace? It seemed that no sooner had she stopped tormenting herself about whether or not to tell Molière the truth about Armande's birth than she was subjected to a veritable cross to bear, one that, unlike the other, she had not brought down upon her own head.

She reasoned and reasoned with herself. A child needed a father's love as much as a mother's. There was no doubt Armande was more attached to Madeleine than to Marie Hervé but after all she believed the older woman to be her mother and she also received affection from Geneviève. In contrast to this plethora of motherly tenderness Armande had been told her father was dead, and she received attention from no other man beside Molière: Louis and Joseph were shy and awkward around their niece. It was perfectly understandable that Molière, believing that Armande was his daughter, treated her like one. If he was more and more strongly attached to this lovely child it was a tribute to Madeleine, whom the girl resembled.

None of these arguments made the slightest bit of difference. It was beyond her control.

She was jealous of her own daughter.

***

The day the troupe arrived in Paris for Easter break of 1653, Armande's welcoming ritual with Molière was executed with less exuberance than usual. Madeleine sent him and Marie Hervé to the market so that she could question the girl alone.

"My goodness, how you've grown," she exclaimed. Armande was a tall stately girl with a dignified profile in counterpoint to a devil-may-care grin. Mother and daughter stood back to back to compare their heights. Whereas the previous Easter the top of Armande's head had barely reached Madeleine's shoulders, now it was even with her nose.

"Soon I'll be taller than you," intoned Armande in a petulant voice.

"I wouldn't be surprised," concurred Madeleine. "Now, my grown-up girl, tell me what's wrong."

"What do you mean?" asked Armande with a suspicious look.

"You know you're incapable of concealing anything from your sister," chided Madeleine. "With Mother you're almost as good at hiding things as I was at your age, but not with me."

The girl threw herself onto the pallet she shared with Marie Hervé. "Nothing's wrong," she grumbled. "And if you can read my mind, why ask me? Why not just read it?"

Madeleine sighed. It was only to be expected that a precocious girl who thought she would soon be attaining the venerable age of eleven would give evidence of growing pains.

"I beg Your Highness's pardon," said Madeleine. "I'm pleased to hear that everything is going so splendidly. Now if you'll excuse me, I must look at fabrics for your new dresses. I was going to ask you along, but I see that you're perfectly content as you are."

She walked away slowly to give Armande the time to call her back. As she was reaching for the door she felt a mighty tug from behind.

"Wait!" cried Armande. "Everything is horrible! Don't leave without me!"

"All right, come along," said Madeleine in a conciliatory tone. "We'll speak of this later."

"I wasn't talking about shopping for fabric," howled the girl, "but traveling on the road!"

The request was bound to come sooner or later and here it was. Madeleine stood at the half-open Dutch door and turned her daughter's demand over in her mind.

Perhaps it was time to give the girl what she so desperately wanted. Armande was headstrong but not flighty and at this age would be less likely to misbehave or fall ill than a younger child. With the fine memory she had inherited from her mother she would be perfectly capable of learning small parts, scullery maids in comedies or sprites in works about the gods and goddesses of yore, roles a traveling troupe had difficulty filling. What possible reason could Madeleine have for refusing her daughter's request?

There was only one, but it was enough. The thought of seeing Molière fawning over the girl day and night was unbearable. Madeleine turned back to Armande and prepared to give her reply and face the ensuing firestorm.

***

It was the evening preceding the troupe's departure. Armande had raged at Madeleine's decision to keep her in Paris but after a long spell of ill temper the girl had apparently resolved to accept the verdict. For the past few days she had been as sweet as a honey tart.

The Fleur-de-Lys was filled to the rafters and when Madeleine entered the dining room at suppertime she could hardly find a place to sit. Molière and Armande were nowhere to be seen.

"I believe they're in the courtyard," remarked Geneviève in a noncommittal tone. "I'm sure they'll be along in a few minutes."

"Yes," chimed in Joseph, "I saw them as well. They were rehearsing something. A song or a number of some sort."

Geneviève looked daggers at her brother. Failing to comprehend what he had said to annoy her, he shrugged and took a mouthful of bread.

"Rehearsing?" echoed Madeleine with a frown. "Why would they have been rehearsing?"

"It doesn't matter, I'm sure it's nothing at all," commented Joseph.

The door of the dining hall flung open and in pranced Molière.

"Ladies and gentlemen!" he proclaimed. "Forgive my interruption of your repast but I have an announcement that cannot wait." Madeleine shot him a look but he avoided her gaze. "Tomorrow we depart for another year of giving pleasure and enlightenment to our compatriots. For the very first time we'll be accompanied by one who, although a newcomer to our troupe, is well known to you all." He clapped his hands and Armande tiptoed in as if walking on eggshells, most likely to make herself look taller. "As you can see," he pursued, gesturing grandly toward the girl, "the sister of our leading actress is budding into a flower as comely as our Madeleine. As of this very day Armande Béjart has joined our ranks. I ask you to welcome her warmly!"

The room burst into applause.

"Molière!" cried Madeleine, standing abruptly.

"At your service," he said with a bow while Armande huddled on his far side.

"A word with you."

After an intense exchange of whispers and much furious headshaking, Madeleine, as pale as a ghost, slunk back to her seat. Molière led Armande to the center of the room.

"The new star in our constellation will now sing a sailor's ditty to show her talents," he said. "I myself will assist her," he added with a blush. He drew in a lungful of air and sang.

> In her little garden Angela strolled
> On the shore of an isle, where the blue sea rolled.
> Many sailors she'd see, to their boats they would cling,
> But one of them looked back and began to sing.

Now Armande timidly joined the song:

Your song is so lovely, please teach it to me!

Molière rejoined:

Come into my boat, Miss, just come and we'll see,
But once in the boat she began to cry.

At this Armande drew in great gasps of air and wiped her cheeks with a handkerchief.

What's wrong, my lovely, why this tear in your eye? he asked.
You have stolen my heart, the girl sang, *and that's why I weep.*
I shall give it back then, he replied, *for you to keep.*

Armande sang her final lines before slumping to the floor of her imaginary boat:

What good is it now, this heart that's been rent?
A heart's not returned like a coin that's been lent!

The hall erupted. Armande had inherited Thomas's precociousness, her voice that of a young woman, her intonation imbued with poignancy. She curtsied gracefully to the assembly, refusing to look in Madeleine's direction. And without further ado she and Molière disappeared.

As if that was the end of the story!

Actors crowded around Madeleine to congratulate her on having such a young sister who sang so beautifully. She fought clear, smiling as best she could to cover her fury. The corridor was empty. She sprinted into the courtyard and found Molière and Armande on their way out.

Molière's face had the defiance of an adolescent accused of a misdeed to which he'll freely confess because he doesn't consider it a crime. Armande looked as though she expected flaming arrows to issue from Madeleine's lips and strike her down.

"How dare you go over my head," screamed Madeleine, "and make plans for this girl!"

"I decided nothing," said Molière, standing his ground. "This wasn't my idea. The girl came to me as the head of the troupe."

"She came to me first," cried Madeleine, "knowing full well that it's up to me. I told her she was too young." She turned to Armande. "And you," she said in a menacing tone, "didn't I make myself clear? Apparently not, for you went sneaking around behind my back!"

Armande's lower lip quivered. She drew herself up and said with dignity, "I didn't go behind your back. I asked my mother for permission and she said to ask Molière."

"Marie Hervé told you you could travel with the troupe?" demanded Madeleine.

"You can ask her if you don't believe me," Armande said with a pout, crossing her arms. "She said she's tired of running after me and it's time I earned my keep." Encouraged by Madeleine's silence she went on. "The only reason I asked you first is that I thought you would help me convince Mother. But when you refused I went to her. So there!"

As Madeleine hadn't replied Molière pitched in, "You'll see, my sweet, she's old enough. Did you hear the girl's voice? What a draw she'll be on the road! We'll put her onstage as soon as possible in plays that have music and add some to those that have none."

Madeleine thrust her hands into her pockets, fighting back tears. Her fingers closed on Thomas's ring, which she always carried with her. Was he the only person she would ever know who put her ahead of himself and all others?

"My opinion is no longer valued, I see," said Madeleine, "so I'll trouble you with it no longer." She began to sob.

"Stay with her," said Armande glumly. "Geneviève will see me home."

Molière took Madeleine in his arms and she felt herself falling under his spell. "There, there," he intoned. "Don't cry. One day she'll know who her mother is, and her father too." The soothing words only accelerated Madeleine's weeping. "Hush," he whispered, kissing her hair. "From now on it will be just the three of us: you and I and our darling Armande."

***

Madeleine and Molière and Armande. They worked together, ate together, traveled together. In spite of the easy camaraderie of theater life they formed a circle of three that others refrained from joining. Madeleine mused that they must appear to be a happy trio, but just as an aging beauty begrudgingly grows accustomed to applying lotions to skin once flawless, each morning as she assumed a painstaking smile she longed for the days when one came naturally to her lips.

Armande's debut as a nymph in Monsieur Pierre Corneille's *Andromeda* was a small triumph. The chorus in which she sang quickly became a solo when the other two young actresses fell silent, unwilling to have their reedy soprano voices compared to her resonant tone. Like her purported sister, the girl was never more cheerful than when onstage, but while audiences were naturally drawn to Madeleine, Armande had a fierce need to be an object of adulation. Madeleine loved the theater; Armande loved being loved.

And how she was adored by her mentor, this girl who with every passing day became more enchanting! When she was actually twelve but her official age was fourteen, she started to be cast in ingénue roles. She quickly gained a reputation for playing love scenes effectively, affirmed by all of her leading men, including Molière. The first time Madeleine was forced to watch the onstage flirtation between her daughter and her lover, she clenched her teeth and vowed that something would have to be done.

That night she confided in the late Armande for the first time in months.

"I don't know where to turn," Madeleine whispered. "I can't bear to see them together. I know he cares for me too, but he lives and dies with her every breath as he never has with mine." A silence. "But if it's simply an awkward stage," she murmured, "when will it end? How much longer shall I have the strength to wait it out?"

This time there was no reply.

***

During the 1657 season the name of Thomas Corneille was on everyone's lips. The previous year his first tragedy, *Timocrates*, had opened, and it was quickly becoming the greatest stage success of the time, rivaling even his brother's *Le Cid*. At Easter, when Molière's troupe made its annual pilgrimage to the capital, Madeleine agreed to take Armande to see the play. As they waited for the curtain to rise, an outlandish thought occurred to Madeleine. This was the very theater that thirteen years earlier had been reduced to ash . . .

"What are you smiling about?" asked Armande. "You told me *Timocrates* was a tragedy. Shouldn't we be thinking of sad things?"

"I suppose you're right," replied Madeleine, "but sometimes life is funny."

"It doesn't seem so to me," the young lady said with a hint of lassitude.

Madeleine patted her hand. "It will when you're as old as I."

"As old as you?" echoed the girl. "That day will never come."

"Yes it will, and sooner than you think," laughed Madeleine just as the consecrated three blows struck against the stage marked the raising of the curtain.

Suddenly, before the actors' first entrances, out of the wings strode Thomas Corneille!

Madeleine hadn't laid eyes on him since before Armande's birth. Celebrity had transformed the plain youth into an attractive man. His elegant attire drew attention to his height. The white tuft he had as a boy had spread, but the tawny locks still flowed gracefully to his shoulders; his gaze remained that of a sage. He surveyed the rows of seats and spread his arms wide, as if to gather the entire hall into a single embrace. Madeleine pulled back into the shadows, wary that he might single her out with that sixth sense of his. Taking care to face forward, he moved from stage left to stage right, his arms held wide to display himself to the entire hall. A sense of drama was one aspect of his character that had apparently survived the years intact.

As the audience leapt to their feet Madeleine remained seated and observed Armande. The girl neither applauded nor cheered but stood in silent reverence, as if a Christian saint had fallen to earth before her eyes. Thomas bowed deeply and left the stage and the ovation abated. Only Armande remained standing.

The play was beginning; Madeleine yanked her down. The girl shook her head as if recovering from a tumble. Madeleine whispered, "What is it, darling? Are you feeling ill?"

"That Monsieur Corneille," answered the girl. "I have never seen a man so handsome! I heard someone say he's the most famous person in France after the King."

"Hush," answered Madeleine, "The play has begun."

Three hours later, when the accolades were renewed, Madeleine would have been hard pressed to recount the play's events, having spent the entire time fretting over Armande's reaction to Thomas. It had never once entered her mind that Armande, unbeknownst to herself, might one day become infatuated with her own father. It was a danger to be avoided at all costs.

But as they were leaving the theater, a hue and cry arose, and there stood Thomas in the middle of the Rue Vieille du Temple, blocking their path! Accompanied by a musketeer for protection, he was thanking the departing patrons. There was no way to avoid him, so Madeleine pulled Armande to her other side and faced away from him.

"Mademoiselle Béjart!" he cried. She sped up but Thomas exhorted the crowd to seize the attention of this spectator unaware that she was being addressed by a man of such renown. She whispered something in Armande's ear and the girl squealed with excitement. They made their way toward Thomas. The crowd parted as if the two were members of the royal family.

"Good evening, Mesdemoiselles," said Thomas. He bowed deeply and kissed first Madeleine's hand, then Armande's. Turning back to Madeleine he gushed, "What an extraordinary pleasure to see you again after so many years!"

"The pleasure is ours, Monsieur," said Madeleine briskly, curtsying and nodding to Armande to follow suit. "Congratulations on your tragedy, which is the talk of Paris."

"Thank you, Mademoiselle," he responded. "I've heard you're a member of Molière's troupe. Nothing could please me more than knowing my play diverted you."

There was a pause. She desperately searched for an excuse to leave but could find none.

Thomas said, "I don't believe I am acquainted with this young lady. May I be so bold as to request the honor of an introduction? Is she a member of your troupe?"

"Yes she is, Monsieur," answered Madeleine. "She's my youngest sister, Armande."

Thomas kissed the girl's hand for a second time, but now her cheeks turned the color of strawberries. He smiled but looked distracted. "I wasn't aware that you had a sister of such a tender age, Mademoiselle," he said to Madeleine. Addressing Armande he asked, "How old are you, my dear?"

"Fifteen in July," she replied, straightening her posture.

"Quite," he said with a smile. "It's a pity you'll be on the road by then and unable to receive my best wishes for the occasion."

"We leave for Nantes next week," Madeleine said quickly, happy to change the subject. "We've thought for years of settling in Paris, but you must be aware of how difficult that is."

"I am, Mademoiselle," he replied, "but if any troupe has a chance for success here, it's yours. If I can be of service, please let me know. Perhaps I can give you a play to perform."

"Oh yes!" cried Armande with delight. "Will there be a part in your play for me?"

"Of course," Thomas said gravely. He turned to Madeleine. "I'm lodged at the Golden Spoon till the end of the week. If you care to discuss my idea, pay me a visit."

With that he gestured to his musketeer to follow and melted into the crowd.

***

Scarcely had Madeleine and Armande entered their room at the Fleur-de-Lys when Armande pulled Molière into a corner and said in a state of elation, "We met the most famous man in France! Aside from the King," she added as an afterthought. "Guess who he is!"

Molière pulled her hat off, smoothed her hair, and kissed her cheek. He stroked his chin to signify puzzlement and replied, "The Prime Minister?" A shake of Armande's head. "The Queen Mother?" She giggled. "Oh," he said, "she's not a man. The devil?"

"No, no!" exclaimed Armande, "You'll never guess! It was Monsieur Thomas Corneille! He wants us to move to Paris so he can write us a play!"

"Those were not his words," Madeleine interjected, causing Armande's features to contract. "What he said was that if we did move to Paris he might help us."

"It's the same thing, Mado, the same thing!" cried Armande. "You always correct me, whatever I say. The most famous man in France said he'll write us a play, with a part for me!"

"That's wonderful news, my darling," said Molière to Armande, giving her a hug. "I met him long ago, when he gave us precious assistance. I believe your sister made his acquaintance before I did, didn't you?" He looked at Madeleine for corroboration and she nodded without comment. He thought for a moment, contemplating Armande's eager face. "But you mustn't count on such promises, my sweet," he went on, "or you may be hurt. Sometimes famous people pledge things that never come to pass. Aren't you content with the parts I've given you?"

"I suppose so," said Armande. "But it's not just the play."

"What else then?" asked Molière.

"Monsieur Corneille is the handsomest man in all of France!" she burst out.

Molière turned toward the wall, his shoulders slouching. Madeleine asked in a playful tone, "Is he handsomer than Molière?"

"You're a monster, Mado!" screamed the girl. "You know that's different!"

"Why?" rejoined the older woman. "I have two eyes in my head, as do you. When I look at Molière and then at Thomas, Molière is handsomer. What could be simpler?"

"Leave it, my lovely," Molière said to Madeleine. "She meant nothing by it, did you, Menou?"

The use of Armande's nickname, now limited to quieting things down when a discussion was getting out of hand, had the opposite effect.

"I am not Menou!" she cried. "I'm no longer a baby! Never call me that again or I'll run away and marry someone who looks exactly like Monsieur Thomas Corneille!"

Madeleine raised her hand to slap the girl but Molière stood between them.

"Please, ladies, you're giving me a headache." He covered his ears with his hands. "Mado," he said, then interrupted himself with an aside. "Armande, do you see how even a grown-up lady can have a silly nickname?" He turned back to Madeleine and went on. "First, I thank you for your generous vote of confidence insofar as my appearance is concerned. I have not seen the younger Monsieur Corneille for years but I am convinced your judgment does not do him justice. Second, if the girl wants us to call her Armande, we shall do so. It is, after all, her name." He now pivoted to face Armande and said, "As for you, young lady, first, I'll thank you not to call our Madeleine a monster, for she is an angel. And second, if you wish to marry a man who resembles Monsieur Thomas Corneille, I wish you godspeed."

He bowed with exaggerated formality and tottered out of the room with the gait of a drunkard attempting to walk a straight line.

Armande flung herself onto her bed and sobbed into a cushion. Madeleine sat beside her.

"I'm sorry if I hurt your feelings, my darling," she said. "But you're old enough to learn that your words may also hurt others. Tomorrow you must apologize to Molière."

"Why, Mado?" wailed the girl. "What did I say?"

"That you found Monsieur Corneille handsomer than Molière is," Madeleine replied.

"But I do. What's wrong with that?" queried Armande.

"Nothing, really," Madeleine replied gently. "It's just that you made it seem as if you were fonder of Monsieur Corneille than of Molière. Monsieur Corneille is a perfect stranger to you and Molière has known you for years and loves you very much. Do you understand?"

Without lifting her head from the cushion the girl muttered, "No, I don't."

"But I do, my darling," Madeleine said gently, "so you must trust me."

She stroked her daughter's hair, searching for words of comfort. It occurred to her that she ought to feel relieved at this unanticipated conflict that threatened to drive a wedge between Molière and Armande, but she couldn't bear the thought of his unhappiness.

"Molière loves you as much as if you were his own daughter," she said to Armande after a long pause. "You must never do anything that will cause him to suffer. Will you promise me that?"

Silence. Armande, a preternaturally sound sleeper, was famous for her ability to drift off in the middle of the most animated discussion. Madeleine pulled a cover over the girl's shoulders and blew out the candle.

CHAPTER 27

In Which a Tapestry Is Discovered to Be Ripped in an Unseemly Place

For the entire week after Armande's infatuation with Thomas Corneille took root, she mooned about the Fleur-de-Lys and pecked at her food as if in the final throes of a wasting disease. Molière, starved of the young lady's adulation, imbibed such quantities of wine that Madeleine oversaw on her own the auditions scheduled for actors and actresses wishing to join the troupe. Something had to be done, but what? A move to Paris, long desired but endlessly postponed? Armande's fixation on Thomas might dissipate if the girl experienced the excitement of living in the capital and receiving the attention of countless men. And was it not conceivable that the frozen knot in Molière's broken heart would melt away in the warm glow of success?

In spite of Thomas's kind offer, after so much murky water had flowed under the bridge would he be willing to come to their rescue yet again? The troupe would soon be back on the road, Thomas leaving Paris to return to Rouen, so it was with a firm resolve but no clear idea of how exactly she was going to proceed that Madeleine set off to visit him at the Golden Spoon.

***

Directly across from the Louvre, the Golden Spoon was grander and boasted a more distinguished clientele than the Fleur-de-Lys; the innkeeper shot Madeleine a suspicious look as she reassured him that she had an appointment with the famous playwright lodged there. As if she and Thomas actually had one, he answered her knock instantly and showed her in. On this chilly day a fire was blazing. In an alcove at one end of the room stood a curtained bed; two walnut armchairs were drawn up close to the hearth. A small writing table, its surface strewn with papers, quills, and an open inkpot, stood next to the window.

"I'm intruding on your work," said Madeleine. "I beg your pardon, Monsieur."

"Please don't call me that," he said graciously, taking a place across from her in front of the hearth. "It is a delight to be interrupted in this way." He blushed. "As agreeable as it is to speak to you in private, I'm sorry to see that your lovely young sister has not accompanied you."

Madeleine fidgeted with a sleeve. "Nothing would have given her greater pleasure," she said. "The reason I've come . . . You've helped us so much already that I hardly dare . . ."

"As I said," replied Thomas, "I am eager to be of service. Among the traveling troupes Molière's reputation is second to none. It is high time you established yourselves here." He thought for a moment. "What would you say if I persuaded Pierre to give you another play and I added one as well? He has written little of late and I cannot vouch for him, but I can for myself."

"I would be most grateful," Madeleine said slowly, "but why? You have nothing to gain."

"Is it not foolish asking why," he said evenly, "when you know?"

She was surprised but not displeased by his frankness. She shook her head.

"It seems to me that with each passing year I know less and less. All I have ever learned is from reciting speeches written by others."

"Who wrote these words that you're speaking?" Thomas asked. "Mine come from my heart."

"And mine," she said, "come from my head, for my heart is not my own. Nor is yours, Thomas. May I congratulate you belatedly on your marriage, of which I only recently learned?"

"Leave that out of this," he replied gruffly. "I had little choice in the matter. And as I told you long ago . . ." She put a hand to his lips to silence him. "All right then," he went on quietly. "I'll provide a play and seek out a patron for your troupe. I'll speak to Pierre and perhaps he will be persuaded. Write to me when you're returning to Paris."

"Mere words cannot convey my appreciation," said Madeleine. She stood and turned away, desperate to escape from the pain in his eyes.

As Thomas showed her out, he paused at the door. "And my ring? Do you carry it?"

She reached into a secret pouch sewn inside her gown and showed it to him. She grasped his hands in her own, dropped them abruptly, and without looking up took her leave.

***

Soon Madeleine, Molière, and Armande were on the road again and to all outward appearances nothing had changed, but it was as if an invisible fourth member had transformed the bright circle of three into a square with shadowed recesses. Thomas's fame having spread across the realm, whenever he was mentioned Armande's eyes glistened and she explained to perfect strangers that he was the handsomest man in France and was writing a play just for her. A hint of melancholy tinged Molière's acting even in the most uproarious of comedies.

As the months wore on and the girl's reverence for Thomas strengthened, Molière's mellifluous voice grew acrid and dry. As in one of the tragedies of passion so prized by audiences, the weight of invisible woes was suffocating his vital force. As the end of the season approached, deciding whether the time was right for the troupe to attempt a permanent return to Paris could be put off no longer. On a snowy evening in Grenoble where the troupe was resting up before a long stay in Lyon, Madeleine broached the matter.

They were lodged in the townhouse of a marquis and had a room to themselves, with two beds for the three of them. After supper, Madeleine sent Armande to Geneviève's room to have her hair braided so that she and Molière could be alone. She mused that in earlier days such a pretext would have been motivated by a desire for intimacy. Molière was already in bed.

"I'm sorry to disturb you," she said, sitting beside him and taking his hand.

He sat up. "Not tonight, my sweet. I'm all done in."

"That's not why I'm here," she snapped, vexed at Molière's habitual refrain. "It is high time," she said slowly after a deep breath, "that we discuss whether to accept Thomas's assistance and move to Paris. If we wait too long . . ."

"What is there to decide? Nothing prevents him from writing us a play if he so desires."

"We can hardly première one of his plays in the provinces," retorted Madeleine. "And he also said he would look for a patron. He asked me to write to him before our return to Paris."

"A patron? Why did no one tell me?" A bitter grin made his chin dimple disappear. "It strains belief that Armande would have concealed such astonishing news about *the handsomest man in France*."

"Armande knows nothing about it," Madeleine said carefully. "When we encountered Thomas," she fibbed, "he asked me to send her ahead before we discussed it."

Molière's head fell back onto the pillow. "Perhaps it *is* time we try our luck," he said with a sigh. "I'm so tired of the road! We could have a place of our own, just the three of us."

"What about the others, Mother and Geneviève, and my brothers?" Madeleine asked.

"We're prosperous enough to have separate lodgings."

"Armande is almost fifteen," she observed. "She and everyone outside the family believe she's even older. Perhaps she would be better off living with Geneviève."

"Why?" demanded Molière.

"They're closer in age," responded Madeleine, "so it's easier for them to talk." She composed her face. "Armande no longer confides in me."

Molière took a straw from the floor and worked loose food lodged between two teeth.

"She can converse with Geneviève to her heart's content. Her place is with us."

Madeleine pulled his head onto her lap and massaged his temples. He closed his eyes and smiled, once again the dimpled Jean-Baptiste she so desperately missed.

"My darling," she said, "Armande's place may be with us now, but sooner or later it will be with another. We can't keep her for ourselves for the rest of her life."

His face froze. Who would reply, the motherless Jean-Baptiste or the haughty Molière?

"I am afraid of losing her," whispered Jean-Baptiste.

Madeleine leaned over and kissed his forehead. "You'll never lose her," she said. "Come what may, you'll always be her . . ."

She could not force the word to her lips. The identity of Armande's father was the most important untruth she'd ever perpetrated but it was a lie by omission: Molière simply assumed from the start that Armande was his daughter. Voicing the lie aloud was now the one thing Madeleine could say to reassure him. Could it, remaining false, comfort him just as well?

Suddenly Armande burst in and threw herself onto the other bed. She had overheard Madeleine's last words. "Who will always be whose what?"

"Never mind," said Molière, sitting up. "We're just discussing moving to Paris."

"Has Monsieur Corneille written my play?" Armande asked breathlessly.

"As I told you before," said Molière, "you mustn't count on him, my darling. He has probably told dozens of people he'd write them plays."

"But he promised!" the girl exclaimed, believing it herself. "All actresses have parts written for them when they're acquainted with great writers." She struck a pose. "I'm almost sixteen. No one can say I'm not old enough to play a leading role. Don't you think I am, Mado?"

Madeleine nodded.

Without uttering a word Molière stretched out once again and rolled over to face the wall. Scowling, Armande put on her nightgown and settled down in her bed. Madeleine extinguished the candle. Molière's breathing, though almost regular, was not quite that of a man asleep.

***

Thomas's businesslike response to Madeleine's letter comprised three items: he reiterated that the time was ripe for the troupe to settle in Paris; he had arranged an engagement of several months in Rouen where he could help prepare them for Parisian audiences; and he requested a private meeting with Madeleine the moment they arrived in Rouen.

The cloudburst accompanying the troupe's entry into Rouen in late April put Madeleine in mind of the Illustre Théâtre's arrival in the Normandy capital fifteen years earlier, but there was no denying that since that time they had come up in the world. Rather than entertaining the masses in the open air of the Saint Romain Fair, they were to perform at the Braques Theater, not far from the Corneille residence. And yet as they settled into the elegant lodgings Thomas had arranged for them to occupy, she felt a pang of nostalgia for the seamy Red Bull Inn and the simpler time when all that was capable of driving her and her lover apart was a difference of opinion about the future of the troupe.

Armande, agog at the notion that she would be seeing her idol and introduced to his equally famous brother, twittered on about the larger roles she would soon receive. She applied rouge to her cheeks and refused to have her bodices altered to mask her now womanly figure.

Upon arrival they settled in for an early night and soon Molière was snoring heavily. Madeleine crept out and made her way through the rain-soaked streets to the Rue de la Pie. As Thomas had instructed, she knocked at the door of a small addition behind the main residence.

A manservant led her to a paneled study, seated her on a sofa, and disappeared. The room was made cozy by wall hangings, a blue wool carpet, and a fireplace all aglow. Shadows cast by the firelight danced on the wall opposite the hearth, weirdly illuminating a Rouen tapestry. It depicted knights and ladies strolling through a garden while Cupid looked down from above, his arrow poised to fell a handsome man gazing at a young woman of Armande's stature.

Madeleine's attention was drawn to the man's midsection where, by chance, the fabric had been rent. She burst out laughing at this comical effect at odds with the pathos of the scene. How vulnerable men were to love's arrows! Women, accustomed to vigilance, had an invisible armor that made them less susceptible to Cupid's weapons. Were not men, believing themselves masters in love as in all else, actually at greater risk? In the flickering light the doomed lover rather resembled Molière. All at once her mirth changed to shock.

Without his even knowing it, could *that* be the nature of his feelings for Armande?

Before she could give it a moment's thought there was the sound of a door opening. She composed her face and prepared to greet Thomas.

Standing before her was Pierre Corneille.

***

The years had not been kind, his comeliness having accompanied his professional reputation into a subtle but noticeable decline.

"It is an honor to receive you, Mademoiselle," he intoned, kissing her hand.

She nodded politely, at a loss for words. "I thank you for your kind welcome, Monsieur," she finally said, "but the honor is mine." She paused. "When will your brother be arriving?"

They sat side by side on the sofa. Pierre cleared his throat.

"Thomas is in Paris today," he said, "and unable to be here. His latest play is soon to open at the Théâtre du Marais. Don't think harshly of him. He didn't know you were coming."

"How is that possible?" Madeleine asked curtly in spite of herself. "He himself suggested the date, and I replied to confirm our plans."

"Nonetheless Thomas is unaware of your arrival," said Pierre. "Don't be alarmed. The invitation you received is genuine and offers a great opportunity, but I must confess it was not my brother who received your letter and corresponded with you. It was I."

"I don't understand," said Madeleine in bewilderment. "My letter was addressed to Thomas. In Paris last year he asked me to write to him. He said he would help us."

Pierre nodded. "Thomas spoke to me of that meeting," he said. "Hardly a week has gone by that he hasn't encouraged me to write a play for your troupe. But he wasn't at home the day the messenger delivered your letter. When I heard it was from you, I took it and opened it."

"I'm flattered, Monsieur," Madeleine replied cautiously, "but why?"

Pierre walked to his writing table and let his weight fall onto the chair beside it.

"Mademoiselle, I hardly know you," he said, "nor you me. But from the moment we met so long ago I sensed you could be trusted as I have trusted few people. Women have trouble keeping a secret. Can you keep one?"

She stifled a laugh, wishing Thomas were here to receive this evidence that Pierre was a typical man. "Of course," she replied. How strange it was to feel pity for one so famous!

"As you know," he began, "it has been six years since I've presented a play. I take pride in my brothers' accomplishments and have not wished to eclipse the attention he has earned."

The words were spoken with a trace of irony. Had Pierre been privy to the rumors about his fear of a rivalry with Thomas?

"That is most generous of you," she said. "We all admire your brother's achievements."

Pierre nodded. "It is time for me to take up the pen once again," he said. "Monsieur Fouquet has been urging me to do so in the strongest terms." The Superintendent of Finances had ambitions of becoming the greatest patron of the arts in the kingdom.

"Have you chosen your subject, Monsieur?" she asked.

"The greatest in all antiquity," announced the aging playwright with a glimpse of his former grandeur. "The unfortunate Oedipus, who unknowingly killed his father and wed Jocasta, his own mother!"

Madeleine smiled to mask her distaste. Among all the dreadful tales chosen by playwrights for tragedies, this was surely the most shocking. She chose her words with care.

"It will be a work of great genius," she said quietly, "and I thank you most humbly for sharing your secret." She paused. "I beg you to excuse my naïveté if I ask whether *Oedipus* has something to do with me."

"It is possible," Pierre said, "that I may offer the play to your troupe."

She stood and prepared to thank him but he brushed her away.

"Don't thank me yet. The play has not been written." She sat again and waited for him to go on. "Jocasta would not be a flattering role for a woman of your great beauty," said Pierre. "Aside from the shame she incurs, she is not a young woman."

Madeleine laughed. "Actresses lie about their age, Monsieur," she replied gaily, "but I have no false pride. I am forty years old. My beauty, such as it was, is a thing of the past."

"Mademoiselle Béjart," Pierre said, "I too will speak plainly. Like you I refuse to feign ignorance of my age. I have an old man's face but harbor a young man's dreams and desires."

Their eyes met. There was a long silence that seemed even more protracted than it was.

"All I know of the dreams and desires of men, old or young," Madeleine finally said, "is that they rarely serve any earthly purpose. Men are not helped by them, but haunted."

"You are very wise, my dear," said Pierre, "and in spite of your modesty every bit as beautiful as you were at twenty-five. Do you recall when I visited you backstage before your debut as Chimène? Your comb tumbled to the floor and you blushed most charmingly."

She nodded, saddened by this memory from a distant past when nothing had yet been achieved but everything still seemed possible.

"I won't deny," Pierre pursued, "that I have consorted with and forgotten many actresses. But I have never stopped longing to watch your hair tumble around your shoulders once again."

She had not seen it coming. To soothe her agitation she walked to the window and listened to the sound of the rain.

"Nothing could be more gratifying, Monsieur," she replied in measured tones, "than to provide pleasure to a man as great as you. But I am unable to do so."

Pierre's eyes dimmed. "Because of Molière?" he asked.

Pain cut across her gut. For as long as she could remember her every action had been dictated by devotion to her lover, and yet hearing the question of her motivation posed, stark and unadorned, exposed a truth she could no longer overlook. At the present time, remaining faithful to Molière meant little. Lovers they were no longer. Lovers they never again would be.

How futilely his heart must be rebelling against its monstrous desires, his head attempting to protect it by attributing his feelings for his purported daughter to mere fatherly devotion!

"Yes, Monsieur," she said, "because of Molière. As you know, your brother has also offered us a play. As precious as your tragedy would be to our troupe, I must decline."

Pierre stood to face her.

"My brother's play, the one you are depending on, is out of reach. It is the one I mentioned, about to open in Paris. Thomas had not heard from you—or so he believed—and thought you had changed your mind, so he made other arrangements."

Madeleine buried her face in her hands. At least there was now an excuse for tears. If she refused Pierre, the troupe would not stand a chance of moving to Paris. There would be nothing to distract Molière from his feelings for the girl he believed to be his daughter, nor to divert Armande's attention from the man who she was unaware was her father. And Madeleine would find herself powerless to save the two people she loved the most from themselves.

Fate was taunting her, tempting her to let things run their course. Why assist the very man who had never loved her as she had loved him?

Because she loved him still.

Loving without reward, my heart remains pure.

Though it was Molière's voice she had heard many times reciting Don Fadrique's lines in Thomas's first play, *The Promises of Chance*, it was Thomas that now spoke to her imagination, Thomas who, knowing his love for her would bring him only suffering, remained as attentive to her needs as if she had given him her heart in exchange for his. Was there any greater proof of love than loving as he had, without hope of receiving love or any other benefit in return?

Her weeping ceased. She lifted her head.

"If my favors·are the condition for your assistance, I shall not refuse."

He took her hand and kissed it.

"Please accept my thanks." He paused. "My pride hoped to avoid it, but it is only right I reveal the truth. If I humbly ask for your favors, it is not as a condition without which I will refuse you my play but as one without which I won't find the courage and inspiration to write it."

CHAPTER 28

In Which Our Heroine Is Reunited with Three Faux Lovers and Sends the True One Packing

And so, without anyone's being the wiser, on that night and at regular intervals during the troupe's stay in Rouen, Madeleine went with Pierre, and little by little his *Oedipus* came into being. In the meanwhile the troupe presented a repertoire of Pierre's older plays, along with comedies Molière had written or adapted during the long years on the road. They were warmly applauded by the audiences in Rouen, strengthening their hopes for Paris, although Thomas's search had not yet yielded a patron. To Madeleine's relief, she saw not the slightest sign that he suspected what was going on between his brother and the woman he himself adored.

In spite of this favorable turn of events, the months in Rouen were trying, each of the members of this inchoate *ménage à quatre* suffering from unrequited love in a similar fashion. Thomas observed Madeleine's every move with his great owl eyes but often found her staring at Molière. She herself took little pleasure in watching her director at work when she found him gazing at Armande, his forced cheerfulness never more artful than when the young woman was fawning on Thomas. Armande's joy at having her heartthrob within reach was such that she forgave him for not casting her in the production of his new play in Paris, but the fact that he responded to her coquettishness with cool courtesy was more difficult to overlook.

One sweltering night in early August, Madeleine granted Pierre's request to join him in the little annex. Afterward, as she was dressing, he sat up in bed and said in an expansive voice, "My tragedy of *Oedipus* is finished! Once you have found a building in Paris and a patron for your troupe, you may schedule the première." He kissed her hand. "My dear, please allow me to express my gratitude once again for your indulgence."

How little satisfaction she felt! She recalled Jean-Baptiste's elation when the Illustre Théâtre received permission to stage *The Liar*. Presently all she could think of was the mask of doom his lovesick face now wore.

"There is no need to thank me," she forced herself to say. "It is I who am grateful."

As she prepared to leave, Pierre called her back.

"Madeleine, my dear," he said, "I would like to introduce you to a gentleman who may be of assistance in finding a patron. He is just passing through. Thomas and I have arranged to spend the day with him tomorrow at our country house in Petit-Couronne. Invite the entire troupe, and make sure your

Molière agrees to come. He's been looking a trifle out of sorts and could use a bit of fresh air, or hadn't you noticed?"

***

Petit-Couronne, five miles away from Rouen on the other side of the Seine, was accessible from the city only by water, the one bridge having fallen into disrepair. On the boat they were crushed together but made the crossing bearable with kegs of hard cider and pixilated jibes about the queasiness of certain passengers, the result of the stiff breeze that made the vessel pitch and roll. Untouched by the general animation, Molière was roused from his indolence only once, when Armande pushed past him. He quickly closed his eyes and pretended to be dozing.

Soon they found themselves on a sunlit prairie sloping up from the river. The Corneille's family residence consisted of a large house and a barn not far from the Seine. The gusts of wind that had plagued them on the river brought welcome respite from the August heat.

Madeleine waved Molière and the others ahead with Thomas and Pierre. She longed for a few moments of solitude before meeting with the troupe's mysterious patron.

Could she exult in the move to Paris under the present circumstances? She had spent the previous night pondering how she, Molière, Armande and Thomas could learn to coexist. She flung herself down in a field, shut her eyes, and drifted off to the sound of rustling grasses.

Suddenly her father, Joseph Béjart, appeared carrying the first Armande, the beloved child she had lost, enfolded in his arms. Madeleine realized with a pang that it had been a long while since she had confided in the spirit of her late daughter.

"My darling child," she asked, "what shall I do about your father?"

Tell him. Madeleine could not see Armande's mouth, which was covered by her swaddling clothes, but she could hear her voice, which to her surprise sounded like her own.

"Tell him what?" she asked in a disingenuous tone.

That the other Armande is not his daughter.

"But why?" countered Madeleine.

He despises himself. You must put an end to his torment. Perhaps he'll marry the girl.

"I know it's the right thing," Madeleine began haltingly. "I should, but I can't."

Why not? What are you afraid of?

"Losing him," Madeleine replied.

But haven't you already?

"Yes," responded Madeleine. "But losing him to your sister? I'm not sure I can survive."

Why? He deserves her.

"I know," Madeleine replied earnestly. "More than anything I want them to be happy."

That's not what I meant. The child's voice took on a hint of irony. *They deserve each other. Don't you see? They won't get along.*

"Still," said Madeleine, "you're right. I must give them a chance. I love them so!"

Far more than either of them loves you.

"That's true," Madeleine concurred, surprised at how matter-of-factly she resigned herself to this sad state of affairs. "Be that as it may, I must bring them together."

Then what are you waiting for? Tell him.

"Who shall I say is the father?" cried Madeleine in desperation.

Joseph Béjart, up to now a mute actor in her dream, interrupted. He pulled Armande's swaddling clothes over her entire face to protect her from the wind.

The truth is best, Daughter, he intoned.

Men. They were good for less than nothing! Why tell Molière about Thomas, whom he already detested because of Armande's devotion? It could only cause everyone greater suffering.

Marie Hervé might have provided more useful advice if only Madeleine had been able to introduce her to Molière's child. Perhaps it was not too late to do so now. Madeleine snatched the infant from Joseph's arms and ran like the wind, but Marie Hervé was nowhere to be found. All at once a mighty gust propelled Madeleine into the air and deposited her in a field.

"How lovely your hair is in the sunlight," said a familiar voice.

Madeleine opened her eyes to find Thomas and Pierre standing on either side of her. She was certain the voice belonged to neither of them; could the owner possibly be who she thought? She sat up in the tall grass and turned in the direction from which it came, but the gray head that bowed to greet her gave her pause. It dawned on her that it was more than a dozen years since she had last seen him, time enough for the transformation. The aging gentleman now bringing her hand to his lips was the Comte de Modène.

***

Out of nowhere a shower blew up and they scurried into the barn, Madeleine and these three men who had each, mostly unbeknownst to the others, been her lover. As they stood waiting for the storm to pass Pierre launched into a formal introduction of the Comte, who caught Madeleine's eye and shot her an amused glance. Only then did it occur to her that he was the individual she had been brought to Petit-Couronne to meet.

"It is a pleasure to make your acquaintance, Mademoiselle," began the Comte. "I have never had the privilege of seeing your troupe but I gather from my honorable friends that you're among the most promising in the entire kingdom."

"They have been far too generous," Madeleine replied with a blush elicited less by the flattery than by the awkward situation.

"Not at all," said Pierre expansively. "If anything we have been sparing in our praise."

"In any event," Thomas pitched in, "His Excellency needn't take our word for it. Monsieur le Comte, I've arranged for you to attend tomorrow's performance of *Le Cid*."

"One of your distinguished brother's most admirable works," rejoined the Comte, and Pierre inclined his head. "Don Rodrigue is a fine role and I welcome the opportunity to see this Molière who is on everybody's lips. I trust that you, Mademoiselle Béjart, will play Chimène?"

"Alas," said Madeleine with a smile, "I am no longer of an age to do so."

"And yet you must have been, once," said the Comte.

"Ah, once!" said Madeleine, avoiding his eyes. "What was *not* true, once?" She laughed to cover her sadness. "Today my role is that of the Infanta, the King's daughter, also in love with Don Rodrigue but unable to reveal her feelings. My young sister will play Chimène."

"She will certainly do honor to the role," retorted the Comte, "although I can't imagine that her youth could surpass your beauty."

Their eyes met. Pierre appeared agitated but said nothing. Thomas broke the silence.

"Be that as it may," he said, "perhaps it is time for Monsieur le Comte to share his mission with Mademoiselle Béjart."

"Mission?" echoed Madeleine.

"Yes, Mademoiselle," said the Comte. "I regret that I myself no longer have a sufficient fortune to offer assistance to your troupe, but I come on behalf of one who does." He paused.

"I am first gentleman of the chamber to the Duc de Guise."

Madeleine could hardly believe her ears. Was it possible that the Duc de Guise, a man from the highest echelons of the aristocracy, might become their patron?

"The Duc has heard of your troupe's reputation," the Comte continued, "but it is actually another gentlemen, a man of his acquaintance, who wishes to bring you to Paris and see you perform."

"No doubt one of the other gentlemen in his service," said Madeleine to mask her disappointment. "Or perhaps a prosperous merchant wishing to make a name for himself by his generosity?"

"Would you call Philippe d'Anjou a prosperous merchant?" teased the Comte.

Was he mocking her?

"Why would the King's brother take an interest in our troupe?"

"Because of its excellence, my dear," declared Pierre, "of which I have been assuring you for weeks."

The Comte bowed to Pierre and Thomas in turn. "Please allow me to thank you for introducing me to Mademoiselle Béjart," he said. "And now, if I may, I'd like to meet with her alone to discuss the details of the arrangement proposed by His Royal Highness."

Pierre and Thomas took their leave. The shower had passed, cooling the air and leaving the fields fragrant. Madeleine and the Comte strolled arm in arm. She listened to the details of his plan of bringing the troupe to Paris and introducing them to the King's brother. She nodded politely but a plan of a different ilk was forming in her mind.

***

They came to a halt on a knoll where tall grasses overlooking the Seine swayed in time with the windblown waves. No clouds remained, and as Madeleine raised her eyes to the horizon and watched the river taper off in a winding thread, she imagined she could make out the buildings of Paris in the distance, just as little Armande had expected to be able to do when they first traveled there together. Her daughter was no longer an innocent child, that much was certain. Madeleine plucked a daisy, wedged it in her hair, and turned toward the Comte.

"It seems I've spent my entire life asking you for favors, Esprit," she said. "I promise this one will be my last."

They sat down on the wet grass. The Comte waited politely.

"I don't know how much Pierre and Thomas might have told you," she began, "but perhaps they have mentioned my youngest sister, Armande, the one who will be playing Chimène."

The Comte nodded.

"No one must ever be told," she continued, "but she's my daughter."

The Comte displayed no greater surprise than if she had announced that she had tripped on uneven stones and accidentally ripped a seam on her skirt.

"Is Molière her father?" he asked mildly.

"No," said Madeleine dully, "but he believes he is, and now he's in love with her, although I'm fairly sure he does not yet realize it. If he ever admits it to himself, it is difficult to imagine what might ensue." She teared up but her mouth held firm.

This time the Comte's eyes widened. "I am sorry for your misfortunes, my dear," he said, "and for his as well, however foolish I find the man. What is it you wish me to do?"

"Let me lead Molière to believe that you're Armande's father," she responded, "so that he is free to marry her if that is what they both desire."

"But why not simply inform him of the true identity of the girl's father?" inquired the Comte. "Who is he?"

"For reasons I cannot explain, I would prefer not to reveal it to you, and Molière must never find out. Please trust my judgment when I assure you that it would only make things worse." The Comte's brow furrowed. "You must believe me, Esprit," she went on. "I do not say this to protect my own good reputation, which I lost long ago. It is of them I am thinking, of my daughter and my . . . the man who once thought he loved me."

"Didn't he?" asked the Comte.

She looked away and said nothing.

***

They joined the others and announced the astounding news. Amidst the laughter and cries of joy, Madeleine grasped Molière's hand and pulled him aside.

"Where are we going?" he inquired genially.

"No questions, Monsieur. We are going where go we must."

She guided him into the barn, pushed him onto a haystack, and sat down on one beside it.

"Do you remember our first time?" she asked. "It was in a barn much like this one."

Molière, visibly moved, nodded wordlessly. It was only here and now, in a place evocative of that magical night, that Madeleine took the measure of her lost happiness. And if she briefly allowed herself to be overcome once again by the tenderness she had felt for the motherless boy, it was to let her heart believe that their love wasn't simply a thing of the past.

"Fear not, my darling," she said. "I have not brought you here for a repeat performance. I am aware of your tribulations. I am here to put an end to them."

His forehead creased. "What do you mean? What tribulations?"

"All in due time," she said. "I have a story to tell and you must listen carefully."

And so it was that as evening fell she offered a fresh lie about Armande's birth, delivered not in Marie Hervé's wheedling voice but in the magnanimous tones of the gallant Jean-Baptiste she would always love but was now setting free. While performing in Avignon with the Troupe du Vent, she said, she had chanced upon her former lover, the Comte de Modène, and gone with him. When she met Molière in Nîmes she was already expecting the Comte's child. She had let Molière believe Armande was his daughter for fear of losing him if he discovered she was not.

He sat as if petrified.

"I'm sorry I hid it from you," Madeleine went on. "It has taken me years to understand that love can't grow from a lie. Perhaps you'll find a truer love with Armande."

"What's that you say?" he gasped.

She sat close beside him and pulled his head onto her breast. "You mustn't be ashamed, my dearest," she whispered. "I can hardly imagine how you've suffered, but it's over now. Armande is not your daughter. If you have had feelings for her it is because your heart sensed it, and now at last you are free to love her if you wish. Perhaps she'll make you happy, as I cannot."

She held him tightly as he wept, as if to protect him from himself. It was to be the last time she'd ever have him in her arms, and she rocked him to comfort herself as much as him.

It was nearly dark when his sobs abated. He lifted his head.

"How did you know," he asked in a monotone, "when I couldn't even see it myself?"

"A woman always knows when a man she has loved loves another," she responded.

"*Has* loved?" he rejoined. "Don't you love me any more?"

The last thing she had expected was to have Molière question her love for him. A moment's thought sufficed to see that it was an opportunity to be seized.

"I'll always be fond of you," Madeleine said carefully. "But time has changed us both. My daughter is a lovely young woman. She is not accustomed to thinking of you in that way," she pursued. Her voice barely held steady. "It may take her time to return your affection. But your love would do her honor," she continued, thankful that the evening gloom masked the stabbing grief she could no longer keep from her face. "As it would any woman."

Molière strode to the door of the barn. A flock of sheep was barely visible in the distance but the sound of bleating drifted down.

"You have not answered my question," he said in a husky voice.

Nor will I, thought Madeleine, but her next response was such that he wouldn't notice.

"For the past three months I have been the mistress of Pierre Corneille."

CHAPTER 29

In Which Implausible Improvisations Beset Brothers and Addle an Actress

---

In Rouen the previews of Pierre Corneille's *Oedipus* went poorly. In spite of the text's brilliance, Molière, recently made aware that Armande was not his daughter but that he had been unknowingly more or less in love with the girl when he assumed she was, mumbled his lines and pulled at his collar as if in fear that the king's incestuous costume might adhere to his skin. After all that Madeleine had gone through to acquire the play, the idea of opening with it in Paris had to be dropped. She was at a loss over how to overcome this setback and relieved when the King's brother, delighted with Molière's play, *The Amorous Doctor*, which they had staged just for him, suggested that for their official launch they present Molière's new comedy, *The Ridiculous Precious Ladies*.

In October of 1658 Molière's troupe was ceremoniously introduced to the King, who graciously offered them the Salle des Petits Bourbons in the Louvre until the Palais Royal theater was refurbished. *The Ridiculous Precious Ladies* was a sensation. They were off and running.

Armande savored the larger roles with which she was now entrusted but seemed to be relishing her personal triumphs even more than her theatrical ones. She had not inherited her mother's mesmerizing charisma but was graced with a pleasant face, expressive eyes and a captivating smile. Light brown curls fell in perfect ringlets on either side of her high forehead. Her figure was lovely, her mien inviting, and her manner of speaking breathy and alluring. As Madeleine had hoped, the fact that the girl remained far away from her idol and now turned the heads of most males in her vicinity had largely distracted her from her obsession, at least for the time being. The few times she still rhapsodized about Thomas Corneille, Madeleine thanked her lucky stars that the man was safely back in Rouen.

As for Molière, Madeleine could tell he wasn't exactly happy, but he certainly appeared to suffer less than in the past. Had he and Armande become lovers? To Madeleine's way of thinking the great advantage of the troupe's lodgings on the Quai de l'École was that they all had separate rooms. What went on each night after her door was bolted she preferred not to know.

Gradually it dawned on her that she was changing from being a star in Molière's troupe and life to playing supporting roles in both. She loved him no less than before, but her warm memories of their long romance were tinged with sadness. No longer of an age to play leading ladies, she now captured the public's attention even in the smaller roles of servants and matrons.

Her family were aging before her eyes. Young Joseph died in 1659; Madeleine missed his sweet face, gentle ways, and even the stammer that she rued having treated with such impatience in the past. Louis lived with his mistress in another part of town but remained part of the troupe, and Geneviève was a pillar of support. Marie Hervé withdrew into fabricated memories of the blissful life she had never led with her late husband.

Molière's relationship with Armande quickly reached a stalemate. The young woman's signs of pleasure at his attention fell short of true tenderness or trust, while his overwhelming adoration and possessiveness once again became a source of torment for them both.

Would they marry? Madeleine reassured herself that she had done all she could. What now came to pass between her daughter and her former lover was not her concern.

***

On an unseasonably mild evening in January of 1662, while strolling through the gardens of the Palais Royal, Madeleine overheard two actors from the Hôtel de Bourgogne troupe exchanging the latest gossip. Pierre and Thomas Corneille were moving to Paris!

She sat abruptly on a stone bench. What might it mean for Armande to live in the same city as Thomas? The theater milieu was small; their paths could not help but cross. Though Armande had not seen Thomas in a long while she continued to speak of him with reverence. It was troubling to imagine what might transpire if they found themselves thrown together on a regular basis.

Madeleine raced home. At this hour the troupe would be on supper break from their rehearsal of Molière's latest play, *The School for Husbands*. She avoided visiting him as a rule lest she find him with Armande. She sprang up the stairs and stood panting in front of his door, more breathless than she would have been in the past. Fortunately he was eating dinner alone.

"How do you do, Monsieur?" she said in the bantering tone they now used.

"Mademoiselle," he said, wiping crumbs from his face and bowing with exaggerated formality. "What a surprise! Will you do me the honor of partaking of my humble repast?"

"Thank you," she said, shaking her head. "I've come to discuss an urgent matter."

Molière ushered her into the *salle*, sparse when the troupe first moved to Paris but now opulently furnished. She took a seat across from him at the dining table.

"The Corneilles are moving to Paris," she proclaimed without further ado.

Molière's face absorbed the shock. "Both of them?" he asked. "Thomas as well?"

"It's only a rumor," she replied, "but I believe it is likely."

"Does she know?" he asked.

"If she doesn't, she will," responded Madeleine. She paused. "Does she speak of him?"

Molière shot her a wretched glance.

"She compares us," he said in the voice of a patient battling an untreatable medical condition. "She asks why I'm not as tall as Thomas, as well dressed as Thomas. Why I lack Thomas's grace, Thomas's manners. Why I can't speak in a dignified way like Thomas rather than playing the buffoon. Every other word out of her mouth is Thomas."

It was worse than Madeleine had feared. Her heart, which Molière had broken, now broke for his. He shook with the shallow sobs of approaching old age, all the more poignant for appearing, deceptively, to lack the intensity of youth.

A knock drew them both to attention. Armande's voice called out merrily, "Come along, old man! We've finished our supper. Will you be keeping us onstage till midnight?"

"Forgive me, my sweet," Molière croaked, "but I'm feeling poorly. Tell the others there's no rehearsal tonight but they're to be at the theater tomorrow morning at ten."

"Yes, all right. Do you need me? Shall I stay with you?" The doorknob turned.

"Stop right there," he barked. "I'll see you in the morning."

"Good night then." Armande's steps could be heard descending the stairs.

Madeleine swallowed hard. "Perhaps it's time you thought about marrying the girl."

Molière sighed. "Even if she would have me, what good would it do? That Thomas is a married man hasn't cooled her ardor. Why should being a married woman rein her in, especially now that he'll be living in town?"

"For a short while at least," Madeleine responded, "as a married woman she would be on her best behavior. In the meantime we've got to think of a way of keeping her far from Thomas once and for all."

"How?" cried Molière in despair. "Would you have me barricade her in her room?"

Madeleine kissed him on the forehead. "No, my dear," she said, "we shall not resort to such tactics. Once I've talked to our darling demoiselle she'll be begging you to wed her. As for Monsieur Thomas Corneille, trust me. I'll think of something. He'll soon be out of reach."

Molière cleared the table without finishing supper. As Madeleine was leaving he said, "Please, Mado, be gentle with the girl. I can't bear the thought of your upsetting her. I know you're not the person in whom I should confide about my feelings for her, but I have no one else to turn to for assistance, not even my own good judgment. She has robbed me of my right mind."

Madeleine nodded. "Have you ever told her?" she asked.

"Told her what?"

"How much you love her," she said, pleased at how calm her voice sounded.

"I've tried to," he said, "but I can't. She'd laugh at me. I don't even know if she really loves me. How can I tell her how much I need her when she might offer not a word in return?"

Madeleine bit her tongue. This was no time to be quoting Thomas's first play, *The Promises of Chance*, to reaffirm the importance of selfless love. Instead she replied, "Forget about your right mind for now. I'll retrieve it for you."

***

There was no time to waste. Armande answered Madeleine's knock instantly and her brow furrowed. Was it some other face she had anticipated seeing?

"Good evening, Mado," she said coolly. "What a pleasant surprise."

"Am I disturbing you?" asked Madeleine. "Perhaps you were expecting a guest."

Ignoring the implied question, the girl led Madeleine to an armchair by the hearth and said, "Molière has canceled this evening's rehearsal. I was planning on having an early night."

Madeleine nodded. "Why did he cancel?"

"He said he was unwell," responded Armande, taking a seat beside her.

"Poor dear, he's not been himself," Madeleine observed. She glanced around the room, decorated at even greater expense than Molière's with an embroidered rug, lace tablecloth, and silk wall-hangings of various hues. Her eyes were drawn to the purple velvet bedcurtains but she drove from her mind the question of what might have taken place within their confines.

Where to begin? Weary of dissimulation, she blurted out, "Are you in love with him?"

"With whom?" asked Armande in a defiant tone.

"Don't play games with me," snapped Madeleine. "You may take on the airs of a great lady with the others but you're not too old for me to take a staff to your rump."

Armande's eyes blazed and for a moment Madeleine thought her daughter might attempt to strike her, but after a pause she replied in a simmering voice, "No, I am not in love with him."

"You do know he's in love with you," Madeleine said, the words not quite a statement.

Armande covered her face with her hands and sobbed. When she was cried out she wiped her face on a towel.

"Of course I know." She brushed the curls from her forehead. "I'm very fond of Molière. He's always been so kind! But I'm not in love. Please don't blame me, Mado. It's not my fault."

"It's not your fault," Madeleine said, "but it is your responsibility. You have not asked for his love, but he is offering it to you nonetheless. What do you intend to do about it?"

"What is there to do?" replied the girl in a monotone.

"Whatever you can to make him happy," replied Madeleine.

Armande's eyes narrowed. "But I told you," she said. "I don't love him."

"If you're patient and kind," responded Madeleine, "you will learn to."

"How can I when he irritates me so?" exclaimed Armande. "Every time a man throws me a glance he pitches a fit."

"Is there cause for jealousy?" inquired Madeleine. "Are you in love with another man?"

Anger pulsed across Armande's features once again. "That is not your affair," she said.

Madeleine sat down at Armande's dressing table and gazed at her own reflection. Here and there, around her eyes and mouth, her otherwise smooth skin was delicately etched. A silvery web in her coiffure was visible in the sea of red. She was forty-four years old and it had probably been coming on for some time, but only now did the mirror's truth reach her eyes.

"Forgive me," she said with a sigh. "I am not here to interrogate you. But if you're sincere in wanting to avoid hurting Molière further, you've got to agree to marry him."

Armande stared. "*Marry* him?"

"Yes, marry him," reiterated Madeleine.

Armande sat lost in thought. The girl was so impulsive that it was not often she had the patience to reason through a question, but her eyes now shone with understanding.

"The way I see it," she said, "I can't take a breath without causing someone to suffer. If I must, I would rather it be Molière than you."

"What do you mean?" demanded Madeleine.

"You still love him," observed the girl, "however little you show it. I know you better than you give me credit for. Molière would be happy if I married him, but it would hurt you."

Madeleine kissed her on the cheek and said, "My only wish is for the two people I love most in the world to be happy. As for what would or would not hurt me," she concluded as she made her way toward the door, "please allow me to quote you. That is not your affair."

Thus it was that on January 23, 1662, shortly after his fortieth birthday, Molière received an unexpected gift: the hand of Armande Grésinde Claire Elizabeth Béjart in marriage.

In his excitement, the official story of his bride's birth—the lie Madeleine had circulated for general consumption according to which Armande had been born to Marie Hervé in April of 1642—slipped his mind. Consequently he repeated the lie that Madeleine had told him as a secret and that he believed to be the truth: that the birthdate was February of 1643. Madeleine took the cleric aside and insisted that it was April of 1642. Eager to avoid a family dispute over a matter of little importance, the priest wrote that the bride was "twenty years old or thereabouts."

The bride herself, who was actually not quite eighteen, remained silent and smiled politely throughout the proceedings. She gave her assent to wedlock with a wordless nod.

**

Pierre and Thomas Corneille moved to Paris in October, just as Molière's troupe was beginning to rehearse his new comedy, *The School for Wives*, due to open the day after Christmas, December 26, 1662. The main character of his play, Arnolphe, was a middle-aged man obsessed with the fidelity of his fiancée, Agnès, whom he had taken as a protégée at the age of four and raised in complete ignorance to be a faithful wife to him later on, too naïve to stray, or so he believed. Nevertheless Agnès—now nearly eighteen and having recently been informed that Arnolphe intended to marry her—had fallen in love with a young man by the name of Horace. In the play's climactic scene in Act V, Arnolphe belatedly attempted to persuade Agnès to marry him, but in vain; in the end she held to her decision to wed Horace, and Arnolphe flounced off the stage in humiliation.

Molière was to play Arnolphe. To Armande's displeasure she had not been cast as Agnès but had to settle for being the understudy to Catherine de Brie, who had been given the role.

The play was an immediate sensation and began selling out. As was the custom, the most prominent members of the audience were seated directly onstage to accommodate the overflow.

On December 31, 1662, the Feast of Saint Sylvester, both Catherine de Brie and Geneviève Béjart, who had the role of

Arnolphe's servant, were ill. Madeleine was called upon to replace Geneviève. Armande joyously received the news that she, too, would be onstage.

When Madeleine arrived at the theater to put on her costume an hour before curtain, she found Molière alone in the dressing room scratching away at a scroll of paper. He was in a state.

"What are you writing?" she asked as she began to disrobe.

"Nothing," he muttered, not bothering to look up.

"Is something wrong?" she queried.

"Armande," he said, without elaboration.

"I know you're accustomed to playing opposite Catherine," said Madeleine, "but there's nothing to worry about. I've been coaching Armande. She'll be effective in the role."

"It's my love scene," he said. "Getting rejected by a character played by Armande . . ." He wiped his brow with a rag. "How can I play the cuckold in front of hundreds of mocking spectators and with my own wife onstage?"

"I tell you, she's perfectly competent," asserted Madeleine in an attempt to sidestep the real issue. "You'll be pleasantly surprised."

He scowled. "Let *her* be surprised for once," he said darkly.

"I beg your pardon?"

The door opened and Louis, in costume as Arnolphe's best friend, Chrysalde, rushed in.

"Tonight's the night!" he cried, out of breath. "They're here!"

Madeleine blanched. "Don't forget," she said, "they must be seated onstage."

Still bent over his scroll, Molière said, "Who?"

"No one," said Madeleine briskly. She turned to her brother. "Are you ready?"

"Yes," he replied. "I've memorized it." He slammed the door behind him.

Molière finally looked up. "What's going on?"

"Nothing," said Madeleine.

"All right then," he mumbled, "do your make-up in the hallway. I must be alone."

He laid his quill aside and silently began reading over what he'd written. In response to Madeleine's inquisitive gaze, he escorted her out the door.

***

When an announcement was made that for this performance the playwright's own wife, Armande Molière, would play the role of Agnès and her sister Madeleine Béjart that of a servant, the crowd shouted its approval. But that could not compare with the uproar that greeted two unexpected members of the public being led to seats onstage: Pierre and Thomas Corneille!

Pierre was looking considerably older; still a respected celebrity, he was not as deeply revered as he had once been. By contrast Thomas, arrayed in all of the latest fashions, was the current darling of the theater-going public.

Success had gone to his head to such an extent that he'd commenced going by the name *Corneille de l'Isle* to suggest he and Pierre came from an ancient family of landed aristocrats rather than being illustrious bourgeois whose father had been recently ennobled by the King. Armande, when she heard the news that the brothers were in attendance, went pale as a sheet.

The play began and soon Arnolphe was onstage discussing his upcoming marriage to Agnès with his best friend Chrysalde. Louis suddenly took center stage. Facing Pierre and Thomas *Corneille de l'Isle* seated a few feet away, he recited the lines Madeleine had provided him:

> *I know of a peasant, Fat Pierre was his name,*
> *A half-acre of land was his sole claim to fame,*
> *But around it he built a ridiculous moat*
> *And calls himself Monsieur de l'Isle, the old goat!*

All hell broke loose. The spectators pointed at the Corneille brothers and made noises of jubilant derision. The pandemonium went on and on, the shrieks of laughter rising in waves that never seemed to diminish. Peeking out from behind the curtain Madeleine discovered that rather than being annoyed at her renegade interpolation, Molière had doubled over and was delighting along with his public in the unexpected drubbing being dealt Thomas and Pierre.

After sitting in a state of frozen dignity and waiting in vain for their ordeal to abate, the two Corneille brothers rose and stomped out. Armande, visibly shaken, collected herself for her first entrance in Act I, Scene Three, but throughout the first four acts of the play she recited her lines as if she were sleepwalking.

By the time she and Molière appeared onstage for the climactic love scene between Arnolphe and Agnès in Act Five, the public had whipped itself up into a frenzy. Armande, rumored to be deceiving her husband, was onstage this evening to listen to Arnolphe's accusations of infidelity!

Arn.: *You should have been on guard against love's desires!*

Agn.: *But how to guard against pleasurable fires?*

Arn.: *Didn't you know how much it would displease me?*

Agn.: *Not at all. Why it should hurt you I just can't see.*

Arn.: *How true! I should be celebrating this night!*
       So you don't love me?

Agn.:   *Love you?*

Arn.:   *Yes, that's right.*

Agn.: *No, alas.*

Arn.:   *No?*

Agn.:   *Would you wish me to lie?*

Arn.: *Why love not me but another, you hussy, why?*

After confessing to Arnolphe in the first part of the scene that she wasn't in love with him, Agnès tried to reason with this belated suitor whom she had until recently believed was simply her legal guardian:

My goodness, I'm not the one for you to blame;
Why did you not, like him, ignite my flame?
I wish quite sincerely that you attracted me.
If that were so, how easy things would be!

Now Molière stepped forward to give his response:

It can be true if only you would try.

But rather than waiting for Agnès's retort as given by the manuscript, he now threw himself to his knees and spoke new lines with an amorous fervor Madeleine had never heard displayed by anyone but Thomas Corneille.

> *Just listen to this deep and amorous sigh,*
> *See these dying eyes, these languid brows,*
> *And leave that pallid beau who scrapes and bows.*

The words, the intonation, the gestures all harkened back to a speech Jean-Baptiste had recited as Don Fadrique in *The Promises of Chance*. Armande stood in shock as Molière went on with his appeal:

> *He's put you under a spell, what else can it be?*
> *You'll be a hundred times happier with me.*
> *You love fine clothes, whatever you want I'll buy.*
> *May the heavens strike me dead if it's a lie!*
> *I'll stroke you, pamper you, pet you day and night,*
> *I'll kiss you, greet you each morning with a peck and a bite.*
> *If only you'll love me you can do as you please.*
> *How low can a man sink? I'm down on my knees!*
> *Nothing in the world could be equal to my passion,*
> *I'll prove it, ingrate, just tell me in what fashion!*
> *Do you want to see me hurt myself, or weep?*
> *Or see my hair shorn off like a bleating sheep?*
> *Do you want me to kill myself? Just nod your head.*
> *You won't believe me, not until I'm dead!*
> *I'm ready to prove my love, o heartless one!*

Molière, not Arnolphe, was courting Armande, not Agnès, buffered by the illusion that the audience was laughing only at Arnolphe and not at him.

Would Armande grant his wish? Unaccustomed to improvising, the young woman stood for a long moment, the deafening laughter of the audience such that her pause appeared natural. Finally she addressed Molière, still on his knees, yawned in an exaggerated way, and said:

> How dull you are! Are you certain you're quite done?
> You leave my soul untouched, you silly bore.
> Why, Thomas with a single word would move me more!

Had Armande forgotten in the heat of the moment that Agnès's suitor in the play was named Horace, or was she taunting her husband? Molière stood and staggered across the stage. He held his hands to his heart and shed real tears, inspiring greater hilarity from the crowd. He then collected himself and finished the play as anticipated, as if nothing had happened.

The curtain calls that night were endless; it was difficult to argue with success. The speech about the Corneilles, for which Madeleine claimed responsibility as a prank she thought the audience would find amusing, was kept in. Arnolphe's strange declaration of passion and Agnès's withering reply were also retained. They never failed to bring down the house even though Catherine de Brie recovered quickly and Armande's performance was a one-time occurrence.

Armande never mentioned Thomas's name in front of Madeleine again. A month later Madeleine chanced upon him on the Rue de Richelieu. When he caught sight of her, he lowered his gaze and hurried on his way.

CHAPTER 30

In Which Madeleine Presents Her Most Magnificent Lie

———

With time it emerged that the first Armande had been right in her prediction: Molière and the second Armande never did get along, he devoured by jealousy for which she gave ample justification. As Madeleine's decline accelerated and she reconciled with the Church, she could not help but wonder if her sacrifice had gone for naught. Had she been wrong to marry off Armande to a man she had not learned to love? Could Molière be content with a wife who so poorly prized his affection? The most pressing question was whether it was too late to put things right. The thought of dying on a failure saddened Madeleine only for the misery she would leave behind.

Several times she began a written confession but quickly discarded each clumsy attempt. Whenever Molière and Armande were at her bedside she tried to glimpse how best to assist them, but no ideas came. At the current rate of her decline she might have little choice but to leave well enough alone. But well enough was not the state of their marriage, alone what each of them would eventually be if she took no action before she died.

***

One day in early February of 1672, several weeks after Father Anselme brought Madeleine back into the flock, Molière and Armande called on her before their rehearsal. With the première of *The Learned Ladies* approaching they were working late into the night and it was simplest to visit her in the morning. Armande carried a bouquet of dried flowers.

"Thank you, my sweet," croaked the patient, weak from coughing. Ignoring Molière's mask of distress she turned to him and asked, "Will you be ready?" The troupe was to preview the play for the King's brother in mid-February in advance of the opening in March.

"If you must inquire, no," Molière replied glumly. "The rehearsals have been dreadful."

"I suppose that comment is intended for me?" snapped Armande.

"Not especially," he muttered. "You have all been equally dismal."

Armande stomped her foot, crossed her arms over her chest, and went to sulk in a corner.

"I'm sorry for this unpleasantness, Mado," she said. She turned and faced her, continued in a pleading tone. "As I told this stubborn ox from the start, it's confusing for me to address a character who bears my own name. If he felt compelled to call the two sisters Henriette and Armande, what possessed him to give the role of Henriette to me and Armande to Catherine?"

"What possessed me," came the testy reply, "is that you're not suited to play my Armande. My Armande remains faithful to the man who adores her."

"A pretty thing to say to your own wife!" cried the young woman. "So *your Armande* is not I, but a creature in one of your precious comedies?"

"Nothing would make me happier," countered Molière, "than if *you* were to be *my Armande*. As the court and the city of Paris can attest, I have not been accorded that pleasure, and I doubt if I ever shall be!"

Armande made a motion to go for her husband's throat, then halted and composed herself as best she could.

"We would all be better off," she said in an ominous tone, "if we left for our rehearsal before we make worse fools of ourselves than usual in front of my moth . . ."

Had Molière also heard the slip? His face revealed nothing. "You may take as much time as you need," he said listlessly to his wife. Then he kissed Madeleine's hand and was gone.

***

Armande added a log to the fire, then settled down in an armchair at Madeleine's bedside. Deep in thought, the young woman put a hand to her forehead.

"My darling . . ." Madeleine began, but she was interrupted.

"Not this time, Mother," said Armande, her eyes averted. "My entire life you have done everything for me. But this I must do for myself."

Mother. Madeleine had born three children and raised one to adulthood. Despite her body's decrepitude, her spirit rejoiced in hearing the word for the first time on a daughter's lips.

"So you know," she said.

Armande nodded and said, "I always have."

"How?" asked Madeleine.

"Why, everything," replied the young woman. "What people said when they thought I couldn't hear. The way you acted and how I felt. Marie Hervé never treated me like a daughter. When Molière approached me, it was no surprise. At least not that part of it," she concluded.

"What did he say?" Madeleine inquired after a pause.

"It was in Rouen," replied Armande, "shortly before we moved to Paris." She hesitated, a blush overspreading her face. "He took me aside and declared his love. I was speechless."

"Had you sensed nothing?"

"Not exactly. Something had been in the air for months but I had dismissed it. Until that night."

Gathering her strength, Madeleine stretched out a hand to caress her daughter's cheek and said, "My brave girl! It must have been a terrible shock."

Armande brushed away a tear. "I had no idea what to say," she murmured. "He said you were my mother and the Comte de Modène, a nobleman you had once been close to, was my father. I had heard about the child you had with the Comte before you met Molière and assumed the Comte was my father as well." Loath to continue, she played with a ribbon on her sleeve.

"So he began wooing you," Madeleine said to encourage her, "but you couldn't bring yourself to tell him that you felt nothing?"

"It wasn't as simple as that," the young woman finally replied. "I'd never thought of him in that way but I was flattered. I probably would have given in but for one thing."

"What?" inquired her mother.

"You," Armande answered, her eyes downcast. "I could tell you still loved him. Men are so easily fooled! I invented a story about being in love with someone else. I don't know if Molière believed me, but he ceased his demands."

"And then?" Madeleine asked.

"Then we moved to Paris," Armande went on. "There was little time to devote to such matters, although Molière occasionally made a scene about some man he suspected of being my beloved. I held out hope that the two of you might be reconciled, until . . ." She broke off.

"Until I convinced you to marry him?" asked Madeleine gently.

Armande nodded. "When he put the question to me I agreed."

"Come into my arms, my darling," Madeleine said, opening them as wide as she could.

For a long while Armande sobbed against her bosom. Then she brushed her brown curls from her face and said, "I'm sorry, Mother, but I must go. In spite of my annoyance Molière was quite right about the rehearsals and there are few passages he can work on without me."

A spell of coughing interrupted the tender scene. Finally Madeleine was able to draw a breath. "Before you go," she said in a whisper, "can you ever forgive me? I've ruined your life by having you marry a man you don't love."

"You haven't ruined my life but given me life," Armande said simply. "It's I who ask for your pardon. If anyone could convince Molière that you were the person he should love it was I, for he'd lost his heart to me and I was the one who had the greatest sway over him, the only one he might have listened to. I did my best but failed in the attempt. For that I am truly sorry."

Before Madeleine could respond Armande kissed her on the forehead and was gone.

***

For days after Madeleine's conversation with her daughter, the surprising wisdom uttered by this capricious young woman who to all outward appearances meandered through life with her head in the clouds was never far from her thoughts: those who are loved have the greatest sway over those who love them. The idea seemed to be suggesting some course of action but what that was Madeleine could not discern. On February 17, 1672, she received her answer.

After a month of chilly rain the morning dawned sunny and mild. Madeleine's bedclothes were soaked in blood but her mind remained clear. This day would be her last.

The realization that God's reprieve was coming to an end filled her with despair. In spite of her best efforts, it seemed that she had squandered the days and weeks granted to set her affairs in order. She would never rest in peace having left Armande and Molière to their own paltry devices. To judge from his sallow complexion and coughing spells, more frequent of late, it wouldn't be long before he followed Madeleine to the grave. Whether he would be refused God's grace was out of her hands, but how could she accept that he would spend his remaining time on earth in the lower circles of hell? As for Armande, would she ever learn the nature of true love if in his greatest hour of need she didn't care for this man who adored her, she who alone had the power to bring him solace?

Whatever little time remained, Madeleine was not ready to give up. If God intended to take her on this very day, it must be his way of saying that she still had time to discover what she sought. She closed her eyes and waited.

The voice of the first Armande had never before come to her unsolicited. So God was capable of generosity toward her after all! Before the end he had allowed her not only to acknowledge the living Armande as her daughter but also to hear one final time from this equally beloved child with whom she hoped to be soon reunited.

She listened to Armande's advice. Her mouth fell open at the simplicity and brilliance of the conceit.

"But can I do it, my darling?" she whispered. "Can I manage it?"

A pause. A smile came to Madeleine's lips. "I know I have, and more times than you can imagine, but that was different. I am no longer the woman I once was."

She nodded at Armande's final response. She drew a hand to her lips, kissed it, and blew the kiss up toward the ceiling.

She rang for Marthe, the chambermaid, and ordered her to bring her a small box stored on a shelf on the other side of the room.

"Fetch Armande," Madeleine said. "Tell her to come straightaway."

Marthe nodded.

"Father Anselme at Saint Paul's," Madeleine went on. "Have him come as well, but not until midday. And take this." She handed Marthe something from the box.

Marthe took the object. She knew why the priest was being sent for but was well enough acquainted with her mistress to know she disliked scenes and mawkishness, so she contained her sadness and said only, "Is this for Father Anselme, Mademoiselle?"

Madeleine shook her head. "Rue des Deux-Portes," she said. "Give it personally to Monsieur Thomas Corneille."

***

Madeleine was awakened by the sound of a key turning in the lock. She prepared herself to greet Armande but there stood Molière.

By his expression she gauged his shock at the blood-soaked sheets and the state she was in. Bowing deeply, he said with barely a tremor, "Good morning, lovely lady."

Even now he used his voice as a weapon against the pain. While they were both skilled at covering their feelings, she hid hers only from others, not from herself. Molière would go to his grave bantering away any matter that caused him unbearable sorrow. Who would understand that about him after she was gone? The hardest thing about dying was that when his time came she would not be there to soothe his suffering.

Would Armande?

"Perhaps you've forgotten," Molière carried on, alarmed by her silence, "that today is our first performance of *The Learned Ladies*." He paused, waiting for her to comment. She couldn't, so he rambled on. "In case you're wondering whether we're finally prepared for this great event, I'm pleased to reply in the affirmative."

Madeleine gestured to him to approach. As her sheet was covered with purple blotches, rather than sitting on the bed he kneeled beside her.

"Fancy the coincidence," he said, his voice careening. "I just crossed paths with Marthe and she mentioned you've called for Armande. She'll soon be here. She takes her time, so it would be safer to say she'll be here sooner rather than later, probably a good thing, because . . ."

His voice faded and he drew a deep breath to regain his composure.

"When she arrives, tell her she may stay with you until mid-afternoon. Our performance isn't to begin until four o'clock."

Madeleine took several shallow breaths to gather her strength and said, "She has read me the script. It's a fine piece of work. Your best."

"How good of you to say so," Molière rejoined, his hope restored, as if hearing Madeleine utter a dozen words was hard evidence that she was finally on the mend. "It ought to be a good play," he continued, "having taken four years for me to compose. You can't deny that I too am slowing down in my dotage!"

Madeleine shook her head, a single tear issuing from the corner of an eye, then grasped his hand and pressed it. At her touch he clutched the icy fingers and pressed them to his lips, and for a long while the room was silent except for the sound of his strangled sobs.

"You mustn't tarry," she finally managed to say.

"I can't leave you," said Molière, his pain for once undisguised.

"Just for now," Madeleine said. "Come back later."

He stood. "Shall I fetch a clean sheet before I go?" he asked. "As I said, Armande will be here in a few minutes, but . . ."

She shook her head again. "There's no need," she whispered. "Bring her with you this evening. We'll all eat supper together."

"Truly?" he asked.

"Truly," she replied.

***

When Armande arrived Madeleine instructed her to change the bed, wash her, and bring a white nightgown. Then she asked Marthe to heat up a pot of mulled wine and bring three mugs.

"Are you expecting a guest?" asked Armande.

"Yes," replied Madeleine, without elaboration.

The two women sat close together. Armande held her mother's hand. Sunlight streamed through the high windows and it seemed that out of respect for death Paris was abstaining from its usual midmorning commotion. Madeleine felt a slight improvement and was able to breathe with less discomfort. It would have been easier to speak now but she conserved her strength for what she would have to say once Thomas arrived.

They heard a knock and the rustle of Marthe's skirts. Suddenly there he stood.

Thomas was in his late forties and didn't look younger than his years but the set of his features retained a solemn innocence. At last the wisdom Madeleine had perceived in his eyes when he was a very young man had come into harmony with his age.

Armande gasped. Madeleine beckoned to Thomas and he approached the bed.

"Thank you," she said.

He took in her dreadful condition and his eyes registered dismay but he said nothing. He leaned over the bed and kissed her hand.

"I believe you're acquainted with my daughter Armande," Madeleine said. "Yes, as most of Paris has long suspected, that's who she is."

Without surprise Thomas bowed and kissed Armande's hand. The usually animated young woman resembled a sculpture. He shuffled his feet, so overwhelmed that he was unable to ask why he'd been summoned.

"It behooves me to be brief," said Madeleine, lacking the breath to laugh. "Monsieur, although I introduced you to Armande many years ago, I shall do so now with greater precision than I could use in the past. Thomas Corneille, allow me to present your daughter. Armande, this is your father."

Silence. Thomas fell onto a chair. The statue stopped breathing.

Madeleine looked from one to the other. "Have you nothing to say?"

Armande stared, her face blank. Thomas stammered, "How is it possible? It was only once that you and I . . ."

"Yes," Madeleine broke in, "we all know how such things come about. Once is enough."

"But I thought . . ." he stammered.

"Many people have thought many things," she interjected, "because I've wished it to be so. I've had my reasons." She turned to her daughter and said, "I deceived you about your age. You'll be twenty-eight years old in July. I hope you're grateful to receive two additional years of life. Perhaps it means little to you now but to me it seems the greatest of gifts."

"If only I could give the time back to you," Armande cried, finding her voice at last, "and keep you from leaving us!"

"Thank you, Daughter," said Madeleine. "I would gladly spend another two years repeating that word, which I've had so little time to utter!" After a moment of reflection she turned her attention to Thomas.

"I'm sorry for the pain I have caused you," she said. "Your love was most worthy of mine, but I was unable to return it. That much you knew, but what you cannot have understood, for I myself had not, is that . . ."

Her voice broke. Could she go through with it? She closed her eyes and imagined the first Armande smiling to cheer her on. She opened her eyes back up, brushed away tears and went on.

"If only my heart had been unencumbered when you offered me yours! My love for Jean-Baptiste was real but blinded me to your devotion. Only in death have I realized that all along the one I should have loved—truly should have loved—was you."

Thomas's gaze fixed upon her with the same intensity that had struck her in the twelve-year-old. As it dawned on him that without warning life itself had changed direction and begun to move in reverse, his lips assumed a youthful smile. The gift he had long ago abandoned hope of ever receiving now illuminated the features of a face grown suddenly young.

"My darling," he exclaimed, "after all these years, can it be?"

His smile remained but his eyes posed a question. He hesitated, as if debating whether or not to give voice to it, and though he decided against it she knew what it was. Other men, convinced of their irresistibility, would not have doubted her words for a moment. But Thomas was not other men.

Was she lying?

She smiled in turn, wondering what her smile conveyed, half hoping it did not reveal the answer and half wishing it did.

"My love comes too late," she said, "but I offer it with a pure heart. Will you accept it?"

Thomas nodded, his eyes glistening.

"Thank you, Monsieur. You're not aware of it," she continued, "but there's no one who has felt greater love for you than your daughter."

Before Thomas had a chance to reply Armande covered her face with her hands.

"My dearest," Madeleine said, stroking her hair, "feel no shame. Whatever you may have believed, your love was pure." Armande took refuge against her shoulder. "Do you think," Madeleine went on, "you were the first girl infatuated with her father?"

Little by little Armande's sobs abated and she pulled away and wiped her face. Madeleine turned back to Thomas.

"After I'm gone," she said to him, "will you pass along the love I've offered you? Will you love Armande in my place, as a father loves a daughter?"

Again Thomas nodded.

"And you, my love," she said, turning back to Armande, "I didn't give you the childhood I would have wished. I deprived you of a mother as well as a father. I couldn't allow myself to show you a mother's affection. And I'm ashamed to admit it, but it's true: for a time Molière's love for you was so strong that it made me forget mine. Once again I ask for your forgiveness."

"Mother," said Armande, "there is nothing to forgive."

"Thank you," replied Madeleine. "One last thing I ask you before I go, and the most important. Use the love that I have given Thomas and that he will pass on to you. Give it to Molière in my place. I loved him, but that wasn't enough."

"But how can I," exclaimed Armande, "when I have never loved him as you have?"

"If you can't love him," Madeleine replied, "make him think you do. There's nothing on earth he will more strongly wish to believe. It's the only thing that will bring him comfort and solace in the months to come. You must find a way. Your father will help you." She paused and looked at Thomas. "Won't you?"

One last time he nodded, his lips saying nothing but his eyes grasping everything.

Madeleine felt a great peace settle over her. As always, Molière's Armande had been right. She had carried it off, her most magnificent lie.

***

When the priest arrived, Armande and Thomas asked if they could wait in the next room and sit with Madeleine after he'd finished; she shook her head, bade them adieu and watched them depart arm in arm with a heart lighter than she's known for years. Father Anselme being ill, a much younger priest had been sent. And before Madeleine had time to gather her thoughts he was standing beside her bed reciting Latin words she knew but whose meaning she no longer understood. All she was sure of was that soon he would turn to her and ask her to make her final confession.

Her final story, the tale of all the stories she had ever told, was at hand.

She had believed that the most important words she would utter before leaving this world would be for Molière. That remained true, but they would be transmitted through Thomas and Armande. It would be up to them to find the right words, to say them for her.

And that, she mused, was as it should be. She could not have shut her eyes with a clear conscience if she had either continued to lie to Molière by having him believe her love for him was a thing of the past, or offered him, in death, the love he had never been able to accept from her in life. And yet the love was there; it had to go somewhere. The best she had been able to do was to give it to the one who needed it most, who had loved her all his life as she had loved Molière. Thomas would pass it along to Armande, who would do her best to love Molière in turn. At the very least she would learn to lie to him in a loving way.

Madeleine's chest tightened with a presentiment of death. She examined the young cleric as carefully as her failing sight allowed. Though his face was unlined, he looked as humorless as Grandfather Pierre Béjart. He glanced at her as his recitation was reaching an end. She ventured a smile and thought she perceived a shift in his gaze. Was he capable of amusement? Might he be made to glimpse the delight that underlay a lifetime of loving falsehoods and how preferable such a life was to one of false love?

He invited her to begin her confession. In spite of her many weeks of reflection she realized that she had nothing prepared and would have to improvise. One thing at least was clear: she would not ask forgiveness for her lies. How wonderfully absurd it all seemed, this life where, as in the theater, loving was not always separable from lying! Was it possible to make the priest understand that the truth was the heart of an onion which, when severed from all the layers of lies and half-truths that gave the onion its flavor, left little taste or nourishment?

Let him judge her as he pleased! God would certainly do so, and she might as well resign herself to it. But as long as she had breath in her body she would be the judge of her actions. And as she contemplated the young man whose life in this vale of tears lay before him, she knew in her heart that her last good deed on this earth must be to teach him, also, the preciousness of a good laugh.

THE END

Postscript

On February 17, 1673, one year to the day after Madeleine Béjart's death, Molière suffered a seizure while performing the title role in his final play, *The Hypochondriac*. He was able to finish the performance but died several hours later. He was refused the last rites but his widow, Armande, convinced the King to overrule the Church's objections so that Molière, an unrepentant actor, might be accorded Christian burial. Popular wisdom has it that to avoid controversy he was buried at midnight.

After Molière's death Thomas Corneille became a close friend of Armande's. She asked him to write a more refined version of her late husband's most scandalous play, *Don Juan*, so that it could escape further censorship and be staged. Thomas's adaptation was the only version of the play performed until the nineteenth century, when Molière's original, two hundred years ahead of its time, was finally revived.

Nearly four centuries after the events of this story, Pierre Corneille is considered the father of French theater, Molière the greatest playwright France has ever produced. The works of Thomas Corneille, one of the most successful writers of his time, have largely fallen into oblivion. The true identity of Armande Béjart's parents has never been established nor the mystery surrounding the date of her birth resolved. Madeleine and Armande Béjart are footnotes of history.

Index